The Fire Witch

A Zvi Jayden Novel

Sasha Marshall

This is a work of fiction. Names, characters, places, and incidents are either the products of the author's imagination or are used fictitiously. Any resemblance to actual persons (living or dead), events, or locations is entirely coincidental.

Sasha Marshall Arts

Atlanta, GA

Copyright © 2021 by Sasha Marshall

Third Edition

Published in the United States of America.

All rights reserved. No part of this book may be reproduced in any form or by any electronic or mechanical means, including information storage and retrieval systems, without permission in writing from the publisher or author, except by a reviewer, who may quote brief passages in a review.

We at Sasha Marshall Arts enjoy hearing from readers.

SashaMarshall.com

Cover Design: Lin'Diana'art

Interior Design: Lin'Diana'art

Formatting: Nola Marie

CONTENTS

PROLOGUE	2
CHAPTER ONE	8
CHAPTER TWO	16
CHAPTER THREE	28
CHAPTER FOUR	40
CHAPTER FIVE	46
CHAPTER SIX	54
CHAPTER SEVEN	62
CHAPTER EIGHT	74
CHAPTER NINE	92
CHAPTER TEN	104
CHAPTER ELEVEN	112
CHAPTER TWELVE	122
CHAPTER THIRTEEN	130
CHAPTER FOURTEEN	136
CHAPTER FIFTEEN	144
CHAPTER SIXTEEN	152
CHAPTER SEVENTEEN	158
CHAPTER EIGHTEEN	164
CHAPTER NINETEEN	172
CHAPTER TWENTY	182
CHAPTER TWENTY-ONE	190
CHAPTER TWENTY-TWO	198
CHAPTER TWENTY-THREE	206
CHAPTER TWENTY-FOUR	214
CHAPTER TWENTY-FIVE	222
CHAPTER TWENTY-SIX	228
CHAPTER TWENTY-SEVEN	234
CHAPTER TWENTY-EIGHT	240
CHAPTER TWENTY-NINE	246
CHAPTER THIRTY	252
EPILOGUE	258

For Drake,
My dragon and my heart, I'm so proud to call you my son.

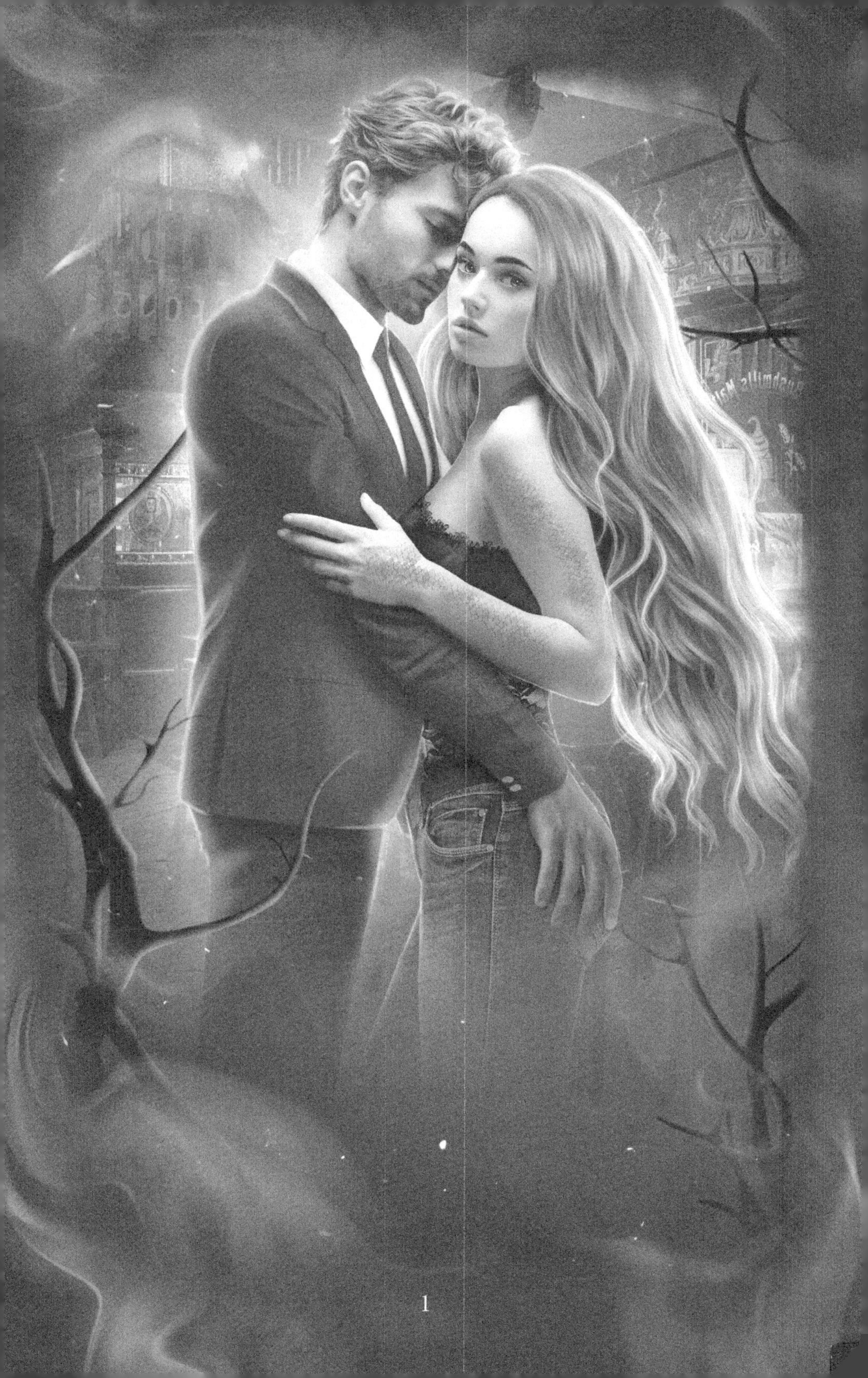

PROLOGUE

Karl

    THE END OF DAYLIGHT savings time and winter combine to make nights longer, a blessing for a vampire—one I have cursed more than graciously accepted for over 600 years. As I reach up and push on the coffin's lid, the hinges squeak as it opens. I crawl out into the evening, refresh myself with a shower, and then I wander onto the front porch with a book in my hand, a collection of essays by Ralph Waldo Emerson. As I take a seat in my favorite antique, white rocking chair, I reach out into the distance, casting my senses beyond me like a net, searching for potential danger. The crickets chirp, the cicadas sing, and the smell of honeysuckle sweetens the humid, Georgia air. I sense another vampire eight houses down, another creature of the night assimilating into human culture.

    The night is peaceful, just as I like it, and makes for the perfect evening to bury my nose in Emerson's *Self Reliance* and let the world around me disappear. When the grandfather clock inside chimes through the screen door at the eight o'clock hour, I decide to move to the kitchen for my nightly cup of coffee, a habit I picked up in 1914 on the eve of the war. Coffee is the closest thing to sunshine a vampire can withstand.

    As the beans brew, I take the time to appreciate the rich aroma, allowing the smell to waft over me. It brings back memories of days gone by when I was very much in love with Maribel. The love of my life has been gone for over fifty years now. I can't seem to move past her, recreating the smell of our long nights together each evening with a simple cup of joe. If I listen hard enough, I can still hear her laugh as she guzzled caffeine to stay awake with me.

    Lost in thought, I move back to the rocking chair and cast my net again, always on the lookout for danger. This time there are two vampires–one of the two ancient and powerful–and a witch. The hair on my neck stands on end as I wait for them to reveal themselves. Anticipation makes me anxious to discover their identities. It's the witch that shows her face–a beautiful face, framed with mousy brown hair that would've deceived me if I'd not already smelled her dark magic.

    "Mr. Ekman," she greets as she climbs the porch steps, wearing a long, black, lacy dress that drags the ground.

"What do you want, witch?" I ask, in no mood to be bothered by a stranger in the middle of the night.

"They say you loved a human woman," she says.

Most vampires would be ashamed of the fact, but not me. The thirty years I spent with my Maribel were the best years of my immortal existence. "I still do."

She smiles at me, lifts one hand in the air, and unleashes a black cloud of dark magic with one target in mind. The small cyclone picks me off the porch for a few moments before it sets me back on my feet and crawls inside my lungs. I sink to my knees as I cough and sputter, choking on the thickness. It consumes me, painfully twisting my bones, contracting my muscles, and invading my mind.

The witch walks over to me with dark black shining eyes. She touches my forehead and whispers an unknown language into my ear with snarled, black words. A mental picture of a male human and his dog filters into my brain, and there's one command along with it.

Kill.

I stand from the porch, feeling stronger than ever before. I begin my journey from my suburban home to downtown Atlanta, zipping through woods and streets at vampiric speed. I reach a parking garage off Decatur Street where my victim and canine have made a temporary home for the night. I'd been homeless many times in my mortal years, living on the streets of Granada. I try not to prey on those in the same position. But tonight, there's bloodlust running through my veins. With each beat of the human's heart comes a fresh wave of the copper scent that causes my fangs to protract in anticipation of tasting the sweet life force on my tongue.

In the back, dark corner of the garage, the sleeping dog wakes and lifts his head. A deep growl emanates from his throat, a warning not to venture closer to the human. Animals can always sense when they're in the presence of a stronger predator. The man rouses from his sleep.

A vampire never has to take a life. It keeps their existence from being discovered. Once they make it past the first year of barely controlled hunger, they can make the experience quite pleasurable, even sexual, for both parties. Depending on the age of the vampire, most need little more than a sip of blood. But tonight, there's no pleasure to be had. The magic coursing through me will ensure that I'll devour the man's soul down to the last metallic drop.

"I was here first," the man says, clearly of the mind that a well-dressed vampire is here to impose on his makeshift bed.

I don't want to kill the man. It's a senseless loss of life. I'd rather go home and finish my java while reading Emerson, but the urge to fully consume the man outweighs all humanity left in my vampire soul.

I don't respond to the man. Instead, I opt for an attempt at fighting the black cloud in my head. I tell myself to walk away, to leave the fragile human being, and allow him to live another day.

"Find your own spot," the man says, his voice dripping with annoyance over being roused from sleep.

I try to turn around and walk out the way I came, but the hungry urge is too strong. I close my eyes and force images of Maribel into existence. If anyone can remind me of the man and vampire I am, it's her.

I step into a small circle of light, illuminating myself.

"What the fuck are you?" the human asks.

I can barely manage words, but I have to give the man a real shot at escaping. "Run!" I growl.

The man quickly slides from his sleeping bag, crab crawls backward and jumps up into a standing position before he sprints across the garage. I fight like hell against the magic's hold. The quick retreating footsteps slap the pavement in perfect timing with the human's heart. The beat grows stronger, harder, and faster as the man overexerts himself as he runs for his life. If I can wait until the man is behind a locked door, maybe I can find some control. A lock won't stop me, but a required invitation to come inside by a human will.

Maribel dances across my vision, a dark-haired beauty with high cheekbones, full lips, and sparkling blue eyes. I concentrate on her scent—a heady combination of jasmine and vanilla. It's a scent that normally calms me quickly. I focus on the silkiness of her long locks, the way her long lashes touch her cheeks, and the smile made to bring man and beast to their knees. But the bloodlust, the sound of my victim's quick breaths, and the stench of the street fill me instead of the beautiful spirit I hope against all hope will save me.

"Maribel," I call out, hoping she'll spare me from this terrible act.

Thought becomes more difficult with each passing moment. My soul fades, buckling under the witch's power. I know what will happen if I give into the darkness—it will take over and I'll rip the man to pieces.

"Maribel," I plead one last time, my voice full of desperation. "Save me, my love."

But her memory slips away, replaced with my only mission.

Kill.

I casually amble out of the parking structure, my senses locked onto my prey, and stalk down a dark alley on the trail of the scent. In the distance, the human bellows as he frantically knocks on alley doors for entry and safety. When I am but five feet away, I stop and wait for the man to turn around to see what awaits him. The moment before the kill is the sweetest moment of the hunt when the lamb finally realizes the blade is about to drop. There's nowhere to turn and no one to cry out for.

As the man turns to face his death, I notice the dog tags around his neck–Patrick Russell. The fog of the magic lifts just enough to realize that the man is a veteran. "You served?"

Patrick puffs his chest out, pride overcoming the fear on his face. "Yeah. You?"

"In another life, being a soldier was the only option for an orphan."

"That's fucking great, man. Are you going to chill now?" Patrick asks warily.

A blackness fills me again, and a cloud settles over us. I reach out with my sixth sense for my Maribel, hoping she's nearby and can help me overcome the forceful magic. It begins to choke me, filling my lungs with needles as I fight against it. My bones begin to buckle underneath the weight as I nearly collapse to the ground. My eyes fill with tears as I realize I'm seconds away from completely losing control. There's nothing anyone can do for Patrick or myself at this point.

With supernatural speed, I close the distance between us. I wrap my hand around Patrick's throat and squeeze as I lift him into the air. Patrick claws at my hands with wide eyes that beg for mercy, but there's no mercy to be had. The human kicks his legs in an attempt to break free, but his fragile, mortal body is too weak to fight against the hold. There's fear in his eyes until right before life leaves him, and then there's the resignation of a soldier—a man who knows death is coming and decides to meet the end with dignity and bravery.

I lower him enough to connect my lips to the carotid artery. I hover above it for a moment, enjoying the vibration of the rapid pulse against my mouth. I possess no restraint as I tear into the neck. A blood-curdling scream escapes Patrick, which only invites me to drink harder and faster. Rivers of the crimson flow down our bodies, soaking the skin and clothing in the sweet elixir. I haven't felt this kind of hunger since the night I first rose as a vampire. Patrick's heart gives out, and as soon as I release the dead weight, the body crumples to the ground. I find myself unsteady on my feet, drunk from overindulging way past my fill. I lean over and vomit most of the blood back up, feeling sick from a combination of gluttony and putrid, dark magic. I purge the spell from my body, and when I'm finished, I look up to find Maribel's ghost beside Patrick's body. Tears stain her porcelain face. I squat over the man's body and reach out to touch her face, but she vanishes into thin air.

    I fall to my knees as I pull at the strands of my hair. Tears cascade down my face, and utter shame courses through me. The guilt threatens to pull me under. "I'm sorry, my love," I whisper to her ghost.

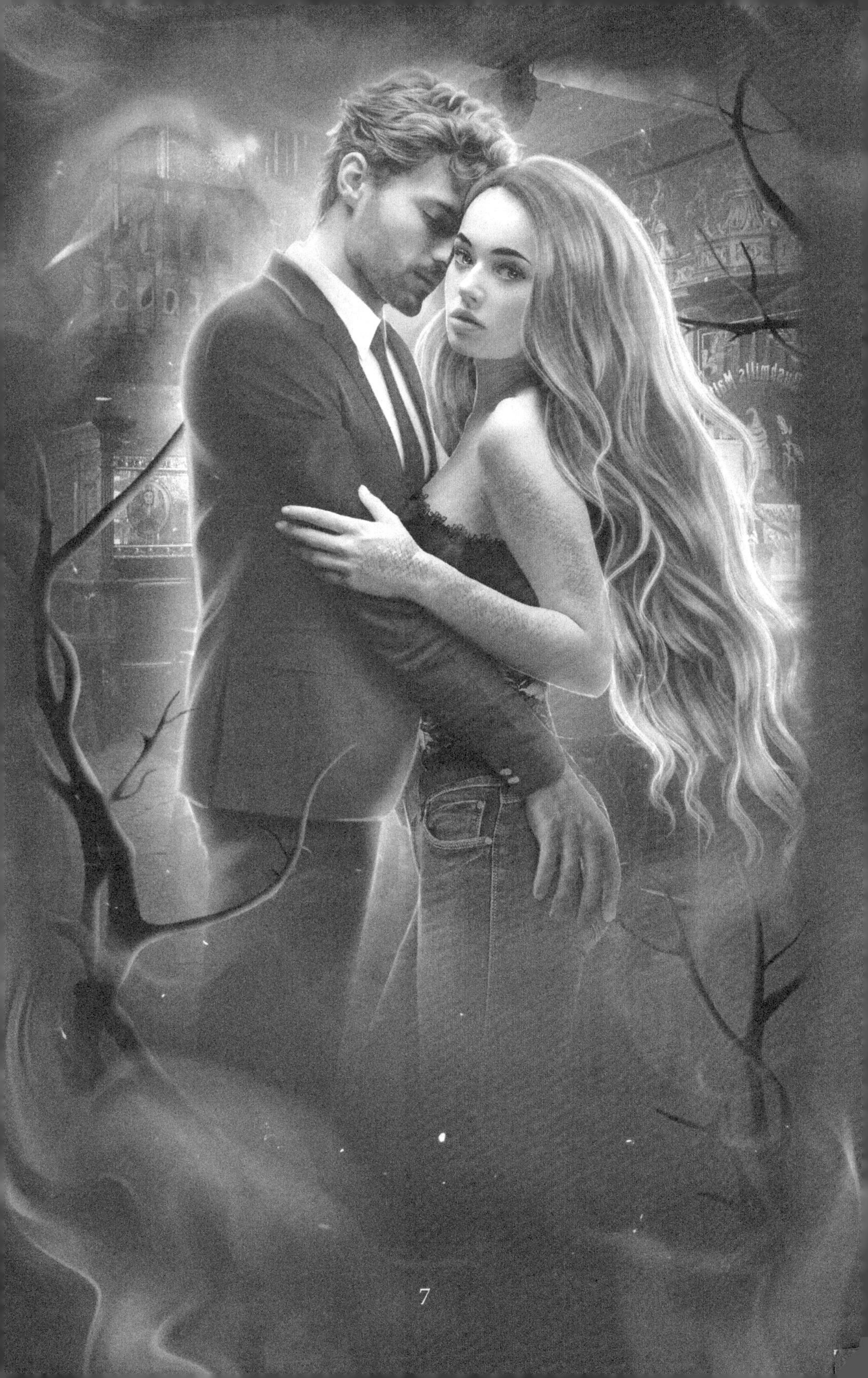

CHAPTER ONE

Zvi

I TAKE ANOTHER SIP of Wild Turkey as I keep watch over The Bar. It's creeping toward eleven. The bourbon isn't curing my headache and neither are the patrons, who are as loud as the music. The place is dimly lit with the house lights turned down. Lighted liquor and beer signs adorn the walls along with music memorabilia. Dank smoke hovers in the air in billowy clouds from those who prefer herbal relief to alcoholic beverages.

The place is owned by my sister, Moe, and myself, and what The Bar lacks in originality in name, it makes up for with the character of its supernatural clientele. It isn't just another watering hole. It can only be accessed from a dark alleyway off Decatur Street in Atlanta, but there isn't a lighted sign above the door directing every Tom, Dick, and Nancy to spend their hard-earned dollars on booze and debauchery. As a matter of fact, no signage exists, but a spell warding off humans does. Humans don't need to discover our existence and ruin their precious little perceptions of their safe worlds, which means a person does not wander into our business by mistake. If a human is ever inside our walls, it's because we want them there.

Thursday night is bike night, and heavy rock and roll pours from the speakers. The dress code consists of leather, boots, doo-rags, and patches sewn onto vests. The place is overrun with wolves who like their pipes as loud as they do their music. I'll never admit it aloud, but I like Thursday nights only slightly better than I like Friday nights, when the vampires and demons come out in droves for 90's night. I love the 90's. It was a great decade for music.

I don't prefer one supernatural species over another though. They're all assholes as far as I'm concerned, and there doesn't exist another being like me. It confuses the hell out of everyone I come into contact with and annoys the shit out of me when I'm bombarded with probing questions.

The bar is packed and the crowd is reaching an eight on my internal drunk-o-meter. If trouble is going to rise, it usually begins at an eight.

Moe and two other bartenders are still pouring beer like it's water, while some of the customers show off their stellar dance skills in the middle of the room. Members from different packs congregate around the pool tables and dart boards, but I pretend not to see the money wagered on each game. Wolves love to gamble, and I don't care as long as they aren't hurting anyone. But I keep watch over the gambling since four different packs are in attendance tonight. They love to fight as much as I do, but I don't fight in my bar where I have to pay for broken shit. I understand that dogs will be dogs, and they just have to be the last one to piss on a spot, but they can do that shit outside in the parking lot.

My job is to knock heads together if a fight breaks out. Most people know not to cross me, but alcohol makes them forget sometimes. I'm coiled tighter than a rattlesnake on a good day and wait for someone to step out of line to justify me putting my fist through their face. Otherwise, I'll go to jail for assault and battery, and Moe said she isn't bailing me out anymore.

I scan the bar from one side to the other and catch the glint of chrome in the middle of the room. An unfamiliar man wades through the dance floor and sticks out like a sore thumb in his gray, fitted slacks and black, button-down shirt. He has to be law enforcement and a supe since he's able to walk through the door. Being a stranger or a lawman doesn't necessarily get your ass kicked in The Bar (most of the time), but the gun at his side is about to put him in a very problematic position. No weapons are allowed in here, except mine, per state law and my decree which is why every head in the place turns to him as he marches toward my dark table in the corner.

I don't care if he has a badge, he isn't special. We don't need a pissing contest in the middle of the place because half of these wolves have priors and claim they're allergic to the police. This stranger might not be the brightest crayon in the box. We aren't off to a great start. Strike one.

He pulls out the chair across from me and dumps my feet from their perch. Strike two. I cock a brow at him as he helps himself to the seat. He's good-looking, a good 9.5 on the scale because a ten just doesn't exist. I'm waiting for Moe to cut the jukebox and holler "dibs" across the joint.

My phone vibrates, and I turn it over to discover a text message from my sister.

Moe: Dibs on that tall drink of water!

Zvi: Damn it! I thought about it first.
Moe: You know the rules.
Zvi: You're an asshole.

I met my sister when I was too young to remember it. She's the same age and lived in the same foster home some fifty miles south of Atlanta. Neither of us remember our parents, and we instantly bonded over our disgust for our foster parents. We lived with a couple who cared more for our monthly government draw check than our well-being. They weren't abusive, just neglectful which was a blessing when we hit puberty. To our surprise we turned into other beings. Moe's a witch who possesses too much magic for her own good. On a blue moon, I turn into a... well, you wouldn't believe me if I told you. We always knew we were different, but orphans never suspect their differences will be about creatures written in myths and fairytales.

I place my phone face down on the table and look across it to find the man grinning at me like he knows something I don't.

"Zvi Jayden," he greets.

I school my face. "Well, now, you have me at a disadvantage, because I have no idea who you are."

He rests his large hand on the table and opens it to reveal a shiny badge with a black star in the middle. "Deputy Hendri Connor, Black Star Division."

Black Star doesn't exist as far as the world knows. It's a secret division of the CIA. Their deputies are supernaturals in charge of bringing in violent magical fugitives. When they can't get the job done, they come to me. I like the extra income and the workout. It's cheaper and more productive than therapy.

"A furball and a cop?"

He continues to grin at me. "Feisty and displays an unwillingness to cooperate."

I shrug. "My reputation precedes me. What else did you hear?"

"Creative with insults, supernatural, nobody can pinpoint your species. You've got a notorious temper on you, and you're as strong as an ancient fanger. Rumor says you heal faster than most supernaturals, and you're suspiciously good at capturing rogue creatures Black Star can't seem to apprehend. You refuse to work with anyone from the Black Star office and slip every detail we put on you."

I lace my fingers together and then crack my knuckles. I chance a look around the Black Star Deputy and find the entire bar looking back at us.

"Mind your own damn business!" I yell over the music and slap my palm down on the table. They all quickly find something else to look at, and rightly they should. I'm hard to handle on a good day and if it weren't for Moe, I'd likely be locked up in Black Star's asylum for all of eternity. I help them catch bad guys and in return, they tend to help me out when I get into trouble… again. "Sounds about right," I reply.

The stranger leans forward where I can see his dark green eyes, brown hair, and tanned skin. He has a nice jawline covered with a five o'clock shadow and an even nicer smile with perfect teeth. His legs are so long his knees touch mine. I'd put him at 6'4 which means he stands a whole foot taller than me. He's attractive in a rugged way, and the scabs on his knuckles tell me he isn't afraid to throw down.

My phone vibrates again, and I chance another look knowing it's likely my sister.

Moe: Why haven't you sent him to the bar yet?
Zvi: Because you're not a bounty hunter.
Moe: I like a lawman. Maybe he'll show me his gun. ☐
Zvi: Why don't you just ask him to whip it out instead of beating around the bush?
Moe: Because some of us know how to soften the blow.
Zvi: I see what you did there. Nicely done.

"Interrupting something?" the Deputy asks.

I place my phone back on the table. Moe still acts like a boy crazy teenager at twenty-eight. I just want someone to take home who'll shut up and take care of business, but everybody wants to know my species. Twenty-one questions kills the mood.

"What do you want?" I ask.

"There was a vampire attack tonight." He runs his hand through his hair and sighs. He looks like he's running low on sleep. "The victim is male, 32, and his body was found in an alley two hours ago about a mile from here. Half an hour ago, we confirmed that a vamp named Karl Ekman is responsible, and he's now Black Star's number one fugitive."

The hairs on the back of my neck stand up. I don't care too much for killers in my backyard, vampire or human. "What's special about this vampire attack?"

"It was very public, sloppy, and overkill. Something doesn't sit right with me about how it all went down."

"So he's the number one fugitive now?"

"You didn't see the amount of blood at the scene."

Vampire attacks happen, not often, but they do occur. "Any leads on him?"

He avoids my question with one of his own. "So, what are you anyway?" The million dollar question. *Moe can have him*. I don't need to be nagged anymore than I already am about my fucking species.

I raise two fingers in the air to signal Moe to pour me a double. Killer vamps and too many questions make me drink… more. There's always a lot of gore when the vamps go crazy. I don't have a weak stomach, but there are some things eyes are not meant to see.

"If Black Star wants my help, get to talking or get to walking. Doesn't matter much to me either way."

My sister, Moe, walks two shots over to our table.

We're like night and day in both appearance and personality. She's a free spirit and that's due to her earthly magic. I'm all hard edges. Moe is optimistic to my rampant pessimism, or as I like to call it, realism. She tries to see the good in people. I believe 99% of the population are self-serving assholes. Her idea of a great day is filled with blues and folk music, thrift store shopping, and wine paired with a romantic comedy to unwind at the end of the night. I *might* smile if I'm on my Fat Boy with rock and roll turned as loud as it can go, and the wind whipping through my hair. Or, if I get the chance to open a can of whoop ass. I wouldn't be caught dead drinking wine if hard liquor can be found within a fifty-mile radius.

My hair is dark purple. I have baby blue eyes. Her hair is a dark auburn and reaches the middle of her back with a fair complexion and bright green eyes. She's taller than me by four inches.

She walks a double shot of Turkey to the table for me and a double shot of something else dark and likely top shelf for the poor unsuspecting soul that Black Star sent my way. "Johnny Walker for the Deputy and Turkey for the sister."

The handsome man looks between the two of us several times, no doubt assessing our many physical differences. "You're sisters?" There's a hint of disbelief in his voice.

Some people ask dumb questions. "Isn't that what she just said?"

My sister glares at me for a moment before she smiles down at the deputy again and sticks her hand out. "Moe Jayden."

I motion to him with indifference. "Deputy…" Then I swallow my shot because I've already forgotten his name.

He stands from his seat and takes her hand gently in his. "Hendri Connor."

That's his name! Huh. "Right. What he said."

She smiles up at Hendri. "I hope there's no trouble."

He and I speak at the same time.

His voice is kind and gentle. "Nothing to worry you with, ma'am."

I mumble, "There's a crazy vampire on the loose. Dropped a body a mile from here. I hate when the vamps go crazy. They make my gut churn. I need more alcohol."

Moe ignores me. "Are you from Atlanta?" she asks him.

"I transferred from the Seattle office," he answers. "I've been here a week, but I'm originally from Louisiana."

She bats her lashes. "I thought I heard southern Louisiana when you spoke. I'd love to show you around our city sometime."

He grins down at her. "I might take you up on that."

"Her bedroom is on the second floor if you two would like to get to knocking boots and get it out of your system, or you can tell me what I need to know to put down psycho Karl," I say.

"Don't mind her. She can make a preacher cuss!" she says and touches the side of his bicep. He looks down at her hand and gives her a look of approval.

He looks at me then back at her. "She's going to make my life a living hell, isn't she?"

My sister, the only person on this earth who gets me, casts a gentle expression in my direction. "She's just a Care Bear."

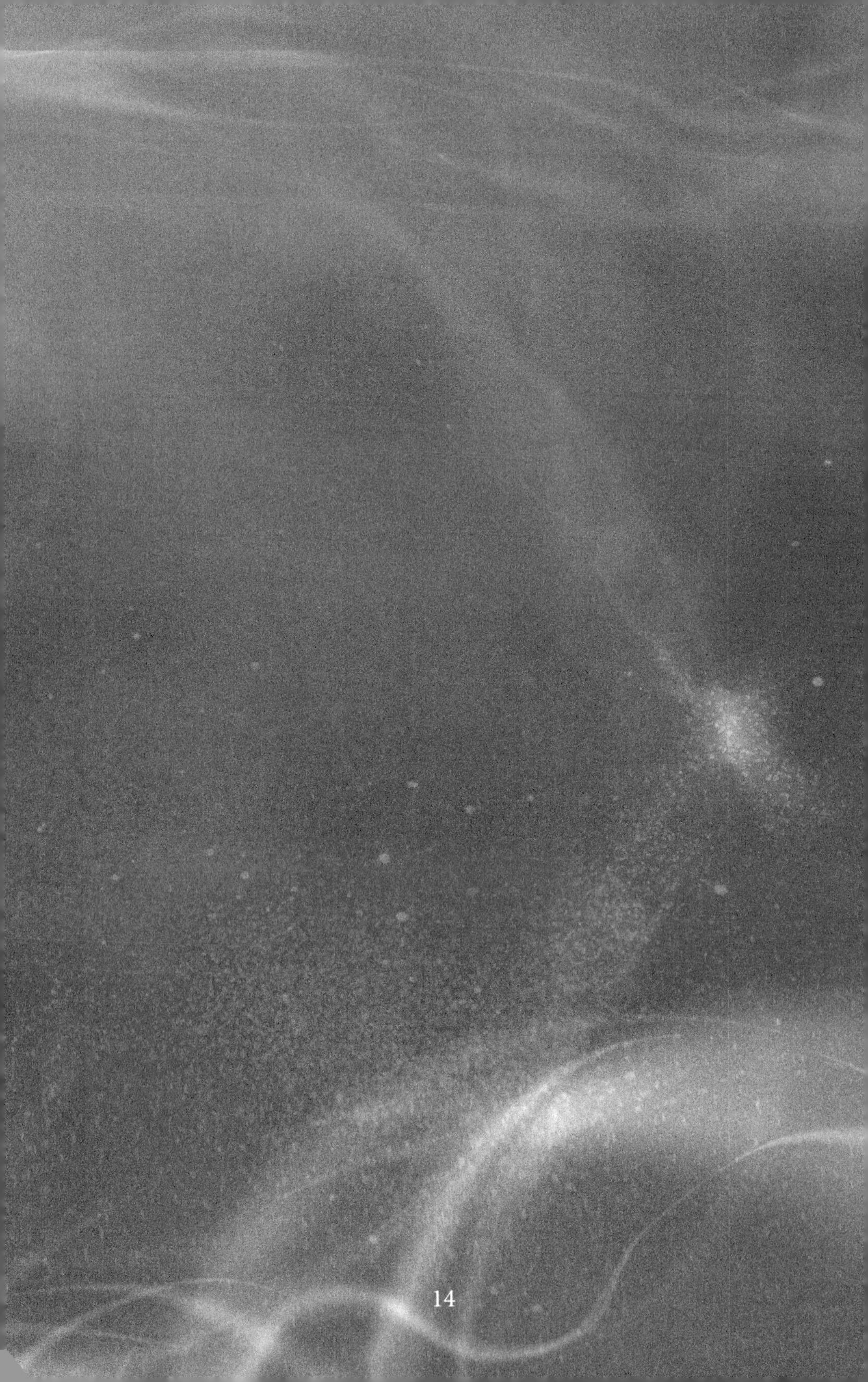

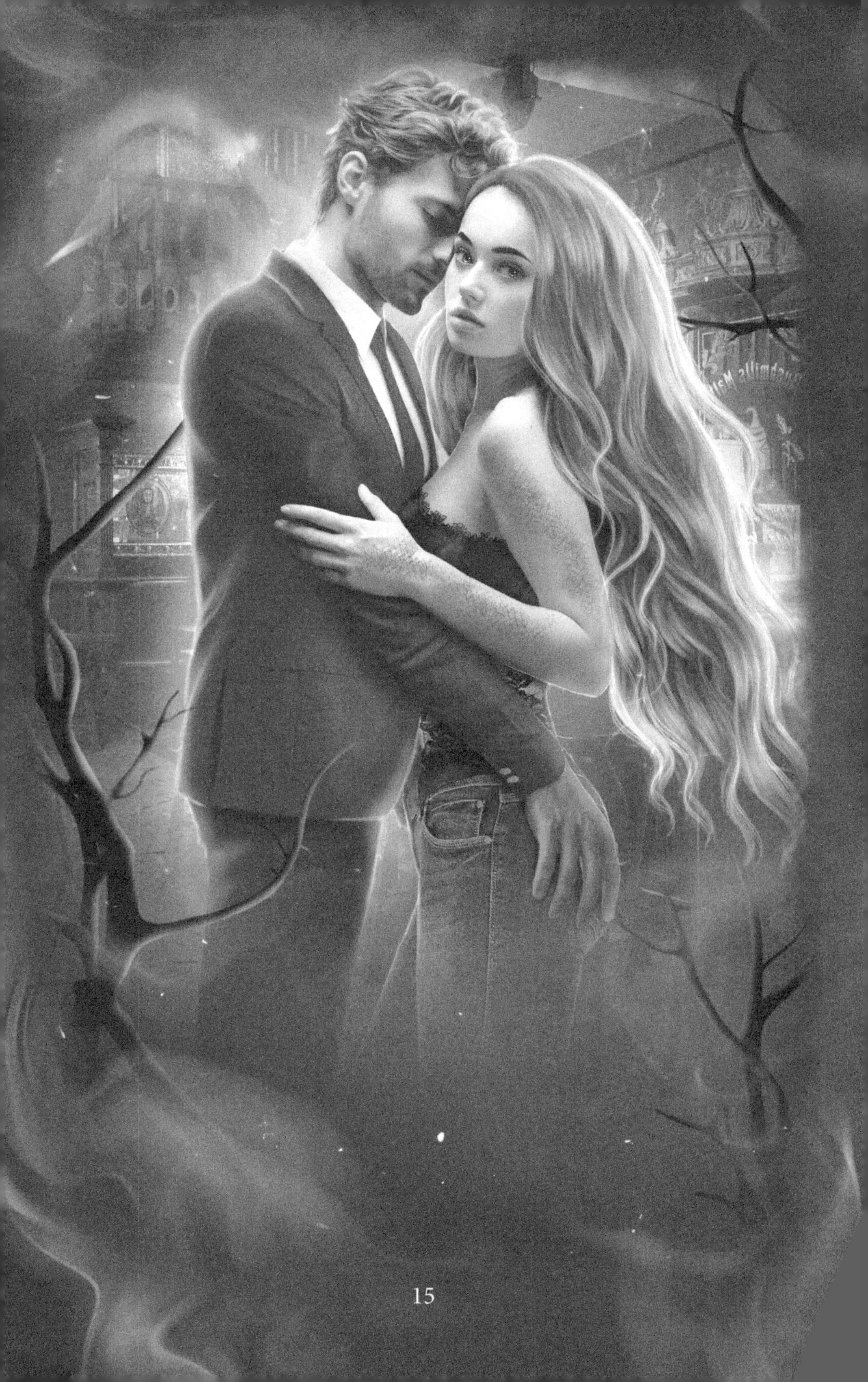

CHAPTER TWO

BEFORE I CAN ISSUE a snarky reply to my sister's comment, someone cuts off the jukebox in the middle of a song. It's a crime to cut a good tune short. The Bar is as quiet as a library, except for the multitude of whispered "what the fuck's". It prompts me to leave my seat in a hurry to investigate and hopefully zero in on the asshole responsible for interrupting the flow of revenue to our establishment.

In the middle of the dance floor stand ten men in perfectly tailored suits. I can smell vampire in the air. Wolves and vampires don't congregate very often or very well. The wolves don't care to get along with other species and need to be contained more than any other type of customer. It's why Thursdays are for wolves, Fridays are for fangers and demons, Saturdays are for witches, and Sundays are for the rest of the shifters.

"I'm looking for Zvi Jayden," says a man in an Irish lilt, but I can't gauge which man spoke.

I march up to a beast of a man, one of the largest I've ever seen, with long, dark brown, sun-streaked hair, and honey brown eyes. He's pretty. He smells old, but not quite ancient. That means he's strong, and he'd be a great sparring partner. I always have some pent-up aggression in need of alleviation. I detect a rare, ancient bloodsucker somewhere in the vicinity, and said vampire would be an even better man to fight. The older the bloodsucker, the stronger they are.

"I'm Zvi," I say with as much attitude as I can muster in a half-drunk state. "Who's asking?"

The beast takes a step to his left, and then the ancient vampire steps forward. He stands at about 6'0 with a strong body, short, brown hair, and fair skin. Large, unique, light blue eyes stare back at me. His face is perfect and a work of art that mocks even the most magnificent works crafted by celebrated and gifted artists. His oval-shaped face holds prominent brows, full lips with a small cupid's bow, a perfect nose, and a strong, angular jaw. The bone structure and chiseled features of his high cheekbones are sharper than the sharpest blade. Half-closed, clear, marbled, light blue orbs are deep-set with thick, long, upper lashes that appear to have been painted with a fine line of liquid liner and a heavy dusting of lower lashes. I've never seen a man I would qualify as a ten, but I'd give this one an eleven.

"Forgive my intrusion," he politely says. "I'm Killian Kavanagh. Is there somewhere private we may speak?"

If I didn't know better, I'd swear the vampire has dazzled me with his vamp superpowers. I know who Killian Kavanagh is, although I've never met him. Meeting him seems to suddenly make me stupid. I'm blaming the bourbon for my unusual behavior.

Fortunately, Moe elbows me in the ribs and rattles my words loose. "Everybody get out! Settle your tabs! See you next Thursday! You don't have to go home, but you can't stay here. Don't drink and drive, or I'll kick your ass. Remember to remove your beer goggles before making any decisions you'll regret in the morning. Have a nice night!"

At once, the patrons grumble but jump into action and head for the bar to settle their checks. I continue to stand in the middle of the dance floor with the vampires, staring at Killian Kavanagh like he's a goddamn unicorn. Moe nudges my ribs once more.

"Right. You can follow me," I tell him as I rub a hand over my ribs.

I head back to my reserved table in the corner of the bar. The overhead lights flash on and nearly blind me, so I yell at the bartenders to cut them off. Half of these people fell out of the ugly tree and hit every branch on the way down, and I don't need their homeliness to be illuminated.

Deputy Connor is still seated at my two-top table. I slide into my seat and let the vampires find their own chairs. I'm hospitable like that.

Mr. Kavanagh sits at the four-top beside me and looks the deputy over before asking, "And you are?"

I almost chuckled at his rudeness. I might like this guy, but not likely since I only like Moe and that's pretty much it.

Deputy Connor is a werewolf, and I know he can smell an ancient vampire as well as I can. "Mr. Kavanah, I'm Deputy Hendri Connor, Black Star."

The vampire seems unimpressed by Connor. "Deputy, please call me Minister. I believe we may share a common interest this evening. I'm here regarding Karl Ekman."

The Deputy looks as confused as a fart in a fan factory. "We just identified him thirty minutes ago. How do you know about him?"

Kavanagh appears bored. "Your office identified him because of me. The reward money also came from me and my associates. I have many resources at my disposal. Atlanta is my home, and I stay informed of supernatural fugitives, especially when they bring unwanted attention to my species or yours. I assume we're both here to procure Miss Jayden's bounty hunting skills?"

Did I mention how creeped out I am by fanger killers? I'm equally disturbed that this hoity toity vampire knows of me. I don't exactly advertise my services.

The wolf crosses his arms over his broad chest. "And you're telling me your interests are purely about public safety?"

Kavanagh looks down his nose at him. "There exists a legion of vampires with interests in public safety and keeping our existence a secret, as is the purpose of your Black Star Division."

"Le Ambrogio?" Hendri asks.

"He's a top-level, delta five bloodsucker, or whatever they call him," I confirm.

Kavanagh speaks with an air of insolence and self-importance. "I'm a founding member of Le Ambrogio."

Isn't he special?

It isn't like we can Google the super-secret vampire society and read the history section on its founding and purpose. It's a global vampire government, and they don't like their kind causing trouble. I've had contact with members of their society, but never someone of apparent importance.

"That's just spiffy," I tell the high-falutin Killian Kavanagh. "Mind if we get on with this? You two already ruined bike night, butchered AC/DC, and took away revenue from our bar."

The beast from earlier finally speaks. "What's bike night?"

Moe jumps in. "A bunch of loud, like-minded people who enjoy riding equally loud motorcycles congregate to show off said motorcycles and measure their dicks and pipes while listening to rock music."

"I resent that," I protest.

"You would."

I roll my eyes. "Can someone give me a lead on Ekman before he kills again?"

The beast hands Kavanagh a thick folder, who then hands it to me. "You'll find updated photographs, contact information, and his history. He was a quiet, law-abiding citizen until a few hours ago. Something doesn't add up," Killian advises.

People come to me for help taking down hard to catch supernatural criminals, and I'm good at what I do. The Black Star Division isn't the only organization that seeks my skills. Moe is my partner-in-crime. It's her magic that allows me to fly in the sky, swim in the waters, and change on land undetected by technology or people. Magic chose her at birth and the force is strong. She can manipulate or draw power from any element of this earth, including blood, which happens to be a rare gift. Most witches can't manipulate blood. She might be able to use the victim's blood and trace it back to the killer. If the vamp ingested even a drop, she'll be able to find him.

"I need the deceased's personal effects," I tell them.

The wolf lifts a brow. "It's at the coroner's office."

"I need it here."

"I can't take unprocessed evidence from the coroner and bring it to you."

"Then I can't fucking help you. Have a nice night." I leave my seat and head for the bar, leaving eleven men looking after me in bewilderment. Bless their hearts.

"She's serious?" Hendri asks.

Moe nods. "She means what she says."

She follows me to the bar and begins to clean behind it with the other bartenders. I make work of wiping and bussing nearby tables. Kavanagh approaches me alone while the other men remain in their seats. "Deputy Connor will bring the items you requested within the hour."

"The quicker the better. I'd like to find him before he goes underground at dawn." We still have about eight hours to find him since it grows dark earlier this time of year.

Hendri walks by us in a huff, no doubt pissed off that he was strong-armed by a vamp to bring the evidence to The Bar.

"Did you hear that, wolf?" Kavanagh asks.

Hendri turns around with a pissed off glare aimed at Killian. "I have excellent hearing, fanger."

And with that he leaves, and the Minister saddles up to the bar in front of my sister.

"Can I get you or your friends something to drink, Mr. Kavanagh?" Moe asks as I watch the encounter closely, ensuring he doesn't get too close to Moe.

"Would you by chance have a Midleton?"

Of course, he'd drink expensive Irish whiskey.

"And for your friends?"

He smiles one of the sexiest smiles I've ever seen. If Moe didn't look so terrified of him, she'd call dibs on him too. "They needn't a thing."

She pours the man his whiskey and places it on the dark, wooden bar. I duck in the back with an arm full of dirty glasses, but my hearing is as precise and sensitive as Kavanagh's.

"She's not quite vampire," he says, and I can hear the swirl of liquid against his glass.

"What do you mean?" That's Moe. She's ride or die. She's the only person who knows what I am, but she'll take that to her grave.

"She has vampire in her and something I've not smelled in many years… I can't quite put my finger on it. Does she require blood?"

"She's not a vampire," Moe argues.

The thought of drinking blood temporarily grosses me out, but his line of questioning intrigues me since neither of us know our parents.

"Vampires can't breed", she reminds him.

"On a rare, blue moon, an ancient can father a child."

"Do you mean a seasonal blue moon?" she asks.

"Yes."

I can change at will, but I'm forced into transformation on a blue moon. Is there any truth to what he's saying?

"I've never heard of a vampire fathering a child."

I can hear the smile in his voice. "I said it was rare."

"You did. How often have you seen this occur?"

"Rarely."

He's frustrating me.

"How rare is rare?" she asks.

He chuckles lightly. "Once in a blue moon."

"You play your cards close to the chest," she says.

"Always."

"A man of few words?"

"I speak when necessary. The world is too full of misunderstandings as it is."

"Ancient *and* enigmatic. Most of the vampires who come in here won't shut up."

"If it is to be known about you or your sister, I know it. Else, I would've never walked in here. I don't believe in being unprepared when interrupting multiple packs of wolves."

He's unnerving me with his observations and knowledge. I like it low key. I don't want people, especially powerful vampires, in my business.

Moe turns the jukebox back on to drown out the silence and lift my spirits. I continue to clean the tables until they're all clear and the chairs are turned upside down on top of them. Killian Kavanagh sits at the bar alone slowly sipping his drink, while his acquaintances remain eerily quiet and still across the room at a table. I don't like them lurking.

Forty minutes after his departure, Deputy Hendri Connor returns with several clear plastic bags sealed with red tape. He throws them on the bar carelessly. I see he has the same attitude problem he did when he left. For about thirty seconds, I wonder if I should rectify it for him.

Each night, we walk our employees to their cars to ensure they're safe. Kavanagh insists on accompanying us as we walk them out.

Once the two women drive off, he turns to Moe. "Do you use your magic out in the open?"

"Moe doesn't get involved in this shit," I answer for my sister.

"You both live above the bar, yes?" he asks.

"You know entirely too much about us, and I'm warning you, it's pissing me off," I caution.

"Le Ambrogio maintains a file on all known supernatural beings. Please do not be alarmed as our purpose is only to preserve order."

"The stories I've heard about your organization don't exactly make me feel warm and fuzzy, Captain."

"I can say the same for you," he counters.

"Best you stick to managing vampires, fanger."

He ignores my comment. "I will accompany you upstairs while my associates entertain the deputy."

"Nope." I pop my "p". "I don't work with anybody. You can keep your ancient ass in the bar, and if you have an inkling that you might come up those stairs, I'd warn you against it. You don't strike me as a man who would walk into a bar known to be full of werewolves without knowing a thing or two about me and Moe. I'm going to assure you that everything you heard about me is true. So help me if one hair on my sister's head is harmed, I'm going to kill your bloodsucking ass."

He grins at me. "I understand."

Moe releases a sigh of relief. She's probably thinking I was considering roasting him in fire, and she'd be right.

I grab the evidence bags where Hendri left them on the bar, and we march upstairs to Moe's second story apartment. My sister stops a few steps up and casts a spell to seal the door. Most witches used latin in their spells, but she uses Gaelic to be sure others can't unravel her magic. It isn't widely spoken, especially in America.

"Séala ó gach duine eile!"

We enter her apartment with the evidence, and I get to work on rolling up an area rug from the living area to uncover the casting circle. Moe collects the quartz crystals she needs for a spell. Next, I light candles around the circle as she sits cross-legged in the middle with the evidence bags. The victim's shirt is drenched in blood, but the pants have very little. She pulls the jeans from the bag.

Her eyes lift to mine with surprise inside them. "I feel another witch's magic pull at me. The magic is weak because it's been hours since the magic touched the item, but I can tell it's a woman who's practicing dark magic. Am I looking for the witch or for Ekman?"

"Why would a vampire transfer dark magic to a victim?" I ask.

She allows a crystal to drop from a necklace over the clothing, and then she chants to draw the magic from the fabric. "Ceangailte agus Ceangailteach. Ceangailte Ceangailte. Féach an Radharc. Éist an Fuaim. Cad a cailleadh. Faightear anois. Ceangailte agus Ceangailteach. Ceangailte Ceangailte. Solas an méid a cailleadh." The candle flames grow taller and brighter as her magic surrounds the clothing. Black smoke begins to rise from the jeans and quickly fills the room until we're choking on the magical fumes.

"Holy shit! It's a compelling spell!" She shouts excitedly between fits of coughing.

I motion for her to follow me as I gasp for air and quickly head for the front door of the apartment.

"I thought only vampires could compel," I say.

Moe's eyes widen in fear. "This isn't good. A witch shouldn't have access to this much power. I have no idea how one woman can contain so much darkness inside her. It'll drive her absolutely mad."

"So you're saying Ekman was compelled to kill?"

She nods. "Likely. I can't think of any other reason that spell would be attached to a vampire."

"Fuck. There's a witch compelling a quiet, law-abiding vamp to kill?"

"Yep," she answers.

I put my hands on my hips and try to sort through the new details, but I still don't have enough information. "How long before this witch goes bonkers and compels every vampire in Atlanta to slaughter half the city?"

She shrugs her shoulders. "It depends on how long she's been practicing on this level with this type of magic. Most witches will go crazy within three or four months of crossing over to the dark side."

"Find the vampire. We need to get him off the street before the sun rises. Then we can concentrate on the witch when the vamps go underground." I chance a look back inside to find smokey clouds swirling around. "I'm going back in to open your windows."

I don't wait for a reply as I zip through the apartment with a speed vampires would envy. Once the windows are open, I turn on a few fans to push the cloud outside into the early morning air. When the room is aired enough that I can see my sister, we go back inside. She goes back to the casting circle and begins to chant again. Dark red droplets of blood raise off the pants and dance in the air in front of Moe. And then the tiny drops merge together and move through the room and out the window with lightning speed.

"It's done. You'll find a blue glowing light attached to the vampire. Grab your go bag. I'll meet you on the roof."

I climb the stairs to my third floor apartment and find my go bag in the bottom of my closet. Then I climb the stairs again, this time past the third floor to the roof. Before I can open the door, I hear Kavanagh's Irish accent. "Nice touch with the door. What is she?"

"My sister," Moe answers, a smile in her voice "How did you get up here?"

"Where is she?" he asks, ignoring her question.

He's throwing a kink into our ritual, and I have to think fast on my feet. I need her to cloak me before I walk onto the roof.

"Ní féidir léi a fheiceáil. Ní féidir í a mheas. Ní féidir éisteacht léi. Ní féidir é a smelt, ag aon duine a lorg. Cloaked mar go bhfuil sí, i bhfeidhm mo thoil. Tá sí cosanta ó litriú, droch-mhianta, agus dochar. Ní thagann aon olc níos gaire ná teacht a lámh. Níl aon fhéachaint léi ach iad siúd a bhaineann le gach solas a fheiceáil. Agus mar a labhair mé, mar sin beidh sé anois," Moe chants.

"You realize I'm Irish and two millenia old. I speak Gaelic," he says.

"How nice for you."

Moe sends me a quick text, unaware that I can hear their conversation.

Moe: Kavanagh is on the roof, but you're already cloaked and protected against magic.

Zvi: I had a feeling he'd be a thorn in my side. I got something

for his nosey ass.

Moe: Do not blow your cover, or I will lock you in a magical bubble again until you've learned your lesson.

Zvi: I hate when you do that. Have I mentioned that you're an asshole?

Moe: It's easier than convincing you to go to anger management.

Kavanah speaks with an air of certainty, "So, you've cloaked her and protected her from evil and magic. What will she do now?"

"You speak Gaelic," she counters with a smart-ass tone.

"Earlier you heard that I am a founding member of Le Ambrogio?"

"I believe I did."

"You two have been on my radar for about ten years. I make it my business to know which creatures reside in the capital of my territory. I will find out what she is, and you two can be helpful or we can do things the hard way."

"Zvi only does things the hard way. Best to learn that lesson early on."

"I'm an ancient vampire tasked with the supernatural ongoings of the country. I'd be wary of frustrating me."

"Well, touch you. Aren't you important?"

"Very," he replies.

Narcissistic much? Vampires are the ultimate a-holes. They think they're glamorous and at the top of the food chain, but no one ever is. There's always something larger, better, or faster. A werewolf's bite is toxic to a vampire, a vampire's bite can rip the throat out of pretty much anything, a demon's bite is venomous to any creature, and if a witch is strong enough, she can wreak havoc on all of them with magic.

This particular vampire is pissing me off.

My sister sends another text.

Moe: I take back what I said about the magical bubble. Somebody needs to knock His Highness down a notch or two.

Zvi: Consider it done. Coming up to the roof now.

While not another soul can see, hear, feel, or detect me, Moe can. We've been bound to each other since we were twelve. If she feels pain, I can sense it. If she's in trouble, I know it, and I can always see her no matter who used magic on her. I can always find her in this dark world.

I emerge from the stairs with a black backpack on my shoulders. I walk straight up to an unknowing Kavanagh and throw a punch to his jaw that knocks him back about ten feet. He lands on his ass and looks a little dazed for a moment before he grins.

"Hello, Zvi. You throw one hell of a punch, muirnīn."

He jumps to his feet and looks around attempting to ascertain my location, but he won't find me.

"If he wouldn't figure me out, I'd fly him to the Atlantic and drop him in it," I tell Moe.

"Please don't," she pleads.

"Oh please do." Kavanagh laughs in utter delight. "Whatever she has planned for me, I'm sure I'd rather enjoy it."

"Are you insane?" Moe asks the vampire.

"Rather fascinated," he answers.

Great. He's enchanted with me. He won't be the first or last man to be so, but I don't think a meddling, rich, ancient, vampire king is going to scare away as easily as the rest. I have a feeling he'll be a problem for quite some time. I'm already regretting that he walked into our bar tonight.

"I'm changing," I warn.

I strip out of my clothing, and pack it in my bag. I concentrate on the constant burning in my gut, and slow my breath. Claws grow from the tips of my fingers and the skin on my underbelly changes to an iridescent color. My bones break, but I don't make a sound. My muscles contract and then expand, ripping and bulging at my flesh until I've morphed forty feet into the air. The rest of my skin changes into dark purple, bony scutes that protect me. I flap my wings in the air and feel the warm breeze against my scales. My wings are colored lilac and fade into a Caribbean blue.

I purr, enjoying the feel of being in my supernatural form. I'm happiest when I shift, something I don't often find in my human form. I look over to find the vampire watching Moe as she looks at me with her neck craned back.

"She's a dragon," Killian guesses. His eyes are open wide in absolute joy. The confidence in his voice almost stops my heart, then my purring ends.

"Shit," Moe curses.

I lean forward and pick up the backpack with my giant left hand, and then I pick Killian up with my right.

"Shit, shit, shit, shit," my sister chants. "Don't kill him!"

Even as a dragon, she can read my facial expressions, and the one

I'm wearing right now is fifty kinds of pissed off. I flap my wings until I gain enough speed and air to lift from the top of our building. I fly into the night with the vampire king dangling precariously in the sky.

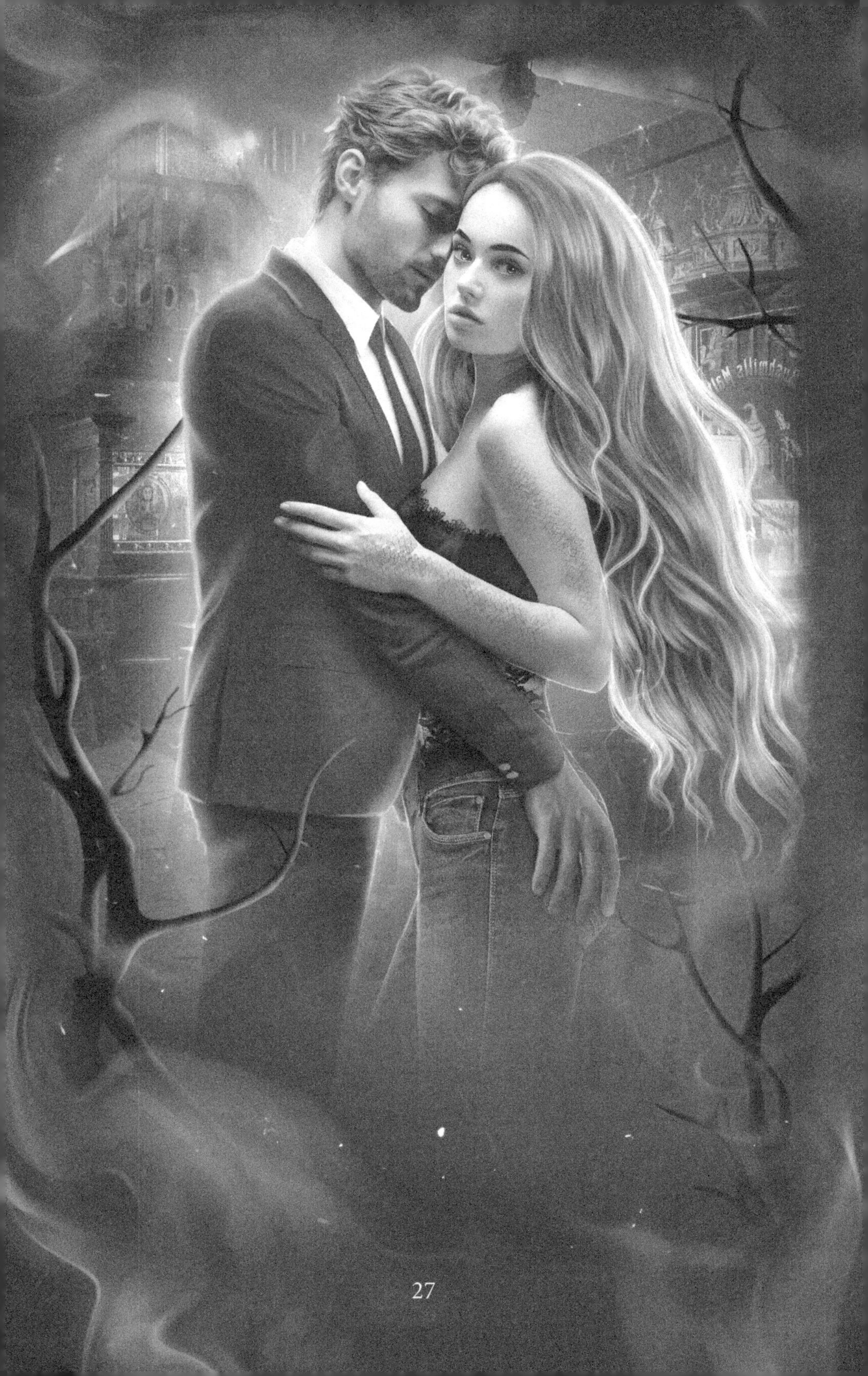

CHAPTER THREE

IF I DIDN'T HAVE a witch and a compelled vamp to hunt down, I'd fly to the middle of the ocean and drop Killian Kavanagh in it. It wouldn't kill him, but he can't move as fast in water as he can on land, and it would take him days to reach shore. I don't have a problem with that, and it gives me time to save the world before I devise a plan to kill him. Unfortunately, ensuring another person isn't butchered by crazy Karl takes precedence. I fly west toward the Chattahoochee River and surprisingly, Kavanagh doesn't fight my hold on him. There's something seriously wrong with this vampire. Maybe he's grown bored in his old age. After a ten-minute flight, I drop him in the river and turn back for Atlanta without a glance spared.

Good riddance.

The October wind is cool underneath my wings. My temperature runs hotter than most, and the air is a welcome relief. I fly over the western portion of the metropolitan area as I look for the glowing, blue beacon Moe attached to Ekman. I fly north and then east before I continue south. I find the beacon twenty miles south of the city and lightly land on the roof of the house.

I quickly change back into my human form and redress. Then I jump to the ground and walk to the front door. I don't feel like using my manners since I'm still pissed about the word "dragon" spilling from that damn vampire's trap, so I kick in the front door without warning.

I hear someone stir toward the back of the house and follow the sound until I come to another closed door which I also put my boot in. Inside stands a middle-aged woman in her nightgown with a frightened expression on her face. She's pretty in an understated way with dark brown hair hanging past her shoulders and powder blue eyes shining from beneath her lashes. She doesn't know what scary is until a person she can't see or use her magic against captures her, tapes her mouth shut, and ties her up. "No!" she screams and flails her arms in the air like a windmill. She starts to chant in Latin, but I've never met another witch who can unravel Moe's magic. My sister is a badass.

I reach into my backpack for duct tape and tear off two pieces... just in case. I tape her mouth shut, which thankfully, muffles her hollering. I don't need another headache tonight. I toss her onto the bed and leave her for a few minutes to check the house for Ekman. I duck in and out of rooms, looking under beds and in closets only to find zilch. I do find several pieces of mail on the kitchen counter addressed to Karl Ekman. This must be his home. I take out my phone and snap a picture of each letter.

The tradeoff for Moe's cloaking spell is that I can't speak to anyone. The spell doesn't have a mute button to flip my volume on and off. The thing is, I'm a dragon, and that means when I'm flying high in the sky I like to let out a good roar or two, really expand the lungs. So, I'm going to have to take the woman with me and question her at the bar to figure out why she's at the killer's house. I venture back into the bedroom to find that the lady has wiggled off the bed. It probably hurt like hell when she hit the floor. Leaning over, I pick her up, throw her over my shoulder, march through the house and out the back door, only to discover the backyard isn't big enough for me to shift. I remember seeing a baseball field a few blocks over and turn in that direction.

Sure enough the field is where I remember seeing it. I throw the witch over the fence. She lands with a thud, then I jump over too. I pick her up and carry her to the middle of the field where I undress, pack my bag, and turn. My energy is beginning to wane from changing twice, flying while hauling a vampire who is too smart for his own good, kicking in doors, and assaulting and toting a witch. I pick up the wiggling witch and take flight once more. I'd like to say I enjoy flying over my city, but it's full of smog and you can't see the stars this low in the atmosphere. If I fly any higher, my hostage will stop breathing, and we need her to tell us why she's at Ekman's house.

Our building comes into sight fifteen minutes later where I gently land and release the woman into a roll across the flat roof. I change once again and dress in the clothes I wore earlier in the evening, so no one is the wiser.

"Did you kill him?" Moe asks.

She's an anxious one. I probably make her that way with my blatant disregard for rules. She keeps me together. I might fall apart when my temper gets the best of me, and it often does.

"Not if he can swim."

"Zvi Rose Jayden! What did you do to him?"

I shrug. It wasn't like I killed him… yet. "Monica Caroline Jayden!!! I dropped him in the Chattahoochee. He's still alive… unfortunately."

"I can't believe he guessed!" She paces along the rooftop. "He's a freaking king! A vampire king! The vampires are going to execute you for treason or something equally awful!"

"Would you calm your tits already? The nervous Nancy routine is giving me heartburn."

She continues to pace anyway. "What are we going to do about him?!!"

"You know the saying, 'If I told you, I'd have to kill you?' Well, that's what I'm going to do," I reply.

"You can't! He's Killian Kavanagh!"

"And he dies just like everything else on this earth."

Then she grows quiet. Moe doesn't do quiet. When she's silent, I get scared because she's plotting something magical. When she's pissed at me, I get put into a magical bubble where I can't self-destruct. I don't like it there.

I change the subject. "Can you uncloak me now?"

"Oh!" Her eyes grow really big and her head goes from side to side, which means she is indeed angry. "You want me to uncloak you, do you?"

"Yep."

I swear smoke is shooting out of her ears. "What are you going to do when he comes waltzing back through our bar?"

"I'm gonna kick his ass and then plot his death. Easy peasy."

Our hostage begins to roll herself back and forth, and her muffled screams start up again. I'm grateful that she takes the attention off me and my mischief. Maybe keeping a rotation of hostages is the key to changing the subject when my sister is mad at me. I'll have to think about it more when I'm not about to torture a person.

I crack my neck and then trudge down three flights of stairs as I carry the witch. When I open the door to the bar, I discover Killian's nine henchmen and the deputy waiting patiently right where we left them.

"Who's that?" the beast asks.

"I broke into a random person's home and found the first woman I thought *might* be a witch," I quip.

He's about to reply when his phone rings. His brows furrow in confusion, and I know the jig is up, because it's likely Killian Kavanagh on the other end of that phone. He must have one of those waterproof boxes on his cell. I didn't account for that and now realize I should've relieved him of said phone right after I punched him in the jaw.

Oh, well. You live and learn.

"Yes, sir," the beast says. "I understand." He looks dead at me with disapproval written all over his face. "We'll wait for you here, Your Highness."

Your Highness, my ass. He was His Lowness when I dropped him in the river.

I don't much like quiet, which is why I like Moe being around. She talks enough for the both of us. It's also why I like my music incredibly loud. I need something to drown out some of the terrible thoughts in my head. Most of them consist of mayhem and those bad boys need some serious antipsychotics. So, I beat the beastly vampire to the punch.

"How is His Majesty?" I ask. He growls at me, making me chuckle. "That good, huh?"

"You should know I have been ordered to stand down or this would be a very different conversation."

"Good to know. How about you make yourself useful and tie this woman to a chair?" I throw the tied-up woman at him, and he catches her mid-air. I'm sure she's ecstatic about that.

Once she's tied to a chair, I walk over to her. "I'm going to take the tape off your mouth, but if you scream, I'll take you up to my soundproofed apartment and torture you until you tell me everything I want to know. Hear me?"

If looks could kill. But within a few seconds, she nods in agreement. I feel glee when I rip off both pieces of tape.

"Two pieces of tape?!!" the witch yells.

I shrug it off. I'm too tired to verbally spar with anyone. "I'm thorough."

"Go get some food and take a nap. I'll take care of this one," Moe says to me.

My brows shoot up in surprise. "Say again?"

"I can slap people around too, you know?"

I motion toward the ten men. "And them?"

"We're all here to stop a killer. I think I'll be okay while you rest."

"She is officially under our king's protection," says the tattooed man in the room.

"Do you have a name?" Moe asks.

"Aleki," he answers.

"I just call him 'the beast' in my head," I offer. "And no way am I missing you torturing someone. I'll be okay for a few more hours."

Aleki walks up to the witch and flicks her nose with a maniacal smile on his face, which I think is an odd thing for a vampire to do. He could've hurt her in many other ways. Huh.

"Where's Karl Ekman?" he asks her.

She spits in his face, and he looks at Moe for help.

"I'll be right back." Moe goes behind the bar and brings back a bottle of vodka and a lighter. And then she pours the liquor over our hostage's head.

"What's your name?" she asks.

"Helen."

"Helen, I'm going to light your ass on fire if you don't answer our questions. Then, Aleki is going to start breaking bones. Understand?" Moe asks, and I swell with pride. I mean, I knew Moe was a badass, but I've never seen her be quite this bad.

She flicks the lighter until a nice, pretty, orange flame dances on top.

"Okay! Okay! Okay!" Helen shouts. "He's my lover. I came over after my shift was over at the diner. He wasn't there when I arrived."

"How did you get inside?" I ask.

"I have a key."

Aleki flicks her nose again.

Weird dude.

"He murdered someone tonight," he tells her.

Her eyes were as big as saucers. "Karl wouldn't do that."

The Deputy jumps in to interrogate her. "Do you know where Karl is?"

"No. I fell asleep while waiting on him," Helen answers.

"We need to take her back home in case he returns," Aleki suggests

Helen scoffs. "That crazy girl kicked in two of his doors. He may already know someone has taken me."

The front door opens and catches my attention. I look up to find a very dry vampire king in a new black suit with a gray tie.

Uh oh.

His poker face is stellar, so I can't get a read on him. I smirk in his direction, hoping to get a rise out of him.

"Sir," Aleki greets and bows.

Moe bows, and I snort at her. I can feel her nervous energy.

He saunters my way until he stands right in front of me. "How are you, Zvi?"

"Tired," I answer honestly.

He has really nice teeth. "Oh? Have you engaged in anything strenuous?"

"I'm sure she's sorry," Moe says to him.

"Cut it out, Moe," I say.

He sends a gentle smile in her direction. "She doesn't strike me as the type of person who is often apologetic, but I appreciate the gesture."

Isn't that the truth?

"You're welcome? Listen, I'm really partial to her." Moe continues.

He looks me over as he says, "I'll take that into consideration. Now, what have we learned?"

Apparently, he isn't overly concerned about my demise. Huh.

Moe is quick to answer, talking a million miles an hour with a slight quiver in her voice. "This is helpful Helen, a witch we found in Ekman's house. She's his lover. He was already gone when she arrived late in the evening after her shift at the diner. She has no idea where he could be. Also, Ekman was under a compulsion spell."

The vampire's head almost comes slap off it turns so fast. "He was under a spell when he killed?"

"Yes," my sister answers. "Dark magic was transferred to the victim's clothing. I cast a beacon spell on the victim's blood and it led Zvi directly to Ekman's house, so he must've returned at some point and left some trace of the blood behind."

"Is this the witch responsible for the compulsion spell?" King Fanger asks.

Moe shakes her head. "No."

I yawn and stretch while they converse about magic and witches. Rather than bother them with the fact that I'm starving and exhausted, I sneak out of the room and head for my refrigerator and bed.

*

My eyes open when I hear something truly awful coming from my stereo speakers. It's very loud, it's pop music, and someone is about to die. I'm going to shove at least one of my speakers up the culprit's ass.

I roll over to find my darling sister sitting on the edge of my bed, staring a hole through my face. I cover both of my ears with my hands and yell, "Turn that shit off, would you?!!"

She cuts the music. "You wouldn't wake up."

"Well, I'm awake now. I should hit you over the head for putting that atrocious song in mine. How long have I been asleep?"

"An hour. You changed twice and you needed it. You were getting too cranky for me to handle."

"Geez. Thanks, sis."

She scoffs. "I wasn't aware that you were delusional about your temperament."

"I'm not. How's the witch?"

"She's sleeping off the excitement in the back room of the bar." She throws her hands up in the air. "Nevermind that. I have great news! I don't think the vampire king wants to kill you."

I roll my eyes. "I'm so glad you told me. Now, I don't have to be terrified and lose sleep over it."

"He's an ancient, Zvi. Some of them are as strong as you. Can't you just admit that you should have handled the situation better?"

Her anxiety never fails to kill my nerves. "I've been the same since we were five. I'm not going to change. I'm not afraid of any ancient vampire because they all have quite the aversion to fire, and I'm a fucking dragon. Seeing things my way yet?"

"You're an asshole."

"I know. Where's His Wetness?"

"Downstairs, cooking you breakfast."

I frown. "Say what?"

"He says they enjoy food sometimes, but it offers no nutritional value."

"Huh. A vampire that eats food. You learn something new every day. I'm going to shower and meet you down there."

"Hold on a sec. I've got something to tell you."

That sounds ominous. "So tell me."

"Apparently, Hendri is a tracker, and his nose was able to pick up on not only my magic but also how strong it is. It makes me nervous."

"Do I need to kick his ass?" I ask.

"No!" she yells. "He… uh… I like him and think maybe he feels the same way. Okay, I know he feels the same, and we're planning on some dinner and maybe some kinky things once Ekman is caught."

"Jesus! I was only asleep for an hour, and you've gone and made plans to do the hokey pokey with a werewolf from Black Star? You do realize that this will bring them closer to our doorstep, which is what we've been avoiding for ten years!"

She anxiously wrings her hands. "Stop yelling!"

I start pacing, but I can't process this information until I have food on my stomach, and apparently, there's a fanger downstairs in the kitchen cooking like it's an everyday occurrence for him. Moe quietly takes her leave without another word. I don't like this, Hendri Connor showing interest in my sister. She's far more delicate than I am. I fear her desire to have a family of her own will get her into trouble with supes like the deputy. I want her to be happy, but I don't want her interest in the wolf to bring Black Star to my door every single day and make my life difficult. I'm a loner and don't care to be a part of a team. That will take away the freedom I love. I have no interest in working for anyone but myself.

    I can see through the windows that the sun has yet to rise. The vampires don't have long before they have to go underground. I need to hit the street to look for kooky Karl as soon as my belly is full.

I take my time showering and grooming before I throw on a crop top, jeans, and boots. I strap a stake around my thigh, a sickle on my back, and my revolver preloaded with silver bullets. Then I make my way down the stairs. My nostrils fill with the smell of bacon, coffee, werewolf, vampire, and magic. Plates of food are stacked high on the bar. I'm a big fan of meats and coffee, not so much on the wolf and vamps. Killian Kavanagh is behind the bar with his suit jacket off and his white dress shirt rolled up at the sleeves. I hate to admit he's the best looking man I've ever laid eyes on.

"How was your swim?" I ask him as I pile my plate high with greasy food.

Moe spits out a mouthful of coffee.

"I enjoyed the flight more, but the swim wasn't as bad as I thought it would be."

His flippant attitude doesn't do a thing to improve my usual cantankerous mood, but his chef skills just might. I sit down beside Moe who's already eating. I dropped him into a river and here he is, smiling at me in genuine good humor. There's something wrong with him, and I have a feeling I'm still going to have to kill him, regardless of Moe's assurances.

    "Are you really going to eat all that food?" Aleki asks.

"Miss Jayden, you have the appetite of a dragon."

My hand tenses around my fork. I start to feel a little stabby. It's fortunate for Mr. Kavanagh that no one in the room seems to take his comment literally.

"Now you're a comedian? You know what? Don't answer that. I want to eat in peace."

The room leaves me to eat in quiet while I try to think of different strategies to catch Ekman.

I look at my watch before I announce, "I want to visit the crime scene after breakfast."

"I'm going with you," Moe says.

I don't require as much sleep as Moe, unless I'm drunk or hungover, but there are already dark circles around her eyes from lack thereof.

I nudge her. "You need to sleep."

"I'll sleep after."

"Fine." I'm not going to argue with a grown woman.

Once my belly is about to burst, I go back upstairs to fetch the keys to my bike and grab my helmet. When I open my apartment door, Kavanagh is leaning against the wall across from me.

"What do you want?"

He looks down at my helmet and reads one of the stickers attached to it. "*If you think you feel good, you should feel me.*" He looks back up at me. "Is that an invitation?"

"Do you have a death wish?"

His stupid, breathtaking smile appears again. I've never been rendered dumb by a vampire before. I thought I was immune to most supernatural forces, but he makes me second guess myself.

"I haven't seen a dragon in a century."

"And you didn't see one today. M'kay?"

"One day, you'll change for me."

"I think you should know I haven't decided whether I'm going to kill you or not. FYI, vampire plus fire equals vampire toast crunch. Now, what do you want?"

"I must take care of matters at Le Ambrogio. If I don't see you before I go to ground at dawn, I have an assistant, a human I trust with my daytime endeavors. In the event you should require something or someone to aid in your investigation, please give Kreston a call. He is under direct orders to be at your beck and call while I sleep."

"I don't need a human to see about me, nor do I want your help. I'm perfectly capable of finding Ekman without your assistance." I check the time on my watch. "How long do we have before the sun comes up and fries your ass?"

"Why do I get the distinct impression that you'd rather enjoy watching me writhe in pain?"

"Pain? No, I'm thinking more along the lines of death."

He leans his head back and laughs, a melodic sound, but then he drops all the pretenses of humor and rushes me. My back is against the wall before I can grasp what's happened. His hand gently wraps around my throat and gives a small squeeze. His lips part, and I can't help but look up at them. He inches in, almost touching his mouth to mine, and whispers, "But I can't fuck you if I'm dead, and I very much want to fuck you before I die my final death, Zvi." My body betrays me, and he doesn't miss my sharp intake of air, or the gasp that leaves my mouth when I'm almost positive he's going to kiss me. A devilish smile crosses his face, a small victory in his eyes, as the tips of his fingers delicately touch my cheek. "Tell me, love, will you fight this or give in to the inevitable?"

I hate that my voice comes out all breathy, affected so much by his nearness and his words. "You can go fuck yourself."

He presses his lips together to hide a smile but does an awful job of it. "God, I hoped you'd say that. Will you watch?"

My rational mind finally kicks into gear, and I realize I've found myself in quite the precarious position with a vampire king.

"Am I interrupting something?" Moe asks from behind Killian, a smile easily heard in her voice.

"He attacked me!" I argue, even though I can't see over his shoulder to her.

She snorts in disbelief.

I raise my knee to get the man off me and teach him a lesson at the same time, but he blocks my crotch shot with both hands. God, he's quick. But it gets his hand off my person. I try to push him over by knocking him off balance, but he recovers far too quickly for my liking. I step out of reach from him and find my sister and Deputy Connor staring at me with big grins on their faces. Shit, there are witnesses. I'm going to have to kill the wolf now, and that's likely to make my sister a very unhappy camper.

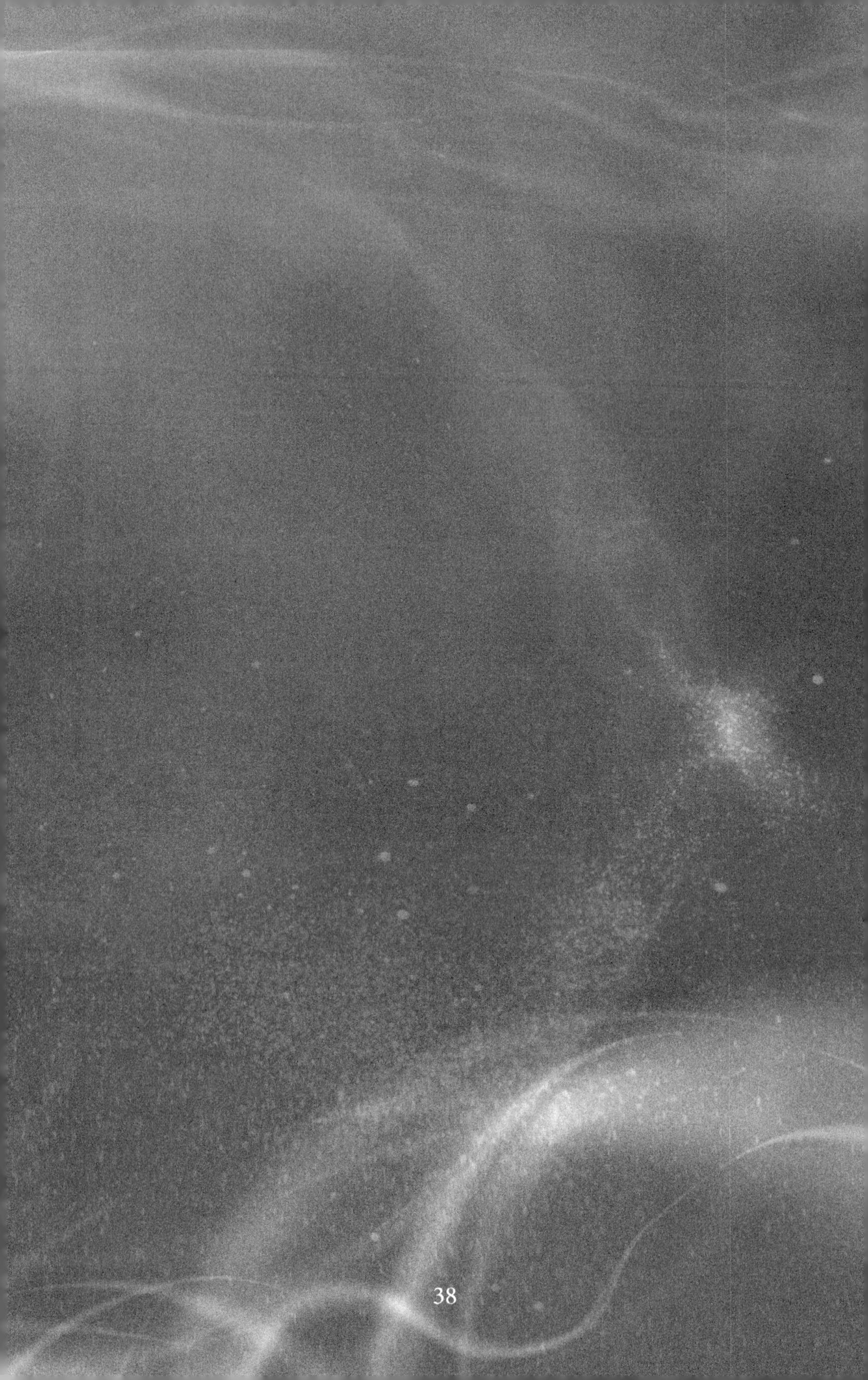

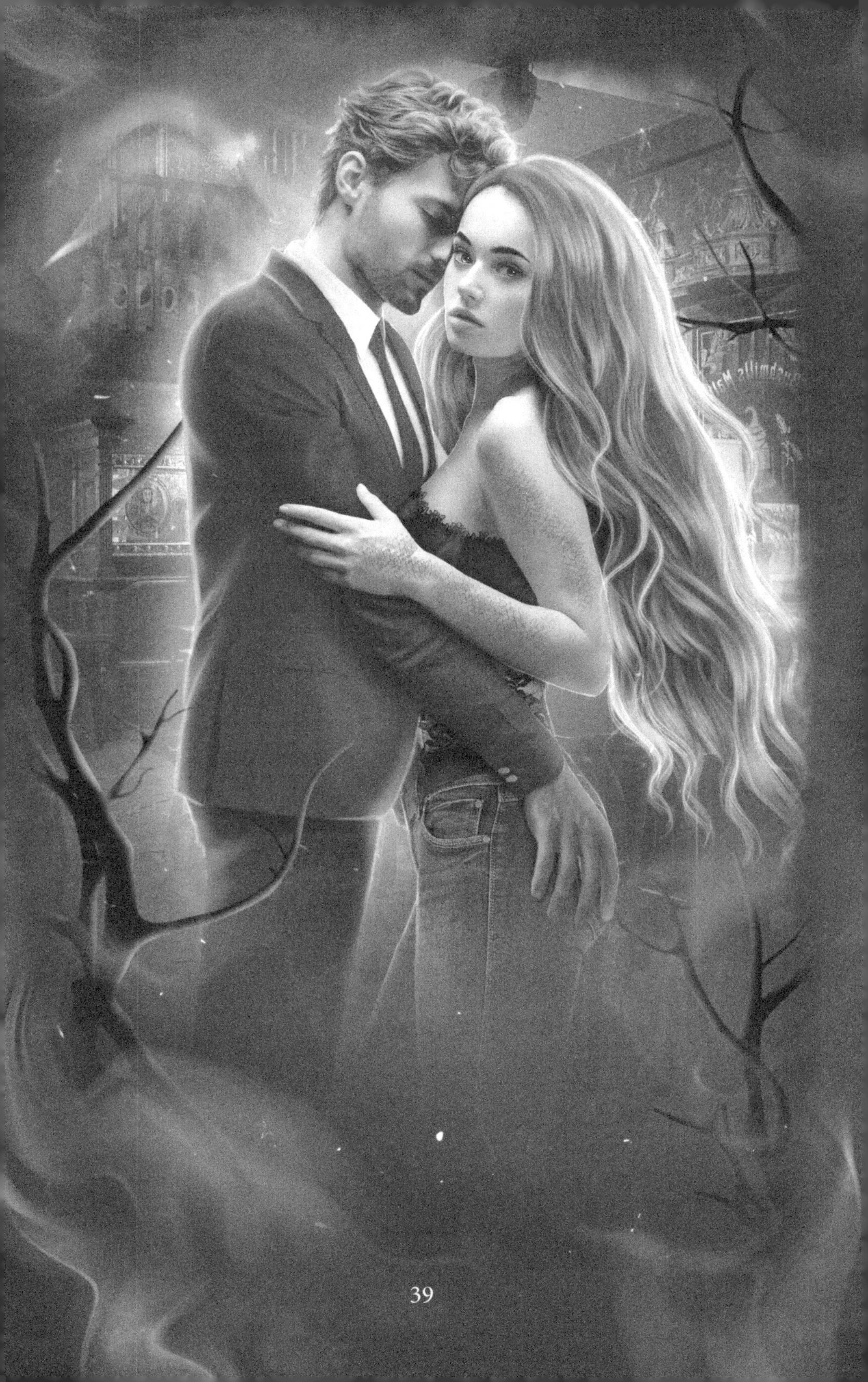

CHAPTER FOUR

I PARK MY BIKE on Pryor Street, throw my leg over, and then Moe and I follow Hendri into the alley. It's taped off with police caution tape, and the area is drenched in blood. There's a metallic smell and the stench of death in the air, and something else that's familiar. I quickly duck under the tape and advise the rest to remain where they are. I walk the area, then kneel down to touch the blood and bring my fingers to my nose. There are two scents. One is human, and the other is a dog. I know both scents well. I stand facing away from the party with my hands on my hips, denial coursing through me as I come to grips with the truth.

"Zvi?" Moe calls out to me.

I remain still and quiet for several more minutes before I speak. "The file didn't have any identification on the victim."

The Deputy replies, "No, but he's been identified as…"

I finish his sentence. "Patrick Russell. Where's his dog?"

"How did you …?" he asks.

The look on my face promptly shuts his pretty little mouth. There are many things in this world that piss me off, but now I'm coming to terms with the fact that I've been taken off guard, and there's nothing I can do to help anymore.

I'm losing my patience. "Where is the fucking dog?"

"Zvi, what's going on?" Moe asks.

"The dog is with animal control," the Deputy answers.

My eyes close as I take calming, deep breaths. "Has anyone claimed the body?"

"Not as of an hour ago."

I leave the marked off area and march past them as I say, "Take me there. I'll claim the body."

I can hear Moe's feet fall on the pavement behind me as she rushes to catch up with me. "What's going on?"

"Ekman killed Patrick. Our Patrick. Can you go get the dog from animal control?" I ask.

Her hands immediately cover her mouth. "No, he'll be in the bar in a few hours to clean the floors."

Patrick, a homeless veteran, was a good man whom we paid to keep our floors clean. With his PTSD, he couldn't hold down a job, but he could work in the quiet of the empty bar while everyone was at home sleeping it off. And he had an excellent work ethic. He also kept up the parking lot for us, and in return, he crashed in our shed in the back. I have no idea why he was sleeping where he's so vulnerable.

I place a hand on her shoulder, letting her know I feel the weight of our friend's loss too. "No, sis, he won't."

Tears fill her eyes to the brim until they spill over.

"He wouldn't want you to cry, but he would want us to make sure his dog isn't euthanized," I say.

She nods her head in understanding and wipes her tears. "Okay. I'll go get Rocky."

When I find numb-nuts Karl, I'm going to put a hurting on him. I don't care if he's compelled or not. He'll burn. Vamps hate to go that way. Those idiots would rather be staked or have their heads lopped off. It doesn't usually matter to me which way the bad guys die as long as they die, but Karl is going to bleed. In this situation, I like that a vampire heals fast. It means I can drag out the torture for a substantial amount of time.

*

My sister and I sit at the bar and nurse our respective drinks after a busy Friday evening at The Bar. It's four in the morning, but it's already been a day. And to top it off, King Saddam Insane walked in. I don't like his lurking.

"What are you thinking about?" Moe asks.

"Murder and torture," I answer.

"Jesus, help us all."

"He won't help you, or Karl. As a matter of fact, I'm going to kill King Fanger over there right after I take care of Ekman."

"I heard that," Killian says.

"You want a fucking cookie?" I ask.

I hope he asks for one, because I'm rearing for a fight after our friend was just murdered. At this point, I'll fight anybody just to make myself feel better. Patrick deserved better than the gruesome death he got. And his dog is now with the perfect old couple out in the country, but he'd still much rather be with Patrick.

The kitchen door behind the bar opens and a stranger walks through. Killian flies over the bar and grabs him by the throat before I can investigate.

"What are you doing here?" he demands.

New Guy is ancient, and he's probably the second oldest vamp in the room. His dark hair is slicked back like a douchebag as his green eyes shine with mischief. He's wearing a navy pinstripe suit with a purple tie. He's quite attractive but he gives me creepy vibes.

"Who the fuck is that?" I ask.

The stranger attempts to pry Killian's hand from his throat as the vampire king struggles to keep his grip.

"Why are you here?!!" Killian asks again.

I can see the stranger's predicament. "I don't think he can talk with your hand around his throat, ya big mosquito."

Killian's guards surround the two vampires and put us right in the middle of the fight. I jump on top of the bar and pull Moe up with me to avoid becoming collateral damage.

"Vampire popsicles!" I yell to Moe.

I hop down from the bar and run into the kitchen to grab our commercial mop bucket, fill it with water, and run back into the bar. Moe holds the bar gun aimed at Killian and New Guy, and has already begun to use the water button to freeze both men into place while her other hand works her mojo. I run toward Killian's group of vampires on the other side of the bar and brace myself.

"Ready!"

"Now!" she yells.

I throw a bucket full of water at the crowd while Moe chants a spell in Gaelic. It falls over them and freezes them into place.

I round the bar and get in their faces. Two sets of eyes look over to me.

"When you thaw out, you're going to sit your asses down and play nice. If you act up, I'm going to lose my temper and Moe is going to turn you all into slugs. They're worse than frogs and much easier to smash on the floor. A little dab of salt and poof, you're dead!"

I have to hope they'll listen since they're unable to speak or give an inclination of the head. I climb back on top of the bar and sit crossed-legged. Moe hands me the bar gun, which I use to shoot water on them to speed up the process for Killian and his friend. He'll have to find some dry clothes a second time today, and I randomly wonder if he owns anything other than a suit.

When New Guy thaws, he pushes the Minister into the bar, then rubs his neck. The Killian Icee falls to the floor with an audible thud, but he springs to his feet moments later.

"Can you turn that off now?" asks New Guy.

I look down at the bar hose in my hand and realize I'm still super-soaking him.

"Oh, right. Totally my bad," I apologize.

He steps forward and offers me his right hand. "Everett Burton. I do apologize for this mess."

I forget what's going on when Killian removes his very wet jacket and places it in my lap, then begins to unbutton his white dress shirt. I can't figure out whether I want to punch him or watch the strip show more, which is just one more reason why I want to kill him.

"Zvi," Moe whispers.

"Yeah?"

He made me stupid again, and yet I can't pull myself out of it.

"Shake the man's hand," she whispers again.

Now, I remember what I was doing. I turn my attention back to the Englishman. "Zvi Jayden." I wave my hand in front of my sister. "She's none of your business."

I hear the Minister's sopping wet shirt hit the floor and like an idiot, I turn to look at His Wetness. He's watching me with a tense jaw.

"Answer my question, Everett," Killian commands. Although, he's still looking at me while he speaks.

I'm in a super sexy land with all my carnal thoughts… about a vampire I'm most certainly going to fry.

"I was visiting a friend," Everett answers.

"Mighty convenient," Hendri says from a booth slap across the bar.

"Whoa! I forgot you were there!" Moe shrieks in surprise.

He shrugs his shoulders. Somebody knows how to get out of dodge when the vamps try to kill each other. Smart man.

"You didn't advise my office you'd be in my territory," Killian says.

Everett is very blasé. "It must've slipped my mind."

Everybody in the room knows that's bullshit.

"Say, you look familiar," Everett says to me.

"No, I don't. I'm not the one you want to use as a pawn. Why are you in my bar?"

Killian answers for him. "He's looking for me. Lord Burton is an excellent tracker."

"Lord of what?" I ask him.

"Canada," Killian answers.

I pry my eyes from the delicious muscles on his lean body. "Well, we're the queens of The Bar, and we'd really appreciate it if you left before I throw you out. That goes for you too, wolf."

"Are you speaking to Kavanagh or me?" Lord Everett asks.

I can tell he thinks a lot of himself.

"Both of you," I answer. "The guards will thaw in about fifteen minutes, and I want all of you out, else I'll mop this place with the lot of you."

"What did you do to her?" Everett asks Killian.

"She's naturally mercurial," the Minister answers, a grin on his face.

"*What* is she?" the newcomer asks.

"Hey!" I snap my fingers to get their attention. "She is right here and none of your damn business."

With that, I maneuver around them to the kitchen door. After I pick up two mops, I hand them over to the two royal assholes. "You mess it up, you clean it up. Bar rules."

Everett looks to Killian. "Is she serious?"

Why do people keep asking that?

"Very," he replies.

The two vampy royals begin mopping behind the bar. Ten minutes later Killian hands over the mops to his minions and orders them to clean the large puddle they left behind. Then they get the hell out of our bar.

"What the hell was that all about?" I ask my sister.

"Something is brewing with the supes," she answers, and my intuition tells me she's right.

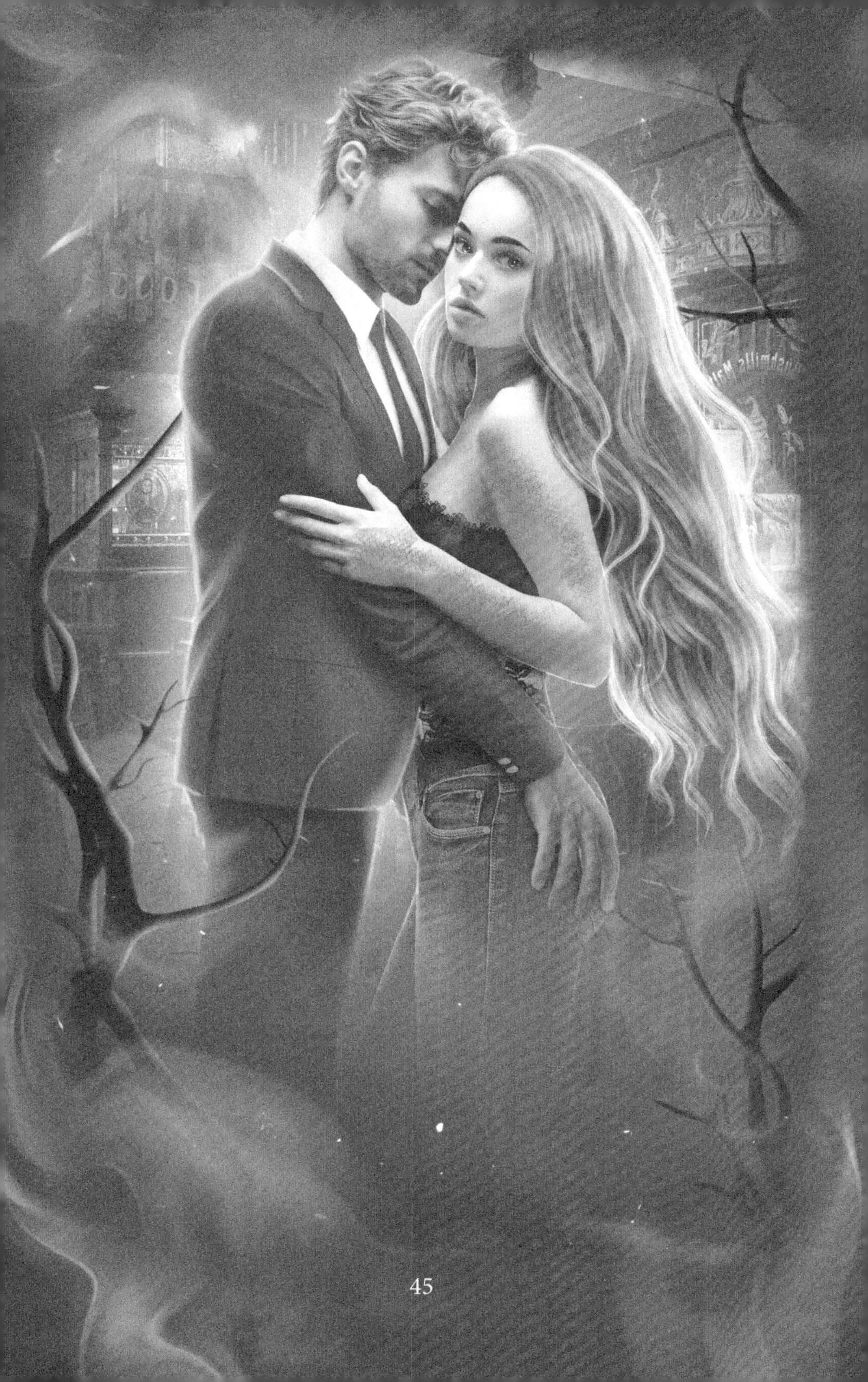

CHAPTER FIVE

I'M WIDE AWAKE AFTER everyone leaves the bar, a part of me waiting for Patrick to walk through the door for his shift. The other part of me knows it'll never happen again, but wrapping my head around it has been more difficult than I could've imagined. I think through the case and the newcomers to The Bar. Our establishment has been very busy with powerful, important supes, and I don't like it one bit. I don't have enough information to go on to try to track down a quiet vampire who apparently spent his time with his witch lover outside the city.

I'm able to sleep after the sun rises, but I oversleep and wake in a panic. We open at five on Saturdays, and it's eight. I throw on the first clothes I lay my hands on and run downstairs in a hurry. There are too many strange people in our bar lately for Moe and the other bartenders to be without protection.

When I open the bar door, Soundgarden croons from the jukebox and the place is half-full of regulars. Moe is behind the bar with our Russian vampire bartender, Milena.

I rarely work behind the bar and for good reason. Customer service means pouring a drink in exchange for money to me, but that's it. I don't care if the customers want to watch another football game, I'm not changing the one I'm watching. Also, I'm not a fan of small talk, and bartenders need to be good at that. I don't understand people's need to talk too much, and I've given up looking for an explanation about the curious behavior of others.

Milena isn't much better, but the vamp customers like her and she can pour a mean bloody mary. However, the two of us left unsupervised may drive away all our business.

"You look like fresh fuck," Milena sneers at me, and I flip her the bird in response.

Moe scowls. "What are you wearing?"

I look down to see my tiny boxer shorts are on backwards. Black rain boots with skulls all over cover my feet, and I'm still wearing the black crop top I wore last night. My hair probably looks like I stuck my finger in an electrical outlet. I also haven't brushed my teeth. I realize people are beginning to stare and it might be a good idea to go upstairs and make myself presentable. "I'll be back." I rush through my usual routine and hurry back downstairs thirty minutes later.

I immediately notice the regular Friday night vamps and demons aren't saddled up to the bar anymore, and they've been replaced by two royal vampires and some of their guards. I glower at the two leading men. I have to get them out of here.

"I can take over," I tell Moe as I come to stand in front of the two eldest vamps in the room.

I pour bourbon into a lowball glass and slam it in front of Everett Burton. The glass breaks into several pieces.

He looks at me in surprise. "I can't drink this."

"Tough shit," I reply.

Moe interferes, "I can pour you another."

"No, you cannot." I contradict. "I told these assholes to get out of our bar and I meant it. They're scaring off the customers." I wave my hand down the length of the bar.

The regulars are whispering amongst themselves at the tables and booths throughout the bar, and all eyes are on the two men who no doubt used their royal status to gain their seating. Other than me, nobody in The Bar is going to refuse these two men or their requests.

Killian is very clearly annoyed with Everett. "I told you this was a bad idea."

Well, I'm annoyed too. Maybe that isn't a strong enough word for what I feel. "You should've listened, leech."

"Why *are* you here?" Moe asks.

Maybe I can speed this up and get them out of here before another brawl breaks out. It's a little early in the night for one, not that I consider time an issue where a fight is concerned.

Everett speaks first. "I thought we were hunting a killer. I've unearthed some potentially useful information."

"No, *we're* hunting a killer." I motion between me and Killian. "I can't handle more than one smug vampire at a time. You should go back to wherever it is you came from."

"As much as it pains me to say, you might want to hear him out," Killian says.

Obviously they aren't friends.

I wave him on to continue. "Go ahead then."

"There are too many around. Is there somewhere we can speak without an audience?"

Killian answers for me and my sister, "You aren't going anywhere with them alone. I've notified you of their protection status."

I'm a fucking dragon. I'm not worried about his protection.

"Let's use the kitchen," Moe suggests.

The two vamps follow us to the kitchen, where they stand as far away from each other as possible. Everett rubs me the wrong way, and I have a feeling Moe feels the same. I'll have to save my questions about him until after he's gone.

"Speak, weasel," I order.

Everett frowns at me but speaks anyway. "I know a witch who has worked with this type of spell in the past. She may be able to help lure him out of hiding."

"Why would we work with a dark witch?" I ask.

"If she's successful, we can capture him," Everett answers.

I don't mess with other witches and Moe stays out of covens for a reason. She practices solitary magic with access to an occasional mentor to avoid power struggles and to keep other witches out of our business. Everett's plan is missing vital details.

"Who is the witch?" Moe asks.

Killian scoffs before he raises a glass to his lips. Then he says, "I can't believe this was your grand plan."

Everett shoots a glare at the king, which I think is rather unhealthy since a king is higher in power than a Lord. "Please forgive King Kavanagh. He and my consort seem to disagree over some past events."

"What the hell is a consort?" I ask.

"It's a fancy word for his sociopathic girlfriend," Killian replies.

"Who is she?" Moe asks again.

"Natasia Portnova," Killian answers.

"You're joking! You don't seriously expect any witch in the Atlanta area to work with her do you?" my sister asks.

I look between them like a tennis match, not feeling warm and fuzzy about not knowing what the hell she's talking about.

She sees my expression and expounds. "He has to be joking! There's no way in hell I'd be caught dead anywhere near her. She was mixed up with vampires ten years ago here in Atlanta and sold out her entire coven in order to save her own head. The vampires butchered every last one of them. I don't know the specifics, but she was banished from the state of Georgia and as word spread about her actions, she's been refused in other states as well. I want absolutely nothing to do with her!"

"Did you kill those witches?" I ask Killian.

Killian sticks his hands into his pockets and levels me with a look I know is meant to show me he's not going to bullshit me. "No, Burton's brother would be responsible for that bloodshed."

I'm not giving Burton an answer until I have all the facts from Killian. There has to be another way. "You and your men are to leave this bar at once. If we decide to use your help, Killian will make contact with you."

I'm suspicious of everyone and Everett, his witch, and Killian share the number one spot. First a dark witch shows up in my city and compels a vamp to kill someone I know. Then Black Star and an ancient royal vampire show up to ask for my help. Another pompous fanger appears in our bar pretending to help, and he just happens to know a dark witch, who I might add, is connected to Killian somehow. And I trust Everett less than I do Killian, and that's saying something.

Once Everett leaves, Moe is the first one to speak. "Natasia Portnova is the last option. I'm not working with a traitor unless it really is the only way to find Ekman."

"Why is Everett really here?" I ask.

"I killed his brother," Killian answers.

"Why did he come to our bar?" Moe asks.

"Every vampire has different abilities. Burton is good at intelligence. He's probably had eyes on me for weeks before he made an appearance. A Minister of Le Ambrogio walks into a bar full of werewolves, and you can be sure it did not go unnoticed by the supernatural community. I unintentionally led him here and for that I apologize. Both of you and The Bar are under my protection."

I snort. I'd totally kick his ass in a fight. How is he going to protect me?

"That guy doesn't give two shits about Ekman. What does Everett really want?" I ask.

"To kill me, take over my territory, and become Minister. I killed his brother, Blaine, ten years ago, right after he killed that coven of witches. He tried to use them to kill me. Natasia was his spy, but I caught onto her before they could follow through with their plan. Blaine murdered the witches to cover his tracks. Natasia fled Georgia and ran to Everett for protection before I could get my hands on her."

"Wasn't she banished from Georgia?" Moe asks.

"She was banished from my entire territory."

"I knew Everett was a weasel," I comment. "You let Natasia get close enough to spy on you?"

He clears his throat in discomfort. "She was in my bed."

"Ah! Dicks make men stupid," I reply.

I can see that Moe is trying to reconcile all she's learned. "Everett wants to kill you, but he's offering to help catch Karl Ekman with the help of Natasia's power. How powerful is her magic?"

"She's a natural-born like you, but her magic comes from a darker place. She's very powerful and quite effective in unraveling other's magic." he says.

"I don't want her anywhere near us then," Moe replies. "Is she in Atlanta?"

"If Everett is here, I suspect she is too."

"Everett simply wants to get close enough to kill you, and Natasia is a liability we can't afford right now. They need to go home," says Moe.

"Can you contain her with your magic or do I have to kill them both?" I ask my sister.

Moe grimaces. "Do you always think about killing things?"

"Pretty much," I answer.

"I don't kill things!" Moe says, then turns to me. "I don't have any experience containing dark magic, and I'm not sure my power is as strong as Natasia's. We would also have to find a way to capture them. The Fire Witch is the only one that can take her power away or unravel it, but the Fire Witch is elderly and in New Orleans. It would be best if we could capture Natasia and take her to   "

"Who?" I ask.

"

I can feel Moe's power. Detecting magic of any nature is a gift I possess and Natasia will meet her match in Moe. "You're just as powerful as her. I've known witches to take power from another and contain it in an object. I'll take care of Everett and bring Natasia to you."

"I've cast a containment spell before, but if her magic touches me, I can be affected by it. Even if I was successful, keeping a dark object puts whoever holds it at risk for theft. There are too many witches who'd want to get their hands on her power."

I smirk. "I think you're both forgetting, I'm pretty good with fire. I can take care of Everett and Natasia with one breath… or I can always drop them in an ocean."

"There's something wrong with you," Moe says to me. "I need to go see my mentor. I'd like to avoid more dead bodies if we can help it. I need help with the spells."

"I'm going with you. I don't want you alone until we can figure out who the players are."

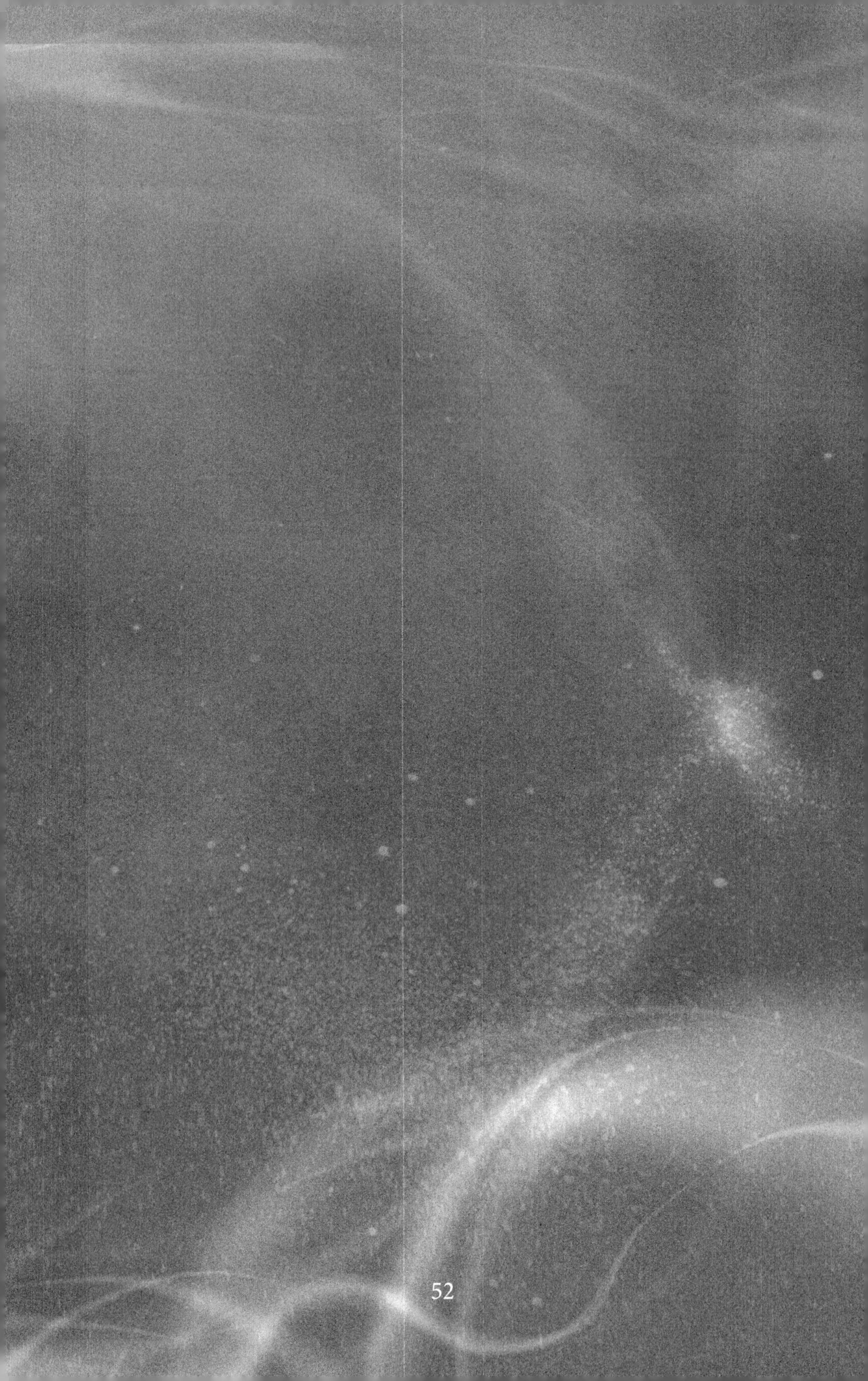

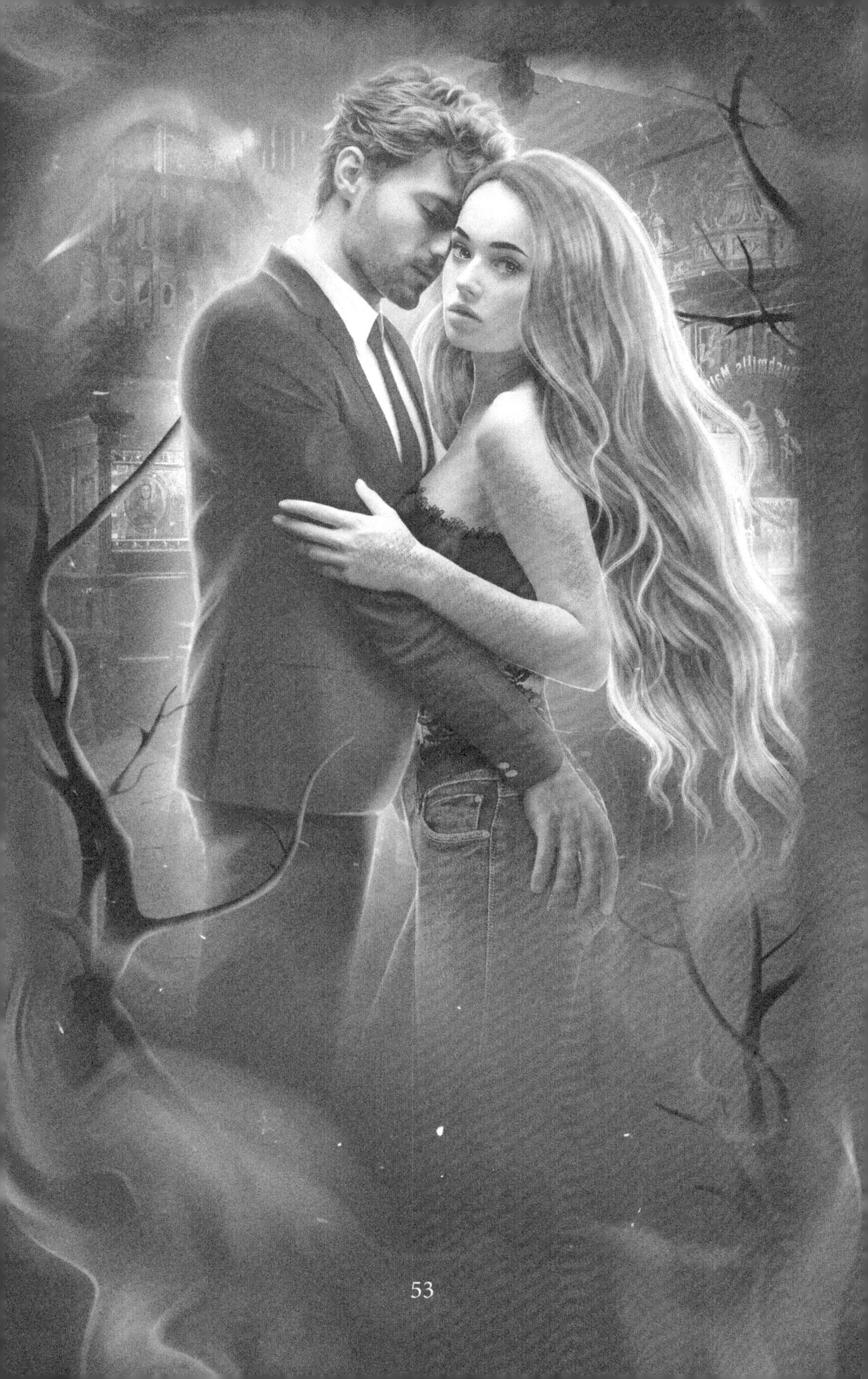

CHAPTER SIX

GRETA IS A WOMAN in her fifties, who has mentored Moe from the age of twelve. She's graying all over with more wrinkles than she should have at her age. Her skin is leathery from too much sun. Her blue eyes are discerning, and not exactly unkind, but they've never been welcoming to me either.

My sister is fortunate that the woman lived next door to our foster parents when we were growing up. She was able to sense the magic in Moe from a young age and guide her in the right direction. Greta's magic is strong, and I've always trusted in her advice. She still lives in the same house on Jayden Street (the name is the one we adopted when we were both of age to change our names) and opens the door at half past ten on a Saturday night with a warm smile on her face.

"I haven't seen your face in months," she greets Moe. I've accepted the fact that I'm not her favorite long ago. I can understand why she bonded with my sister and not me. They're both witches after all.

"The bar and Zvi keep me busy," Moe says.

Her home always smells like sage and sugar cookies, and tonight is no different. She offers me a plate of cookies and a mug of coffee as we sit on her couch.

"You said you had an emergency over the phone?" Greta asks.

"Yes. Do you remember Natasia Portnova?"

"I knew Natasia. She was always a nasty little thing."

"I suspect she's back in Atlanta with Everett Burton, and I need to contain her magic without also being turned into a nasty little thing."

"I know Everett Burton too. I was a member of her coven but left before she talked them into using dark magic. She practiced magic for Everett's brother, Blaine. I didn't approve of her ways, and I left and became a solitary practitioner. I thought Killian Kavanagh had banished her from Georgia."

"He banished her from his territory," I reply.

Disapproval is written all over her face as she asks Moe, "Are you practicing for Killian Kavanagh?"

"He's helping us apprehend a vampire that was compelled to kill tonight. I still only practice for myself," Moe says.

She leaves out that she also cast spells to cloak me. Greta knows I'm not human, but she stopped asking questions about me when we were kids.

"You should be careful with Killian Kavanagh. Vampires like him want powerful witches like yourself on their payrolls. Stay as far away from that one as you can. He's dangerous."

I don't doubt for one second that Killian is dangerous. He holds considerable power and has the strength of an ancient vampire. He also has dangerous enemies that are now in our lives. The more people who come around asking about me, the more likely it is to get out.

"My magic is still pure," she assures the older woman. "Do you have a containment spell for something as forceful as Natasia's magic?"

Greta nods. "You'll need the power of four, fire, and a mason jar to contain the dark magic."

"A mason jar?" I ask.

"It's the south, honey. You don't need an old relic to contain it when a mason jar will work just fine."

"What's the fire for?"

"To destroy the magic once it's in the jar. You don't want that kind of foulness lying around for some idiot to get a hold of," the older witch answers.

We have fire in spades.

I have one last question. "Do you have a mason jar?"

It's the one component we don't have.

"Let me get you one." She leaves the room and enters the kitchen before she returns with the jar.

"I have one more favor to ask," Moe says a little nervously.

"Yes. I'll help you take away that snake's power," she answers before my sister can ask for her help. "Call me when you're ready."

We thank her for her help and hurry back to the bar in hopes that it's still standing. I feel like I've been running all over hell's half acre since I woke up.

When I enter The Bar, everything seems in place. Milena scowls from across the bar at a customer.

"Where is Helen?" I ask.

"Tied up in Zvi's apartment. Why?" Milena deadpans.

Roxana, a witch and our best bartender saddles up to us, and Moe quietly tells her about our visit. "I need four witches to complete the spell to take Natasia's power."

"Why do you have a mason jar?" Roxana asks.

"We're going to put her power in it," Moe whispers.

Roxana gets back to work as my sister and I make our way to my reserved table.

"Four witches and a mason jar… it sounds like a really bad title for supernatural porn," I quip and chuckle.

"I need you, but I haven't figured out how to harness your magic and keep you cloaked at the same time," my sister says to me.

I grin so big I think my face might break. "I get to breathe fire?"

"Yes. You'll have to be careful though. Anyhow, I'll leave you to your good mood," she replies. "It's time to convince Helen to help us before she runs as far and fast as she can get away from us."

*

I don't particularly care for demons in The Bar. Some of them drool worse than a mastiff when they drink, and I'm the lucky girl who gets to clean it up. Their drool smells like rotten bologna and alcohol doesn't help the aroma. I tried to order some of those bibs that barbeque joints offer, but Moe said it was offensive. I think it's practical, and she isn't the one who has to clean up after them. They drink more than other beings which means they spend more money on alcohol, so I can't complain about the income. Most of them are congregated around the dart boards in the back and using each other as the board instead. A collective hoot goes up and then they smile at their buddies as they throw the metal tips at their faces.

Freaks.

"Thirty points for the eye!" one yells.

I need to sanitize them with bleach when this long night is over. I have a high pain tolerance, but that game is just plain stupid.

Moe comes back down to the bar with an unhappy expression on her face. She looks meaner than a wet panther, and her sights are set on Milena. I'm not afraid of much in this world, but that look can mean unpleasantness for the recipient. She's the one person who can put me in my place that I won't in turn beat the shit out of. I deserve more than a magical bubble at times, and Moe knows how to torture me best… with silence.

"Helen is no longer handcuffed to your refrigerator, but fears for my safety since she believes you two," she points to me and Milena, "are 'two bricks shy of a load'. Somehow, I managed to console her, and she's willing to help us contain Natasia. You have to be nice to her," she decrees.

"I handcuffed her to the refrigerator so she has access to food. Humans need food," Milena explains like we forgot that little bit of information.

Moe puts her hands on her hips and turns her full attention on me. "You will be nice to her."

She sure is cranky tonight.

"I'll do my best," I reply.

Moe pulls Roxana to the kitchen to most likely talk her into joining her secret Power of Four Club and gift her with their new secret decoder ring. Not five minutes later, Hendri Connor walks in with a grim expression on his face. I know what he's going to say before he says it.

I don't want the entire bar to hear about this and witches are nosey as all get out. I motion for him to follow me upstairs, but before I can unattach my ass from its seat, that damn vampire king walks in for the second time tonight. Of course, every head in the place turns in that direction. That happens when you're the head honcho traveling with a fleet of warriors.

Killian finds me across the dimly lit room and the right corner of his mouth slightly lifts in amusement until he sees the deputy standing next to me. A frown mars his beautiful face, which puts a smile on mine. I rather enjoy his displeasure. He leisurely covers the space between us, his soldiers carrying the rear. "I've missed you," he says loud enough for the entire bar to hear. Not that he had to shout it. Our patronage has excellent hearing.

I narrow my eyes at him and turn to the deputy. "Let's move this upstairs."

Killian is right behind us. Once we're inside my apartment, Hendri and Killian look around with their judgmental eyes. I don't care if it is a mess, I'll clean it when I get good and damn ready.

"We have another victim," Hendri finally says. "The victim is another male, forties, and he was drained from a large gash in his carotid."

I stretch my stiff back and notice both men getting an eye full of my stomach. There's not an explanation of why I find this far more irritating with the vampire than the wolf, but it's a thing. I also find it difficult to interpret why I find this far more tantalizing with the vampire than the wolf. The deputy is a good-looking man. He certainly did it for me in the few moments before Killian glided in with a small army. Hendri is a southern boy with a charming smile, attention to detail (he's a cop, and he searches people... well not as in people like people people.... for a living and they mostly had the same parts), he looks as physically capable as me, but I bet he's a mama's boy. I can see how much influence a woman has had in his manners. I'd tear his heart out and eat him alive.

Killian Kavanagh is the godfather to Hendri's down home charm. He fulfills the bad boy role like a well-dressed billionaire. He's well-spoken, refined, vintage, and temptation divine. I know he's as strong as me, though I'd never admit it aloud. And his strength gets my engine running, but I absolutely, positively fucking hate it.

I pick at a speck of dirt inside my fingernail. "Another male victim."

Killian clears his throat when he manages to tear his gaze from the skin of my midriff. "Where was the body found?"

"In the parking garage by the alley where Patrick was killed. The victim used the lot when he met up with some friends at a paranormal book convention earlier this evening," Hendri answers.

I snort. They both cast their judgmental eyes on me again. "How ironic."

"You can see the whole thing go down on camera this time. The human security guard saw it live and called it in. We had to erase his memory of the events. He was quite shaken."

My interest is piqued. "You can erase people's memory?"

"Black Star provides their deputies with a short-acting medication for these instances, yes."

"Can I get some of those?" I ask. "And do they work on vampires?"

I can use them on Killian, and he won't remember the whole dragon thing.

"They don't work on vampires," he answers.

Killian grins smugly at me.

I stretch again to see what their reaction will be. Hendri looks away, clearly not interested in me. Killian licks his lips. I flush a little, but just a little. "We need to focus on where Karl lays his head. Someone in this city has seen him."

The deputy is holding the folder out and looking at the picture. "Black Star can circulate his photo in the media and see what falls out."

I shake my head. "No, we'd have to sort through every idiot who called the tip line for the reward money. We don't want to alert him or the public to the fact that he's a vampire. He's too unpredictable under the influence of magic. We need to stop him before he strikes a third time."

The deputy's phone rings, so he takes the call out in the hall, leaving me with the last person I want to be left alone with.

"I need someone in the bar watching the girls' backs," I tell Killian.

He gives me a brief nod and retrieves his phone from his suit jacket. He quickly types something into it and then returns it to its previous location. "Aleki has taken over your duties."

We wait in awkward silence for the deputy to return, although I expect the vampire king to make it more uncomfortable by opening his mouth. To my surprise, he doesn't.

Hendri returns with a file on the new crime tucked under his arm and hands it to me.

The most recent victim from tonight is on top. I immediately recognize the name.

Heath Rutherford.

My spidey senses start tingling. There is something much larger going on here than I first suspected. I flip the page to see a photograph of the alpha from the Scarlet Moon Pack. He was in The Bar last night. I hold up a copy of his driver's license to Hendri. "He's not human. He's the alpha of the Scarlet Moon Pack. No one at Black Star caught this?"

"It's after hours and the paperwork was faxed over. I didn't get to the crime scene until after the body had been moved. It was moved out of the public eye quickly, but now I know why I smelled a wolf at the scene. I thought it was another law enforcement officer."

"How did he get the jump on an alpha?" I ask.

"Why would an alpha attend a paranormal book convention?" Hendri asks.

This could mean that someone knows entirely too much about my acquaintances. I shiver when I think of the one person who Karl Ekman can take from me that would tilt my world on its axis. I have to protect Moe first and foremost.

Hendri's eyes grow as big as half dollars. He asks the question that I'm thinking. "Where *is* Moe?"

We both run from my apartment, fly down the stairs, pass through the steel door at the bottom and stop short of the bar. She isn't behind it. Why the hell isn't she behind it? I scan the barroom for her, but there are too many people here to find her. The music is too loud to hear her voice. Hendri also looks for her. Killian is right behind us, texting someone- probably feuding with Everett on social media or some shit, while I'm about to have a nervous breakdown and tear this place apart.

    I tear through the crowd as I search for her brown hair, but to no avail. The room starts to spin, my heart rate skyrockets, and I break out in a cold sweat. My eyes are wide with fear as it grips my throat. Someone grabs me by the elbow and spins me around. I'm too close to vomiting to rear back for a punch. I meet the beautiful, light blue eyes of Killian Kavanagh as fear continues to course through my veins. Showing weakness in front of him isn't acceptable, so I do my best to school my face into something close to passive. I must not have done a very good job, because there's sympathy in his eyes. Gently he pulls me into his chest and holds me there in the middle of the dance floor before leaning down to whisper in my ear, "Moe was in the kitchen. She's alright, macushla."

    For the first time in my life, I stand still and let the moment just exist where a man holds me, and I let him. We sway as he holds me tighter to his body. I know people must be staring at their vampire king intimately holding me, the temperamental woman who doesn't let anyone but Moe in. Worse is I enjoy being locked in this flash of time with him. Once the song is over, everything will return to normal. I'll be the grumpy, sarcastic hard ass, and he'll be a royal pain in said ass. When the song is over, he grabs me by the hand and leads me to the bar where Moe is standing and looking at us with a grin on her face. I tear up when I see her face and forget all about the man holding my hand. She walks to the side of the bar, lifts the bar flap, and waits for me. I pull myself from Killian and hug my sister tightly, relieved that she's safe and healthy.

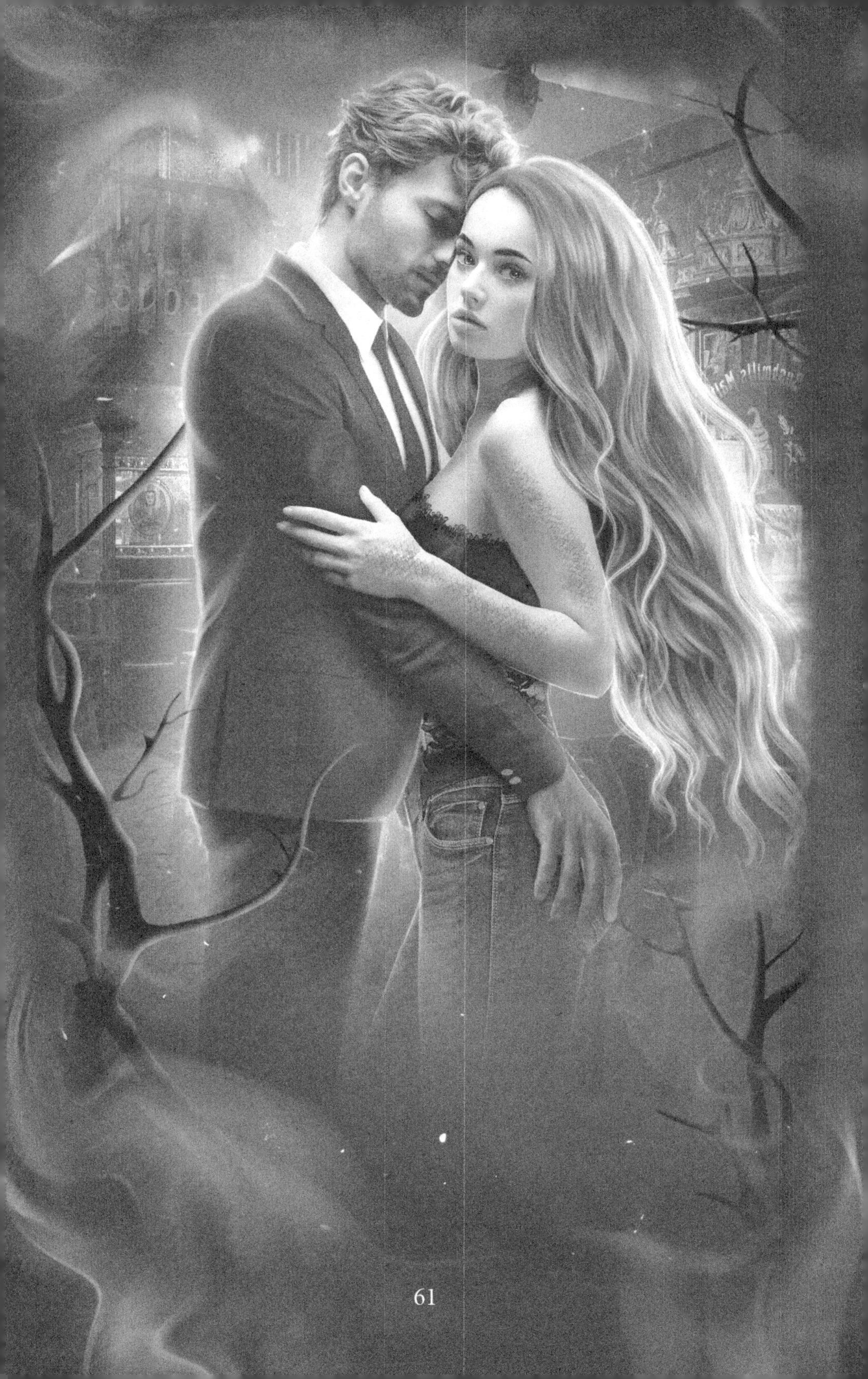

CHAPTER SEVEN

LATE MONDAY AFTERNOON, I wake to sunlight streaming through my tall windows and immediately turn over and throw the covers back over my head. A crumpling sound underneath my forearm has me awake and searching for the source. I reach under the duvet and pull an envelope out. My name is written on the front in a beautiful script. I look around the room to figure out how someone managed to get an envelope in the bed without me waking and mauling the culprit to death, but everything looks as it should be. So I open it and remove a handwritten letter.

My darling Zvi,

You are quite beautiful when you sleep. It's the only time I believe you've ever been nice to me, and I rather detest it. I miss your smart mouth while you slumber. Still, watching you in the stillness of the morning has set my soul on fire with a burning desire I've not known since I first became a vampire.

Do you have an inkling of just how many women can pass through a vampire's immortal life in two centuries? Droves of women, none off which held my fancy for longer than a few months. Yet, I've found in the past decade that I'm completely fascinated with stories of a certain bar owner and her witch sister. How can it be that one tiny woman can strike fear into so many hearts? And how do I find a way into not only her life, but also into her bed and heart?

I ponder these things while you're lost in your reveries. I'd like to think you're dreaming of me when you release the most delightful purr I've ever heard. Perhaps, you're dreaming of what it would feel like to melt in my arms, where you very much belong. Or should I dare ask, are you fantasizing about what it will be like when I make love to you? Because I dream of these things during my waking hours while you sleep, often observing you with my own eyes.

The sun shall rise soon, my dear, so I must leave you now. Even in death, my soul will yearn for yours.

Always,

K.K.

That motherfucker! I can't believe he slipped in here while I was sleeping. I spring from my bed and check each window only to find each one of their locks engaged. My front door is bolted and the fire escape is broken, not that it would stop a vampire. I stand in the center of the room and spin around, looking for some other point of entry that he must've used, but there's nothing else. There's only the locked windows and the door. Something isn't adding up, and I've not had enough coffee to process this just yet.

I grab my favorite mug with a chipper message, "Good morning, I see the assassins have failed again". Carrying the mug and the letter with me, I march out of my front door and down a flight of stairs to Moe's second story apartment. I don't bother knocking. I always come in for coffee each afternoon.

"Fuck!" I hear and catch a glimpse of Deputy Hendri Connor's johnson and tight ass as he flashes across the studio and dives into Moe's bed.

My sister giggles loudly and pulls the cover back for him to climb underneath.

"Fuck, I need drugs, not coffee," I mumble as I cock a brow at my sister. "You're slutting it up."

"Sorry about the streaking," Hendri says. "I had no idea the door wasn't locked."

I wave him off, already forgetting the incident as I head to the coffee pot. Moe sets her coffee maker timer every night, so we always have a fresh brew when we wake. I'm a little perturbed when I reach the appliance and find no java goodness. "Is the coffee maker broken?"

"No and neither are your hands," Moe says, sass in her voice.

I turn around to glare at her. "Fine. I'll make it." I decide to tell her about my stalker watching me sleep and leaving me notes while I wait for caffeine.

"He left you a note?" she asks. "Read it to me."

"No. It's a stupid note. Plus, I'd rather burn it like I'm going to do to that meddling fanger." I hear kissing noises and almost gag. "Can y'all knock that shit off until I leave?"

The kissing, thankfully, stops.

"You know," my sister begins. "You could always choose to feel a little flattered that he's taken such a deep interest in you."

I turn around to find them both getting out of the bed. I think about being flattered for about 2.5 seconds. "Nah."

"Would you like to do some yoga with me today?" Moe asks.

"I'd rather fight someone."

She rolls her eyes. "Yoga is good for the soul. It'll help calm the mind."

"I'd rather beat someone's ass. It calms my mind just fine."

After I enjoy a few cups of brew and discuss the case with the two of them around Moe's scarred oak dining table, I hit the streets to revisit the crime scene and try to turn over some other stones before the vampires wake and Karl strikes again. I have no luck finding any additional evidence or information, so at sunset I make my way back to The Bar and up to Moe's apartment to report on my lack of findings.

Moe's coming out of her door as I hit the top step, and then suddenly, something feels amiss. I can't put my finger on what it is, but my spidey senses are tingling again.

"Shhh," I tell her.

Moe rolls her eyes at me and starts to open her mouth, but I quickly cup my hand across her face.

"Did you hear that?" I whisper as softly as I can.

"Mnoh, I mhdidn'tmh mhear manthingmnh." I forget that my hand is still covering her face and give her an apologetic glance as I remove it.

"Hear what?"

"There's something downstairs."

We start down the stairs as gingerly as possible, keeping mind of the loose board on the third to the last step and stop. The air smells of old iron ore and a slight musk, and something else that makes the hairs on the back of my neck stand up. Whoever or whatever is in the bar isn't to be fucked with, or just maybe they are. A crooked smile splits my face as I turn my head to look at Moe.

Moe speaks in Gaelic and the door at the bottom of the steps blows open, knocking down several bar stools as they slam into the wall. Tables fly across the floor then lift into a wind tunnel in the center of the room. As she picks up the jukebox to send it into the air, a sudden gut-wrenching grip hurdles through my core, causing me to double over. Moe reaches out for my arm and doubles over too. Once I'm upright again, I turn to lunge through the door but Moe grabs my belt loop from behind bringing me abruptly back to the landing. The expression on her face makes me turn back around to see why her eyes are nearly popping out of her head. We both stare as all of the bar furniture stops mid air, the wind tunnel frozen in time, no longer swirling like a deadly tornado. And there leaning against the jukebox is a stranger who appears to be bored out of his mind.

"You know this guy?" I ask.

The man walks halfway across the room to us and smiles. "It's a pleasure to make your acquaintance, Zvi." He motions his hand toward the bar furniture still hanging in the air. "I take it darling Moe, is responsible for this beautiful disaster."

Moe and I quickly look at each other with WTF expressions on our faces.

I don't know who this dude is, but he seems to know us. He's tall, athletic, and dressed in a cape that would look great on Halloween, but he's a little early for the holiday. He wears a tailored tuxedo that likely costs more than our bar. He could be a model with his wavy dark brown hair combed to the side in an out-of-date style reminding me of the 20's era, a perfect five o'clock shadow, and whiskey-colored eyes. His bone structure is impeccable. I'd put him around my age or a few years older.

Apparently, the vampire freaks came out early this year. I have to wonder how he made it past Moe's spell. No one has ever wandered in before, so maybe he's a kooky witch.

"The joint's closed. Time for you to go, Dracula."

He gives me a fangy smile full of good humor and speaks with an accent I can't place. "The humans do their best to replicate vampires, but they never get it quite right, do they?"

He's right about that. Humans come up with some harebrained ideas about supernatural beings. They aren't my favorite creature by any means, but they're creative little things.

I appreciate the lengths this guy goes through to play his character. He has the cape and authentic fangs. The man put down some serious dough on his look, but he sadly lacks a top hat to complete his outfit. That bums me out a bit.

It suddenly dawns on me what he said. "Humans?"

Dracula's facial expression morphs into one of pure amusement. "Ah, yes! Also referred to as breakfast, lunch, and dinner."

Maybe he's a real vamp, but he doesn't smell like one. They all have their own personal scent mixed with a distinct fanger smell, all designed to invite their victims closer. His scent is pleasant with the smell of cloves and sandalwood.

"You don't smell like a vamp."

"No, no, I wouldn't."

I arch a brow. "Are you a few bricks shy of a load?" Crazy people don't always know they're batshit, but it's worth a shot to ask. As he leans his head back, he barks out a fit of laughter that makes me think he does indeed have a few screws loose. It's full of absolute delight and completely over the top. I don't care for people who are that fucking happy.

He points a finger in my direction, his eyes wide. "Oh! Look! I see the dragon in you now! I had to see it to believe it. I can smell the magic of your fire two streets over, but the glow in your eyes confirms it." He looks at me with wonder in his eyes. "My gods, there's still a dragon on earth."

All this talk about dragons is starting to piss me off. He's talking too loud and breaking his jaw so it'll be wired shut is starting to seem like a real good idea.

Moe jumps into the conversation. "You sound like a crazy person. You need to leave before we call the cops."

I snort. Like we need the cops with her magic and my strength.

Dracula doesn't seem to be bothered by Moe's threat. "Then I shall leave you. It was a pleasure to make both of your acquaintances."

There's no way in hell I'm letting him skedaddle off after spouting that mess. "Hold up!" I yell to stop him from moving. "What's all this dragon talk about?"

"Pardon me, I apologize if I'm mistaken," he says and bows. "I haven't smelled a dragon in centuries. Perhaps, I remembered wrong."

I don't believe him. He wears a smirk and has a devil may care attitude that promises deception and… sex. I'm overwhelmed with the scent of warm chocolate, and I need a taste of him like I need my next breath. Something is happening to me, and I'm not in full control of my mind. Is he in my head? I desperately crave him. My middle grows wet as I try to fight against the attraction to the circus freak to no avail. My breasts feel heavy and swollen, and the need to squirm takes over.

Moe stands in front of me and snaps her fingers several times. "Hello?!? Zvi!! Where the hell did you just go?"

I shake my head to clear it of his influence and look around my sister to him. "What was that?"

There's a jovial expression full of adoration on his face as he stares back at me. I now understand why people are so damn curious about my species. I don't know how to protect myself from him if I don't know what he is, and that only serves to rile my temper. Only way to find out what he's made of is to get this party started. I crack my neck and knuckles, gently push Moe to the side and charge him. We crash land into the sheetrock behind him. I raise up enough to land a punch square in his jaw. He grunts, and I wish it didn't turn me on.

I clear the cobwebs from his meddling in my head again and throw my fist into his nose. Blood spurts out like a gusher, and that's when I smell death. He's most definitely a vampire, and the most ancient thing I've ever smelled. Something's different about him though. While mind control is not new to vampire gifts, I haven't encountered another bloodsucker whose gift was strong enough to invade my brain barrier. This guy has me panting at the drop of a dime, which means I'm not in control of me, and that's never happened before. I'm not a fan of it whatsoever. I jump up and pull him from the floor, then wrap my hand around his throat and squeeze.

He lays there unmoving and unwilling to fight back. His fingers outstretch slowly until they softly graze my cheek. "You are far too precious to harm, my love."

I release him and slam him into the ground. "I'm not your love."

"The things we could do together."

"Hey, buddy," I point between us, "*we* aren't doing anything together. Stay out of my fucking head!"

He smiles at me. "Did you not enjoy yourself?"

He knows damn well I had. What woman doesn't love good foreplay?

Hendri walks into the bar and looks our guest over. Distaste is written all over his face, and a snarl escapes his throat as he readies himself for combat. I can see why Moe likes him. He's an alpha with a nice ass. What's not to like?

Dracula holds his hands up in surrender. I guess he doesn't want to chance a werewolf bite. It makes a vampire deathly sick for years. (Pun intended.) "I wish you no harm, wolf."

"And the girls?" Hendri asks.

"I'm quite smitten with them! You need not worry, friend."

Hendri's growl is deep and menacing. "We're not friends, vampire."

Well, I guess that settles that. The deputy doesn't seem to be enthralled with the guy, and that's normal between vamps and wolves, but I can tell Hendri senses that something is off because he keeps looking between me, Moe, and the weirdo bloodsucker.

He lifts his chin at the wall damage. "What happened?"

"A simple misunderstanding is all," says the deader.

I roll my eyes. I don't misunderstand the fact that he came onto me using mind control as a way to coerce me into a state of bliss and confusion. I also don't miss my fist going through his face. Just as I begin to feel normal again, the warm, tingly feeling buzzes through my body once more. It too is accompanied by the sweet smell of chocolate. It's really hard to stay mad at the guy when every single cell in my body is on the precipice of an orgasm. The next thing I know, I want him like I want my next breath, and I have the overwhelming urge to be close to him.

My feet begin to lead me toward him when Killian and his small, mobile army walk through the doors and interrupt my progress. His beautiful blue eyes land on me, and he takes in the sheetrock dust covering me before he frowns. "Are you harmed?"

I shake my head and nod toward the bleeding vamp who's also covered in white dust, and Killian surprises me by bowing immediately to Count von Count. (I have to laugh to keep myself from counting to ten in the Count's voice.)

"Master, you're bleeding."

Hold the front door. *Master*?

Master waves it off. "There's been a misunderstanding between the lovely Zvi and I."

Misunderstanding, my ass. He turned me into a pile of goo without my consent, and judging by how Killian's eyes roam my body and the angry look on his face, he knows exactly what his master has done.

The king schools his face and then offers Dracula a smile. "I see you've met my consort, Miss Jayden. Zvi, meet my master, Gio Swan."

I barely manage to hold back a gag. I understand immediately that he's trying to lay claim on me to prevent Gio from further harassing me, but *consort*? Can't he say he's my boyfriend or better yet, a booty call? Consort implies privilege in their world. Vampires are organized, political creatures. I don't want to be responsible for anyone but me and Moe. I also don't want their drama.

The three men and Moe stare at me while I process his move.

"Zvi," Moe whispers.

Right.

I suck at pretending, so I muster the biggest smile I can which probably makes me look like a lunatic. The thing that irks me most is that I don't have a choice but to play along. While it isn't the way I would've picked, maybe this little scheme of King Fanger's will hold gorgeous Gio back from any further manipulations on my libido.

"Come here, macushla," Killian says in an authoritative tone, and my stupid, treacherous nipples pebble.

I snap out of my little stupor and take myself across the room to him. He wraps an arm around me as he tucks me into his side and smiles down at me like he's genuinely happy to see me. Why does he have to smell good?

There's surprise in Gio's voice. "You've never taken a consort before, my child."

"What can I say, my lord? Zvi's beauty and strength captivate me."

Yada. Yada. Yada.

Gio sounds bothered by our fake relationship. "Yes, she's truly special."

Bro code, G. Bro code. At least I hope there's some sort of code of honor between a master and his children. Otherwise, this pseudo relationship and my poor acting skills will no longer be needed, and I'll have to walk around in a constant state of need. That isn't going to jive. No way is anyone witnessing me at my weakest, nor do I want any witnesses to me dating Killian. I shouldn't be linked to anyone I plan to burn to a crisp. I'm private like that.

Killian grips my hip tighter. "What brings you into town?"

Gio's smile is brilliant. "I learned there was a dragon alive and well here in Atlanta. To be honest, I didn't believe it until I saw your beloved's eyes glow. I wish you would've written and told me of her nature."

Killian's body goes stiff against me. "Yes, well, Miss Jayden is a very private woman, but dragons have been extinct for hundreds of years."

Now we're getting somewhere.

Gio laughs over the top again. "Ah, you know how rumors are. I can't remember which little birdie told me."

I have the sudden urge to strangle the hell out of him. I can tell he likes to play games and that chaps my ass. There wasn't enough time to both catch Psycho Karl and entertain my fake boyfriend's daddy and his games.

I'm thinking of launching myself across the room again and beating Gio to a bloody pulp when Killian interrupts my thoughts. "Can I order you a drink, Master?"

"I thought you'd never ask." Gio walks through the suspended furniture and saddles up to the bar as Moe walks behind it to prepare a drink.

Killian takes his hand from my hip and interlaces our fingers. "Please excuse us for one moment. I need a moment to share some dinner details with Zvi."

I find Moe's eyes, and she gives me the nod to play along. Hendri's watching Gio like a hawk, and the older vampire is sizing up my sister. I can't say I care for the way he's looking at her, but Hendri can protect her with his bite.

Killian leads me up the stairs to my apartment in silence. I know whatever he has to say to me would have to be written down in order to avoid Gio's super vampiric hearing. I can probably hear just as well as a vamp, but I've never met a fanger this old. He might have other gifts in addition to his cocoa glamor routine and hearing capabilities.

When we reach my door, I unlock it and walk in first. I don't make it three steps before Killian grabs my arm and twirls me around to face him. Then he turns us both and presses my back against the back of the door.

He has a crazy look in his eye that I don't identify until it's too late. His voice is a deep whisper against my lips. "You will *not* fuck him."

Telling me what to do is a sure way to get on and stay on my shit list. I give him a small push, but he's rooted to the spot. He runs the tips of his fingers across my cheek. "I know you want to fight me, but I'm trying to protect you from the most powerful vampire alive. He's Ambrogio, the first vampire. He does not operate in the mainstream like the rest of us, and he's capable of true horror. Don't ever turn your back on him, macushla."

I try to whip up a snappy comeback, but it's really hard with him so close to me. "I'm not your darling."

He grins. "No?"

I feel the same warmth I felt earlier when Gio spread through my body and heated my face. "He's doing that thing again!"

"It's me you feel inside."

Does he have to sound thrilled about the idea? Before today, I've been immune to vampire manipulations, and now, my hormones have been hijacked twice by two different ones. "Stop the glamor hit," I borderline plead.

He presses a soft kiss to my lips and then moves over to my ear. "Feel me," he says. "What's different this time?" His lips touch the spot right below my ear causing a shiver to crawl down my spine. "Close your eyes and concentrate on your five senses."

I'm so uncomfortable that I listen to him and close my eyes in hopes that I'll find relief.

"What do you smell?"

I squirm against him. "Sex."

"Yes." He lifts me until I can wrap my legs around his middle. He kisses me again. "What do you taste?"

I moan against his mouth. "Whiskey."

"What do you see behind your eyes?"

All I can see is him. He's everywhere I exist. He doesn't leave an inch of me untouched. I feel covered, cherished, and heavy with need. "You." The softness of his lips invaded my senses.

His tongue slips inside and touches mine. "Tell me what you hear, macushla."

The word sounds like a song rolling off his tongue. "You singing."

He pushes himself into my middle and grunts. The sound is like music to my ears. "Do you feel me?"

I moan too loud for my taste. "Yes!"

"What do *I* feel, macushla?"

"Longing. Desire. Adoration."

"That's for you."

He grinds himself against me and the pleasure from it almost makes my head explode. He has completely invaded me. I've never felt something like this before- an all-consuming need that I can't fight past.

A knock comes at the door and interrupts our progress. Killian drops the glamour, and it feels like I hit a brick wall. I'm breathing hard and overheating from the exertion. I'm sure I look like I'm doing what I was just doing.

"It's Moe," my sister says.

Killian closes his eyes for a moment and touches his forehead to mine. "You will not fuck him, because you're mine."

Again, I can't muster the energy to argue. No words come which probably gives him the wrong impression. Whatever.

He gives me one last enthusiastic kiss and places me back on the ground so I can open the door. The look on Moe's face is full of fear.

"Did he harm you?" Killian asks.

She shakes her head. "No, but he gives me the creeps."

Killian pulls me to him and kisses me again. A whimper escapes me before he pulls away. Moe's never going to let me live that down. "I'll take Gio back to my place to get him away from you both and see if I can get some information from him. If he's throwing the word 'dragon' around, then he's not the only one who knows. I imagine you'd like to know who the players are."

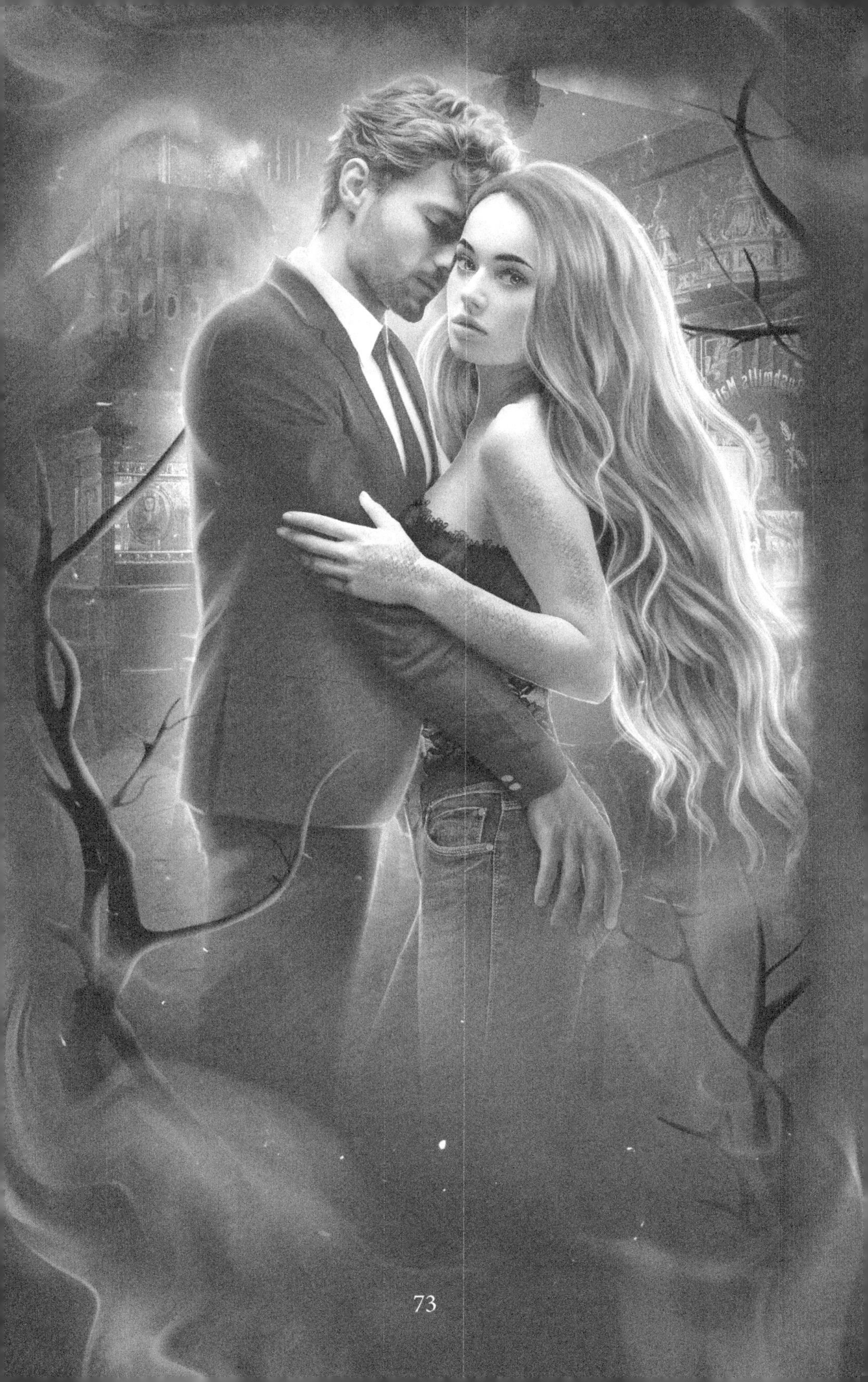

CHAPTER EIGHT

KILLIAN SHUTS THE DOOR behind him, and my sister immediately begins to tease me. "Bow chicka wow wow! Are you okay?"

A sour expression crosses my face. "I'm going to take my time peeling the skin off his body."

"That's not what I expected to hear. You look like you enjoyed yourself. What are you complaining about?"

I pace the aisle I cleared in between the clothes that litter the floor. "I didn't ask for that! He's such a dick! Twice! Two vamps! Two of those fanger bloodsucking maggots glamoured me! I. Was. Not. In. Control. Do you hear me?!"

"Do maggots suck blood?"

"Not the fucking point! Jesus, Moe!"

"What? It's a good question! I'm going to Google that later. Exactly how many names do you have for vamps?"

I tick off fingers as I go through the list of my favorite insults. "Fanger, bloodsucker, leech, tampon, mosquito, deader, dust cunt for starters."

"You're going to piss off a really important person one day."

"Can we focus on the important part where I said two vampires glamoured me?"

"That is a problem. You not being in control is not a good thing. It makes you unpredictable," Moe says.

I have to tell her everything Killian told me so she knows what we're really dealing with here. "I need to tell you something about Gio."

"Can you stop pacing? You're making me nervous."

"No."

She sighs. "What do you need to tell me?"

"Killian said Gio is short for Ambrogio."

"Like Le Ambrogio the organization?" She asks.

I nod and continue to pace the worn path. "The very one. Kavanagh said he's the first vampire, and of course he's the strongest. He also said not to turn your back to him."

"I've heard of Ambrogio before," she says and pulls her phone out to likely Google the guy. I look over her shoulder to see the search results lead her to the Greek mythology of Ambrogio. "In 450 BCE, an Italian human named Ambrogio fell in love with a beautiful goddess named Selene, and she fell for him, but the sun god Apollo loved Selene. Out of anger at their match, Apollo cursed Ambrogio to walk in the light of the moon because Apollo's sun would burn his flesh. It was a plan to keep the two apart. Ambrogio then sought the help of Hades who offered to help him recover his soul, telling him that he had to bring the silver bow of Apollo's sister, Artemis, back to the underworld. Ambrogio gained favor with Artemis, the goddess of the wilderness, and he stole her bow. Before he could take it back to Hades, Artemis realized what he'd done, and she cursed him with an allergy to silver. Ambrogio pleaded with Artemis to have mercy on him, and she did. She took pity on him and gifted him with the strength and speed of the gods and wild beasts, and he was almost as strong as her. He was also gifted with immortality and shared this gift by exchanging blood with a human."

"I wonder how strong he really is," I ponder. Something doesn't add up, but I can't put my finger on it. Maybe it's the sudden emergence of new people in our otherwise quiet lives. I already don't trust anyone outside of Moe, and this is making me suspect everyone. "Where are all of these new people coming from? First it was Killian and his vampire thugs. Burton showed up and is suspected to be in the company of Natasia Portnova, who's a psycho witch and not even supposed to be here in Killian's territory. Now, Killian's daddy is here. I feel like I'm waiting for the other shoe to drop."

"I feel it too," she says. "Some serious shit is about to hit the fan. Shoot! I forgot he's still here."

"Who?"

There's a sadness in her eyes. "Hendri. He showed up, ya know?"

I put my hands on my hips. "Aw, shit. You've got that broken little Bambi look in your eyes. What is it?"

"He showed up with the rest of the new people. I don't think it's safe to trust him."

"Hendri seems like good people, sis. You've trusted him so far. Let the guy breathe a little until he gives you a real reason to suspect him. I'll keep an eye out to make sure he's on the up and up."

She tilts her head to the side like a dog would and looks at me like I've been abducted by an alien. "When did you become the positive one? Who are you and what have you done with my sister?"

"Don't you need to get downstairs?"

She laughs. I follow her out of my apartment door and head down to the bar. Downstairs, Hendri sits at a bar stool and sips a glass of whiskey. A folder lays beside him on the counter, and upon seeing it, I know why he's come.

"Please don't tell me there's another body," Moe pleads.

"I wish I didn't have too, cher. Who was the dick head in the bar?"

I crack a beer open and take a swallow. "Gio is Ambrogio, who also happens to be the very first vampire. He's Killian's master, which means Killian is some sort of real vampire royalty, buddy." *Buddy*? Whatever those two vampires did to me must've fried my operating system. I get back to the task at hand. "Who's the victim?"

Hendri opens the folder and slides it across the bar, and I gag from the absolute horror I see in front of me. A young woman is the victim this time, and her face is clawed beyond recognition. The violence significantly escalated with this murder. The magic being used on him is getting blacker and nastier, and that will only make it that much harder to find him. Not that he's been a peach to find thus far.

"Justine Baldwin," Hendri answers.

"I know her," Moe says. "She's a witch."

"He killed a human first, then a werewolf, and now a witch," I summarize.

"Zvi knew the first victim, Patrick; you both knew the werewolf, Heath; and now you know Justine," Hendri adds. "I doubt this is a coincidence."

I flip through the pages until I come across Justine's driver's license. She was a beautiful, young woman with light brown hair and powder blue eyes. She had her entire life ahead of her.

I can feel that knowledge weighing heavy on Moe as tears brim in her eyes. "It's my fault she's dead."

I slam a hand on the bar to snap her out of it. "You did not kill that girl. Ekman and a witch did this. It sucks that these people may have been murdered because they know us, but we didn't harm them."

Before I can come up with some possible theories, Killian walks back through the front door. I jump over the bar and zip across the room in a blur, and then I bulldoze the vampire like a linebacker, and then I punch him in the dick. He might be a vampire, but he's still a man, and that hurts like hell. Killian rolls over to his side and cups his crotch in pain.

"If you ever glamour me again, I'm going to fry you to a crisp, only after I peel your skin from your body."

Killian gasps for air for a few seconds before he finally struggles to his feet. "He can't glamour you when you're already glamoured by me. Would you rather him have done it instead?"

I shoot him a look that says "screw you", and lift a brow. "What's option C?"

"I'd like to request your presence at my home tomorrow night for a dinner thrown in honor of my consort. The dress code shall be formal. I've scheduled my personal shopper to be at your beck and call all day. My master must believe that we are together, or you'll no longer be under my protection as he precedes me in age and will pursue your company."

I can see me and Gio getting along like a house on fire. I'd be the fire and rage, and he'd be the antagonistic gasoline that makes me blaze out of control. It's best we avoid that, so I guess we're going to dinner tomorrow night. This won't be easy with zero acting skills.

"It won't work," I tell him. "Too many people in your organization equals too many leaks in your ranks."

Killian looks like he needs a drink. "I assure you that my people know exactly what's at stake with Gio being here. They want him gone as much as I, and I don't want you anywhere near him. I'm doing the best I can with him showing up out of the blue, but I need you to work with me. My people will play along."

Moe places her hand over my mouth as I open it to say something insulting. "What time should we be there?"

*

Killian's personal shopper, Liz, is a beautiful, red-headed woman with long locks and dark green eyes. She's probably around thirty-five. "Mr. Kavanagh is very generous," she says. By the way she says it, she's obviously talking about more than his money, and she's a beautiful woman, so she's probably already rode his meat rocket. "You have an excellent ass—very muscular and strong."

I'm not going to make it through this dress-up party if she keeps talking about my ass while I'm half naked. She stands up from measuring my waist and grabs my boobs, and I growl. "These are excellent too."

Moe jumps up and gently pushes her away before I can backhand her. "No touchy touchy."

Liz seems to pick up what she's throwing down and moves back to her rack of clothes. "Mr. Kavanagh has an excellent eye. He guessed your size over the phone."

A little shiver runs through me when I think about him knowing my size from jacking me against a wall. Ugh. I force myself to think of hunting from the sky, but that gives me a little thrill too. I hate him for screwing up my hormones.

Liz brings me a black sequined dress with lace cutout sleeves. "Try this one on. I think it's the one!"

I glare at her because the last time I wore a dress I was five. "I'm not fucking wearing that. Do you have some dressy jeans?"

She clears her throat, signaling her discomfort with my request. "Mr. Kavanagh requested formal wear."

I put my hands on my hips and take a deep breath. "Do you see Mr. Kavanagh here? No. If he isn't wearing a dress then I'm not going to either." I can feel the tickle, pull and warning of my sister's magic—her and that magical fucking bubble. I think better of the bubble and hope she gets mad enough to put me in one, then I won't have to go to this dinner. Vampires are quickly becoming my least favorite species. "Do it," I dare her.

"It won't get you out of the dinner," she says and puts her hands on her hips. "Put on the freaking dress, Zvi."

"Can you put a spell on me?" I ask.

"What kind of spell?"

"Like 'opposite day' for my personality," I answer. I'm not delusional about my flaws, and I hate social gatherings. I get enough socialization at work and the rest of the time, I just don't want to be bothered by anyone. If she doesn't cast a spell on me, then I'm going to show up as the real me and dinner will be ruined. I have a feeling that Moe, despite the circumstances of the evening ahead, really wants to wear one of these dresses. She just might do me real harm if I don't do something to get me through the evening.

She touches her chin as she gets lost in her thoughts. "I can't believe I'm considering this, but I think I have a spell that will work. You need to be sure you want to do this though because when magic messes with the psychology of the brain the results can vary."

That doesn't sound good. "What does that mean?"

"It means the results depend on your personality and opposite traits can mean anything. I can't know which parts of you will be affected."

"How long does it last?" I ask.

She hesitates. "Four to six hours."

What can go wrong that can't be fixed in four to six hours? Especially if I'm the opposite of me? I can be good and play the part of dutiful consort and hopefully get Dracula to skedaddle on back to where he came from. I take a big, deep breath and release it. "Okay, do it."

Moe looks unsure of this. "Zvi, you need to make sure this is what you really want. I won't be in a position to use the true strength of my magic without vampires catching on which means I won't be able to undo this. It'll just have to wear off."

What's the worst that can happen?

*

There's a slight buzz just under the surface of my skin, one that lets me know Moe's magic is alive and well as it courses through my body. I've changed my mind about the dress and heels as I glide my hands over the sequined material. I have to admit I look good in it, and I like the snug fit although it isn't much good in a fight. If the slits were high on both sides, I could make it work.

"Would you stop feeling yourself up and get in the limo?" Moe asks.

I climb into the limo Killian sent to take us to dinner. Once I'm inside, I cross my legs and take the stiletto off my foot. "Are these made of wood? They make pretty convenient stakes if you ask me." I aim the shoe at Moe's forehead and take a fake practice throw at her. She flinches then frowns. "I bet I can hit a deader right between the eyes at ten yards. I'd probably need a few practice throws first."

Hendri sits next to Moe and pulls her hand into his own before he releases a big sigh. "This is going to be an interesting fucking night." I'm a bit surprised that Killian extended a dinner invitation to a wolf, but I figure he has his reasons, and I should trust those.

With traffic, it takes about fifteen minutes to make it from downtown to Buckhead. The limo enters an estate neighborhood with tall gates that actually keep people out. We pull through the gates when they open and drive around a cul de sac at the end of a quiet street. Killian's home has a private home gate made of ornate black iron. Beyond the gate is a light red brick courtyard with a fountain in the circular drive. The gate quietly opens to reveal the massive architectural piece built with white bricks and black trimmings, and the drive off to the side of the house is full of expensive foreign cars. Vampires have always been flashy creatures who like big shows of wealth.

The limo stops in front of the house, and a dark-skinned man in a black suit and a massive blade on his back opens our door. Moe and Hendri exit first and since his ass is in my face, I reach out and give it a good pinch and say, "Moe! You could bounce a quarter off his ass!" He turns to look at me in horror and then hurries out of the vehicle to get away from me. I follow them out and come face to face with one of my movie heroes. "Blade is that you?"

"Blade?" the attendant asks.

Hendri chokes down a laugh as Moe pulls at my arm to move me along, but I remain rooted to my spot. It's not every day I meet someone as badass as me.

"He's a super-duper mofo who rids the world of vampires. Well, come to think of it, you probably wouldn't like him at all since he'd cut your head off with his blade," I say and slice my finger across my throat as I stick my tongue out as far as it will go.

The only thing that moves on his bored face is his mouth. "Excuse me?" He sounds personally offended that Blade would chop his head off.

"Touchy subject?" I ask.

He grunts.

I pat his chest with my hand. "Good talk," I say and turn to walk to the door where another gentleman waits for us.

"She's talking too much," Moe whispers to Hendri. It's cute that she thinks I can't hear her. I ignore it since I'm in such a good mood.

The vampire at the door, who I assume is the butler, wears a kind smile on his face, and I can't help but walk up to him and wrap my arms around his neck. I hug tightly and enjoy the closeness. This feels so good. I wonder why I didn't hug people sooner. When the butler clears his throat, I realize I've been hugging him a little too long. I'll have to learn all the rules about embraces before I try that again. I lean back and give him my biggest smile. He looks a little horrified at first, then he smiles back.

"Geez, Harley Quinn much?" Moe mutters.

"You're fucking crazy, aren't you?" the butler asks as though he'd genuinely enjoy it if I were?

I shrug my shoulders. "I mean… technically? I guess you could say I'm crazy. I don't usually get along with others very well, but now, I want everyone to be as happy as me."

Moe snorts. "I should've put this spell on her years ago."

The butler turns to look at her. "What?"

"Nothing," my sister answers.

The butler seems to be amused by me, and he places my hand through the crook of his arm, and then leads me through the door. "I'm Sebastian, milady."

He wears a suit well, and the light blue of his tie matches the beautiful, brilliant blue of his eyes. His dark hair is short and expertly tousled on top, and he has just enough hair on his face to call it a beard. Sebastian's a tall man with a broad chest and shoulders and from the hug, I can tell he has a tight body. Yum.

I shake my head at the term. "I'm no 'milady', and you're sure as hell no butler," I tell him. "I'm Zvi."

"The Minister said you were perceptive. As the Minister's consort, you will be shown respect by our kind as order decrees. We have also been notified to never ask your species, but I've always been a rebel, so I'm going to ask anyway. What are you?"

"An order was decreed?" Hendri asks, but Sebastian waves him off without making eye contact, which I find a little rude to be honest.

"A demon," I tell him.

He laughs. "No!"

I laugh right along with him. "Could you imagine smelling like that?"

"How dreadful!" We both join in a chorus of loud, raucous laughter that echoes through the large rooms. We walk through a massive hallway that leads to another wing of the house. The floors are hardwood throughout the parts I can see. We seem to walk forever to our next destination. We finally come to a set of large, mahogany doors and beyond it, I can hear voices—I count at least 100. I frown and look back to Hendri to find him also concerned about the number of vampires in the next room. The music drowns out a lot of their conversations, but I can feel the waves of excitement coming off the fangers. I suddenly feel nervous. Moe must feel it too because she gives my hand a quick squeeze of support.

"I've got you," Sebastian says and opens the door. The entire room goes silent, including the strings playing in the corner. Everyone turns to look at us at the same time, and I just about shit my pants. I swallow hard.

Sebastian repeats, "I've got you." I don't know the man from

Adam, but something tells me I can trust him.

He holds my hand in his as though I'm royalty, and it makes me want to giggle. "Presenting Lady Zvi Jayden and her guests, Miss Moe Jayden and Mr. Hendri Connor."

No one says a freaking word. Not one. Instead, they stare back at me. Several of them look me up and down as though they're looking for every single one of my flaws. Hendri and Moe are mere afterthoughts. It's intimidating as hell to walk into a nest of snakes. I decide I don't want to do this consort shit anymore. Before I can escape, Killian steps forward and takes my hand from Sebastian and also presents me to the crowd. What am I, Miss America? No one oohs or aahs, throws things at me, or boos me out of the room. I guess I should be grateful for those things.

He closes the space between us and leans forward to kiss my cheek, whispering in my ear, "You're stunning this evening, macushla."

I'm so incredibly happy to see him that I throw my arms around him and bury my face in his neck. He goes stiff against me, but no one seems to notice because there's a few "aww's" coming from the crowd behind him. I couldn't care less that someone else is in the room because all I need to feel safe is to be close to him.

"You smell good," I say louder than I probably should, which elicits a few laughs from the crowd.

"Um." He clears his throat in apparent discomfort. "Darling, let us go meet our guests." He snaps his fingers. The noise of the room returns to normal, like a light switch was flipped back on. The strings begin to play again, conversations continue where they left off, and luckily, no one stares anymore.

I meet so many people that my eyes begin to cross, and I'm relieved when the dinner bell rings. Moe, Hendri, and I follow Killian to one of the round tables. "We'll sit here for the evening," he says and pulls out my chair for me.

I take in the other guests at the table as I sit. To my right, there's a man with familiar blue eyes and long, strawberry blond hair staring back at me, curiosity shining in his eyes. I hope he doesn't get on my nerves.

He offers his hand across the round table, and I cordially accept. "Shaw Benton."

"Zvi Jayden."

"You're Lady Zvi Jayden now," he whispers to correct me.

"Is that supposed to imply I'm a consort?" I whisper back.

"It means you are someone of a great deal of importance," he says.

I play shove him and twist a piece of hair around my finger as I laugh. "Oh my! Bless your heart for saying so!"

A strange look passes over the man's face. I frown at him, but a very good-looking Sebastian takes my mind off it as he joins us, seating himself on the other side of Shaw. Killian takes the seat to my left, and Moe is sandwiched between him and Hendri. Aleki takes the seat next to Hendri, and we're served soup in fancy china bowls.

I notice one last seat is still open and just as it has my attention, Gio glides over and fills it. "Ah, beautiful Lady Jayden. I'm incredibly happy you could make it to have dinner with me this evening."

He really is a strangely handsome man, and I give him my biggest flirty smile. Killian clears his throat, and I look over to him to find him giving me a barely perceptible shake of his head. Whatever that means. I figure he's jealous is all, so I slip my hand over his thigh and rub as close to his dick as I can without touching it to make him feel all better. Hendri kicks me under the table, Moe stares at me in horror, Sebastian chokes on his soup, and Killian grabs my wrist to still it. Maybe it's too early in the night for him?

"Gio, you must be a proud papa! Isn't he the sexiest thing you've ever seen?" I make a swooning sound and stare at Killian's exquisitely beautiful face.

"Are you quite alright, Lady Jayden?" Gio asks, concern etched on his face.

Gosh, he makes me nervous. "Oh! That… darn… Game of Thrones! Did anybody else see the ending?"

"The ending was a sellout!" Sebastian passionately says. "Jon Snow was supposed to sit on the iron throne."

"With the dragons," I add, but everyone knows the dragons could've won the throne without any help from those other weaklings.

Moe purses her lips. She sure is acting strange tonight.

"All three of them?" Sebastian asks.

I vigorously nod my head. "Of course."

Killian elbows me. I turn and mouth "what?" to him. There's a slight shake of his head. "Do you not like GOT?" I ask.

"Of course, darling." Something tells me he's placating me, but I let it go and get back to my conversation with Sebastian.

Sebastian puts an elbow on the table and leans in. "Favorite character?"

"The dragons," I answer.

"Other than the dragons?"

"Well, there are three of them, so they're my top three favorite characters."

Moe's nervous voice jumps in after a fake chuckle. "Love that Jon Snow."

"I'm more of a Tyrion Lannister guy myself," Hendri adds, and Moe shoots him a glare.

"Can you believe they killed two of them? And Drogon is all by himself!" I say and find that I'm feeling pretty emotional about it.

Killian clears his throat. "Lady Jayden is quite taken with those characters. She's always had a special place in her heart for those creatures."

"Creatures?" I ask.

He looks at me with wide eyes.

"Is there something in your eye?"

Those beautiful blue orbs close in what appears to be extreme frustration.

"Do you need something to flush it out?"

They open with a pleading expression. "No, darling. Why don't we talk about something a little less intense?"

The wait staff removes the soup and salad is put in its place. "Why are all you vampires eating food?" I ask. Killian squeezes my thigh. "Ow! What's wrong with you?!" The entire room turns to look at us. I give them a wave that a pageant queen would be proud of, and they turn back to picking at their food.

"Ow?" Killian whispers and looks at me like he's just now seeing me for the first time.

"What's wrong with her?" Gio asks.

"Where's the garlic for the bread?" I ask and several gasps ring out through the room. Whoops. Vampires aren't allergic to garlic, but it has a very foul odor to them.

"You described her in a much different manner, Minister," Shaw says.

"Are you high?" Aleki asks.

"Killian," Moe says his name as a plea.

"Macushla, let's see to my eye in the study," Killian says and stands with a hand outstretched to me. I stand and accept it, and the rest of the table also stands in a show of respect.

"Is that what they call it now?" Hendri mutters under his breath.

Shaw is preoccupied with Killian's hand on the small of my back and oddly enough, he appears angry about it. Maybe he doesn't like me as a consort for his king or minister or whatever Killian is to them. Killian slightly bows and asks our guests to politely excuse us. The table of guests stand and also bow. I'm not exactly sure about this consort thing. Am I a queen or something? Either way, I bow back and almost trip over my own feet. Fortunately, Killian catches me as I dive for the floor before he sets me to rights.

His study is on the other side of the spacious and cozy mansion done in all hardwood floors, distressed woodwork, and dark board and batten panels. Each door is wide and massive as we pass them in halls. I wonder which one is his bedroom. What does it look like? Is it warm and cozy like the rest of the house?

We reach our destination. He opens the door for me and waves me through before he follows me and closes the door behind us. There's a large wooden writer's desk at the other end of the room. In the center is a fireplace and two bulky, tufted, dark brown leather love seats with metal nailheads.

My heels sound against the hardwood as I walk to his desk and sit in the plush, executive leather chair and spin myself around in it. I wonder if he feels like an all-powerful vampire when he sits here. When I grow a little dizzy from the chair, I stop and look at his desk. There's a lamp, phone, calendar, a closed laptop, and two manila folders with mine and Moe's name on it.

"What's this?" I ask and open my file. There's a picture of me that's at least seven years old. In the photograph, I'm straight-faced and no nonsense, dirty blonde hair, and a chip on my shoulder.

"We keep a file on every known supernatural creature."

"It lists me as a witch." I point out.

"Yes, macushla. I told you your secret is safe with me. Not even my people know the truth."

"I'm not a witch, though." I don't want to be involved in a situation where I'm expected to perform magic.

There's reverence in his voice. "No, darling, you are not a witch. You are far rarer than that."

"Why are we here?" I ask.

He looks at me with heat in his eyes. "Buiochas le Dia, you are positively striking in that dress."

He's pretty striking in his suit, the black of the material seems to amplify the blues of his eyes. "Being your consort makes me horny."

The only response that I receive for my honesty is the flare of his nostrils. "What's wrong with you this evening, sweetheart?"

"Moe put an opposite spell on me, so I could play your doting consort."

He comes to stand behind me and the chair. "You have me confused. I don't want a doting consort, Zvi. I want you the way you are." His hands find my shoulders and gently massage. "You are strong, beautiful, intelligent, witty, loyal, good, and a force to be reckoned with. I like strong women, not a compliant consort who refuses to challenge me. You're not afraid of me."

In one swift motion, I stand and shove the chair to the side. Killian spins me around, picks me up by my hips, and places me on the desk. Looking into his gorgeous blue eyes has me feeling all sorts of things— anxiety, desire, and the need to rip both of our clothes to shreds. My breaths come quickly with him standing so close to me. My internal fire licks my deepest corners. His fingers gently snake their way up my neck until he wraps a hand around my throat. Killian closes the small space between us and presses his soft, cool lips against mine for a moment before he slips his tongue inside to dance with mine. The moan that escapes me elicits a groan from him.

Something feels like it breaks inside me when his hand finds its way to the open slit of my dress. I almost come off the desk when he squeezes the top of my thigh. I place both of my hands on his chest and shove him back toward the discarded desk chair. His knees hit the seat and down he goes. Before he has a moment to adjust, I'm on him like white on rice. I straddle him and shove his face in my cleavage.

"Fuck," he murmurs against my skin and simultaneously thrusts his pelvis up. His lips find my neck and chest and then another guttural moan tears itself from my mouth. He grips my hips and lifts us from the chair with ease. The next thing I know, my ass is on his desk and the items from it hit the floor as he clears it with both hands. He puts a hand over each breast and squeezes and then he moves lower, and presses his fingers into my thighs, and slowly they push my dress higher.

"Lift your ass, macushla."

I obey and find my dress pushed as far as it will go. My black, lace panties snap on the sides. His head disappears between my thighs and the first thing I feel is him blowing on my center. His tongue swipes up my middle, and I'm about to shout when a knock comes at the door.

"Fuck! Not again!" I whine.

"Yes?!" Killian calls out in frustration.

"Your Highness, the staff would like to know if you'll take your dinner in the study," Sebastian says.

Who the hell is thinking about food at a time like this? "He's already eating! Go away!" I yell.

Killian gives me a wide, perfect smile and chuckles. "Sebastian will find great humor in this."

I don't care about what Sebastian thinks. I currently have a one-track mind, and it's only concern is an orgasm. "Can you get back to it?" I impatiently ask.

Killian's grin grows wider as he dips his head once again, but another knock comes at the door. I slap my hands on the desk in annoyance. This pussy isn't going to eat itself.

"Zvi?" Moe calls out.

"Yeah."

"I'm uncomfortable in there without you," she whisper-shouts. "Are you okay?"

"Screw it," I say and sit up. Killian backs away to let me off the desk. I walk to the study door, pull my dress down, and open the door. "No, I'm not okay. You are the second person to interrupt us and now I have blue bean."

Hendri stands behind my sister while wearing a knowing grin. "There's a lot of people here to see you," he reminds me.

Killian comes to stand behind me. "What did you do to her?" he asks Moe.

Moe crosses her arms across her chest and narrows her eyes at him. "What she asked me to do. You put her in an impossible position. She didn't think she could make it through the dinner as herself. She wanted to be the opposite of her. I thought that maybe she was right, but I can clearly see I was wrong."

"Can you fix it?" Hendri asks.

"It has to wear off. She'll be back to herself in a few hours."

I don't know that I can wait a few more hours without exploding with need in front of everyone, especially with Killian looking the way he does. It doesn't help that he's standing behind me with his hand resting on my hip as though he's claiming me. Both Hendri and Moe look down at his hand in surprise, but I don't care what they think about it. His hand feels like it belongs there.

"Gio's getting antsy. I don't trust him or a room full of vampires as far as I can throw them. I'd very much appreciate it if you'd come back to dinner and keep an eye out," Hendri says.

"The entire room is watching him because he has real power to hurt a lot of vampires and other creatures. I assure you that no one wants him here. He does not inspire love or loyalty, but instead he rouses the deepest fears of every creature he crosses," Killian says.

"Is the myth true?" Moe asks.

"Parts of it," Killian replies. "I don't have time to get into that right now."

Hendri places his hands on his hips. "I don't know them. I somewhat know you and as your guest, I expect not to be eaten alive by a room full of vamps."

"She can't go back out there like this," Killian tells him.

"Do you have some lavender or chamomile tea?" Moe asks.

Killian shakes a finger at her. "No more witchy business." He turns me around to face him and holds my face in his hands as though I'm precious to him. "Sweetheart, listen to my voice."

I begin to feel lighter but heavy with vampire magic at the same time. Warmth sneaks into my veins and coils tight around my nerves. I'm deeply relaxed by the time I pick out the scent of his magic again. It smells of sex and tastes of whiskey as he invades every cell in my body and mind. Killian sings a song in a foreign language that sounds like a lullaby, sending me into a deep calm. I can feel his longing so strongly that a ball of emotion forms in my throat. I want to cry and smile at the same time.

"Yes," he whispers against my lips. "That's how much I want you."

His words strike a chord deep inside me and enamorment comes over me. I feel connected and bonded to him in every way possible. It both scares and excites me.

"Zvi," he whispers again. "You are beautiful and perfect the way you are. You are enough, my macushla. Come eat and dance with me."

I quietly agree. "Okay." I'd follow him anywhere.

As the buzz of the spell wears off, it's replaced with Killian's vampiric glamour. I don't fight against it, much too tired from the day and long night. We make it back to the table just in time for the main meal. I smile and laugh with Sebastian, kick Hendri under the table every chance I get, ignore Gio the entire time, and speak with Shaw Benton at length about music. Killian's right hand rests on my thigh all evening.

"Come dance with me, Zvi," Killian says into my ear. I let him lead me to the dance floor. Soon, Hendri and Moe follow us as do others. I rest my hands on his shoulders and look up at his handsome face. I could stare at him all night, and I do until sleep takes me under.

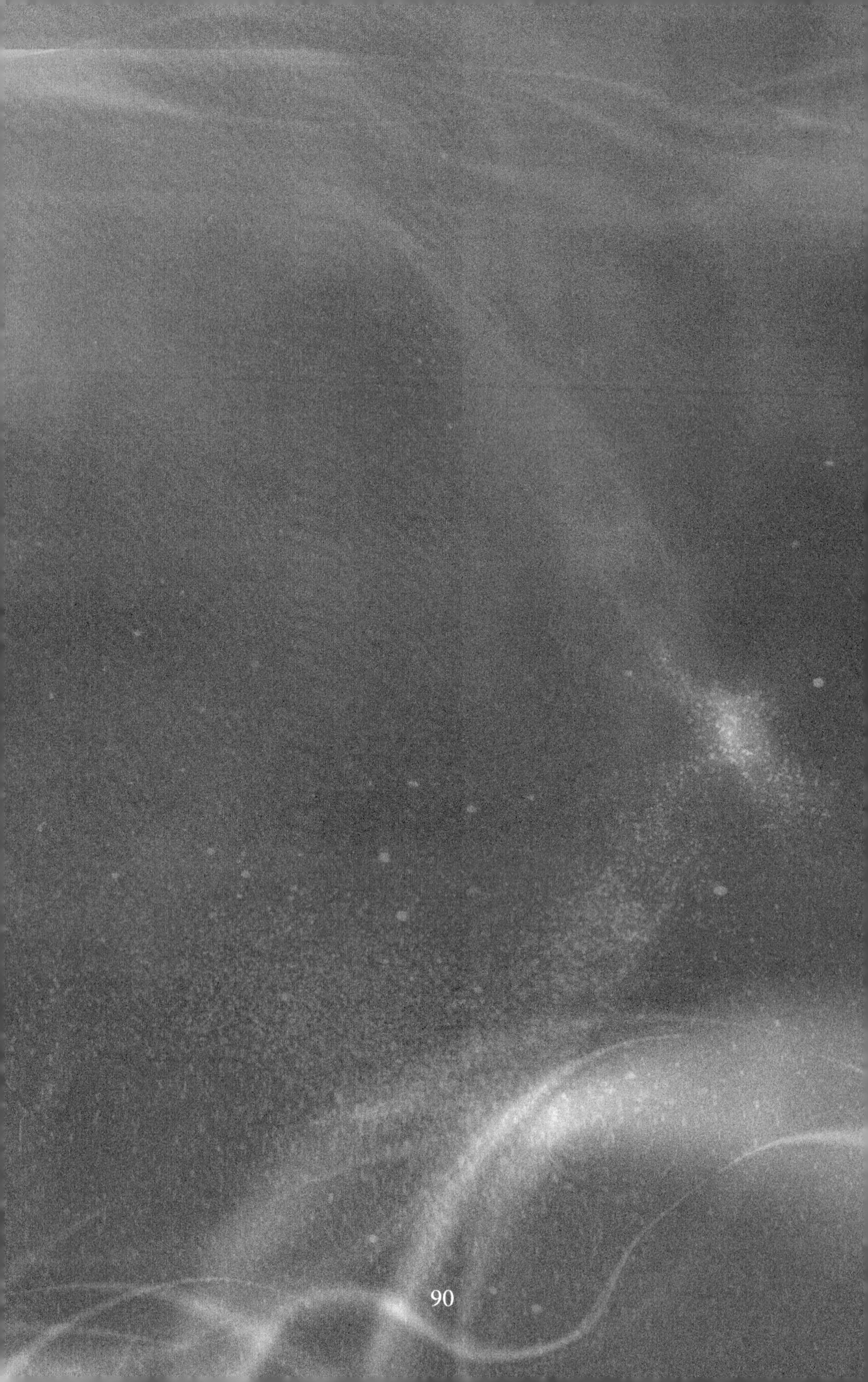

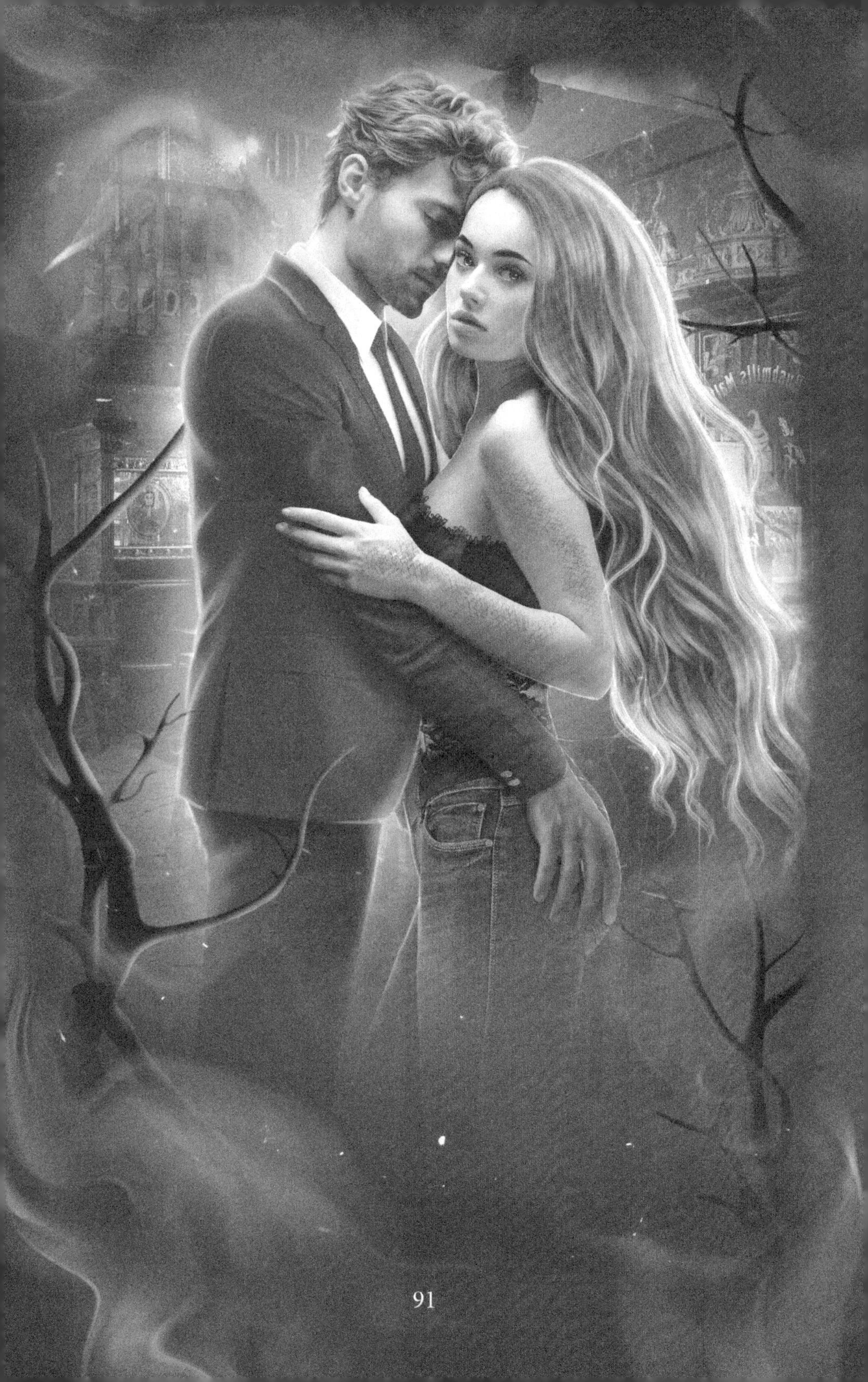

CHAPTER NINE

THERE ARE CERTAIN THINGS every person tells themselves, even if only subconsciously, will never happen to them. I don't have to tell myself subconsciously that I'll never end up in Killian Kavanagh's bed because that *will never happen to me*. Well, it fucking did. I'm currently staring at his empty side of the bed as I lie on his high thread count, dark gray sheets (which are super-duper soft by the way). Falling in love with sheets is now a thing for me, but I wish I never knew what all the fuss was about because that means I wouldn't be in his bed while wondering what I was thinking last night when I asked Moe to put a freaking opposite spell on me (or whatever the witchy variety call it).

While I lay in his bed all alone, I have a few minutes to gather my wits and make it through the cringe-worthy details of last night. I cover my face with my hands, too embarrassed to even look at myself. I loathe me at the current moment. I don't know who I'm more upset with—me or everybody who's a witness to the atrocities of battle I incurred yesterday evening. And vampires are so freaking snooty that I'll never live this down, which leads me to believe there's only one thing to do about it. I hope his back yard is big enough for me to change and breathe fire onto his house. Boom! No more stupid witnesses. Problem solved… except Moe and Hendri saw it too.

"Shitsicles!" I yell as I remember I put my finger on Hendri's ass and pinched it as we were exiting the limo. I hope Moe doesn't know or she's going to kill me.

I won't allow myself to lay here any longer when the memories of Killian and I come to the forefront of my mind.

Buiochas le Dia, you are positively striking in that dress. I'm not a fan of the dress I still happen to be in. It's a small miracle I'm wearing it now because the sequins are scratchy as hell and the dress is so tight that my ribs are punching my kidneys. Good times. I need to get out of this thing pronto.

I don't want a doting consort, Zvi. I want you the way you are. He tells all the lies. I'm the worst candidate for a political position such as consort. Vampires aren't nice creatures. Oh! And he called me a creature last night! I thought he wanted me the way I was. Liar, liar, pants on fire.

You are strong, beautiful, intelligent, witty, loyal, good, and a force to be reckoned with. I like strong women, not some compliant consort who refuses to challenge me. You're not afraid of me. All of those things are very true about me. Last night, it sounded a lot more like flattery because I was all breathy and acting like a dimwit. He also got the last part right. I am not afraid of him because this creature right here can kick his ass.

I walk into a large closet with dark wooden drawers and hanging spaces. Rich people have nice shit in their houses. There's women's clothing on one entire side of the room starting with formal wear and matching shoes. There's also business suits, jeans, band tees. God. I really like these bands. I might steal some of these shirts. I'm pleasantly surprised to see they're all my size. If he buys clothing for all his women that would make me feel a lot more like an escort than a consort.

Zvi, you are beautiful and perfect the way you are. You are enough, my Macushla. Come eat and dance with me. Oh, the tickle of his breath against my ear and throat is enough to make a girl... ahem, ahem, ahem... damn it! Look what he's done to me!

I have to get the hell out of this dress and into some clothes I can move in, call an Uber, and slip out the back. After last night, I'm going to have to change my name and move away anyhow, and I might as well make that happen today. I need to pack, get a new ID for me and Moe, sell all the shit at the bar for a down payment on a new place, and get a truck to haul what we want to keep. If I have to sell my Harleys because I had to pretend to be his consort, I'm going to lie low for a few years and when he least expects it, I'll be back to stick a Harley Davidson up his dead ass.

Wasting not a minute more, I search for a zipper on the back of this wretched piece of torture but quickly discover I can't reach it. I can't stand being in it another minute, so I pull it over my hips and up to my boobs where it catches. A long strand of my hair yanks when I pull the dress higher.

"Grrr."

I try to maneuver the dress back down, but it's stuck. I push and pull and do it some more to try to get it to give one way or another. I'm twirling and dancing in his closet, bumping into things, then I stub my toe and almost come out of my skin, it hurts so bad. I pick it up and hop around the room while I'm continuing the pushing and pulling method which just isn't working. And I start to panic. It feels like I can't breathe because I'm suffocating. The sequins are rubbing my face and if there's small, tiny cuts on it when I get this dag blasted material over my head, I'm hurting Killian (even more than I already am) for sending me the stupid thing. I try to force it over one more time and then I give up. I'm exhausted and breathing heavily over something as simple as taking a dress off. It can't be this hard for other women to get dresses off or they'd never wear them. Maybe it's the aftereffects of Moe's spell or Killian's glamour… and then I remember he glamoured me last night, and a burning rage starts to fester.

"You vag teasing motherfu…," I begin.

"Whoa!" says a familiar voice. "Do you always use such offensive language this early in the evening?"

"Yes," I matter-of-factly answer.

"I take no issue," he says, and I wish I could place the voice.

Sarcasm drips from my words. "That's good."

"Landing strip, huh?"

"Excuse me?" Not seeing is really getting annoying.

"The landing strip is a classic that keeps coming back each and every decade. Good choice."

This dude is starting to piss me off more. "What are you going on about?"

"Lady Jayden, it appears that you have lost your underwear, which I would not know if it were not for the major struggles you seem to be experiencing in removing your clothing. Perhaps, I can be of assistance."

I'm not wearing any underwear because as I recall, they were ripped from my body by that… "Motherfu…"

"I prefer to be called 'Daddy', if you don't mind," he says.

He must have a death wish. "I hate vampires, and if I'm going to call you anything it will be 'Deady'."

I pull at the dress again and when that doesn't work, I push it down. Nope. A button catches in my hair and pulls at it again, the sequins are squeezing my face like a vice grip, and my pussy is out in the open for everyone in the mansion to see. I'm going to jump up and down and throw a temper tantrum as soon as I get free.

"Do you mind?!" I ask.

"You want me to leave?"

"No!!! God, no!"

I hear him chuckle, at what, I'm not sure. "I could go and fetch the Minister."

"No!!! Don't do that!!!" I order. "Can you please cut me out of this thing?"

"Dear, that dress has a $12,000 price tag. No, I cannot cut you out as it would be appalling to do that to such a brilliant cocktail dress. They're hard to find, you know? His other women knew how to appreciate and care for such an item."

His other women? I take a deep breath to keep from rupturing an aneurysm. I don't care how much it costs or about his other women. I need a pair of underwear and something to wear so I can beat it. I drop to my knees and search around for the heels I saw earlier, and once I find them, I start to hurl them in his general direction.

I hear it the moment it hits him and bounces off the floor. "Ow! Stop that this instant!"

I continue to fire off shoes at him until he gives me what I want. "Cut me out of the dress or eventually one of these heels will go through your heart!"

"You're deranged! I liked you much better last night!"

"I was not myself." I seethe. "Now…"

"What is going on in here?" Killian asks.

Oh. Now he wants to come and be helpful.

"I am not your escort!" I shout.

"What did you say to her?" he asks the other man.

"No, no, no, Minister Muerto! This is what you did!" I bend over at the waist and try to get the dress off one last time and fail and so does my patience. I kick to the right, then to the left and throw punches above my head since they're still stuck in the arms of it. I close my mouth and scream as loud and as hard as I can so that no one else will come inside and also see my landing strip.

"Get out, Sebastian," Killian orders.

"Peace, Sebastian," I add and throw the peace sign above my head.

"Stop that," Killian says.

"Are you talking to me?" I ask.

"Yes." He grabs my hand and pushes my fingers together. "That's saying 'fuck you', this," he turns my hand palm out, "is 'peace'."

It takes me a minute to find my words. Let me rephrase. It takes me a minute to wade through all the profanity, insults, witty comebacks, and death threats to find my other words. "Can you please get this dress off me?" I'm glad I can't see his face, not while he looks at my naked body. I was mortified in front of Sebastian, but Killian is another story. This likely looks like weakness to him, and I never want to show him any. The best thing I can do is keep pretending I'm not standing here with my snatch hanging out in the wind.

His hands touch my ribs and slide up my sides to the dress. He's so close that I can smell the coffee on his breath and a rich amber cologne wafting in my direction. Some of the spell is lingering around because I get goosebumps where his hands touch and a little wet at the scent.

"How pissed are you this morning?" he asks as his fingers reach into the neck of the dress which is somewhere around my head. I choose not to respond. I want his murder to be perfectly executed, and I can't do that if I'm this angry. I also want the element of surprise on my side, so if I don't say anything. He'll think I'm okay and not see me coming.

"Zvi?"

I keep my mouth shut.

"Darling?"

I am not his freaking darling.

"Macushla?"

Oh, he's pushing it this morning.

"I'm going to take your silence as an indicator of the level of your anger."

More like rage.

"I know that wasn't you last night, Zvi."

That's the nicest thing he's ever said to me. Good. We're already on our way to pretending it never happened.

"The button at the top of the zipper is hooked in your hair." I already know that, panty thief. I feel a tug and then the hair is ripped from my scalp. I clench my jaw to keep myself from reacting in an explosive manner.

"Sorry about that," he says. "I thought I got the hair loose."

Once the button is undone, I can finally pull the dress over my head, and I chunk the damn thing at him when I do. I hope his next woman likes it. The left side of the closet calls to me to get clothed and get out of dodge. I refuse to make eye contact with Killian while I'm naked… or ever again. I open the top drawer and find matching panties and bras with La Perla tags on them. I don't know much about name brands, but I know their lingerie costs a bazillion dollars. I pull them on and search for a pair of jeans and find them all to be upscale designer denim. I roll my eyes at how pretentious Killian is and find the Tom Petty shirt I saw earlier.

He clears his throat. "I hope the clothes are to your liking."

"There are a lot of clothes here. Don't you think it's a bit weird that all your women wear the same size isn't it?"

His eyebrows rise in surprise. "All my women?"

"Yes. Sebastian said your other women like the clothes you buy them. Doesn't that cramp your player style? Having your women know about each other?"

Killian throws his head back and laughs. "I believe Sebastian is teasing you to get a reaction." His laugh dies down as he looks at me with longing in his eyes. "Were you jealous, Macushla?"

"What?! No! I just don't want to feel like I'm…"

"Please finish your sentence," he whispers.

"Like I'm…"

"You want to feel like you matter, that you're important and wanted."

Yes. "No."

"There's never been another woman in my bedroom, much less my closet. They don't get that close, Zvi. I don't buy them clothes unless they attend an event with me. I sure as hell don't send a personal shopper to them with $12,000 dresses."

I don't know what to say, so I change the subject. Avoidance is perfectly healthy. "You called me a 'creature' last night!"

"I did not. I called a character from a television show a creature!"

Whatever. I'm still mad about it. "You ripped my panties!"

"Yes. I shouldn't have touched you at all while you were under the spell. I didn't touch you inappropriately again all night, and in case you didn't notice, I bought you drawers full of lingerie to replace them."

"Touché."

He puts his hand in his pants pockets and waits for me to deliver the next complaint, but everything that forms dies on my tongue.

"Thank you for being willing to go to extreme lengths to play my consort, but I meant what I said last night-- I want you the way you are."

He's insane. I'm insane, but he's more insane for liking me and completely mistaken about how he feels. Moe's the only person who likes me for me. She's the only person who's ever truly accepted and seen me.

"You don't know me," I tell him.

"I know you better than you know yourself, love."

I don't care what he has in the file he keeps on me. I don't believe he knows anything more than the basics. Moe and I live a quiet life outside of the bar. I should've looked further into the file last night, but I've established I was acting like a dimwit.

When I don't respond, he continues. "You keep yourself shut out from the world because at some point in your life someone hurt you deeply and you never trusted again. Your interior is not as hard as your exterior because I can see you. All of you. You make sure no one ever gets close enough to hurt you again, and while I would normally condone such behavior as safe and realistic with most people, it's not with me. I'd never hurt you, Zvi. I have looked far and wide for a woman of your strength, intelligence, and beauty. I never knew you were living under my nose for years. I'm not about to let you slip through my fingers now. I feel something when I'm near you that I cannot explain, and I've not felt a whole lot of anything for a very long time."

"Where are you getting these romantic notions about me? I've not done anything to lead you on."

"You didn't have to. All you had to do was drop me in a river to get my attention, and you have all of it now," he says.

"I don't know you. People have to earn me, and only one other person has been able to do that."

"Moe."

"Yes."

He sets his shoulders proudly. "I will earn you then."

This isn't coming out right. "I don't want to be earned by you. I want to be left alone like I always have and go on living a simple life with my sister."

"*You* are not simple. I will earn you."

This isn't going as expected, so I just drop it. He'll get over me and move on like all the other ones who thought they wanted a little hellraiser in their life and bit off more than they could chew. "Can you take me home?"

He takes a step toward me. "Zvi…"

"Please don't say another word," I plead.

He lets out a heavy sigh, puts his hands on his hips and then looks down at the boots on my feet. "I thought those boots were perfect for you."

"You bought these boots?"

He waves his hand around the closet. "I bought you all of this."

My heart unexpectedly thaws for him. "Why?"

"If you are ever with me for work or pleasure, you'll have the very best of everything. You're currently working as my consort because my master came into your bar with knowledge he shouldn't have. It's my duty to rectify the situation as best I can until it's resolved. As far as my people know, we are together, and you'll need certain clothing for that."

"And the jeans, tees, and boots?" I ask.

"They reminded me of you. Take what you like, and we'll get you home."

I do take a few band tees to go because they're the shit, and then I follow him through his ridiculous mansion to a thousand car garage (or something like that). He turns the light on to reveal sports cars and vintage vehicles galore, and then I spot a 1970 black Dodge Charger in the corner. I have a feeling I'm going to steal this car soon and drive to my heart's content. There's no way he can handle that much American muscle, so I'd be doing him a favor by taking it off his hands. Killian reaches inside his suit pants to click the lock on what looks to be a brand new BMW SUV. Out of all the cars he owns, this is the one he takes? I roll my eyes. He definitely doesn't deserve the Charger if this is the crap he drives.

He opens the passenger door for me, and I duck under his arm to get away from him quickly. While I wait for him to walk around the car, I look behind me to find all the entry and exit points and any security he has on the place. There's an alarm panel by the first bay door, and I imagine there's a code to get in. I'll have to disarm the security system, which means I'll need a hacker. It looks like I might have to steal, intimidate, and/or kidnap one.

I turn to face the windshield as he lifts his door handle and find him with a smile on his face. "Macushla, you are absolutely fascinating to me. Where have you been my whole life?"

"That makes you sound like a pedophile."

He laughs and backs us out of the garage. "Is that what it feels like when I'm between your thighs?" I squirm in my seat and hope he doesn't notice. I'm not going to dignify that with an answer because if I give it anymore thought I'm going to be even madder. When I was acting like a dimwit, I threw myself at him, and he rejected me. How dare he not have sex with me after the party!

Fine! I'm answering. "Do you enjoy being a tease because I think it makes you a total dust cunt."

Another roar of laughter spills out of him. "Dust cunt? The things you say with that pretty mouth of yours."

I'm offended that he isn't offended by my beautifully constructed insult, but I don't reply in hopes that he'll stop talking to me.

It doesn't last long. "Are you under the impression that I did not desire you last night or every night since I've met you?"

"Oh no siree! You've had two chances to get at this right here!"

He scoffs. "Each time we've come close to being together someone has interrupted. Also, you were glamoured once and under a spell the second time. I want you willing, darling."

"Too bad I'm not a corpse humper. Why would anyone be attracted to a 'creature' like me?" I ask.

"You're going to bring that up again?"

Is he serious? "You bet your ass I am."

"You know that I was referring to the characters in the television show you were all speaking of."

I look at him like he's grown another head. We were both there when he said it. "No. I don't know that. I'm a dragon and therefore, a 'creature'."

"Well, I've never wanted to fuck a computer-generated creature," he says. "We both know how much I want to fuck you."

I open my mouth to reply but my hooha starts short-circuiting my brain, and I forget the words.

"No insult or witty comeback, love?"

I glare at him. "Let me out of the car."

"That's ridiculous. We're two blocks from your place."

I open the car door and get ready to tuck and roll onto the street when he slams on the brakes. "Are you mad?! Close the door!"

Once the car comes to a complete stop, I shoot out of the seat and set about my own course home. He can take his ass home and get out of my hair, except I can hear his feet sound on the pavement behind me and cars honking for him to move his car. I look behind me to find him on my tail. I take off running.

"Get in the car!" he yells.

Screw him. I keep running. He's still chasing when I turn a corner and run straight into an old lady. Shit. I help her pick the items up that spilled from her bag of groceries, and of course that slows me down. Killian almost catches up to me when I take off again and run inside an old movie theater.

"Ma'am, you have to pay for a ticket!" the lady at the box office says.

    I look to see if there's a lock on the door when I push through but find none. I pick the nearest door and enter a movie already in screening and run into the mostly dark room. With a look to my left, I see Twilight is playing on the big screen. I can't freaking get away from the vampires. I seriously need to come up with a sparkly vampire joke for Killian.

    My feet take me up the steps to the sixth row from the bottom, and then I dive into the aisle and army crawl across the floor. Something wet and sticky coats my arm as I pass a guy with smelly feet. I'm going to hope that's soda and not something else, or I'm really going to murder someone today. A hand latches onto my ankle and pulls me back, so I kick whoever it is (most likely Sir Bites A Lot) in the face and find purchase to get to my feet. I jump three rows and just miss the grabby hands of that anemic asshole. "Hey! Look your pretty, sparkly cousin is in the movie!" He's stupid enough to fall for it which gives me even more of a head start. I run out of the theater and back to his waiting car that now has a cop parked behind. I jump into the driver's seat like a maniac and take off while beeping the horn at Stake Bait. I look in the rearview mirror to see him standing in the middle of the summer night on an asphalt road in Georgia with an angry cop behind him.

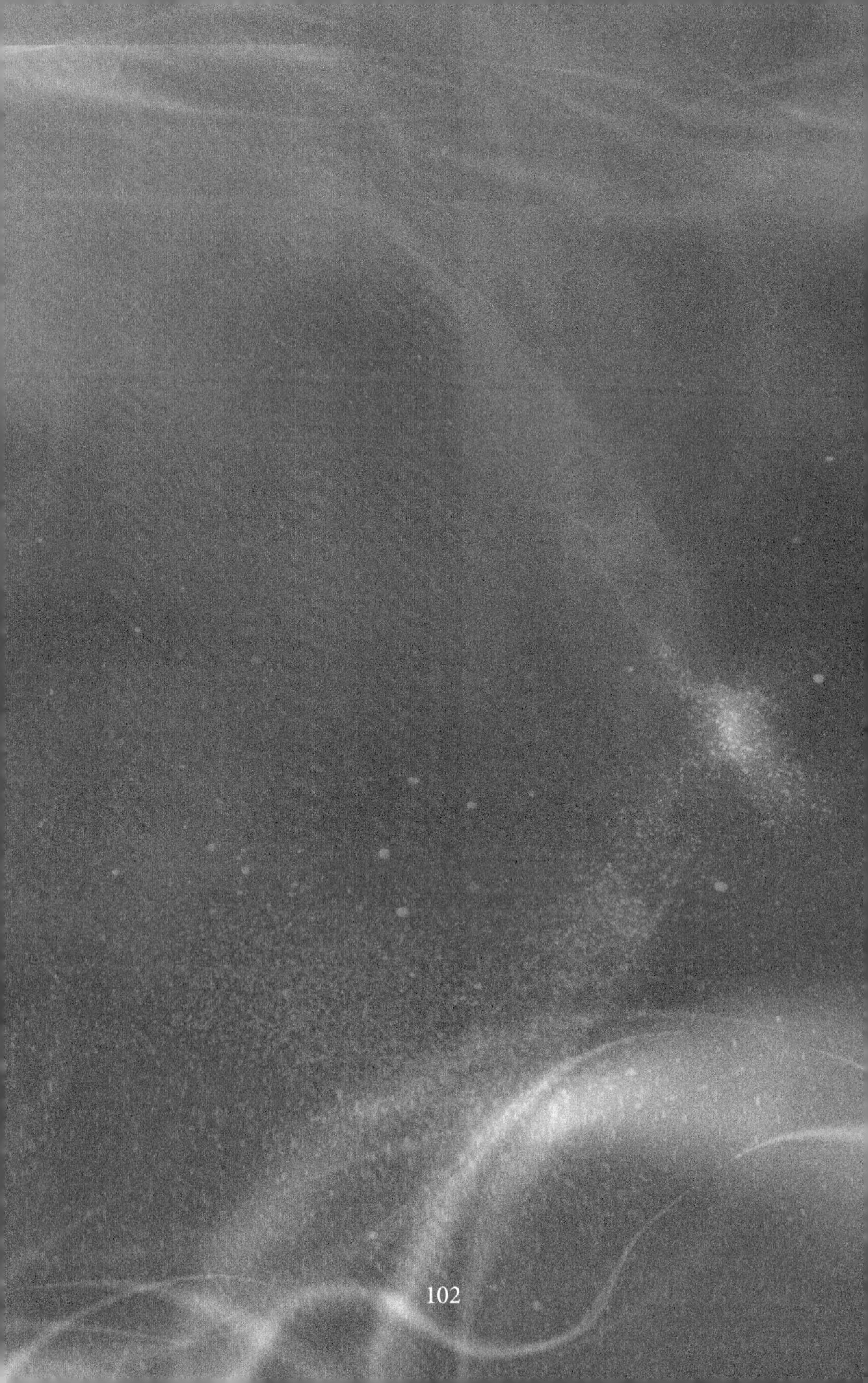

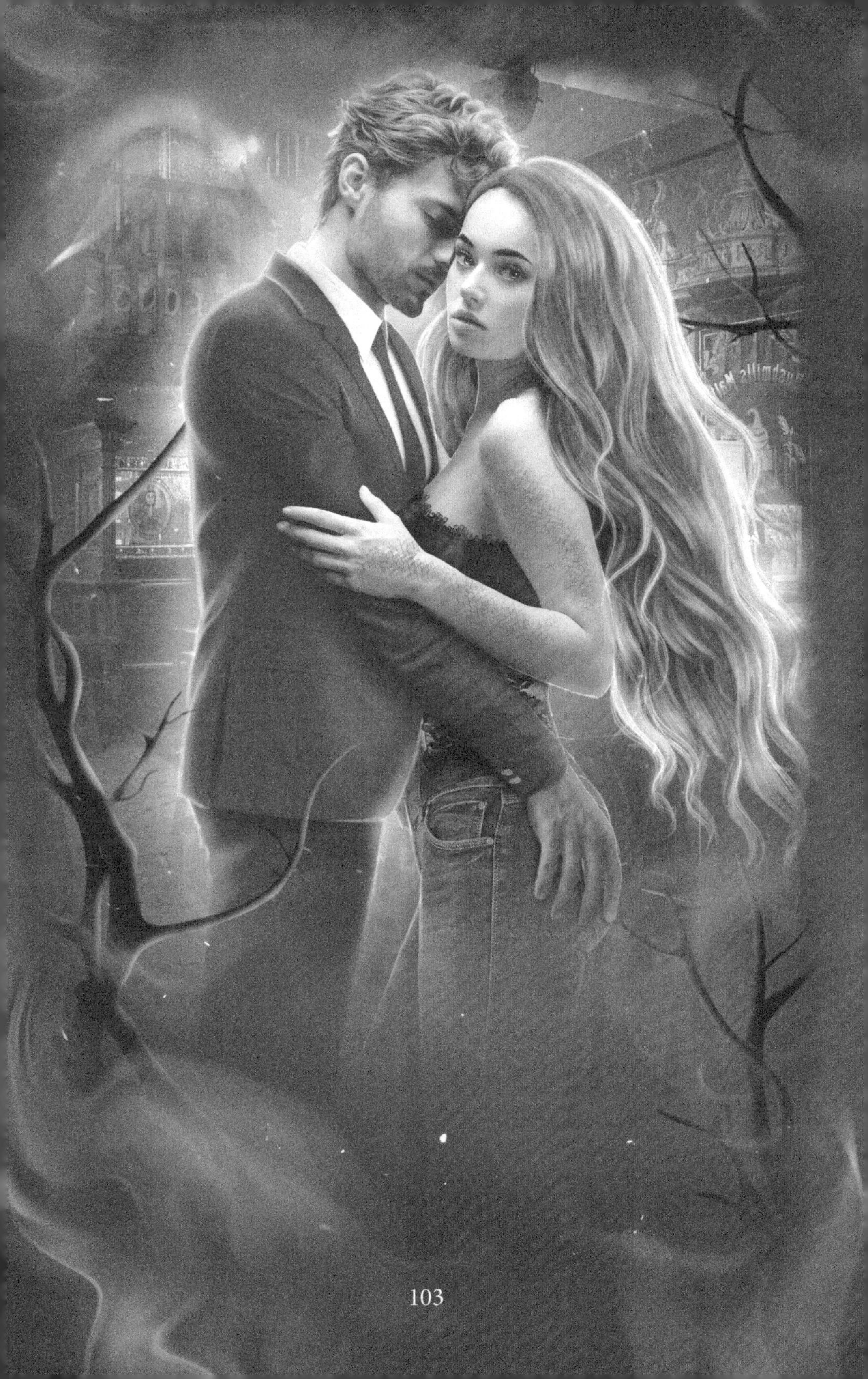

CHAPTER TEN

I GET A LITTLE air under two of the tires as I round the corner into the parking lot before coming to a skidding halt across the pavement. I hope the fanger melts on his way to the bar. I skip into The Bar, which will only be empty for another few hours, and find Hendri saddled up to it with a long look on his face.

"Where's the Minister?" he asks.

I shrug my shoulders. "Why would I know or care?"

"Does he drive a black BMW SUV?"

"Not sure."

The deputy turns to take me in. "What was that?"

I look behind me to see what I missed. "What was what?"

He touches his throat. "The hitch in your voice."

"Means she's lying," Moe says as she walks in from the kitchen. "What'd you do?"

I don't like lying to my sister, so I don't make a habit of it. "Um?"

"Why are you smiling like that?" she asks me. Then she turns to Hendri. "Is it a psychotic smile or one that says she's happy and she has a full belly?"

He thinks about it for a few seconds. "Definitely a little psychotic."

"How does she seem?"

He shrugs his shoulders. "Happy? Why?"

"She did something," Moe answers.

"Care to explain that a little further, babe?"

"The crazy smile usually means she did something she wasn't supposed to do. I need to see if damage control is needed."

"Okay?"

He's not getting it.

"The last time I saw Zvi smile like that, she was happy because she stole a Salvador Dali painting from a private collector in Florida."

Hendri gives me a 'are you kidding me?' look. "Should I be hearing this?"

I think my sister momentarily forgot her new beau is a cop. "She returned it a few months later."

A big, heavy sigh escapes his chest, and I can tell he's wondering what in the hell he's gotten himself into with the Jayden sisters. He rubs his hands over his eyes then puts them on his hips. "You really are a pain in my ass. Why on earth did you chance getting caught? It wasn't a smart criminal move."

He has no idea how smart of a criminal I am, but he doesn't need to know that. It dawns on me that Moe will never be able to tell Hendri about me. There will always be secrets to keep. I don't know how that will affect her relationship with him. I hate that for her.

"Did you really return the painting?" he asks.

I snicker. "I grew tired of it and wanted to steal another painting in New York."

He shakes his head like he can't believe what I'm saying, but he knows me well enough after a short time to know it's entirely possible for me to operate outside the law. "Your sister is an art thief," he says to Moe.

Maybe he needs some more time to process this. "I'm simply a borrower. I like fine things."

"Things? Plural?"

Moe huffs. "She doesn't just borrow art. Miss Cranky Pants has to find something with a high value to make it worth the time. She gets her kicks from stealing shit, but she always returns it."

He stands from his stool and makes his way to my sister. He wraps his arms around her in a tight hug and kisses the top of her head. Moe looks like she wants to melt into a big puddle of lovey dovey goo. "You get I'm feeling shit for you, right?"

"Yeah, I hoped," she says breathily. "I'm feeling shit for you too."

I march around the love birds and duck under the bar flap. I need a pot of coffee with a big splash of jack. All this romance is making me nauseous. I'm grateful to find a fresh pot of java brewed behind the bar, and because I expect another guest here soon, I also grab a low ball and pour two fingers of Midleton into it. I place the bottle beside the glass and wait.

"I only know one person in the world you'd pour a Midleton for," my sister notes. "Where's the Minister?"

I smile from behind the bar at the happy little couple in front of me. "You guys are just so stinking cute together."

Moe blinks at me. Hendri cocks a brow.

"What did you do?" she repeats.

Before I can answer, Killian comes through the front door and smiles at me like he's actually happy to see me. My happy go lucky mood is officially over. "The powers of glamour can get a man out of anything," he says.

"I hoped the cops would take you to jail for the night and help you see the error of your ways. Maybe I need Black Star to throw you in the clinker."

"Tsk. Tsk. Macushla, you will not rid yourself of me so easily," he tells me.

I slide the glass of whiskey to the other end of the bar and Killian uses his vampiric speed to catch it before it crashes onto the floor. The vampire looks at Moe, then at Hendri. *Yeah, Oh Scary One, I noticed what you drink.* His eyes find me again, and I see the same tenderness in them that I found in Hendri's a few moments ago when the wolf looked at Moe.

I hop over the bar and grab my extra strong coffee. Within the blink of an eye, the vampire is next to me, all up in my personal space. He sits beside me and tucks a piece of hair behind my ear. "How was the drive?"

"You could've picked a better car," I tell him and slap his hand away. "Also, you need to work out— you're slow in your old age. I left your ass in the wind."

"What happened?" Moe asks.

Killian moves my long, purple hair over my shoulder, and I swat at him again. "Zvi stole my car after I chased her through a theater, and then she left me stranded with the cops in downtown Atlanta to answer for. I had to glamour them to keep from going to jail."

"That's what you did? You stole an ancient vampire's car and left him without transportation in the middle of a busy street? Why did you do that?!" my witchy sibling yells.

"He called me a 'creature'. And he went crazy weird and bought me a whole closet worth of clothes."

"Oh my God, he bought you an entire wardrobe! Thank heavens you stole his car and showed him who was boss!"

I cast a glare down the bar.

The front door swings open and Greta and Helpful Helen walk through it. We have to start locking the door during non-business hours to keep people from walking in unexpectedly, especially these days with a killer on the loose and gunning for the people we know.

Greta almost dances as she walks. "Toodles, everyone."

"Good evening," we all say.

Helpful Helen throws a little wave in the air. Since she's deathly afraid of me, Moe suggested she bunk with Greta who was more than accommodating.

"How's the roomie thing going?" I ask.

Greta saddles up to a hightop table and that's when I notice she's a bit shaken up. "Natasia Portnova came by in the early hours of the morning. She attempted to recruit both of us to help with some sort of spell she has in the works."

"There's no way this spell isn't connected to the case," Hendri says, and he's right. It's no coincidence that she showed her hand.

I hate to think of it, but she needs to consider her safety options. "Greta, she'll know you're connected to Moe, and that puts a target on your back. Be very careful around her."

Greta waves that off. "She did this a decade ago when she recruited all those witches and left them in the wind when Blaine showed up to cover his tracks. I'm not falling for the same old song and dance she's got playing."

I huff. "I wish this Natasia would stop by the bar so we can go out into the parking lot and throw some bows before I smash her skull open and her brains leak out all over the asphalt in a beautiful, bloody mess."

"Darling, that's beautiful," Killian says.

"I'm not your darling."

Everyone else is looking at me like I'm crazy as hell, and maybe that was a bit over the top and graphically violent, but no one says a word. I chuckle at the quiet of the bar.

"We should create a board and see what we have," Hendri finally breaks up the silence. "Let me run to my car and get the files." He leaves his seat and is out the door in no time.

Killian moves the dart boards to make space on the wall for us to pin items for the case, and everyone gathers around.

Hendri returns and starts us off. "Let's start with victim one—Patrick Russell was murdered in a parking garage three blocks from here. The vet suffered a laceration to the neck made by a vampire bite where the carotid artery was severed leading him to bleed out. He was a thirty-five-year-old white male and a homeless war veteran that knew and interacted with Zvi and Moe regularly." He hangs a picture of Patrick in his Marine dress blues.

"The funeral is tomorrow at the Basilica of the Sacred Heart of Jesus at seven, when the vamps can come out and play," I say.

"I thought he didn't have any family?" Hendri says as he rifles through his folder.

"I paid for his funeral. He was a good Catholic, and I thought that's how he'd like to be buried. The Marine Corps is sending some soldiers out for the ceremony. He'll be interred at the Georgia National Cemetery in Canton."

"Thanks for letting us know so we can make plans to be there." The deputy continues, "Victim two—Heath Rutherford was murdered the next day. The wolf was a forty-two-year-old Hispanic male. He was the alpha of the Scarlet Moon Pack. He was in The Bar the night before the homicide. I've reached out to the pack and they've advised that his public funeral is tomorrow at his home at two o'clock. His pack burial will be private." Wolves are very traditional and private about their funerals. In their time of mourning, they don't care to deal with humans.

"Our latest victim is Justine Baldwin. She was a twenty-six-year-old white female and was found murdered in her home. Her funeral has not yet been set, but I think we should stake out those funerals to see if anyone we know shows up." Everyone is in agreement on the stake out, even Killian. "I'll scope out the location today and have a plan put together. Killian, could you spare a few men for the operation?"

The vampire picks up his phone and types out a text message. "It is taken care of," he says.

"I'd like to address a few more things in the case if I can," I begin, and when no one objects, I continue. "Since Patrick was murdered, we've had three new vampires enter our lives, and two of them are very powerful. But not all of them are connected to me and Moe. Gio showed up out of nowhere with information he shouldn't have, and he's fascinated with us. He just happens to show up in the middle of these murders and says he's here as Killian's master. I'm not sure how he's involved, but I have a bad feeling about him. Everett and his crew showed up here at The Bar right after Patrick was murdered and he's an old acquaintance of Killian's. Everett's also linked to Natasia."

"Who's the third?" Helen asks.

"Karl," Moe gently reminds her.

"Ah, right," she says as concern washes over her face.

Hendri jumps in after her. "I believe there's a fourth person to add to that list—Shaw Benton. I noticed at the dinner that he watched Zvi like a hawk. Also, he seemed to grow angry when Killian touched

Zvi."

Killian immediately comes to his defense. "Shaw is not linked to any of this."

His reaction reminds me that perhaps I've been a bit too open with him and the Deputy. I have to remember Killian has valuable knowledge I can't trust him with. As soon as this case is over, I'll need to reassess how to handle him. I hope Moe does the same with Hendri.

Something about the way he said it makes me sit and take notice. "How do you know?"

He's confident and brisk with his reply, and it's obvious he wants to shut down this line of questioning. "It is not my place to share Shaw's affairs, but I can assure you he is not linked to any of the murders or the new arrivals." There isn't any sense in arguing with him, so I let it go, but my suspicions and doubts remain at the front of my mind. If we meet him again, I'll have to watch him like a hawk.

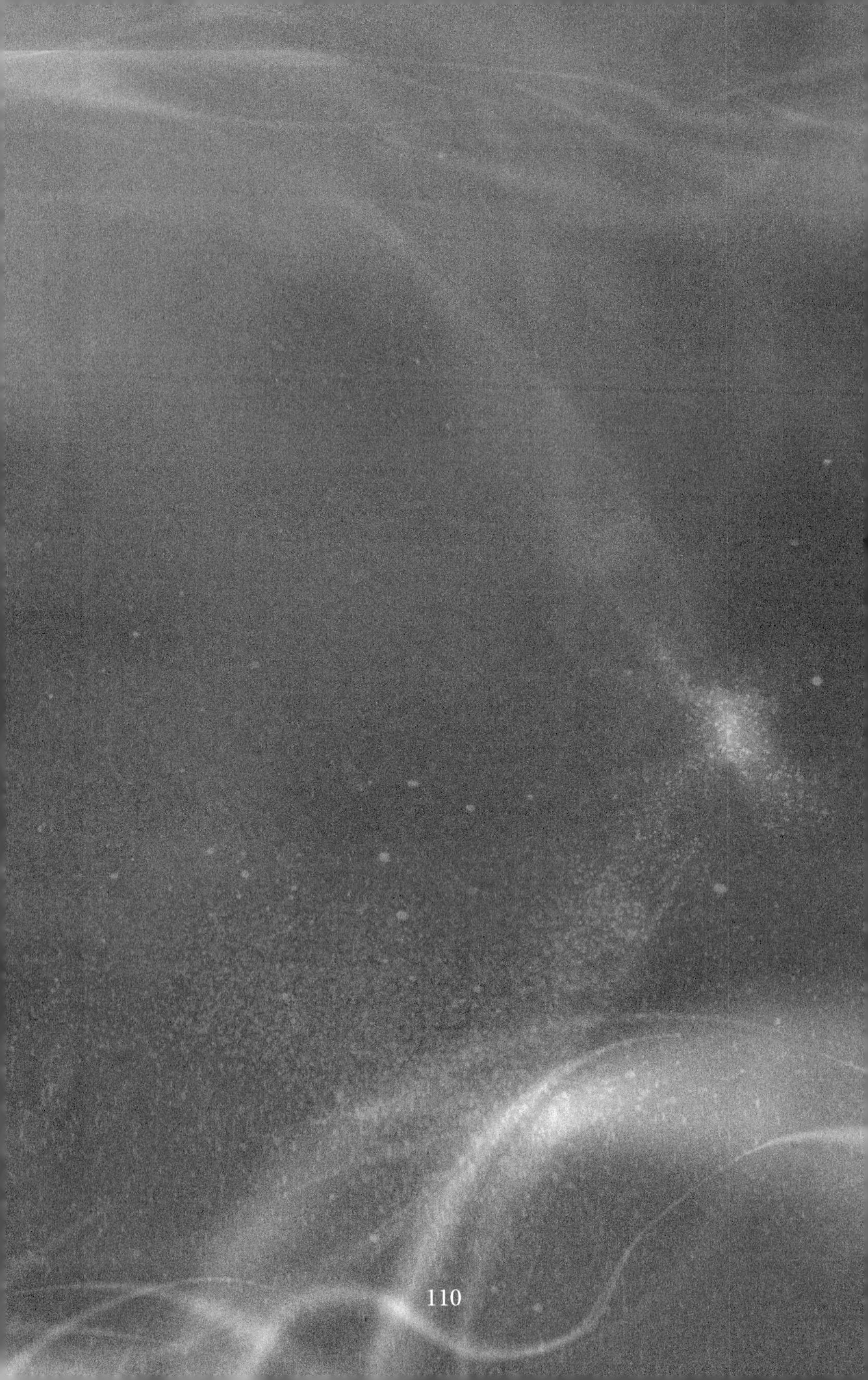

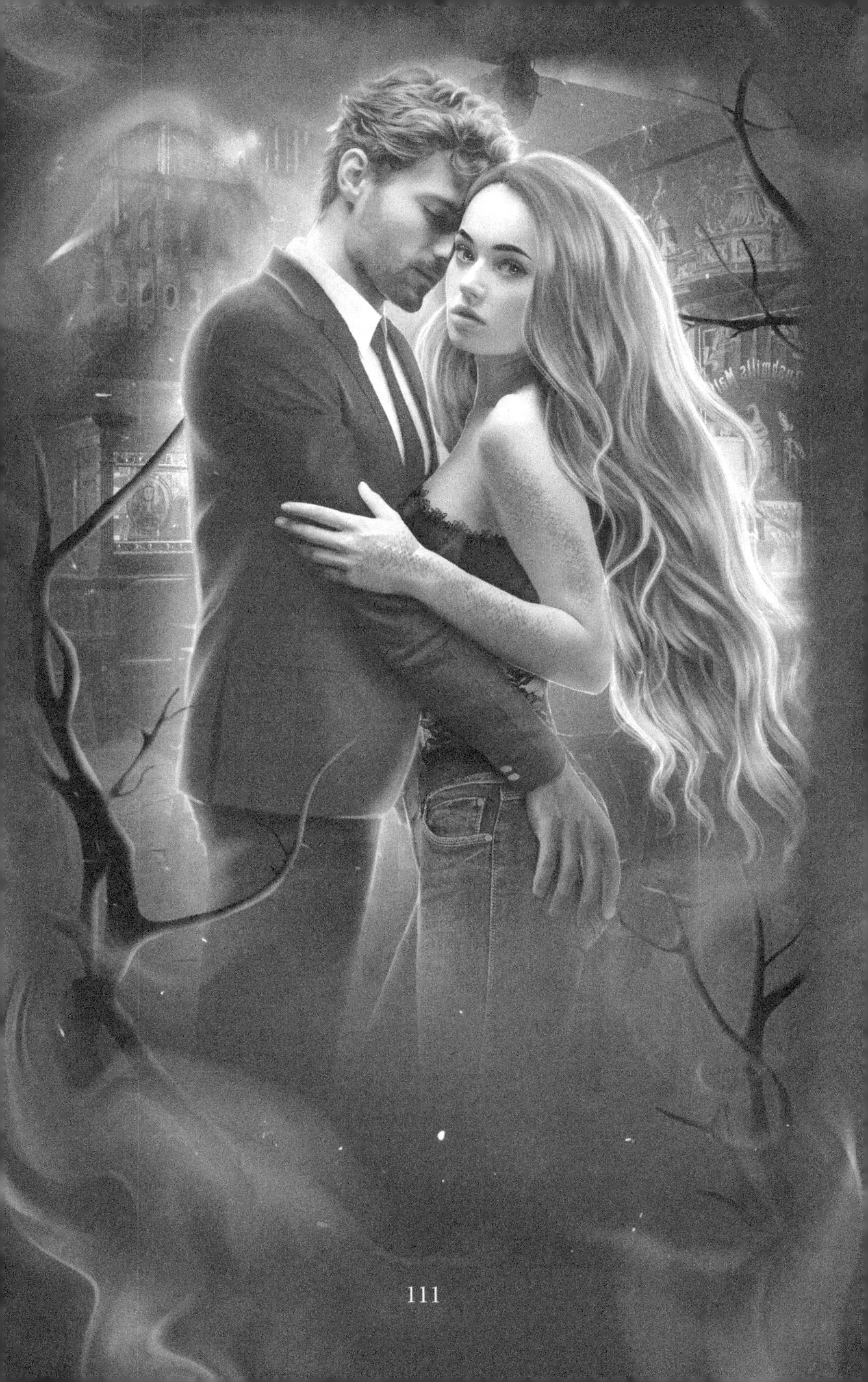

CHAPTER ELEVEN

THE CEMETERY IS QUIET at an hour past dusk. Funerals are exceptionally shitty when a veteran dies alone and has no one to say goodbye. It's even more effed up that Patrick's funeral is attended by supernatural strangers who have to make special arrangements for a night funeral. A dragon, ten vampires, three witches, and a wolf are the only witnesses to the final time the world will acknowledge his life, and he deserves to have someone here who loved him. At least he has our motley crew. Two unsuspecting human marines fold the flag as the taps play the last salute to Patrick.

After his urn is placed in the small square hole, everyone quietly walks to the front of the grounds while the groundskeeper shovels dirt on top. I don't waste any time throwing my leg over my fat boy and turning the engine over. While I wait for an informant—mine, Hendri's, or Killian's—to spot and snitch on Karl, I plan on shifting and enjoying a long, relaxing flight over the mountains of north Georgia. I might even take a dip in a cold river, anything to get my mind off the recent deaths of innocent people.

As I lift the bike and flip up the kickstand, Moe waves me down. After setting the bike back down, I turn the engine off. Moe approaches a little out of breath, her hair sticking to her neck from the ridiculous humidity index. Summer in the south is an intense heat that makes it hard to breathe sometimes. It makes a motorcycle helmet almost unbearable, so I pull it off and hang it on my mirror.

When my sister reaches me, her face is full of concern. "Hendri is on the phone with Black Star. I won't know anymore until he finishes his conversation."

Killian approaches with Greta and Helen. Killian's nine-man army remains by the three black Hummers they drove into the cemetery. We watch as the deputy pockets his phone, turns to us with a grim expression, and walks over to us. Just before he reaches us, the hairs on the back of my neck stand at attention, and Hendri's eyes grow wide. A second later, a gun racks behind me, and my nose tells me it's a vampire at my back.

With Killian's super hearing abilities, he hears the sound and turns but then glances behind me. "What are you doing, Kreston?"

Kreston? Ah, yeah. Killian's human errand boy. But Kreston doesn't smell human. He smells like a vampire. "Hey, Corpsicle, take that off me or you're going to get the ass whooping of your life."

"You're coming with me," he says, voice trembling. He pokes the gun into the back of my neck, which makes me want to break his fangs off and watch him cry like a bitch.

I goad him to see what he's made of. "You won't shoot." He's shaking like a leaf and so is the gun in his hands.

"Darling, please don't provoke him," Killian pleads. He isn't doing a great job of hiding his emotions right now. His eyes are full of terror, and his body is stiff as he moves toward us.

"Zvi, please," Moe adds.

"They say you're a dragon," Kreston replies, and I look around to find every set of eyes on us.

"What are you doing, Kreston?" Killian asks. "Who turned you without my consent?"

A non-humorous laugh escapes the newly created vampire as he jabs the gun into my spine. "I don't need your permission to do anything. I waited for you to turn me for over a decade! I was loyal and dependable. I did everything you asked! I protected you and all of your secrets!"

I raise my hand to see if it's my turn to talk. "Um? That's great, Krestor. Now you're a vamp and you get the last laugh. Can you please remove the gun from my back before I shove it up your ass?"

"Kreston. My name is Kreston. All you supes think you're so much better than humans."

"I don't care if your name is Bob, if you don't get that out of my back, you're going to have a bad day."

"Are you a dragon?" he asks.

There's way too many people talking about me being a dragon these days, and there's also too many ears around to hear him. For the life of me, I can't figure out how anyone I know, other than Moe and Killian, ever got close enough to suspect my species. It isn't like I have any friends or family in my life, other than my sister, and she wouldn't tell a soul. I scan the others standing in front of me to seek out any nervous behaviors, and I note all but one of them is new to my life. Except for Greta. She's known us since we were little kids playing next door. She always preferred Moe over me, and I was okay with it, because I eventually had everything to hide from her.

I don't know if the older woman ever saw me change. There were times when we first discovered our second natures that Moe struggled to contain her magic as I struggled to change. Maybe I wasn't always covered by magic like we thought. I can vaguely remember some sightings, but no one ever believed a person saw Bigfoot, and they definitely never believed someone who claimed to spot a dragon. She's the only person here who could be responsible unless Killian was overheard talking about me by his bodyguard. I look at Killian to see him focusing on Kreston. I look back to find Greta's eyes are watching Moe, and then they slide over to me where they squint into a glare. Bingo.

I can believe she'd stab me in the back, but not Moe. What makes it worse is Moe is a fellow witch, and when witches bond it's almost impossible to break.

"You traitorous bitch," I say, venom dripping from my words.

Moe follows my eyes to her lifelong mentor and back to me. Her big green eyes widen when it dawns on her that Greta is responsible in some way for the gun in my back. "Aleki, grab her!"

The vampire seizes the witch and all hell breaks loose at once. Killian zips past me and slings me to the ground just in time for me to escape the bullet fired from Kreston's gun. Hendri's gun is aimed at Kreston until a group of unknown vampires dash from the tree line. I hear Moe scream and look up to find her tussling with a female fanger. Gaelic words flow from her mouth, and a big cloud of dirt and dust forms into a small cyclone that surrounds her attacker. I have less than a second to appreciate her work before Kreston lunges for me. We both hit the ground so hard the air is knocked out of my lungs. I struggle to turn onto my back because the vamp's hands are wrapped around my neck from behind.

All I can smell are vampires around me and it's difficult to separate the good guys from the bad since I'm not really sure who is on our side anymore. I finally free my left arm and throw it backward into his nose which knocks him off. Sebastian pounces on him and breaks his neck. It won't kill him, but it will knock him out for a few hours. I imagine Killian and his men will want him alive for some good old-fashioned torture. Once I jump to my feet, I rush to my sister, grab the female bloodsucker, and use all of my strength to snap her neck before I rip her head clean off her neck. Blood spurts all over Moe and the body falls to the ground before disintegrating to a large pile of ash. Good riddance.

"Are you okay?" I ask her. I can't tell if she's covered in the fanger's blood or her own.

"Yeah, but Aleki isn't. Go!" Greta has frozen him in a spell.

Across from us, Greta's moving her hands to weave the water from a nearby sprinkler head and then she wraps it around him and turns the water to ice. Witches love to do that to vampires for some reason. Aleki is frozen in place, so I start toward him when Moe screams again. I spin around and find another vampire tugging Moe in the direction of the thick tree line where Everett and an auburn-haired woman stand and watch the scuffle. I zoom across the graves to rescue my sister. I kick the vampire in the side of his knee and smile when it gives an audible crunch as it cracks into pieces. He drops to his other knee and rolls to his back while holding the injured area.

Everett zips from the tree line to Killian and tries to jump him from the back while Killian is otherwise engaged in combat with two other vamps.

"Zvi, help Killian!" Moe yells and runs to help Aleki with Greta, Helen on her heels to offer aid.

By the time I reach Killian to help, he has ripped the hearts out of two vampires' chests and turns around to face Everett. I knew he was a bad guy when I met him, so I'm ecstatic that my vampire is winning. My vampire? I must've bumped my head. He's so not my vampire or my anything for that matter.

A gray cloud surrounds the two vamps, and then the red-haired woman across the field moves her hands along with her words and magic. I instantly know the woman is Natasia Portnova. I don't have any idea what that gray cloud does, but it can't be good if it's hers. I fly across the field to the woman and tuck my shoulder at the last minute as I ram into her like a bull. She flies into the air and lands with a thump. A quick jump later and I'm straddling the heifer with both of my hands around her throat. As I choke her out, she thrashes around, gasps for air, and claws at my hands. Finally, the witch goes limp, but she's still alive. I need time to torture her before I can end it.

I leave Natasia and make a mad dash for Killian who is still in the middle of a gray cloud about twenty-five yards away. Past him, Aleki is free and putting down the rest of the vampires left and right like a warrior. Hendri is just behind him twirling stakes around like a pro. There's a large pile of ash on either side of him as the only trophy of his kills. Moe's managed to use her magic to place the magical purple bubble around Greta. Helen is nowhere to be found. The rest of Killian's army are fighting back the bad guys, and Moe runs over to Natasia and puts her in a purple bubble too. Better them than me.

Hendri shifts as a new group containing five vampires approaches him. A tall, male vampire with long black hair, dark eyes, and dark skin jumps Hendri in the middle of his shift. I rectify the situation for him by flashing over to them and throat punching the fanger. When Hendri has completed his transformation and we've taken out all but one vampire, I leave him to clean up the last one by himself and run back over to Killian and Everett.

I circle Killian and Everett as the magical cloud disappears and wait for a better visual to ascertain how best to kick Everett's ass since Killian can't seem to get it done. I wait for Everett to exploit a weakness of Killian's or get a lucky shot in, so I can go in for the kill shot. I can't allow the Lord to kill the King when I've been promising myself for days that I'd get the honor. I also need the Minister alive to take care of all these bad guys because I'm not interested in the cleanup job. My gig is always in the fuck shit up department.

Both men end up on the ground and roll around like a couple of idiots, ruining both of their expensive as shit suits. Suit jackets get pulled over heads, gut punches are thrown, shins are kicked, and they choke each other out.

I get bored. "Hey, dickheads!" They both grunt in reply.

"She's talking to you," Everett tells him.

Killian gains leverage and shoves Everett backward until he trips on his feet and tumbles back where he hits the back of his skull on a gravestone on his way down. His body lands and crumples against the headstone. I cringe. Ouch. That's going to take a while to heal since there's likely major brain damage. Vamps always heal from it, but they're too weak to protect themselves for several days. His noggin' is going to hurt tomorrow, and he'll wish he was still unconscious. I skip over to the body to check out the gore and discover a wicked amount of blood. "Gnarly." Killian dusts himself off and I chuckle at the condition of his suit. "He almost kicked your ass."

"I'm glad you find humor in the situation."

I snort. "Someone's cranky."

We walk over to where the others have congregated and look around at the bodies lying around us. Hendri, now clothed and once again human, is covered in sweat from the exertion of battle, Moe is wearing blood splatters, Aleki is smiling in the wake of his victory,

Helen is cowering behind Moe, and Killian's men are still in a fight stance awaiting the next threat.

"What was that?" Moe asks, still out of breath from the fight.

"Kreston was trying to take Zvi," Killian answers.

"Two vamps tried to take Moe, and Natasia tried to take you," I tell him.

Hendri starts pacing. "I need to call this in."

Shit. The last thing I need is Black Star up my ass in the midst of people getting murdered and multiple kidnapping attempts.

"Is that necessary?" Minister Killian Kavanagh asks.

The wolf's right brow cocks up in surprise. "Yes, it's fucking necessary." His face is getting redder by the second. "What kind of question is that? I have a job to do." His eyes roll back in his head, and then he drops like a potato sack.

Moe is instantly on the edge of hysterics. "Oh God!" She runs to him, and I follow, then turn him over to find his lower back soaked in blood. I have to rip his shirt to get a good look at a broken stake around his kidney and the jagged wound where blood continues to pour from.

"Killian," I call as I wave him over. "He needs your blood if he's going to survive."

Moe objects. "He wouldn't want vampire blood."

Killian sneers at the thought of giving up his precious, ancient blood. There's only one other older vampire in the vicinity and he's currently in a coma. If Hendri's to survive, he'll need the powerful magic in an ancient's blood. "Save your macho, fanger superiority for when we have time for it. If he doesn't get blood powerful enough to heal him quickly, he's going to die within a few minutes from blood loss."

"Oh, God," Moe repeats as tears form in her eyes.

I take the deputy's pulse and find it beating rapidly. His skin is clammy and his breathing is shallow. He's got less than a couple of minutes when his lips begin to turn blue. "Now!"

Killian hesitates for a second, but he finally bites into his wrist then drips red droplets into Hendri's mouth. I keep my finger on his pulse, and it begins to slow as he loses more blood by the second.

"Please be okay," Moe pleads as she quietly sobs.

His heart weakly beats until it stops, but I don't say anything at first. I give it a minute and hope he'll come to. If he goes, I suspect it would break my sister's heart. My hopes for him dwindle with each passing second, and eventually, I find Killian standing above us, so I give him a slight shake of my head.

"Moe," I gently call.

"I know," she quietly whispers. "He's gone." She leans over his chest and cries out for him. They just met, but I can tell Moe already felt something for him in a big way. I'm about to back off and give her some space to be alone with him before we do what he wanted and call it in to Black Star. Considering the number of vamps that attacked us, it's probably best we use as many resources as we can to stay safe. A sputtering noise has me refocusing on Hendri when the sound escapes him once again as he gasps for breath. "Hendri?" Moe calls out to him. When he doesn't open his eyes, I roll him over again and find the wound has healed over. Then I roll him to his back and feel his pulse return in his wrist. It's beating strong and steady, but his breaths are still labored from pain.

Shit if he died and vamp blood brought him back, then it means…

"He's okay," I tell her, and I hope like hell it's the truth.

She closes her eyes and sighs in relief then lays her ear on his chest and listens to the thump of his heartbeat. "Thank heavens."

Hendri sits straight up with wide, fearful eyes as he hyperventilates. He throws a hand over his chest and reaches around his side with the other only to find it covered in blood. "Did I get staked?" he asks.

"Not important," I tell him. "You're okay now, but you're going to need some help standing for a few hours."

Vampire blood makes werewolves a little drunk for a while, and no wolf in this world wants other wolves to know he drank the crimson martini. Let's just hope he's not about to start craving blood. Worse, a vamp not only healed him but saved his life. Or, the blood can kill him if Killian so desires since fangers have the ability to secrete a toxin in their blood if they're forced to feed another. I look across the park at him and hope like hell for Moe that Hendri's just going to be a little stoned for a few hours.

Moe and I help him up. He laughs. "I feel pretty unsteady. Vampire blood?"

I ignore his question. "I need you to call this in. Can you handle that?" I ask.

His phone drops after he pulls it from his pocket, and Moe has to help him pick it up and dial the right number. Apparently, when Black Star is called they show in under fifteen minutes. Dozens of black SUVs speed into the cemetery, and two helicopters fly overhead as one searches for the culprits while the other monitors all activity around it. The government sure knows how to shut shit down, including us. Hendri doesn't have enough brain cells to help us out. It seems like hundreds of deputies swarm the area before they separate us into different vehicles to prevent us from talking to each other. I can only hope like hell no one says the word "dragon".

Hendri opens the back passenger door and slides in beside me. "Need you to level with me. Was Kreston right about you?"

I stare straight ahead and remain silent.

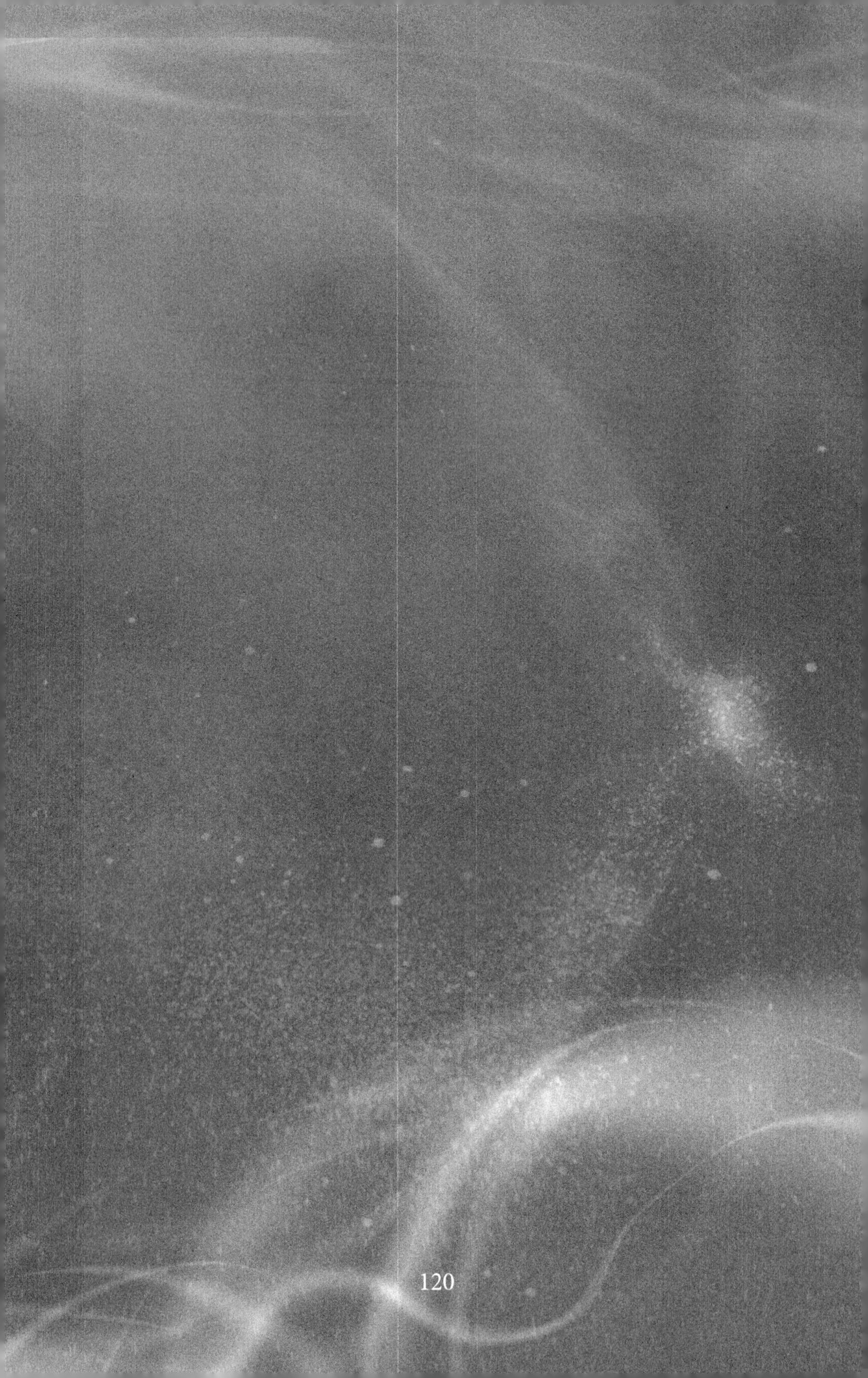

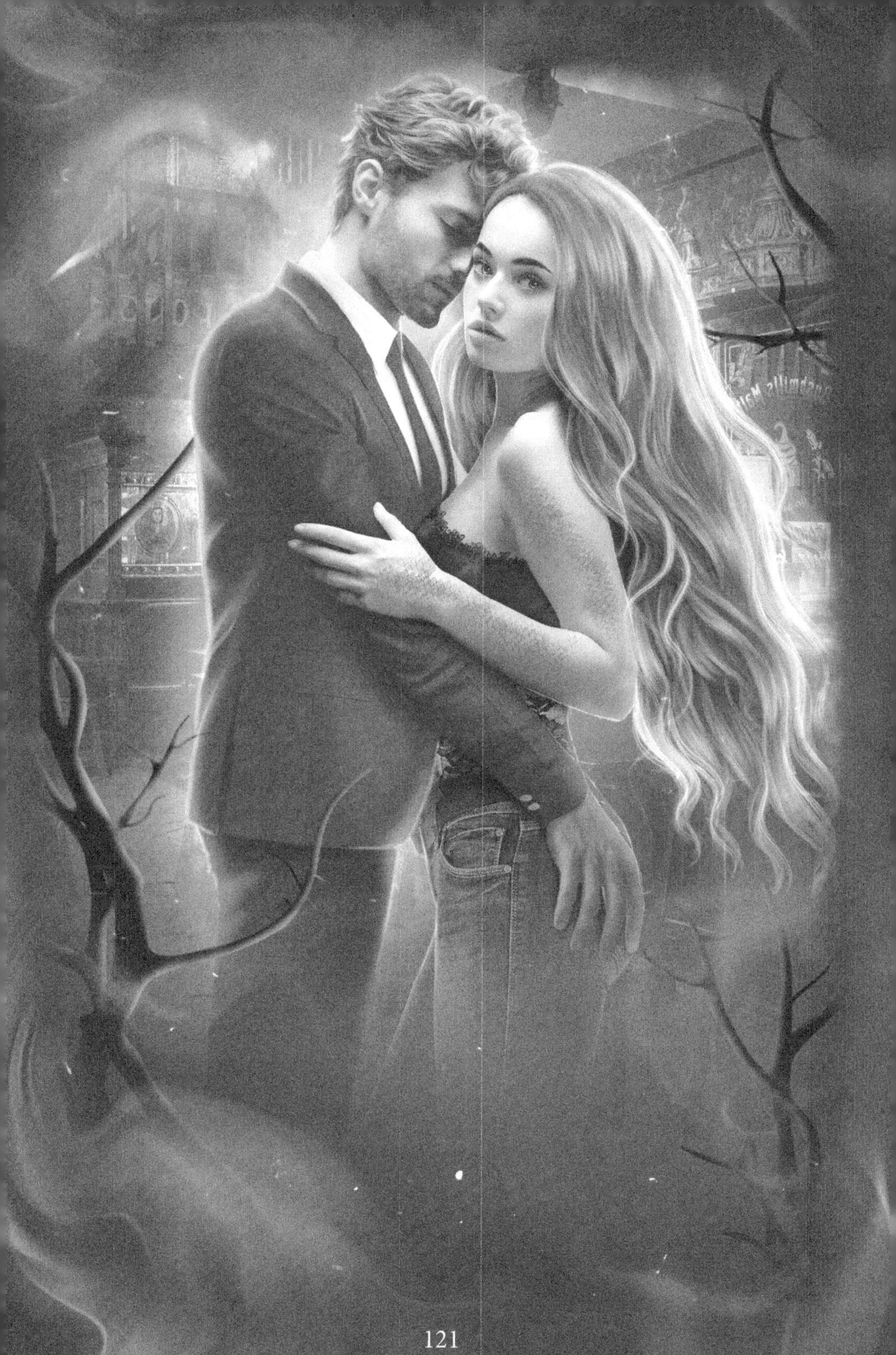

CHAPTER TWELVE

SINCE I'M ON THE side of the good guys this time, I expect to be treated like one, but it seems Black Star has helped me out of one too many situations for them to believe I didn't instigate the attack in the cemetery. This is unfortunate because I've been stuck in an interrogation room with nothing to do but be pissed off. By the time Detective Morris and Detective Renault join me, my mood has declined from extreme satisfaction from winning the fight into a state of supreme disenchantment.

"Can we get you anything, Jayden?" Renault asks. The guy is a wolf of extreme proportions with a body built like a linebacker. He played for The University of Georgia several years back, which is the only reason I ever cut him some slack. The deputy has mocha-colored skin and a short haircut trimmed close on the sides. He has eyes the color of seafoam, and if I were into wolves, I'd probably climb that tree, but he's too strict about rules like laws, so we'd never get along.

Morris is a supervisor with Black Star, and he's also a wolf. Sometimes I fantasize about setting him on fire. He's in his fifties, ornery, round, red-faced, and he's always being extra. "Guess what I heard just before I came in here?" Morris asks.

"The name of a good beta blocker? Dude, you look like you swallowed a ghost pepper. You're a heart attack waiting to happen."

That earns me a sneer. "No, smart-ass. I hear you've got people thinking you're a dragon."

I give him a toothy grin and flash my glowing eyes at him. They're back to normal before either man knows what hit him. Morris jumps out of his seat, and the metal chair falls over with a loud clanging sound. "What the hell?!" he yells.

Renault is still in his chair looking me over with a discerning eye. "Are you really a dragon?"

I snort. "What do you think?"

He considers it for a moment before he speaks again. "I think dragons haven't existed for centuries and you're some kind of weird shifter we don't often encounter." He's right about the second part. People will talk themselves into believing anything.

"Sure. That sounds plausible."

"What are you?" Morris asks for the millionth time over the last decade I've been on their radar.

I shrug my shoulders. "A weird shifter you don't often see." If Morris could get away with it, he'd punch me in the nose. He'd get his ass beat, but he doesn't really seem to care that I'd humiliate him. Renault looks like he's satisfied with my answer, and it's probably because he's already told himself that dragons don't exist. There's no talking him out of it. I'm okay with that because it's one less person up my ass about the dragon thing.

"Why am I here, boys?"

Renault jumps in first. "Can you tell us what happened this evening at the cemetery?"

"Sure," I say. "I went to a funeral and then got into a skirmish."

"That skirmish was a full out battle," Morris replies.

I glare at the older wolf. "I didn't start it."

"Who did you attend the funeral with?" The younger wolf asks.

"I went by myself on my motorcycle."

Renault doesn't miss a beat with his follow-up question. "Other than yourself, who else was in attendance?"

I begin to count everyone on my fingers. "Kavanagh, Connor, Greta, Helen, Kreston, Aleki, Sebastian, and seven other vampires I don't know the names of. There were also two Marines and a groundskeeper there."

"Did the humans see anything?" Renault asks.

"I guess it's hard to know seeing as I was busy keeping me and Moe alive."

"What about Kavanagh?" Morris jumps back in.

I give the biggest attitude I can muster. "What about him?"

The older deputy grins at me in ill humor. "Did you not also try to keep him alive? He and the other vamps tell me you're his consort now."

I'm going to tear Killian's tongue from his mouth the next time I lay eyes on him. Why on earth would that bloodtard tell Black Star that nonsense? I have to fake a breakup with him now so people don't think I've gone soft. "I'm not his consort, and I did try to keep him alive, but he threw homeboy into a coma before I could."

"He's demanding to see you," Renault says and waits for my reaction.

Pah-pah-poker face in place. I wonder what Minister Muerto wants now, but I don't give these two a reaction. "Can I go now?"

"Deputy Connor has linked the victims to you, your sister, and your boyfriend." I roll my eyes at the paunchy man. Morris isn't going to let me go without running that trap of his some more.

I'm growing tired of playing twenty questions, so I let the boyfriend comment pass. "Tell me something I don't know."

The door opens and Hendri walks through on unsteady legs. He takes in the scene in front of him and scowls. "Zvi is my witness and informant. I'll take over from here."

Neither of the other deputies hides their unpleasantness at having to end this conversation. I'll have to do something nice for Hendri for saving me from those dodo brains. The two dogs leave the room with one last glare pointed in my direction. "I'm glad you're okay," Hendri says, and then he shocks me by pulling me into a hug. A second later, he quietly whispers, "Don't say a word about the case until we leave the building."

Whatever. "Can we stop hugging now?"

He releases me, and I find a lopsided smile on his face. "I want to introduce you to someone." I follow him out of the small room, down a wide hallway, up some stairs, and into a door marked, "IT Department".

We march through a narrow aisle separating cubicles until we come to the largest cubicle. A small Indo-European man with dark brown skin swivels around in his chair to face us, and the oddest smell hits the olfactories. "You smell funny."

"Zvi!" Hendri admonishes me.

"I'm tracking," I tell him. I fully understand that I've been rude.

"Zvi, this is Rishi. He's a tech genius for Black Star. Rishi, Zvi is well known for being quite the sparring partner. Rishi would like to learn some self-defense moves, and I thought you could learn some patience from teaching Rishi how to not die."

Rishi looks quite terrified of me as I sit on his desk. "The scent you smell is wererat," he says.

"Never met a wererat, but I assume you can get into some tight and small spaces."

He grins at that. This guy is perfect for a job I have in mind. "Now you have."

"I need a hacker to penetrate an alarm system, but you being a wererat could be quite useful in this situation," I tell him.

"Leaving now," Hendri announces and walks away.

Rishi is a small, meek man who looks like he might cry if he killed a bug. I just hope he doesn't puke in the car. "I'm willing to pay a couple of grand for your services." The money doesn't really sway him because he's looking at me like I might bite his head off.

"I'm assuming this is illegal." He leans forward and whispers, "Are you a witch?"

I slightly shake my head. "Nope."

"Demon?"

"Negative."

"Vampire?"

"Hell to the no."

He leans a little closer and sniffs me. "You don't smell like a wolf, vampire, demon, or witch, but you smell greatly of magic. You have to also be a shifter we don't often encounter."

I blow out a breath and rethink kidnapping this guy. Maybe he'll stop talking when there's duct tape over his mouth. I just need him for his mind and typing skills, not his nosiness. So I pat him on the back a little too hard, and a big woosh of air leaves his lungs. "See ya in two days, Ratatouille."

I'm surprised at how big my grin is after the day I've had, but I'm getting some revenge on Kavanagh for being… well, him. I have a little skip in my step after the long, eventful day and something that feels a lot like happiness. Nothing like the promise of a good theft to lift my spirits. I receive several suspicious and guarded stares from the offices I pass by. I come upon the last rookie, Deputy Logan Carter, they stuck on me before Connor became my keeper. Before I can say "hello" to the guy and have a chuckle about all the things I put him through, he ducks into his office and quickly closes the door. I can't help but laugh a little.

Once I make it to the lobby, I find Moe, Killian, Hendri, Helen, Sebastian, and Aleki sitting around in the leather chairs Black Star has in their waiting area. When I meet the Minister's gaze, I slice my finger across my throat, and the idiot grins bigger than I've ever seen. He stands and becomes a blur of speed as he closes the space between us. Then I'm in his arms, and his lips are on mine. I want to object to the contact. He goes in deep with his tongue, pushing against my own, and for some reason mine moves back. He has to be glamouring me again because I want to rip his clothes off and have my dirty way with him. Instead, I grab the lapels of his dark blue suit jacket and pull him in closer. Standing on my tiptoes, I graze my teeth across his bottom lip and then suck to soothe it. I'm about to tear his jacket to pieces when a round of applause brings me back to my senses, and I'm immediately filled with more anger toward Kavanagh. I wrench myself loose of his embrace and take a few steps back. I don't know how many eyes are on us, but I can feel all of their stares as heat crawls up my neck to my face. Thoughts of violence and taking care of witnesses crosses my mind, but this is not the place to do that. I'll have to hunt them down individually, so I meet every shocked, terrified, and grinning face and lock in the names on their building IDs.

Moe steps toward me from the left and calls out to me in a concerned tone. "Zvi?" She's scared I'm about to lose my shit, and she's right, because I'm talking myself down as we speak. The only way I'm getting this vamp out of my life is murder. Plain and simple. There's no way around it.

I glare at Killian whose lips are parted from the kiss. He wears an expression on his face that's more than lust. I stare back at him to try to decipher what it is beyond the yearning I can see and feel from him, but I'm interrupted by Hendri. The wolf puts an arm around me and leads me from the building. It's probably best he did. I let him guide me away because I'm not sure how long I was going to stare at the lunatic inside, but I know that I liked it, which is further reason to keep my distance from him. If I give in to him, I'll inherit all of his vampire political problems. There's also the fact that I'm not keen on anyone trying to get close to me.

Hendri leads me to one of Killian's Black SUV's where we both lean against the hood and wait for the others. "I know you're tough as nails, but I need you to hold it together. Moe needs you, and any error in your judgment could put her at risk of harm. I don't pretend to understand what's going on with you and Kavanagh, but I can clearly see he's smitten with you. You have your reasons for fighting it, but darlin', you're doing just that, which tells me that you're feeling something too. I don't pretend to know a lot about love, but I do know you don't let a good thing go. For a fanger, he's alright by me, but don't you go and repeat that." He briefly chuckles. "Guess what I'm saying is that you're the strongest woman I've ever met, and it's understandable that you don't want to be in a relationship where a man is weaker. You need a man to challenge you and understand your ruthlessness, and I don't imagine that a doormat man appeals to you. That being said, you aren't going to find many outside of an ancient vampire to fit the bill. Also, you wouldn't like any of the other ancients I know, especially the kings, queens, and ministers. Kavanagh seems okay as if there's still some humanity left in him."

I take in what he's saying and let it mull over in my head for a while. "The only relationship I've ever had is with my sister. I don't have time to worry about somebody else."

He grins at me. "It's going to be fun to watch you fall."

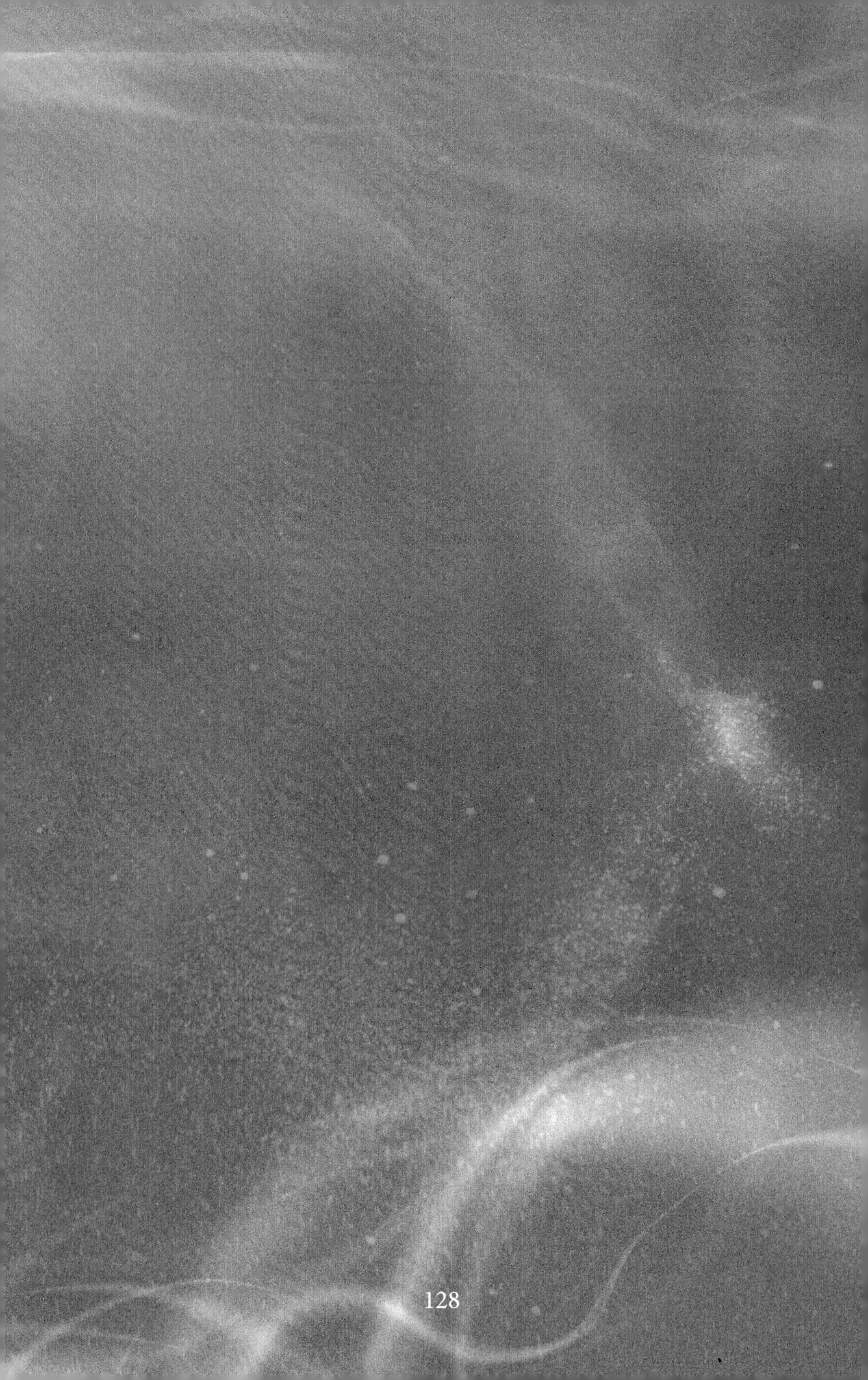

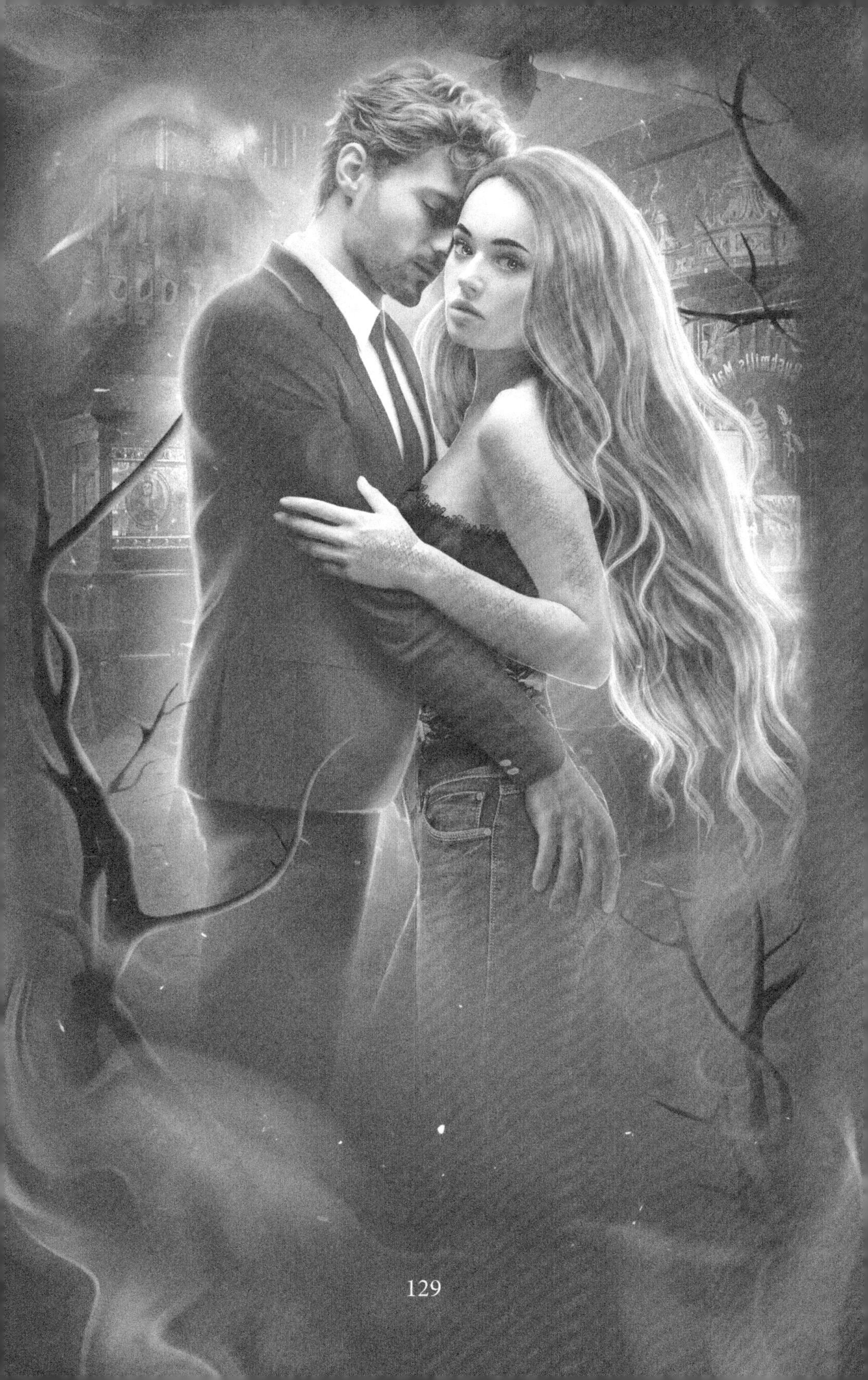

CHAPTER THIRTEEN

THE RIDE BACK TO The Bar is quiet in the back seat of Hendri's government-issued black Tahoe. Moe's sorrow over Greta washes over me. If the old hag wasn't already in jail, I'd invite her over for a nice cup of coffee laced with eye drops. Maybe then she'd understand just what a piece of shit I think she is. I don't like when people make my sister sad.

As the Deputy pulls into our back parking lot, the rain begins to fall. Seems like the right ending for a long day. I'm tired down to my bones. There's a lot of developments to sort through, but I don't have any more brain cells left to do the heavy lifting.

When the car comes to a stop, I open the door and step out into the humid air. I need a shower and my bed. My hackles rise when a tortured moan echoes through the lot. Alarm bells ring in my head. I step away from the vehicle and turn around slowly until I can decipher which direction the sound is coming from. The foul smell of demon blood fills the air, and if the smell is this loud, it means there's a good deal of blood nearby.

I place a finger to my lips as Hendri slips from the vehicle to join me. Another inhuman moan comes from the general area of the dumpster in the south part of the lot. I take a running start and jump on top of the commercial, green can, ready to throw down at a moment's notice.

"Lady Jayden?" a voice cries.

The area behind the can is pitch black, giving me no clue as to who I'm speaking with.

"Just Zvi," I say. "Who's down there?"

"It is I, the demon Roglak Uz'gan."

"Roglak? You okay, homie?"

Roglak is a regular at The Bar, and he often provides parking lot security on the nights demons aren't allowed inside. He takes his pay in spirits.

"I was attacked by a vampire."

He's got my attention. "Yeah? Can you come from behind there so I can see you?"

"I am not wearing my skin, Lady Jayden. I do not wish for you to see me in my demon form."

Demons aren't pretty when they aren't wearing their skin, which is much like a sheathing. It looks like human skin, although demons make sickly-looking humans. I've seen some ugly things in this life, so I'm not afraid of a little demon nudity.

"I can't help you if you don't come from behind there," I tell him.

"He cut my arm off with a sickle," Roglak explains.

Yuk. No wonder I could smell his blood in the air. "It'll grow back."

"Hurts."

"Yeah, life hurts, Roglak. You've been around a long time, and one doesn't survive as long as you without understanding life is full of pain. Thing is, I don't have any words of compassion to offer you, demon, because I'd screw it up somehow. But I can offer you a place to drink your beer while you heal. I'll even buy you your own keg as a 'Get Well' gift from me and Moe."

"You'd do that for me?" He asks, surprise in his voice.

I wave it off. "Yep. You got it. We like to take care of our employees and all."

"Will you allow the wolf to aid me?"

"Yes." I wave Hendri over. "Our friend and sometimes employee is behind here. He was attacked, likely by someone we know. His arm was severed, and he needs help. He'd rather I didn't see him without his skin. Would you be a doll and help him out?"

The Deputy crosses his arms over his wide chest. "You want me to go behind a dark dumpster in a dark alley with a demon?"

Demons are known tricksters. They like to toy with others and often find a great deal of glee in doing so. But they can also be ferocious warriors if you anger one. There's a bleeding demon on our hands, and Hendri won't see it coming if Roglak lashes out in pain. "Yeah. I'm asking you to help my friend. Why? Are you scared?"

"Reverse psychology doesn't work on me. You're going to have to try harder if you expect me to willingly help your friend."

On cue, Moe moseys up to us. We both turn and glare at her for getting out of the car. "What's going on?"

"A vampire attacked Roglak and cut his arm off. He needs assistance, but Hendri won't help him."

Hendri grunts in disapproval. I wink at him, and Moe pouts.

"Fuck it. Fine. I'm doing it." He huffs, kisses Moe on the forehead, and hustles over to Roglak.

I try to hide my victorious smile.

It takes twenty minutes longer for Roglak to regenerate his skin. It'll take much longer for his arm to do the same, but he finally walks out with Hendri, who is covered in stinky demon blood. I'm glad I'm not the one dating him. Roglak is extremely tall at well over six feet in height. He's skinny as shit and walks with a slight slump to his shoulders. His hair is ash blond and cropped short at the sides while left long on top. He's nude underneath a long shirt with The Bar spread across it, but I try not to think too hard about his junk.

We finally manage to get everyone inside the bar and before the demon can tell us what happened, the nosiest vampire in the world makes another appearance with his small army. He whisks through the door, zips through the room, and comes to stand in front of my table in the back. "Are you quite alright, Macushla?"

"What are you going on about now?" I ask.

"The Deputy said there was another attack, and I wanted to make sure you were well."

Moe sighs beside me.

I roll my eyes. "I'm fine. We were just about to get into the details with the demon, Roglak Uz'gan," I advise in an impatient tone. When Killian doesn't move, I blink up at him. "*What?*"

"It is nothing, darling."

"Roglak, can you share what occurred when you were attacked?" the Deputy asks.

"I was watching the lot for Lady Jayden and Miss Moe when a vampire launched himself at me out of the blue. He was fighting against magic and…"

"Whoa! Wait. Back up," I say. "How do you know he was fighting against magic?"

"Yes. Well, I could smell the black magic on him. Also, he was shouting at me to run. It was clear to me he did not want to harm me. He produced a sickle from thin air, it seemed, and then my arm was gone."

"Did he say anything other than 'run'?" Hendri asks.

"Yes. He was mumbling about demon blood," Roglak answers.

"Why would a fanger want demon blood?" I ponder aloud.

"A vampire wouldn't drink from a demon," Killian says. "It would be the equivalent of eating spoiled meat." He frowns at the thought of the substance. "Demon blood is quite corrosive."

"Can you describe the assailant?" Hendri asks.

"Yes. I know exactly who it was. It's the vampire everyone is looking for— Karl Ekman," the demon announces.

I had a hunch this was about ol' wacky Karl. "Thank you, Roglak. Can we get you anything to help the healing process?"

"I would appreciate gauze for a makeshift sling."

Moe touches the demon's shoulder in a gesture of comfort. "I'll go get the gauze for you now."

Killian takes Moe's seat beside me. "Forgive my dramatic entrance." He glares at Hendri. "The Deputy was not clear that a demon had been attacked. I jumped to conclusions at his message and feared the three of you were under threat again."

"Blah, blah, blah."

"I see you're still angry with me," the Minister says.

"Stop telling people I'm your consort. And don't kiss me again."

"I'm afraid I'm not capable of either. You may ask me anything else."

A sniffle to the right of us interrupts the next insult. It dies on my tongue when I realize Roglak is crying. "You okay there, buddy?"

"I am simply happy to watch two people fall in love. All the carnal thoughts it inspires have made me emotional."

"Sex makes you cry?" I ask just to clarify.

The demon smiles with his freakishly sharp, pointed teeth. "Yes! The lust between you is palpable."

I feel the tug of Killian's glamour at the edge of my mind. I'm sorry I asked.

Moe returns with the gauze to wrap the remainder of Roglak's arm close to his chest. She pats him on the shoulder again. "All ready to go."

After Moe and I walk Roglak to the door, we head back to my table and put our heads together.

"How is Karl still under a spell if Natasia is in lock down at Black Star?" I ask Moe.

"The spell must be original and specific. I don't know if it's time activated or compulsion activated. In other words, does Karl kill at a certain time every night, or does Karl need to meet a set of parameters before he can shake the curse?"

"How do we know which it is?" Hendri asks.

"I don't have enough information. I can't fight against a spell when I have no idea which components are involved. Also, I don't know enough about black magic to write a spell reversal," she replies.

"I can't believe I'm about to say this," Hendri begins. "But I think it would be a good idea if you two ladies stayed at Killian's estate. Karl was in the parking lot of The Bar tonight, and it's entirely too close for my liking."

"I concur," the Minister adds like I give two flips what he thinks.

"Nuh-uh," I say. "I want my own bed."

"Done," Killian says and snaps his fingers. Two vamps go upstairs to most likely take my bed to Killian's.

Moe snickers at my lack of an immediate snarky reply. And the point goes to the deader. I didn't see it coming.

Fine. I'll go. I march upstairs behind Killian's do-boys and pack a bag in silence.

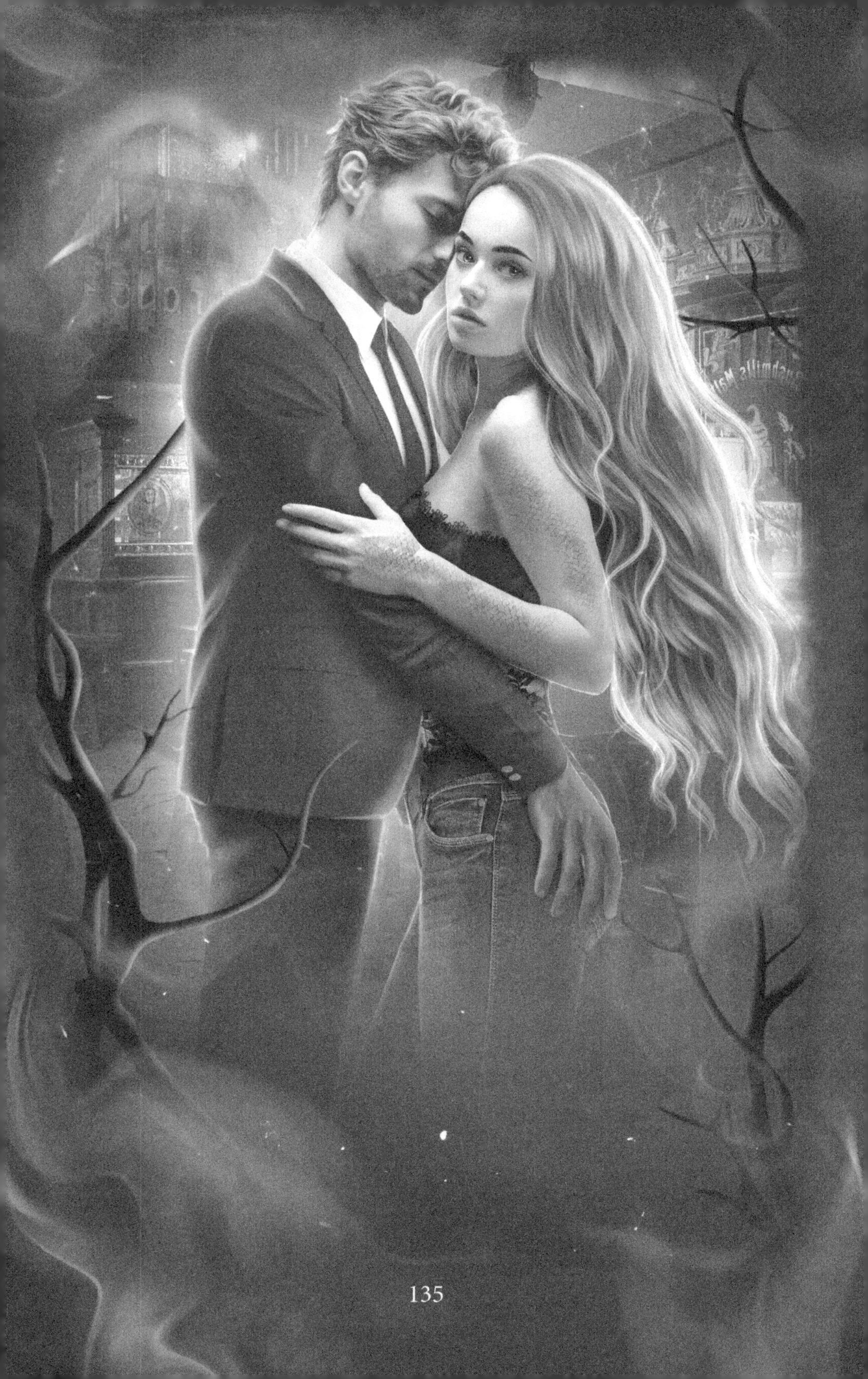

CHAPTER FOURTEEN

NOT ONLY DID KILLIAN'S goons bring my bed to his house, but they also moved his bed out and replaced it with mine. Being a consort might not be so bad all the time. Killian and Sebastian say good night and moments later, Moe and I crawl into my bed. We both toss and turn, unsettled from the events of the past week, but at some point I close my eyes and find a few hours to rest.

I wake to the stench of demon again. I'm never getting the smell of Roglak's blood out of my pores. A sharp point jabs the end of my nose. My eyes are immediately wide open and unblinking.

A childish male giggle erupts somewhere nearby. "I bet you thought you was a goner!"

The blade moves. I sit straight up in bed, scanning the room for the giggling demon and his weapon. I find him lounging in a royal blue armchair in the corner of the room - dressed in a suit two sizes too big for him and holding a sword as big as him. His tie is crooked and torn, but his chest is puffed out in pride. His legs are thrown over one of the arms of the chair in a hapless manner.

"Who the hell are you?" I ask.

"It is I, the demon Zarzos Dig'Dred."

My eyes narrow. "Right. And why are you in the bedroom watching us sleep?"

He giggles again. "The Minister has hired my brother and I to guard you and Miss Moe while he sleeps."

A demon bodyguard makes sense. Their bite is nasty business to any race. It'll drive a human crazy before it kills. As far as babysitters go, I'd rather have a demon than any other being. Demons know how to have a good time.

Zarzos looks like a skinny, white meth head with cirrhosis of the liver. His long, stringy hair needs to be washed like last year, and his smell is indicative of bad hygiene. Demons don't like water, which is why they all smell. At least this one has the drooling under control.

"Where's your brother?" I ask.

Zarzos speaks in his native demon tongue and the master bedroom door opens moments later. Another demon, also in a suit two sizes too big, walks through. "It is I, the demon Barzul Dig'Dred."

Barzul looks exactly like his brother, only slightly taller and with short hair.

Zarzos giggles and tugs at the jacket's lapels. "The Minister said we should be professional, so we borrowed some of his suits." Zarzos stands and twirls around as though he's wearing a dress instead of what's likely a high-end suit. "What do you think?"

I stifle my laugh. The Minister is going to get a kick out of the demons wearing his suits, and I hope I'm there to see the look on his face when he realizes they're ruined. "You look amazing."

"Huh?" Moe asks as she comes to life. She lets out an abrupt scream when she sees Zarzos and Barzul.

"Calm your tits," I tell her. "Minister Blood Turnover hired Zarzos and his brother as our bodyguards."

Barzul bows. "It is a pleasure to serve you, Miss Moe."

Zarzos laughs. "Blood turnover! I declare we'll be the best of friends!" Then he stands in the armchair and jumps up and down in what appears to be Killian's Italian loafers.

"Not smelling like you do, amigo. Shower first," I command.

Barzul and Zarzos both hiss at my suggestion.

Moe turns up her nose and points to the bathroom. "Both of you."

"May I wear my suit again?" Barzul asks.

I crawl from the bed and stretch. "No, we're burning it and starting over."

I shoo both demons into Killian's immaculate, stark white master bath. They begin to strip, having absolutely no modesty, but that's a demon for you. I turn around because I'm not sure what demon junk looks like, but I don't aim to find out today.

I step outside of the bathroom and leave Zarzos and Barzul to it. A note on the corner of the night table catches my eye, so I venture over and pick it up.

Lady Zvi,

I hope this letter finds you well and rested. By now, I assume you've met Zarzos and Barzul. They are very dear, old friends of mine. Please take them with you if you must leave the estate. While I'm very aware of how strong you are, Macushla, it never hurts to have a friend at your back in times like these.

My home is your home. I encourage you to use it and run it as you see fit in my absence. Please try to stay out of trouble until I rise at dusk. I would be devastated if harm were to come to you.

Always,

K.K.

I stick my tongue out at the letter before I fold it up and place it in my back pocket.

"They have to shower every day," Moe tells me in a sleep-laced voice.

"I'll see to it." I have a feeling Zarzos is going to be a lot of fun, but no one likes the smell of a demon, except maybe a demon.

I sit in the armchair while Moe snoozes off and on. When Zarzos and Barzul finally emerge, they're both wearing fuzzy, white robes that likely cost as much as a small country. Zarzos' hair is dripping water down the robe, but he looks as pleased as can be. "We're clean, Lady Jayden."

"Zvi," I reply. "Just Zvi. Thank you for showering. While in our employment, you'll need to shower at least once a day. Preferably twice a day."

Zarzos shakes his head like a dog and throws water droplets all over the room to let me know what he thinks about the business. If you've never seen a demon shake his head, it's like an exorcism, next-level sort of visual. Barzul pouts like I shot his puppy, but I cheer them right up. "Who wants a fresh, new suit?"

Their eyes light up like it's Christmas morning. Zarzos claps his hands and jumps up and down like a pogo stick. Demons are easy to make happy. They follow me into Killian's custom-made closet and rifle through the racks until they find a suit that tickles their fancy.

Zarzos chooses a blue pinstriped suit and a bright green tie that clashes with the suit. "How do I look?" he asks.

"Professional," I reply.

Barzul chooses a plain, black suit. I notice an Armani tag on the inside of the suit jacket and let loose a whistle. Killian is definitely going to love these guys wearing his suits.

"What shall we do today, Lady Jayden?" Zarzos asks.

"We're hunting."

"What for?" Barzul asks.

"I need dirt on Gio. I figured we'd find his room, rifle through his things, and see what shakes out," I answer.

Zarzos raises his hand and jumps up and down. "Oooh, me, me, me, me! I want to go!"

I like this guy. "Yeah? Okay, but Barzul stays with my sister."

"Yes!" Zarzos yells.

After I tie their ties, Barzul sits in the armchair while Moe continues to doze.

Zarzos and I wander around the mansion for thirty minutes before we locate Gio's room. The only indication Gio's been occupying the room is a black cape hanging on the four-poster bed. Me and the demon creep in until we're sure it's empty. Once I've established it's just Zarzos and I, we start to plunder through the closet, dressers, drawers, and under the mattress. Zarzos pulls the entire mattress from the bed and uses his claws to shred it in his excitement.

"Whoa there, buddy! It's Killian's bed," I remind him.

Zarzos laughs. "Ah, yes. Well, I will buy him another bed. Shall I clean up my mess?"

I wave off the ludicrous suggestion. "Nah, leave it for the creepiest vampire of all to clean up."

The demon giggles again. "I like you, Lady Jayden."

"I like you too, Zarzos Dig'Dred."

Together we empty the bureau of drawers and sling the contents all over the room. We even dance for a little while in the middle of the mess just because I don't like Gio. He may not be tied to Karl or the murders, but he's guilty of something.

While Zarzos dismantles the dresser, "just in case", I check the cape. It surprises me to find a pocket inside the garment. The tips of my fingers touch the edges of a thick piece of paper. I take care as I pull it from inside the cape. A faded color photograph from several decades ago stares back at me. In the picture are Killian, Shaw Benton, and two young women who can't be more than 25. Shaw has his arm wrapped around the blonde woman. He looks down at her with unadulterated happiness written all over his face. It's clear he's in love.

I study Killian, the vampire I'm now linked to for all intents and purposes. His hair is longer than it is now, but still trimmed close to the ears and neck. He and Shaw look the same. The woman standing beside the Minister musters a smile for the person on the other side of the camera, but I can tell it's forced. I want to know why. Normally, I wouldn't care, but there's something striking about the women in the photo.

"Did you find something?" Zarzos asks.

I fold the picture and put it in my back pocket. "No," I lie. "A receipt is all."

"I'm not having fun anymore," the demon informs me.

"Right. Moving on then. I've worked up quite an appetite."

"I bet you're beautiful when you're gluttonous," he says, hand on his chest over his heart.

"Awww, thanks, homie," I say and punch him in the shoulder. "Let's go eat some groceries."

Considering I didn't go to bed until dawn, it's already late and dinner time. My stomach is going to eat itself unless I put something in it. We venture back to the master suite to grab Moe and Barzul for dinner.

There's a gazillion staircases in Killian's house, so when Barzul leads us down a back staircase to an industrial kitchen complete with a guy in a silly white hat, I almost faint from relief. Judging by the aroma wafting in my direction, it appears dinner is served. It means I don't have to cook dinner… or microwave dinner. And it smells far better than anything I would've come up with.

"Good evening," greets the man in the white hat. "Dinner is ready. The Minister advised the lady of the house will choose the dining area for the evening."

"There's a beautiful garden out back," Moe says, her voice sad.

If it's where my sister wants to have her dinner, then it's where we'll go. "The garden it is."

The chef snaps his fingers and several waiters in all black attire pop out of somewhere in the back and start mobilizing food. I follow Moe to the garden as Zarzos and Barzul guard our backs.

We spend the early evening hours watching Zarzos chase lightning bugs while I pig out on an entire turkey. Moe barely eats, and I almost say something, but she needs a little while to grieve the loss of Greta. I don't like it, but I get it.

After dusk, Killian, Sebastian, and Aleki find us lounging in the garden, bellies full from too much food.

"Doesn't gluttony look beautiful on her?" Zarzos asks Killian.

Killian's megawatt smile would knock me on my ass if I wasn't already on it. "Yes. I see the two of you got along well."

"She's my best friend," Zarzos says, serious as a heart attack.

The Minister's right brow cocks up. "Is that so? I wasn't aware Lady Jayden had a best friend."

Zarzos giggles. "It's 'cause we just met."

Sebastian chuckles at the demon. "Lady Jayden," he begins, his unidentifiable accent thicker tonight than usual.

"Zvi. Please call me 'Zvi'."

"Lady Zvi." He compromises with me. "I believe Master Gio would have a word with you regarding your daytime shenanigans in his bedroom."

"I'm busy," I tell him, and Zarzos snorts. "I need a word alone with the Minister."

Killian closes the space between us, presses a kiss to my cheek, wraps an arm around my waist, lifts my feet from the ground, and then we're running through the trees at vamp speed. A blur of nature passes us by. It's made up of greens and yellows and browns. The earthy smell in combination with the high speed flight ignites me. I feel alive for the first time in days. Before I feel like I'm truly soaring, we stop in the middle of the forest. I take in the lush green surroundings and the sounds its creatures make.

"I dreamt of you," Killian says, a little too close for my liking.

He leans forward intending to press his lips to my cheek, but I stick my hand in front of his face to halt his progress. "No so fast, vampire."

He talks into my hand. "Are you still angry with me for kissing you?"

"Yes." I lie. It seems forever ago that we were at Black Star. "But it's not what I wanted to speak with you about."

"I see." Disappointment is clear in his voice. "Then how may I be of service?"

"Shaw Benton. What's your real connection to him?"

"Why do you ask?"

It doesn't feel right to give up the photograph just yet. "I'm simply trying to put everyone who's come into our lives into clearly labeled little boxes in my head. I still don't know how Shaw fits into the events of the past week, but he does. I don't believe in coincidences, and it's no coincidence he showed up when everyone else did."

He tucks his hands in his suit pockets. "It's a coincidence, Macushla. Can't you just trust me?"

"No. I trust Moe and only Moe."

With a heated look designed to relay his sincerity, he says, "I will earn you, Zvi." Silence stretches between us. I look away to avoid the awkward moment. If I wait him out long enough, I think he'll cave. It takes less than two minutes for him to crack. "Shaw is also my master's child. I am older than him, but I've known him many centuries."

"Did Shaw show up with Gio?" I ask.

"He came to my home when I called and asked for help with entertaining our master. He has done an excellent job keeping Gio out of our hair. Has he not?"

Maybe Gio has the picture of his children and the two women for sentimental reasons. The explanation doesn't quite fit Gio's personality though. My list of questions is growing with no answers on the horizon.

"I suppose he has," I admit.

"Tell me, were those my suits Zarzos and Barzul are wearing?"

I smirk at him. "You told them to look professional. They took you seriously. By the way, those are the second set of suits of yours they're wearing."

Killian's jaw tenses. "Four suits, you say?" I laugh, and a brilliant smile spreads across his face. "Dia, Macushla. I could listen to you laugh for hours."

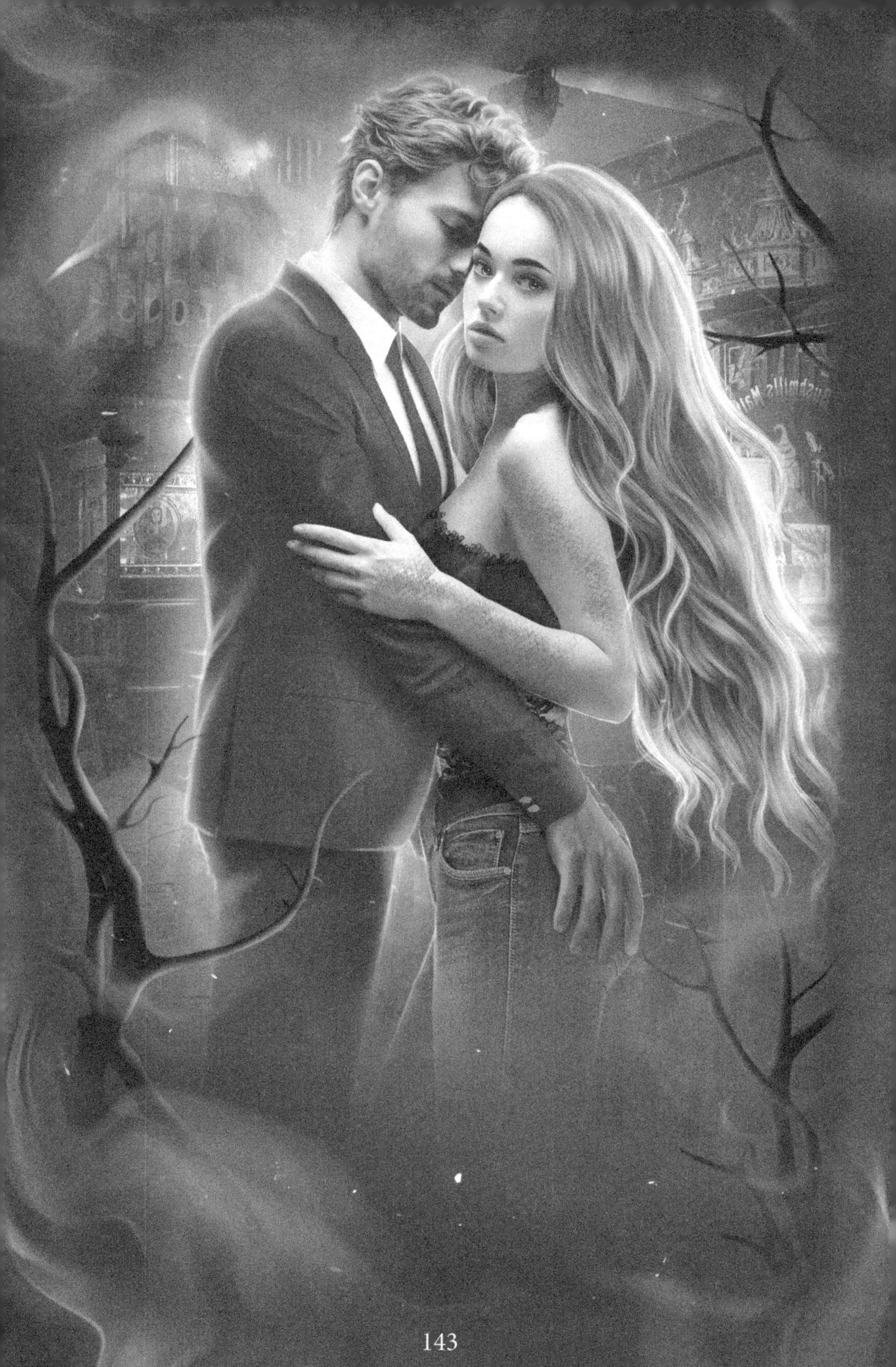

CHAPTER FIFTEEN

THE KAVANAGH ESTATE RUNS like a well-oiled machine during the evening and early morning hours. It's full of vampires and demons, each with a job to do and a reason for being there. Some stand guard with weapons spanning the course of centuries. I've never seen so many pieces that catch my eye. The air is thick with tension as everyone, including me, waits for the next shoe to drop. With Karl on the loose and under the curse of black magic, anything could happen.

I take a moment to step inside a half bath and pull out the photograph for another look. I didn't notice the two women holding hands before. Were they secret lovers? Sisters? Friends? The dark-haired woman, the one standing next to Killian, could be a past lover.

A knock comes at the door. "Lady Jayden? The minister has requested your assistance in the throne room this evening," Sebastian says.

"Tell me the pretentious twat doesn't actually have a throne room," I reply as I open the door.

Sebastian grins at my insult. "The Minister does indeed have a room dedicated to serving the common vampires in his territory."

Zarzos skips down the hall, freshly showered and rocking a slim-fit suit tailored to his scrawny body. His lavender tie is straight and tight. "The Minister taught me to tie my own tie. Barzul didn't quite get it down yet."

"You look nice, Zarzos," I reply.

"Very debonair," Sebastian adds.

Then Zarzos pops the collar on his suit jacket and grins. "Better."

Sebastian frowns at the sight.

I nod my head. "I agree." I totally dig this cat's style.

The three of us venture down the long hallway as Sebastian fills me in on the throne room business. "Once a month, the Minister opens the throne room to the public. During The Reception, as we call it, the Minister settles feuds and disagreements of all varieties, annuls vampire marriages, witnesses certain contract signings, approves vampire turning applications, and listens to newly proposed legislation."

"Sounds boring as hell," I reply.

Sebastian chuckles like he knows something I don't. "It is anything but boring, Lady Jayden."

At the south end of the mansion, through a set of intricately carved mahogany double doors, is the throne room. I expect it to look something like a black room of torture, but it looks more like Buckingham Palace. Killian's throne room is probably better than Buckingham Palace. I scan the room in under one second and count bodies. Thirty-six vampires and twenty-four demons.

"The Lady Zvi Jayden," a deep voice announces.

Oh, geez. I halfway expect a trumpet to also announce the fact that I'm walking through the room in case any of the guests are blind and can't already see it for themselves.

Killian beams at me as I close the space between us. When I reach him, I ask, "You rang?"

Zarzos giggles behind me.

"Please," he says and motions for me to sit next to him on an honest to god throne.

I lean forward and whisper, "You want me to sit on that?"

"Yes Macushla," he whispers back, amusement dancing in his eyes. "I'd like you to rule beside me."

I ignore his last words and take a step up the dais and sit on the throne—a light blue and gold, tufted chair. I let out a whistle. "Ain't this fancy?"

Killian reaches over and lays his hand on top of mine. I almost snatch it away, but I eye Gio amongst the guests. Damn it.

"Shall we begin," Killian asks.

I nod, not sure what I'm in store for, but I discover The Reception is a bunch of whiny vampires who want something from Killian. It's sad that so many beings want him for what he can do for them. And yet, he's patient. He listens to everyone, and more importantly, he's fair. From what I can see, he's a good leader, and there's something insanely attractive about it. I sneer at my thoughts and tune back into The Reception.

"Lady Jayden," greets a vampire that comes to stand in front of us. His dark hair is slicked back like he stepped out of 1955. "The rumors of your beauty have not done you justice."

"Ugh," I gag under my breath.

Killian clears his throat.

Right. I need to behave more queenly. "Thanks, homie. What brings you to our neck of the woods?" I ask and lean forward to show I'm listening.

"I'm here to follow up on my application for turning my beloved," he says, "and enter a plea on her behalf to speed up the approval processing time."

"Why would the Minister do that?" I ask.

"My human lover suffers from a rare autoimmune disorder. Her breathing is impaired and soon she will require a ventilator. She won't be able to move in a few months and will spend her final days confined to a hospital bed on life support."

I'm not sure what the process or turnaround time is for the application process, but I know vamps rarely approve turnings.

"Your application is approved," I say and a collective gasp goes around the room.

Every eye in the place goes to Killian. He gives no indication what he's thinking or feeling until he says, "Lady Jayden has spoken."

And just like that, it's done. The guards lead the vampire to another room, likely for paperwork and the next fanger comes to stand in front of the dais.

"Presenting Lord Johann Krahl, from Minnesota."

Lord Krahl bows in front of us, his long, platinum blond hair is tied at the nape of his neck. "Minister, Lady Jayden, thank you for seeing me this evening. I am seeking a divorce from my husband, the Lord of Michigan."

"Have you notified your husband of your petition?" Killian asks.

"My husband is here with me," the Lord replies.

Kilian motions for a guard to bring the spouse inside the throne room.

"Presenting Lord Pierre Auclair."

The husband saunters in with his shoulders slumped, honey brown eyes full of regret.

"Mr. Auclair, do you contest the divorce?" The Minister asks.

"Yes, on the grounds of love!"

My eyes roll of their own accord. Here goes the soap opera.

"I made a mistake," Pierre cries.

I'll bite. "What happened?"

"I was unfaithful with an old lover," he admits, head hung.

"Have you tried marriage counseling?" I ask.

The room erupts in laughter. Pierre and Johann stare at me in confusion.

They think I'm joking. "Can you forgive Lord Auclair, Lord Krahl?"

"I've tried, "Lord Krahl answers.

"He's taken me back three times. I need one more chance," Auclair decrees.

"You've taken him back three times?" I ask.

"Yes, Lady Jayden," Krahl answers.

"Go to marriage counseling. Present proof of the counseling if you come back. And shit or get off the pot. Take him back or let him go. Next!" I shout.

The guard ushers the confused bloodsuckers away. I think I have a knack for this consort thing.

The crowd goes quiet as the next idiot is announced. "Presenting Lord Arvel Abril and his servant, Miss Viola Cole."

I turn to Killian. "Servant?"

Killian nods as if everyone has a freaking servant. "Yes, Macushla." Then he looks down at the two vamps in front of us. "Lord Abril, you've lodged a complaint against your servant to extend her servitude for another ten years on account of repeated insubordination."

"That is correct, Minister," says Lord Abril, chest puffed out and pointy nose in the air.

I dislike this dude.

"How long has she been his servant?" I ask Killian.

He opens a file folder and skims the page. "Fifteen years."

Geez. "What did she do to deserve that sentence?"

"She didn't pay back a large sum of money within the appropriate time period as agreed on by both parties. She could never supply even part of the money; hence, her 15 year sentence with the offending party."

"Lord Abril, can you describe the nature of Ms. Cole's insubordination?" Killian asks him.

"I require her to ask for her food."

Hold up. "Say that again?"

Abril glares at me. "She's a servant. She gave up the right to have her food when she likes it."

"Type O makes me sick," Ms. Cole defends. "He only allows me to have Type O. While I absorb nutrients from the blood, I often vomit when I drink it."

Some people and their complete lack of decency make my blood boil. "Lord Abril, you're an asshole. Ms. Cole is relieved of her duties immediately."

Lord Abril's jaw looks as though it might break from the tension. "I want to speak to you alone, Minister."

Killian gives the slightest inclination of his head and the guards start for the hoity toity fanger.

"I want to speak to someone else at Le Ambrogio!" Abril shouts.

"Well want in one hand and shit in the other and see which one fills up faster," I deadpan. I pause for dramatic effect. The vampires eat it up. "Next!"

I'm killing this royal gig.

A young woman in a black shawl bursts through the doors with a slew of confused vampires behind her. She slams the doors and throws her hand up to freeze the doors close with a spell. She turns around and plasters her back to the door. Every being in the room is ready to lunge at her and take her down at a moment's notice, including me. Her shawl is torn, her dark brown hair is a tangled mess, and she's covered in blood spatters. Yet, the beauty's shoulders are squared as she looks on at a room full of warriors with a dare in her eye. "I mean you no harm. I'm here to speak with Lady Jayden."

"What is the meaning of this?" Killian asks as he stands from his throne.

The witch comes to stand in front of us, swords pointed at her the entire way, and looks deep in my eyes. "There's so much love in one photograph, yes?" And then her eyes roll back in her head as she crumples to the marble floor like a sack of potatoes.

"Move!" I yell at the guards standing between me and her. I push through them to reach the girl. Killian is at my back as we both kneel down beside her.

"Aleki," the Minister calls for his bodyguard. "Carry the woman to the state guest chambers. Sebastian, call the Olid healer."

Aleki hoists the girl into his big, beefy arms, and the sea of spectators part for the formidable Polynesian warrior. Killian and I trail behind the guard to a guest room with Zarzos at my back. The beast lays the witch on the ivory duvet, and steps back for me to jump in and assess her. The girl's eyes pop open and search her surroundings, wide and full of fear.

"It's okay," I tell her. "You're safe."

She reaches for my face, and on instinct, I jump back.

"I will not harm you, child," the witch says.

I need a witch in here. "Aleki, can you get Moe?"

Aleki slips from the room without a word.

When I look down at the witch, there's no longer a twenty-something girl in the bed. An old, frail woman with olive skin and curly gray hair sits in her place instead.

Zarzos removes his sword at the same time Moe and Aleki rush in.

"No, Zarzos," Killian says, commanding but gentle. And then he bows to the woman. "Amelie-Madeline Delon."

"Who?" I ask.

"The Fire Witch," Moe whispers.

"Well, shit," I mumble under my breath.

"Things are starting to get interesting around here."

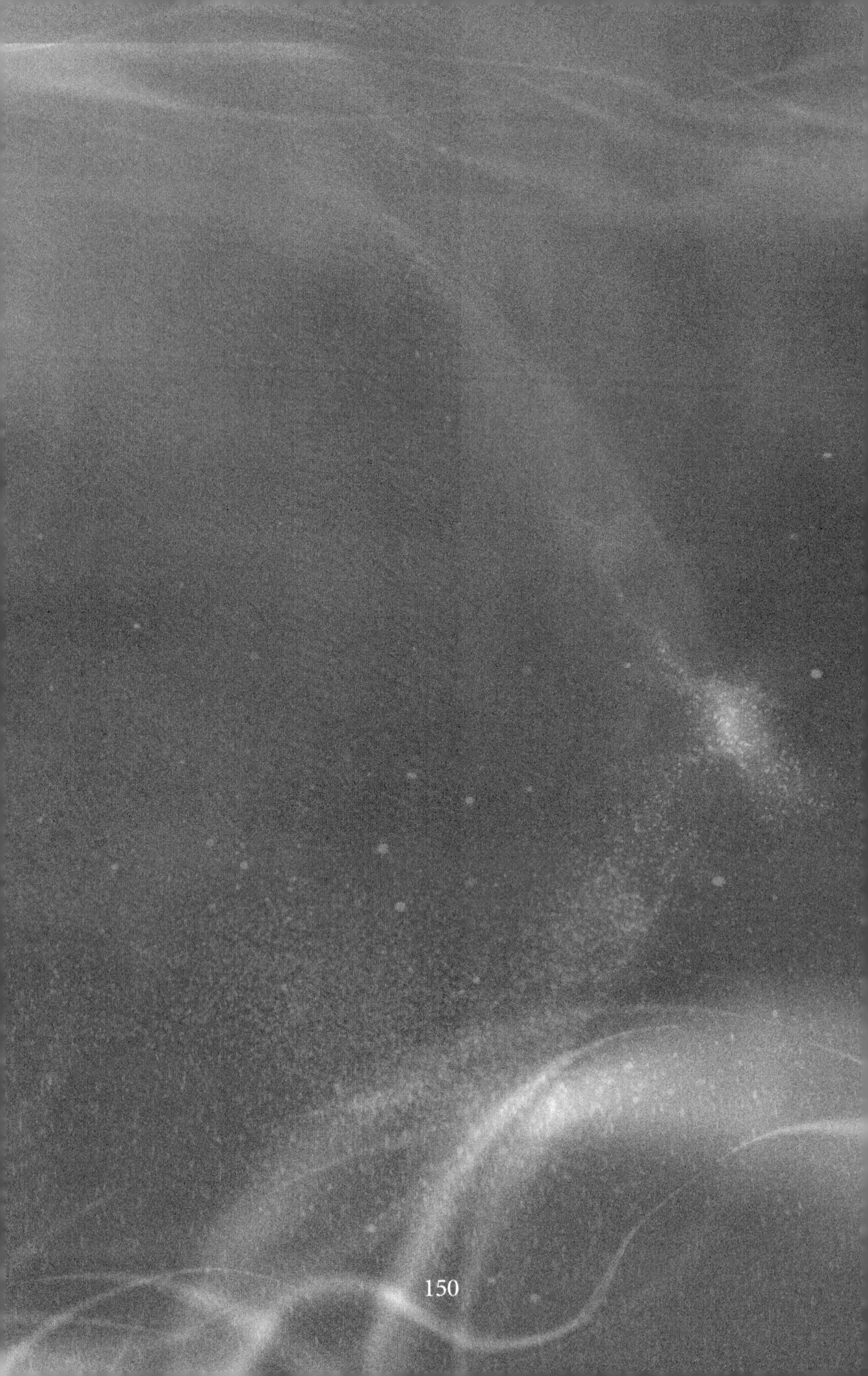

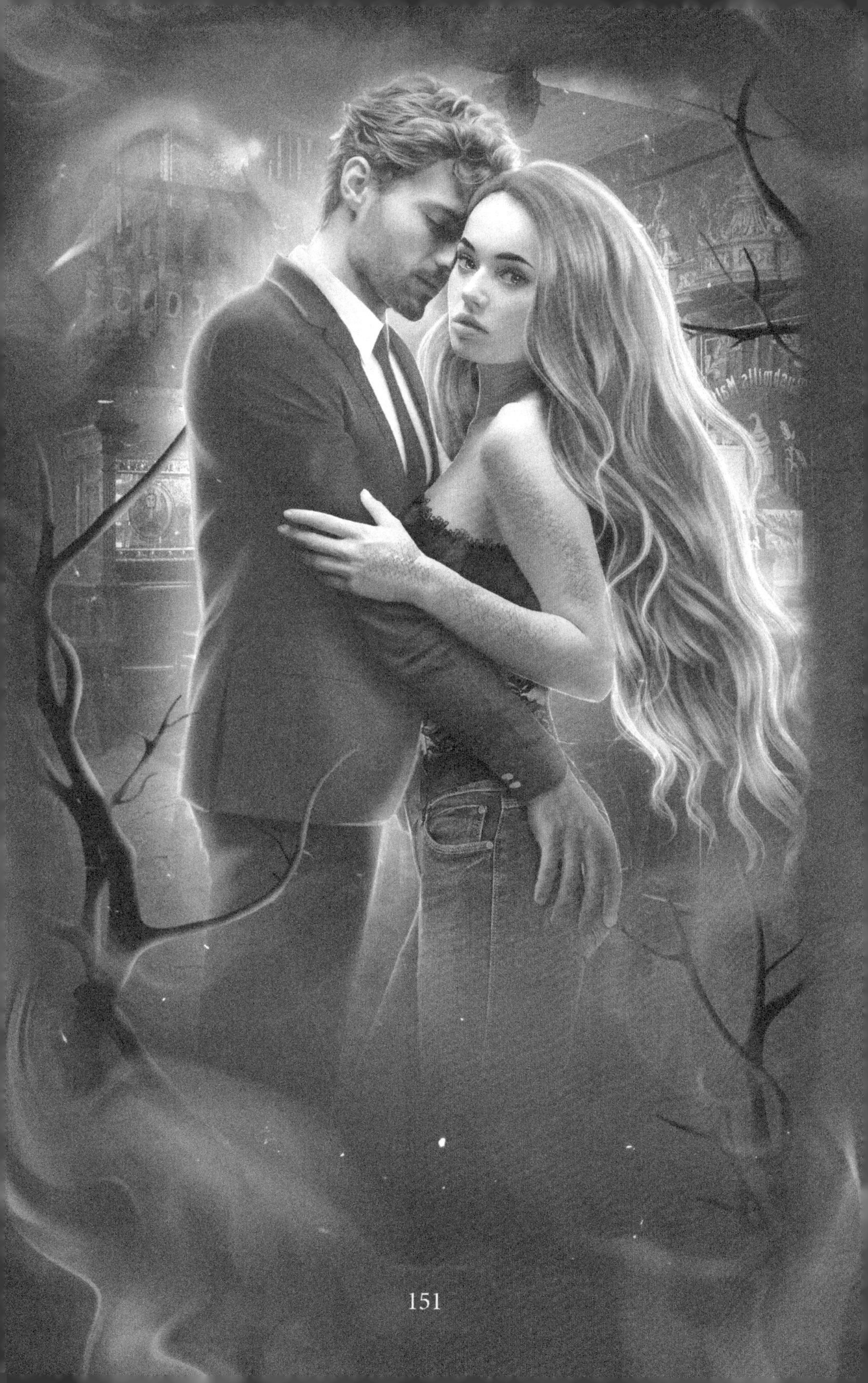

CHAPTER SIXTEEN

I DON'T KNOW A hell of a lot about the Fire Witch, except she's the most powerful witch on the planet. I've heard of her taking a witch's power as punishment for bad deeds, but not much else.

"Come, beautiful girls," Amelie-Madeline says and pats the edge of the bed.

Moe crawls into the bed beside the witch and sits next to her like she's known her for her entire life. I hesitate to join them, always untrusting of strangers, especially these days.

"Zvi, I've known of you since your mother conceived you. I wish you no harm, child," she repeats.

I find Killian to my left. He closes his eyes before he opens them and nods for me to go to her. "She won't harm you, Macushla."

"Leave us, vampire," the Fire Witch commands.

"No," Killian replies. "You'll turn her against me."

Amelie-Madeline sighs. "It's not your fault, Minister. I've told you this for close to thirty years."

Killian finds me, pleading with his eyes, though I'm not sure what he's pleading for. "Macushla," he begins, but his words die on his tongue as though he can't find them. He resigns himself to the witch and leaves the room.

My attention resets on the old lady. "You sure know how to make an entrance," I say.

The woman laughs.

"Will you tell us what happened to you?" Moe asks as she studies the blood splatters on her.

Amelie-Madeline pats Moe's leg. "Vampires attacked me and my guards. Those traveling with me are now dead along the interstate some forty minutes south of here."

"We were attacked by vampires at a funeral, and I have the feeling it's not a coincidence either," I say.

"But Everett, Natasia, Kreston, and Greta are out of the picture," Moe replies.

"There's someone else playing at it," I begin. "Did you recognize any of your attackers?"

"No," Amelie-Madeline answers. "It happened very fast. I was sure I was going to die."

We can add an attack on an uber powerful witch to the list. How do we know she isn't involved in all the craziness around us? "Why are you here?"

"What I have to say to you girls isn't easy to hear. It's going to take time to digest, but you're both resilient, and I have faith you'll take this knowledge and better the world and your lives in service to others."

I already don't like the sound of this.

"Your mothers are from New Orleans, born and raised. They were best friends from the time they could walk. I've never seen two people more inseparable than those two. I've heard the two of you are similar, and I can't express how much it warms my heart."

"How did you know our mothers?" Moe asks.

The Fire Witch takes a long look at Moe, pausing to study her features. "Do you not see yourself in me? You were born Monica Delon, and I am your great-grandmother. Zvi, I was to be your godmother before, well, we're getting there."

I know I can be an asshole a lot of the time, but I don't mean to be when I blurt out, "Where the hell have you been all these years?"

"Zvi," my sister admonishes.

I stand from the bed and start pacing as I try to rein in my temper.

"It's quite alright," the woman replies. "I know it isn't easy to digest."

"And Killian? What's he mopey and panicked about?"

"You have to understand there was a war going on in the magical world when the two of you were conceived. I was hiding from a faction of witches aiming to relieve me of my power. I was almost burned alive in my home, and I couldn't protect your mothers anymore with a target on my back. I sent them to Killian. They stayed through their pregnancies, and just before they delivered they went missing. The four of you were never seen or heard from again. I wasn't sure if you girls made it to birth."

"So we end up in foster care? Where are our mothers?" I ask.

The older witch nods. "Yes, it appears you ended up in a dire predicament. It would've been much better if you'd been raised by supernatural beings who could properly teach you about your power and magic. I haven't a clue where your mothers are. They weren't supposed to leave this estate. They disobeyed Killian's order and left to buy baby clothes. The girls were smart enough to take demon bodyguards with them, but they were murdered, and the four of you were gone without a trace."

"What's my mother's name?" Moe asks, hanging on her every word.

"Caroline Delon. Zvi, your mother is Lena Drake. You are the spitting images of your mothers."

The walk down memory lane has been swell, but I'm more worried about current events than the past. I can revisit the past any time. "Why are you here?"

"With Caroline gone, Moe is the next in line for Fire Witch." She lets the information sink in before she continues. "She needs the fire of a dragon and the blood of five. Your fates are linked. It is fate, after all, that has kept the two of you together and bonded as sisters your whole lives."

The woman cringes in pain and grabs her side. Blood pours from around her hand. Moe crawls off the bed to get help.

"Killian's already called for an Olid healer," I tell her.

I rip Amelie-Madeline's shawl and get a good look at the deep wound in the general area of the kidney. Shit. It's a lot of blood. Moe answers the door when a knock comes at it as I rip the shirt and begin to pack the wound.

"I'm dying anyway, child," the Fire Witch says.

I ignore her and continue to work when the Olid healer comes to her aid. Olids are natural healers and hail from the realm of Olidean. No one has ever been there outside of Olids. Tall, lithe, and graceful, the beautiful doctor with exotic blue-black straight, silky, long hair checks the old woman's pulse in her wrist. "Hello, Amelie-Madeline, I'm Dr. Windsong. I've spoken with your physician in Louisiana and have been brought up to speed on your health. I'm afraid at your age, general anesthesia isn't an option. I'll need to numb the area to suture the wound.

"I'm already dying. Can you buy me a little time to spend with my girls?" she asks.

Dr. Windsong sighs. "If I give you my blood, its power will transfer with your magic to the next Fire Witch."

I hold my hands up. "Wait a minute. I thought Moe was supposed to be the next Fire Witch?"

Amelie-Madeline has a coughing fit before she's able to respond. "It has been tradition for the Delon Dynasty to produce heiresses for two millennia, but the first witch to perform the Fire Ritual shall become the next Fire Witch."

This just keeps getting better. "What, pray tell, is the Fire Ritual?"

The old woman coughs again. "The successor must take the blood of a human, wolf, witch, demon, and ancient vampire. Then she must walk through the fire of a dragon."

I place a hand on my chest. "I'm assuming the dragon is implying *moi*, since I'm the only one alive?"

The woman laughs. "Oh, no. The dragonborn live in Dracaena."

"Drac who?"

She cringes again. "There's an island in Indonesia where your realm can be accessed. The dragons would love for their princess to visit her kingdom. Your name means 'beautiful' in your native tongue."

I scoff. "Princess?"

"And it appears you're also a vampire queen," she adds.

"I'm neither. I'm just Zvi." This shit is getting out of hand.

The old woman's eyes slowly close, and Dr. Windsong pushes me aside like an Amazonian linebacker. I regain my balance and move further out of the doctor's way as she bites her wrist. She places it to the dying woman's mouth. The following five minutes seem like an eternity as we wait to see if it works, and it does. The hole in her side begins to close and a bright white light shoots from within her.

Gnarly.

"She'll heal from this, but she is unwell. Use the time you have with her to say goodbye," the healer advises.

Moe crawls on the bed and snuggles up on her great-grandmother's right side and sniffles. "But I just found her."

The only real connection to my mother or my people is dying.

"What's wrong with her that your blood can't cure?" I ask the doctor.

"She is very old, too old to contain the magic inside her body any longer. The same will happen with the granddaughter as she ages past the century and a half mark."

"She'll live a freaking century?"

"At least, and as long as she's smart and completes the Fire Ritual before anyone else."

Great. There's a time crunch, like we need anything else on our plates at the moment. The doctor takes the woman's pulse again and eases away from the bed.

"How long does she have?" I ask.

The Olid shoots me straight. "A few days at most. Her pulse is very weak."

"When does Moe complete the ritual?"

"When Amelie-Madeline dies." She takes her exit after she delivers the blow.

We might have two days at most to make this happen.

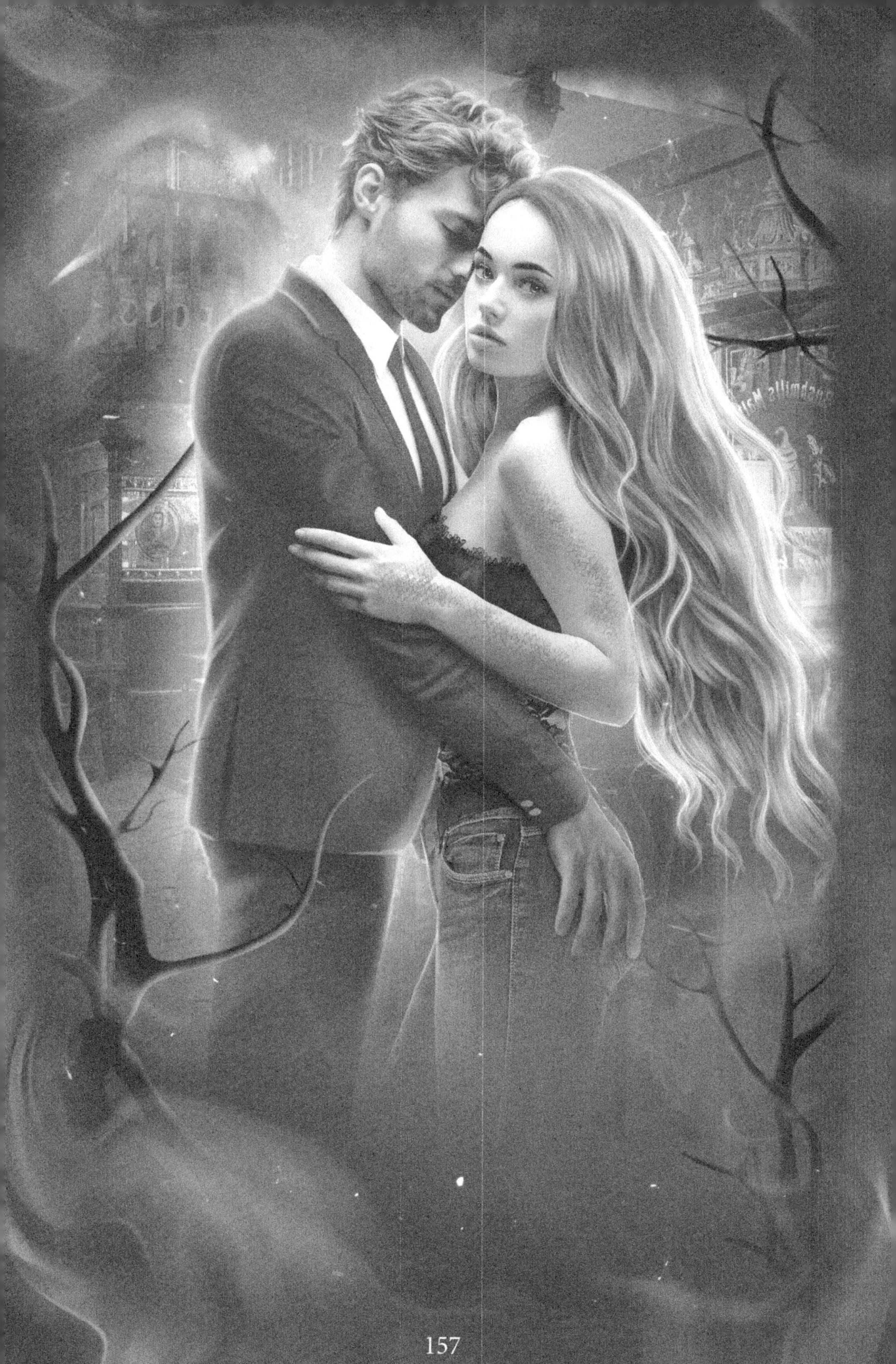

CHAPTER SEVENTEEN

I LEAVE MOE WITH her dying grandmother and head out for fresh air. Just outside the door, Killian, Zarzos, Aleki, Sebastian, and the doctor wait for news.

"She's hanging on," I tell them. "She's in and out."

"She may not fully regain her faculties," Dr. Windsong says.

I cross my arms over my chest as exhaustion overcomes me. "Can we talk?" I ask Killian.

He pulls my hand in his and guides me into a room filled with big, comfy leather chairs, and a beautiful fireplace at the center. He closes the door behind us and comes up to press his chest to my back. His arm wraps around my middle, and his lips come to my ear. "Are you angry with me, Lady Jayden?"

I surprise myself. "No."

"You knew my mother then?"

"Yes, Macushla. I met her when she lived here."

"What was my mother like?"

The scent of Killian's glamour invades my senses. I relax under his touch as his hands move to my shoulders to massage the tension out. "That's it, beautiful. Relax for me while I tell you how much your mother loved you. From the moment she discovered she'd have you, you were the reason she existed. While with child, she sang you lullabies and nursery rhymes and promised to teach you the colors and counting. She was very proud to be your mother."

"Was she beautiful?"

"Very. You were made in her image."

"What will happen when Amelie-Madeline dies?" I ask. "Will others know?"

"All supernatural beings will know something has happened. When she dies, her magic will seep into the earth. Things will be quite chaotic until another witch is made. Typically, this time period is short, but the Delon's have always had a witch in line to complete the ritual as soon as the magic seeps into the earth. It's important we ensure Moe becomes Fire Witch."

A light bulb goes off. "She said the Fire Ritual requires the blood of a demon, an ancient vampire, a witch, a human, and a wolf. What if Karl is collecting blood for a witch?"

"Natasia," he says, disdain dripping from his voice.

"She's trying to become the Fire Witch."

"Well, we don't have to worry ourselves with the likes of her. She's in a Black Star cell."

*

Zarzos and I find an array of prepared food in Killian's industrial kitchen and spend some quality time together chowing down. However, my appetite is ruined when Count Dracula walks in with a creepy smile on his face. I really want to set his cape on fire while he's wearing it.

I let loose a loud, most unladylike belch. "What do you want, Freak Fest?"

He leans against the door jamb, not a care in the world. "I'm curious if you found what you were looking for in my chambers?"

I smile at him, happy he's perturbed enough to go out of his way to ask me about mine and Zarzos' adventure. "You travel light."

"Ah, yes. One doesn't need material things to find true happiness. I'd be ecstatic just to feel the sun on my skin again without ending up as a pile of ash. There's no amount of money or possessions that can buy real happiness."

"Waxing philosophical today?" I ask.

Gio focuses on Zarzos as if he's just now noticing my bodyguard. "Introduce yourself, demon."

"It is I, the demon Zarzos Dig'Dred."

Gio lifts his nose in the air as he name-drops his own name. "Ambrogio."

"I know who you are, vampire," Zarzos replies in a voice a few octaves lower than his normal, playful tone. And to show Gio what he thinks of him, he reaches over his shoulder and draws his sword. "The minister has ordered me to protect Lady Jayden against anyone who may cause her harm, including himself. If I must end you and your entire species, I will not think twice."

When Zarzos goes badass, he really shows up. But wait, what? "The entire species?"

Gio cackles at my question. "Yes, dear. If I meet my end, so do the world's vampires. They were formed in my image and directly linked to me by a bond of blood. So you see, Lady Jayden, your precious Killian would no longer exist."

He's untouchable to every vampire on the globe. How am I supposed to fight him? I can't kill him without upsetting the balance of magic. And there's also Killian to consider. I roll my eyes at myself. I need to shut up about Killian already.

"Wonderful," I deadpan and walk toward the stairs to get away from him before I end an entire species. Gio steps in my way. I stand on my toes and get in his face. "Try me, motherfucker."

"What's going on here?" Killian asks as he walks into the kitchen.

"I've simply asked the lovely Zvi to return the photograph she stole earlier in the evening," Count Chocula says.

I growl in response.

"What photograph?" the Minister asks.

I pull the picture from my back pocket and hand it to him. He frowns at it. "Zvi, this is your mother," he says and points to the blonde-haired woman standing by Shaw. He turns to Gio. "How did you come by this photograph?"

Gio smiles. "A little birdie is all. Say, Lady Jayden, how would you enjoy it if I returned the favor and plundered in Moe's bed tonight as you did my chambers earlier."

I growl again and hear Zarzos draw his sword again. Killian crams his body in between us. "Macushla, please go with Zarzos to check on Amelie-Madeline. I need to have a word with my master."

I need a word with his master too, right after I snap his neck and tie him up for a little fun and torture. But until I can figure out how to capture and detain the most powerful vampire alive, torture will have to wait.

I curtsy. "As you wish, Minister." I wink at Gio before Zarzos and I venture up the back staircase to check on Moe and her great-grandmother.

When we reach the guest suite, I find the door ajar and Barzul missing from his post outside of it. Zarzos once again draws his blade and uses his foot to push the door open. I pull my sickle from my back and follow him inside.

Back to back, we enter and turn around 360 degrees. Nothing jumps out at us but an empty room. There's no Barzul, Moe, or Amelie-Madeline.

"There's a note," Zarzos says and walks over to the pillow as my stomach turns upside down, waiting for the bad news. "They're in the garden."

My sky-high anxiety drops several notches at the news. "Let's go."

We zip through the estate and back through the kitchen to take the back door to the garden. As we walk up behind my sister, the demon, and the Fire Witch, I hear Moe ask, "What's it like to be the Fire Witch?"

I hang back and give Moe the moment with her family. Barzul nods his head to let us know he sees us, and then he stands guard behind where the two witches sit on a wooden bench.

"You're scared," the old woman says.

"Yes," Moe admits. "I'm scared of drinking blood and walking through fire, but I'm most afraid of how this will change my life."

"There's no need in fearing the unknown, girl. Yes, your life will change, and it will change in a big way. But it's important to remember you're going to be one of the most important people on earth. Your entire reason for being will change. As for what it's like, I remember feeling a warm white light come over me, and then I heard the ancestors chanting the incantation with me. Every cell in my body felt at peace. And then it was over, and I had to learn to live with the large amount of magic coursing through me."

"Does it hurt?" My sister asks.

"It is uncomfortable to possess so much power at first."

"Will I need to move to New Orleans?"

I hope we're not moving, but a fresh start in a few states away might be what Moe and I both need after everything that's occurred in the past week.

"No, my dear, you may live wherever your heart desires, but the magical have migrated to Atlanta in droves after Hurricane Katrina. I believe they need you here."

"What happened to our mothers?"

The old woman sighs. "I tell myself Caroline and Lena are living in Dracaena together, waiting for their daughters to find them."

It's all the old woman offers. A miniscule drop of hope.

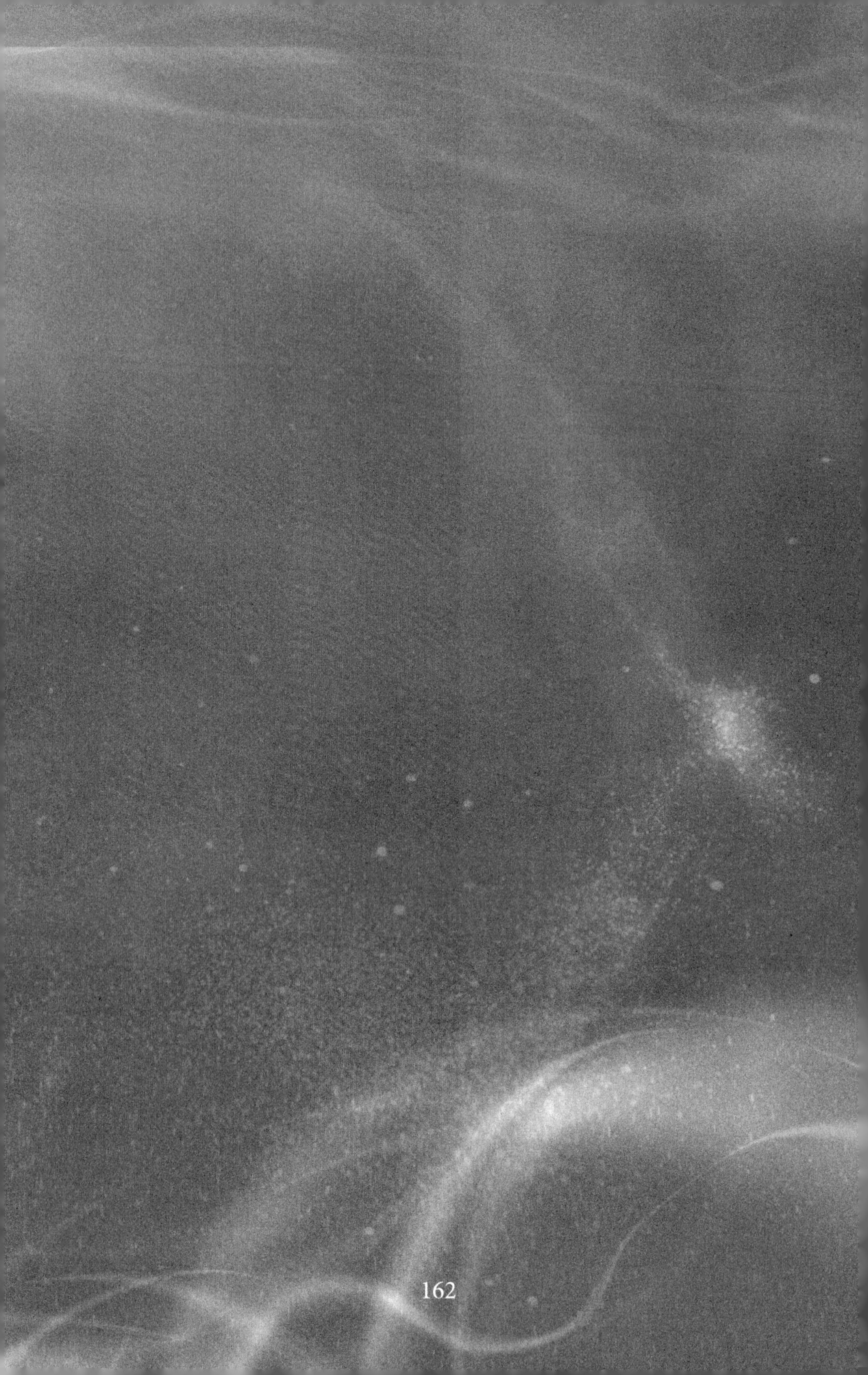

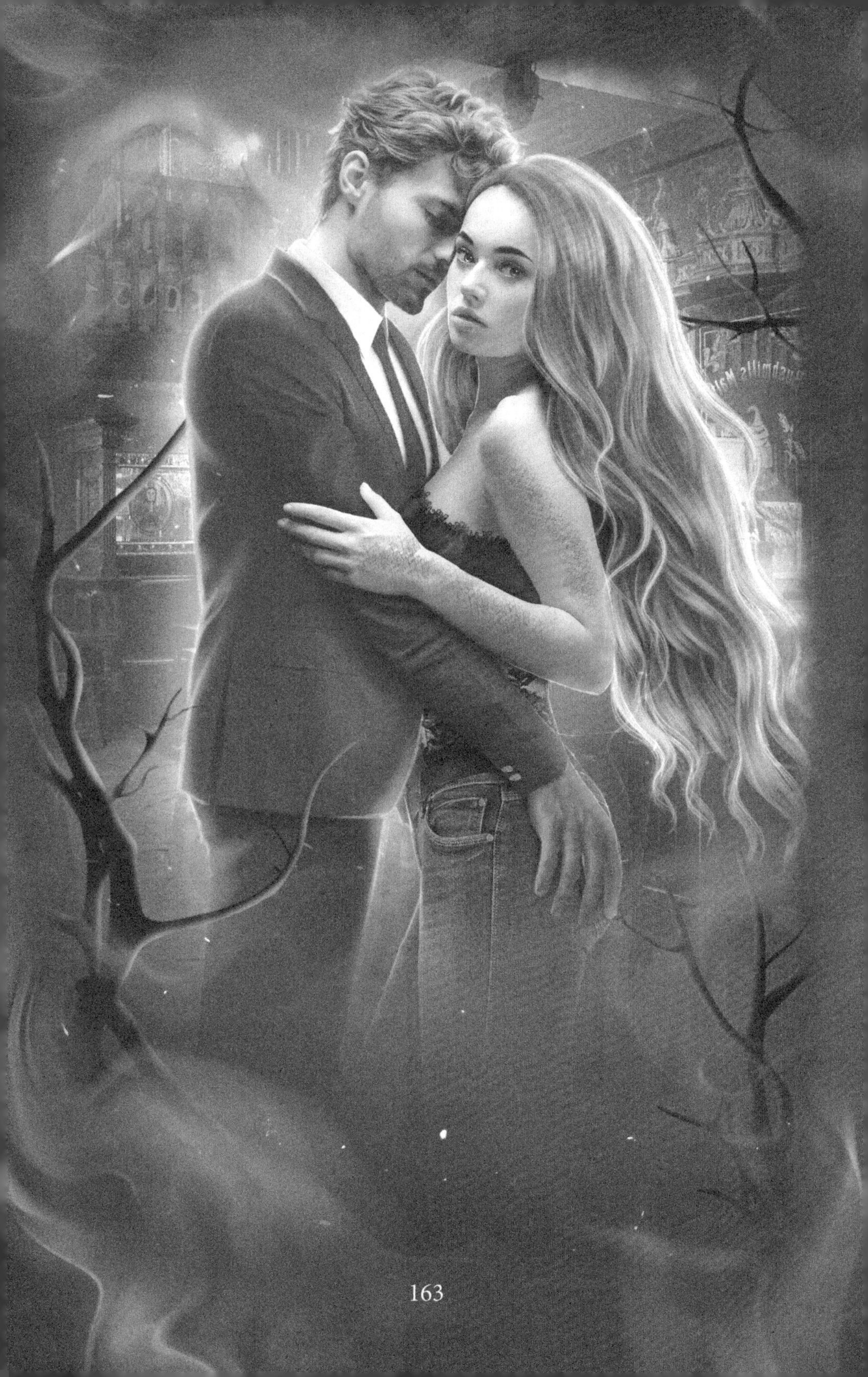

CHAPTER EIGHTEEN

I NAP FOR A few hours when the vamps go to ground for the day. I'm able to rest knowing Zarzos and Barzul are standing guard. When I wake, I nab a shower, and then I venture down to the kitchen for one of my favorite activities, grubbing. When Moe joins me, she has Zarzos and Hendri in tow. The wolf looks like he needs a hot meal, a shower, a shave, and a bed.

"Long night?" I ask.

"I don't sleep well during a big case," the Deputy replies.

"Dude, you need to close your eyes for at least five hours a day," I tell him.

Moe pats him on the back. "He needs food first, and then we're crashing in your bed."

I point my finger at my sister and then the wolf. "No hanky panky in my bed."

Zarzos giggles as he eats a raw steak. He mutters something in demon and laughs at himself.

"Too tired to even think about it," Hendri says as he takes a seat on a stool.

I plop an entire ribeye in front of him, and his eyes show signs of life. After Moe and the Deputy eat, they head to the master to catch some zzz's. Zarzos and I relieve Barzul and take watch over Amelie-Madeline who murmurs in her sleep for hours. Me and the demon take the time to go over the case from beginning to end since he's coming into the fold in the middle of everything.

"What do you know about Shaw Benton?" I ask.

"I don't know much, Lady Jayden. He's a quiet vampire. Never causes any trouble. I believe he lives here in Atlanta."

"I didn't hear of him until this week. I always worry about what the quiet ones aren't saying," I say.

"You suspect he's involved?"

"Something about him showing up when he did doesn't sit right with me, and Killian won't say much. Shaw was in the photograph with my mother."

The door almost splinters as it flies open. Zarzos and I both draw our respective weapons. Hendri and Moe walk through, eyes wide with alarm.

My sister runs to me. "Are you okay?"

"Bored as hell, but yeah, I'm okay. What's up?"

Hendri puts his hands on his hips and sighs in frustration. "Someone hacked Black Star and broke Natasia out."

No, no, no. I'm not playing this sick game anymore. There are too many unknown players. I don't know who we're fighting any longer. If I can't figure out who I'm up against, then I can't get inside their heads to gain the upper hand. I'm fighting a losing battle.

"Zvi?" Moe calls.

"Yeah?"

"You good?"

Nope. "Yep." We know Natasia wants to be the next Fire Witch, but she's missing the blood of an ancient vampire and the fire of a dragon. No big deal, right? I just won't breathe fire on the heifer. Easy-peasy.

Killian, Sebastian, and Aleki zoom into the room and take in the scene. "I've received word of the escape and murders," Minister Zippy Pants says.

Hendri rolls his eyes. "I was getting to the murders."

Killian steals Hendri's thunder. "Everett, Kreston, and Greta were murdered in their cells."

Zarzos nods as if this makes sense to him. "Loose ends."

"I concur," Killian replies.

I have many questions about the situation. "What time did it occur?"

I see the light bulb go off over the Deputy's head. "Just after dusk."

"Then," I begin, "it's either a fanger or someone who wants us to think it is."

"What does a vampire have to gain from the Fire Witch?" Hendri asks, and everyone looks to Killian to answer.

"We should ask Amelie-Madeline," he answers. "Has she been alert today?"

"The witch sleeps," Zarzos replies.

Moe climbs onto the bed beside her great-grandmother and checks her pulse. "It's weak."

With Natasia on the loose we're running out of time. "We need her to hang on until I can collect the ingredients for the ritual. Is there a spell you can place on her to keep her from passing to the other side?"

"Nothing I've ever done, but I can ask…," she starts, but she doesn't finish her sentence.

Greta.

"Is there anyone else to ask?" Please say yes.

"I know someone," Killian offers and pulls his phone from his suit jacket. He taps on the screen for a few seconds and slips it back in his pocket.

*

I check on Moe and Amelie-Madeline every hour. The Fire Witch has not regained consciousness, though Moe patiently waits for it. I get ahead of the curve and develop a plan to push Natasia completely out of the picture. I need blood from willing donors, mix it up, add a splash of bourbon for taste, and have Moe drink it. Then I'll breathe fire on her and bam! She'll be the new Fire Witch.

Natasia is missing an ancient vampire's blood, a required ingredient in the Fire Ritual. I pull Zarzos aside once I've ironed out the simple plan in my mind. "Can I have a few drops of your blood?"

He giggles. "I knew I smelled a vampire in you."

"What do you mean?" I ask.

"I mean because you're half vampire you would want my blood. It's a bad joke. My blood would make you very ill."

"I'm not a half bloodsucker."

Zarzos giggles again and bops me on the end of the nose with his finger. "You cray."

I shrug. "I know, but I'm not a freaking fanger."

Zarzos skips around in excitement. "Whatever you say, Lady Jayden."

I don't have time to worry about this nonsense. It has to move to the back burner. "Can I have some blood to help Moe become the Fire Witch?"

He stops skipping. "Whoa. You want to use my blood to make a Fire Witch?"

"Is that a big deal?"

"Yes. The Fire Witch inherits certain abilities from the human, demon, witch, vampire, and wolf's blood. And the dragon's fire. She is the keeper of magic and shall essentially become more than just a witch, she'll be the only witch to truly harness the power of fire."

I don't know if I like the sound of this. "What kinds of abilities will she inherit?"

"Hard to know without knowing the abilities of the other donors."

I'd be lying if I said I'm not afraid for my sister and the journey she's about to take. Life is going to change in a big way.

"You'll donate the blood then?"

He bows. "I'd be honored."

"Perfect. Thank you. One down, four more to go. Let's go find the beautiful pain-in-my-ass."

We look high and low and almost give up looking for Killian, but then I remember the throne room. It sits nestled on the front part of the home with an interior and an exterior door. The Minister sits on his blue and gold tufted throne, elbows on his knees, fingers steepled, and lost in thought. Why does the bastard have to be so damn good looking?

"You found me," he says. "No one ever thinks to look for me here." I walk inside and pause. "I come here when I want to be alone." I turn to leave him to his peace. "No, please stay."

Zarzos slips from the room, sensing we need to be alone. There's something in Killian's voice, something I can't immediately identify, but it draws me closer.

"I first heard about you in this very room," he begins. "A demon placed a request to speak with me about a menace in our community. I heard him out, though I don't make a habit of interfering in demonic affairs. The demon in question asserted that a woman of unknown species attacked him and pulled his teeth out until he supplied her with the name she wanted."

I remember the demon well. It was my second job as a bounty hunter. "He gave up the name if you're wondering."

Killian leans his head back and roars in laughter. "Yes, I heard. But then I heard of you again, and again. And again. All tales of a mighty unknown species robbing beings of their teeth and dignity. Eventually, a vampire you trapped in his own coffin and threatened to set on fire gave me your name."

He walks down the three steps of the dais and comes to stand in front of me. He reaches up and tucks a strand of hair behind my ear. "I believe I was captivated by you before I ever laid eyes on you." His thumb swipes across my cheek. "And I had to have you from the first moment I saw you."

I laugh in his face. "Is this the part where I fall madly in love with you?"

He chuckles at my response. But then the smile falls as he grips my wrist and spins me around to face away. His chest touches my back as his free arm wraps around my middle. His lips touch the lobe of my ear. "Pretend you don't want me. I'll play your game and show you I'll follow you to the ends of any realm you may go. I know people have let you down your entire life, Macushla, but I'm not going anywhere."

A click at the interior door has both of us turning toward it. Zarzos sticks his head in. "Forgive the intrusion, Lady Jayden, Minister. Ms. Shani Woolridge is here at the Minister's request."

"Who?"

Killian touches his hand to my hip. I remove his hand and break two of his fingers in the process. He grunts in response. "The witch who will hopefully help give Amelie-Madeline more time."

The beautiful woman in question has light mocha skin and long dark braids. Her black snakeskin pants are painted on, a parrot could rest on the gold hoops of her earrings, and she could stake a fanger with the heels of her sky-high ankle booties. I dig her style. It takes us a moment to reach her in the foyer of the main entrance, and with each step her impatience seems to grow into a loud mixture of sighs and lip smacks. "Motherfucker, I don't have all day."

Once we're standing in front of her, Killian bows slightly to the witch. "Thank you for coming, Shani. It's wonderful to see you."

Shani looks me up and down, flares her nostrils, and cocks a brow. "What the fuck are you? Never smelled the likes of you before."

The Minister smiles and explains, "Lady Zvi Jayden is my consort."

She doesn't bother to hide her surprise. "Hmph. Why am I here, Kavanagh? It's late."

"A fellow witch is in dire need of your assistance."

She holds a long acrylic nail in the air. "And you think I'm the witch to call when your friends need help? I'm not your do-girl, vampire, and while I'm on the subject…"

I interrupt her. "It's Amelie-Madeline Delon."

Both of her brows raise. "Come again?"

"The Fire Witch is in my guest bedroom. She's dying," Killian confirms.

"Take me to her immediately," Shani replies as she snaps her fingers.

We lead the witch to the guest bedroom and knock on the door. Barzul opens it and allows us through. Amelie-Madeline sleeps on the four-poster bed with Moe sitting beside her on top of the duvet.

"Shani?" Moe asks, clearly confused but obviously familiar with the woman.

Shani frowns. "What are you doing here, girl?"

"Amelie-Madeline is my great-grandmother."

"Holy shit," Shani says. "So, you're the next Delon Fire Witch?"

Moe holds her chin high. "Yes."

"How can I help?"

Moe brings her acquaintance up to speed on Karl Ekman, Natasia, the murders, and the Fire Ritual my sister needs in order to become the next witch in her lineage to be Fire Witch. "We need to buy her more time. Outside of human sacrifice, I don't know a way to prolong her life."

Shani cuts her eyes over to Killian with an odd expression on her face, and then she quickly returns her attention back to Moe like it never happened. I don't know her well enough to be able to judge what that meant, but there was something there, a silent communication between Killian and the witch. Killian's face is schooled and impassive. There's likely not going to be an honest answer from him if I ask what the silent exchange was all about, so I'm careful to watch them both.

"I'll take care of it. Focus on spending time with your grandmother," Shani tells my sister before she turns to me. "Can you gather the blood components of the Fire Ritual so that we can be ready for it when the time comes?"

Zarzos giggles at the reminder of us using his blood for the spell and bounces on his feet in excitement. I nod in agreement and take my leave with Zarzos on my heels.

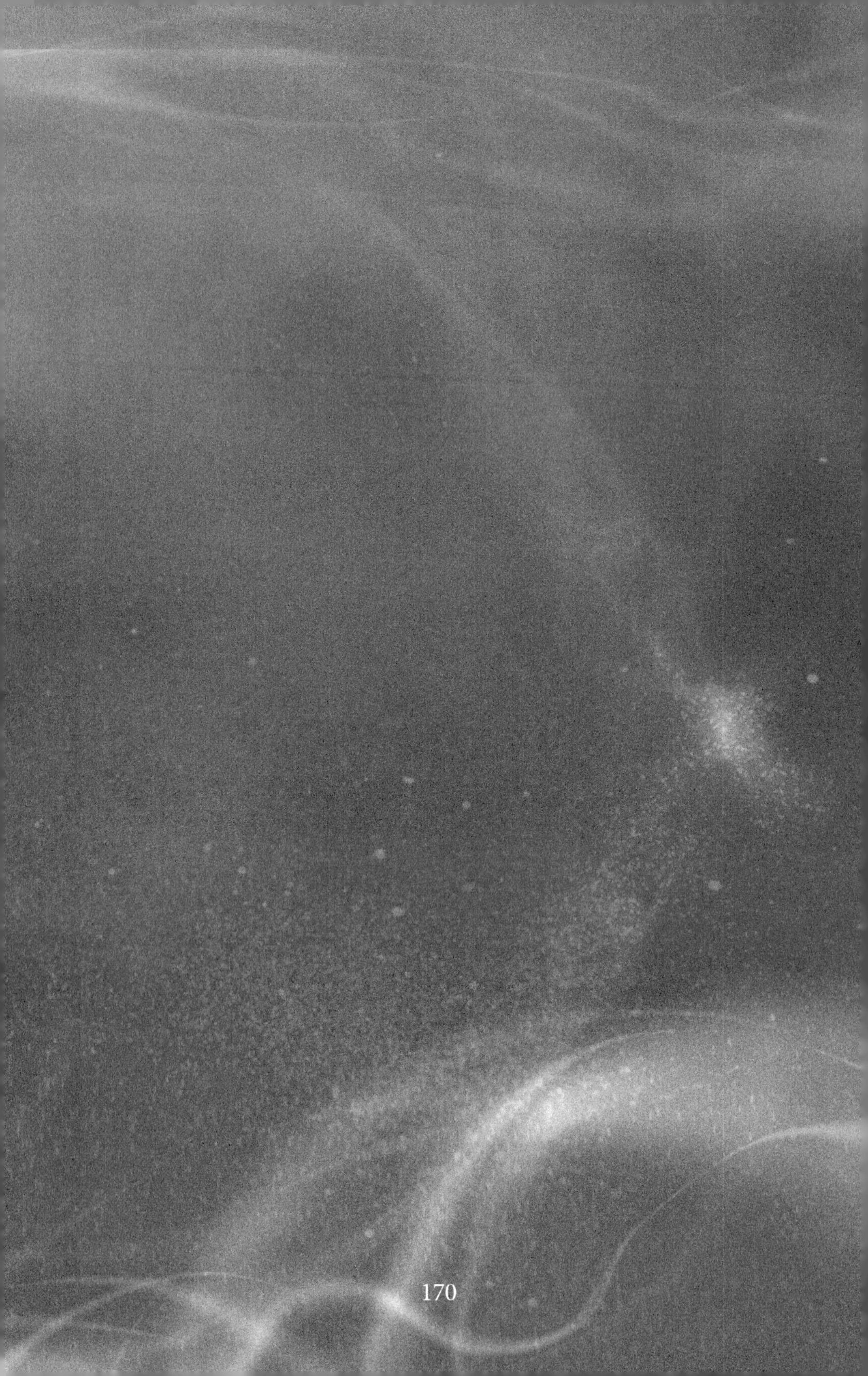

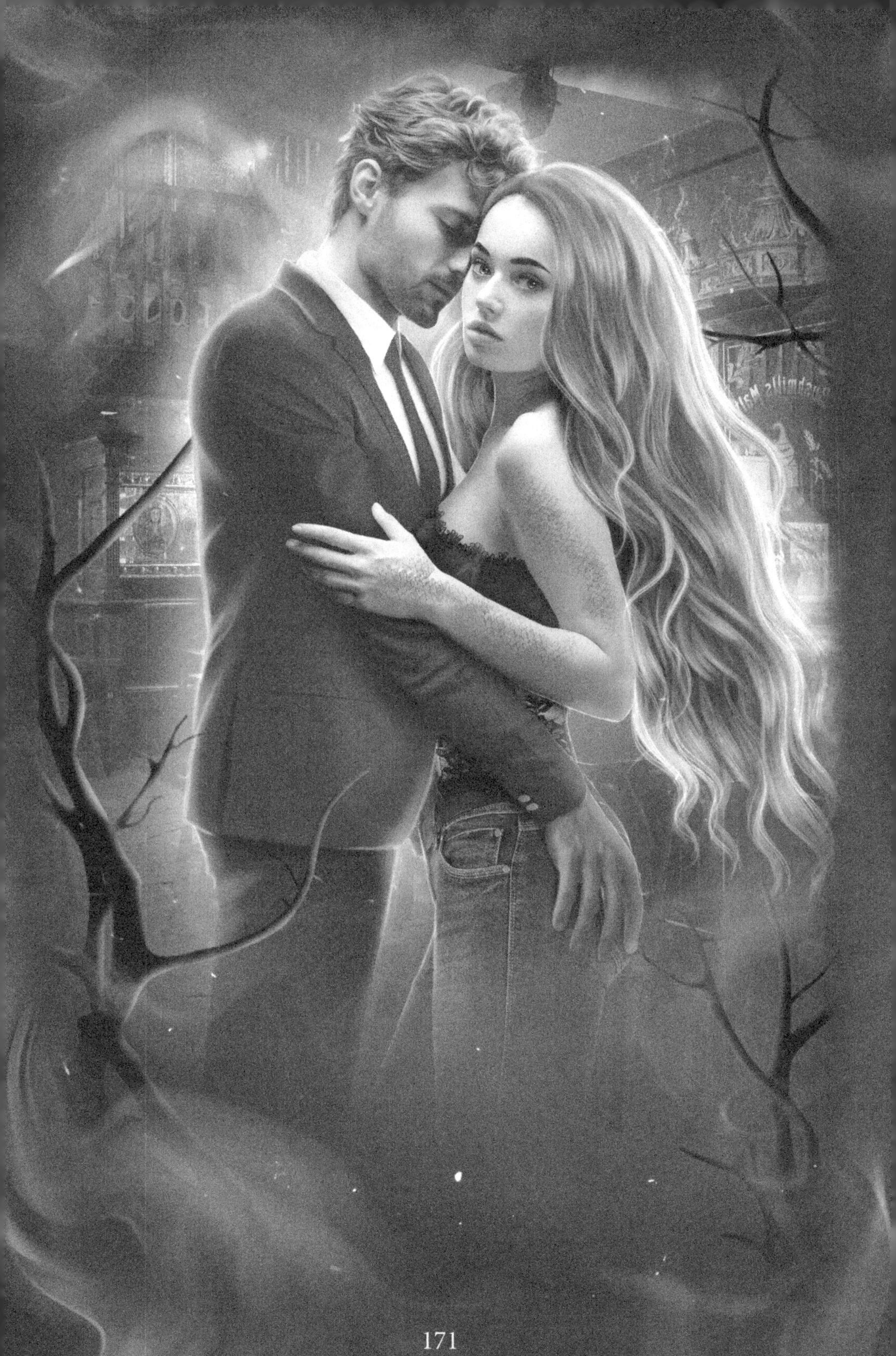

CHAPTER NINETEEN

"WHERE ARE WE GOING, Lady Jayden?" Zarzos asks as we walk through the halls of Killian's mansion.

"Kitchen." My answer excites him, but we're not going for grub this time. "I need a jar for the blood."

He laughs. "You can't store demon blood in glass or plastic, silly. It'll eat it away like acid."

I stop in my tracks and spin on my heel to face him. "What the hell am I supposed to put it in?"

"The Minister will have something for us."

We turn around and meet Killian at the bottom of the grand staircase. "I was just coming to look for you."

"Do you have anything that will hold the blood?" I ask him.

"Yes," he says and leads us to his office. On the way to our destination, he walks close by, his fingers grazing mine every so often. When we reach the office, he opens the door and allows Zarzos to go inside to check for intruders. While the demon is busy, he reaches out and tucks my hair behind my ear.

I swat at his hand. "Stop it."

"What's bothering you, Macushla?"

I don't bother pretending I don't know what he's talking about. "What was that between you and Shani?"

He drops his hand from my cheek. He's going to lie. "What do you mean?"

I narrow my eyes at him and make up my mind rather quickly, I'm not playing his game. I don't answer his question and instead walk into the office as Zarzos comes to tell us all is clear, and then he waits outside to guard the door. Killian walks past me to a locked cabinet behind his desk. He opens the doors, reaches inside, and produces a goblet.

"Dragon Ore from your native land of Dracaena. It was a gift to me from your great-great-great grandfather, Nicodemus, some time ago," Killian answers. "Dragon Ore will contain and preserve the blood mixture until Moe can drink it."

He hands it over to me. The black metal is cold to the touch. I revel in the feel of a piece of my familial history. Later, when there's time, I'll ask Killian about Nicodemus. A hundred questions form in my mind about a man I just learned of seconds ago, but we don't have a second to waste until Moe becomes Fire Witch. "While we're here, I need both of your donations."

I invite Zarzos back in, and the demon and vampire take off their suit jackets and roll up their sleeves. The scent of their blood fills the air. I nearly choke on the stench of Zarzos' blood, although he doesn't seem to notice the smell at all. I've never seen someone so ecstatic to give a blood donation.

"What are your gifts?" I ask the demon. "What will Moe inherit from your blood?"

"It's hard to tell, Lady Jayden. She could be quite the trickster." Zarzos laughs maniacally at the idea, and a little over the top, but I like that he offers no apology for being himself.

When it's Killian's turn to donate, I slice a small cut across his forearm with the blade I keep in my boot and watch the small crimson river flow into the goblet. He watches me intently throughout the process, his eyes never straying from mine. When his vampiric healing closes the wound, I turn away from him and his stare.

"I need Hendri's blood," I say, and after the two men put their jackets back on, Killian locks up his office, and then we head for the guest bedroom where Amelie-Madeline lies.

Barzul and Aleki are posted outside her door when we arrive, both soldiers on watch for the king of vampires. Inside, Moe sits beside her grandmother, and Hendri sleeps in a corner chair, his legs thrown over the arm of it. Shani walks in a circle sprinkling a white substance on the floor to create the casting circle. She's placed four unlit candles around it and drawn unfamiliar signs inside.

When Hendri picks up on our scent in the room, his eyes fly open and quickly take in his surroundings. He settles down when he sees he's safe.

"I need your donation," I tell him.

He doesn't hesitate to leave his chair and offer his forearm to me, but before we can get down to business, Sebastian escorts a young, fair-skinned woman with freckles covering her face and long red hair framing it.

"Miss Woolridge's guest, Miss Hannah Stockton."

Hannah hesitantly steps inside when Sebastian moves aside to present her to the room. The girl can't be more than eighteen. She offers a timid smile and a little wave. "Hi."

Shani returns her smile and welcomes the girl. "Hannah, welcome!"

Something about the uncharacteristically upbeat tone in Shani's voice causes me to take notice. My back stiffens and the hair on my neck stands at attention as I slowly walk backward to the outside perimeter of the room to keep a closer eye on everyone. There's something in the air that doesn't quite sit well in my gut, but for the life of me, I can't pinpoint what it is.

I take in the room and everyone in it. Moe is focused on Amelie-Madeline and is paying attention to little else. Aleki stands guard in front of the door, his eyes focused on Shani standing in the middle of a casting circle at the end of the four-poster bed. Hendri is easing into the opposite corner of the room, his eyes bouncing between me, Shani, and Moe. The suspicion in his green eyes matches the overwhelming feeling in my bones.

Shani outstretches her hand to encourage the girl to come closer. "Please, dear, come."

Hannah takes in the rest of the room as the smell of magic fills the area. I'm keenly aware something is brewing, but without knowing Shani, I have no way of knowing which way she's going with this thing. Past Hannah, I level a glare on Killian. His blue eyes are stuck on me, but they give nothing away. He seems calm, cool, and collected, but I don't trust it for one minute.

To Killian's left is Zarzos, his hand crossed over his chest as he reaches to the opposite shoulder for his blade and settles his hand on the grip, ready for battle. If my guard and Hendri are also feeling the pull of Shani's unfamiliar magic, then I'm trusting my gut.

As Hannah reaches the casting circle and steps inside, a thick dark, sapphire blue cloud begins to rise around the two. Shani begins to chant an incantation in an unfamiliar language, neither Gaelic or Latin, as the flames on the candles around the room begin to dance like they've been brought to life. The witch circles the girl as she continues to speak in a low voice as she calls on her ancestors. The lights in the room begin to flicker as Shani seemingly produces a long, serrated knife from thin air. My hackles raise even more, and I take a step toward the circle. With the lights going in and out, I can only take in part of the scene, but I do not miss Shani stepping behind Hannah and raising the blade to her throat.

"No!" I scream and lunge at them as quickly as I flash over to the circle, but I'm stopped by the blue cloud of magic. It turns into a wall that prevents me from entering the circle, and there's nothing I can do to stop the witch from slicing across the girl's throat.

I scream and fight against the magic to gain entry to the circle to try to save the girl from the blood spurting out of her neck and the fear and horror in her eyes as she panics and holds her hands over the wound to staunch the bleeding. Nothing I do helps me get to her. I stop fighting against the cloud and turn to find Moe. She's my only hope, and I find her a few feet to my right chanting in Gaelic, already attempting to help Hannah.

Past Moe, Hendri has shifted. The large, gray wolf is snarling and snipping at the magical cloud as he attempts to get to Shani. Zarzos is slicing his blade at the cloud from the other side of the circle. Aleki and Killian do nothing to help. In fact, both vampires have their eyes locked on me, watching and waiting to see what I'll do next. And then it dawns on me, they both knew this was going to happen. The look that was exchanged between Shani and Killian a few hours ago was a mutual agreement and understanding on human sacrifice.

As Hannah's lifeless body crumples to the floor like a sack of potatoes, I zip through the room at my quickest speed and lunge at Aleki first. If I try to take Killian out first, I'll have Aleki to contend with anyway. Killian speeds across the room and jumps between us at just the right moment and wraps his arms around me. All three of us go down from the sheer force of our impact. Aleki goes through the sheetrock, and Killian and I immediately begin rolling around with me trying to gain leverage to inflict some sort of pain on him, but he's strong.

"Macushla," he says, "it had to be done."

"No!" I scream at him. "No, it didn't!"

I manage to pull my knees to my chest and bury the bottom of my boot in his abdomen before I push him off me with all my might. I spring to my feet and go after him. I find where he's landed against the side of the bed and lunge again, but Zarzos and Aleki rush between us before I can get the party started. I have no issue putting the beat down on Aleki, but for some weird reason, Zarzos makes me stop.

"Move!" I command him.

He bows to me. "I can't do that, Lady Jayden. My job is to protect you. If you harm the Minister, the vampires will retaliate, and there are far more of them than there are of Barzul and I."

I settle on Killian standing behind and between the vampire and demon. His blue eyes shine with sympathy, but there isn't the first ounce of regret there. "You knew she was going to kill her!" I shout at him.

"We had to save Amelie-Madeline, and subsequently, the world, Lady Jayden. I cannot apologize for sacrificing what is necessary to preserve order in our worlds." His blue orbs beseech me to understand, but I can't see past the horror in that poor girl's eyes.

I turn to the circle. Hendri continues to snap at the now invisible barrier. Shani stands in the middle of it, her arms covered in innocent blood, and she also offers no apology for her actions. Her strong shoulders are held as high as her chin.

"It was the only way," she tells me as the knife falls from her hand and clinks against the hardwood floor.

I work my jaw and attempt to reconcile what my eyes saw with reality. I've seen violent deaths, and I've killed, but it never gets any easier to watch the innocent die a premeditated death. "Get out and hope like hell I never see you again," I tell the witch.

She shifts her attention to Killian. "You guaranteed my safety, vampire."

He slightly nods in understanding. "I shall escort you from here myself."

"And your consort?"

"Lady Jayden shall understand in time."

I cock a brow at him. "I shall?"

"Zvi, Macushla, please try to understand when it comes to you or yours, there are absolutely no boundaries I won't cross in order to protect you."

Moe walks over to Hendri and rubs her hand down his back to bring him comfort, and then she kneels beside him and lowers her forehead to the side of his neck. "Shhh, it's okay. There's nothing we can do to save her now."

I avoid looking at the poor girl lying there with horror still laced in her open eyes. "You made this mess," I tell Shani and Killian. "Fucking clean it up." I turn to the wolf and Barzul. "Protect my sister." And then I leave the room to find a place to cool off before my temper gets the best of me.

I zip through the mansion and outside, and then I march into the garden with a huff. "I should turn around, go back, and fuck 'em all up."

"Your eyes are glowing. So, it's true?" asks a male voice.

I spin around to find an unfamiliar vampire sitting on a bench across the wide garden. Between us is a beautiful, albeit risqué, fountain with a naked woman in the middle.

"Where did you come from?" I'm in no mood to deal with another fanger at this point. "It's not smart to sneak up on a person."

"Especially not a dragon," he says.

He leaves his seat on the bench and steps under a garden light. He's dressed in navy slacks, a red, white, and blue plaid oxford, and an ivory sweater is draped around his neck like he's Mr. freaking Rogers. His light brown hair is cropped short on the sides and a few inches longer on top. His blue eyes shine like sapphires, and his demeanor is calm, cool, and collected.

"Be careful of the words you use, vampire."

"I'd do almost anything for you to turn your fire on me, Lady Jayden."

It dawns on me why I've never met this vampire before, but then his scent is somewhat familiar. "What's the earthy smell surrounding you? It almost smells like magic."

"Black magic," he says and cringes as though it hurts to say the words.

It takes me 2.5 seconds longer to figure him out than it should. "Karl?"

He bows. "Lady Jayden. I'm supposed to take you. I do not wish to bring you harm. Please fight against me when the time comes."

"You really can't control it, can you?"

His lips thin into a sad line. "No, I'm afraid I cannot. It pains me greatly to have taken the lives I've snatched away in the last week."

"Was it for the blood?" I ask.

"Partly. There are many pieces and powerful people in play."

"Natasia."

"Yes."

"Shaw?"

Confusion flashes in his eyes for half a second and then he schools his features. "I'm not allowed to utter their names, but I can say they need your fire."

The scent of black magic invades my nose to the point where the pungent, earthy smell overwhelms me. I bend over at the waist and heave. Before I know what's happened, Karl is standing right in front of me. I straighten and stare him in the eyes, but they're no longer sapphire blue. They're black and empty of intelligent life.

"Fuuuuccccckkkkkk, you snuck up on me there, scooter." I bend back as far as I can to duck as he throws his first punch. "And crazy

Karl returns!" I manage to dance backward to escape another punch. I feel the wind off the second one. "That was close, Karl. I really don't want to hurt you, homie."

I dance around zombie Karl and watch him go from slow-motion movements to robotic, skilled, vampiric flashes of movement. I throw a few punches only to have him block each one.

"Lady Jayden!" Killian yells. I drop my guard for one second and Karl lunges at me. I was already killing Killian, but I am most definitely shanking his ass now.

Karl and I fall backward to the ground with him on top of me. His hands wrap around my throat and squeeze before my back can hit the ground, and the choking commences. I fight for air in my lungs and expend all my energy prying Karl's hands away from my throat. He releases me when his head is pulled backward.

I look past him to see Zarzos holding his head like a vice as he prepares to remove the head from the body with sheer force. "Zarzos, no! He's innocent!"

Karl's sapphire eyes are once again visible and in them is the fear of death. "Lady Jayden?"

"Zarzos, please."

The demon turns his nose up in distaste. "He won't stop until the spell is complete." Then he spits on the ground as an insult. "You stink, vampire."

I press my lips together to keep from laughing at a demon calling someone else stinky. "He's right, Karl. You need a bath."

"I must return to my master," he says, defeated and scared.

Zarzos releases the vampire and Killian steps up to us to help me up. I flip him the bird instead of taking his offered hand. "Go fuck yourself." And then I leap to my feet.

"Zvi," Killian whispers, his voice desperate and pleading.

Zarzos giggles as he walks a circle around Karl. "What do you think of my suit?"

Karl, whose head was previously at risk of being removed by the demon's own two hands, looks to me, and back to Zarzos. There's a quiver in his voice. "I think it fits you well. Is it tailored?"

Zarzos grabs his lapels and holds them. "Yes," he says in a serious voice that sounds nothing like his own and is quite British, "the Minister had it tailored for me." And then he laughs and returns to his normal tone. "Whoever thought of a demon in a suit?"

Killian's phone rings. "Yes?" he says into the receiver. "I see." He ends the call, pockets the phone, and sets his sights on me. "The Bar has been vandalized. We need to mobilize immediately to have you and Moe over there quickly."

"Who called?" I ask, curious as to who knew my bar was trashed before I did.

"I have a man on The Bar each night," he answers as if that is the end of the discussion.

I step in front of him as he turns for the mansion. "Why?"

He stops and searches my eyes, for what I'm not sure. He reaches for my face, but I duck out of his reach. A frustrated sigh escapes him. "There was no other way to keep Amelie-Madeline alive." I look away from him and over to Karl. I much prefer the poor guy to the vampire standing in front of me. "It's not easy to be king."

"Heavy is the head that wears the crown?" I ask, snark fully on blast.

"I don't expect you to understand yet, but as my consort, there will come a day when you must make a decision that could cost someone their life. It is never an easy decision to watch someone die to keep another alive. It's never going to become easier to watch an innocent girl die. If the girl hadn't died, the entire world would be full of the Fire Witch's power and up for grabs. Until that power resides solely in your sister, I will stop at nothing to ensure it happens."

"I'm not in the consort business anymore."

He takes a step forward and closes the space between us. His hands come to rest on my shoulders. "You're not relieved of your duties, Macushla. Not until my death, and even then, you will still be a vampire queen."

I stare him down while also talking myself down from ripping into him. Rage courses and pulses through me as I fight to control it.

"Minister," Moe says from behind me. "Please allow me to speak with my sister?"

He reaches for me again to do something stupid like caress my cheek, so I lean out to meet his hand and bite it. He snatches it away and his brows knit in pain but doesn't make a sound.

"Zvi," Moe admonishes. "You're not a wild animal!"

She says the dumbest shit sometimes, but I let it go in order to stare down Killian like the dog he is. "I'm coming for you, vampire."

Killian walks away without another word and leaves me with Moe. I turn to her. "How is Amelie-Madeline?"

"Who is that?" she asks about the vampire Zarzos is leading toward the mansion.

"Karl Ekman."

She turns around to get another look at the back of the small group of men. "No shit."

"Dude, the black magic thing following him around like a dark rain cloud is some serious shit. No way he's old enough to take me over, and he got the drop on me."

Her brows reach her forehead. "He what?"

"He was seriously about to fuck me up. Zarzos had to intervene. He was wicked strong. Can magic do that?"

"Yes, both white and dark magic can increase strength." She pauses to turn her attention back to Killian, Zarzos, and Karl. "Did you hear about our bar?"

"Minister Asswipe just informed me."

My sister's eyes dance, taking in my face, gauging my mood. "Zvi, there was no other way than sacrifice to extend life. I knew that. I hoped there was another answer I wasn't thinking of, but deep down, I think I knew what Shani was going to do. If you're going to be mad at the vampire, you'll have to be angry with me, too." I almost respond with an insult, but Moe cuts me off and grabs my hand to pull me toward the house. "Now, let's go see what the bartenders found when they opened tonight."

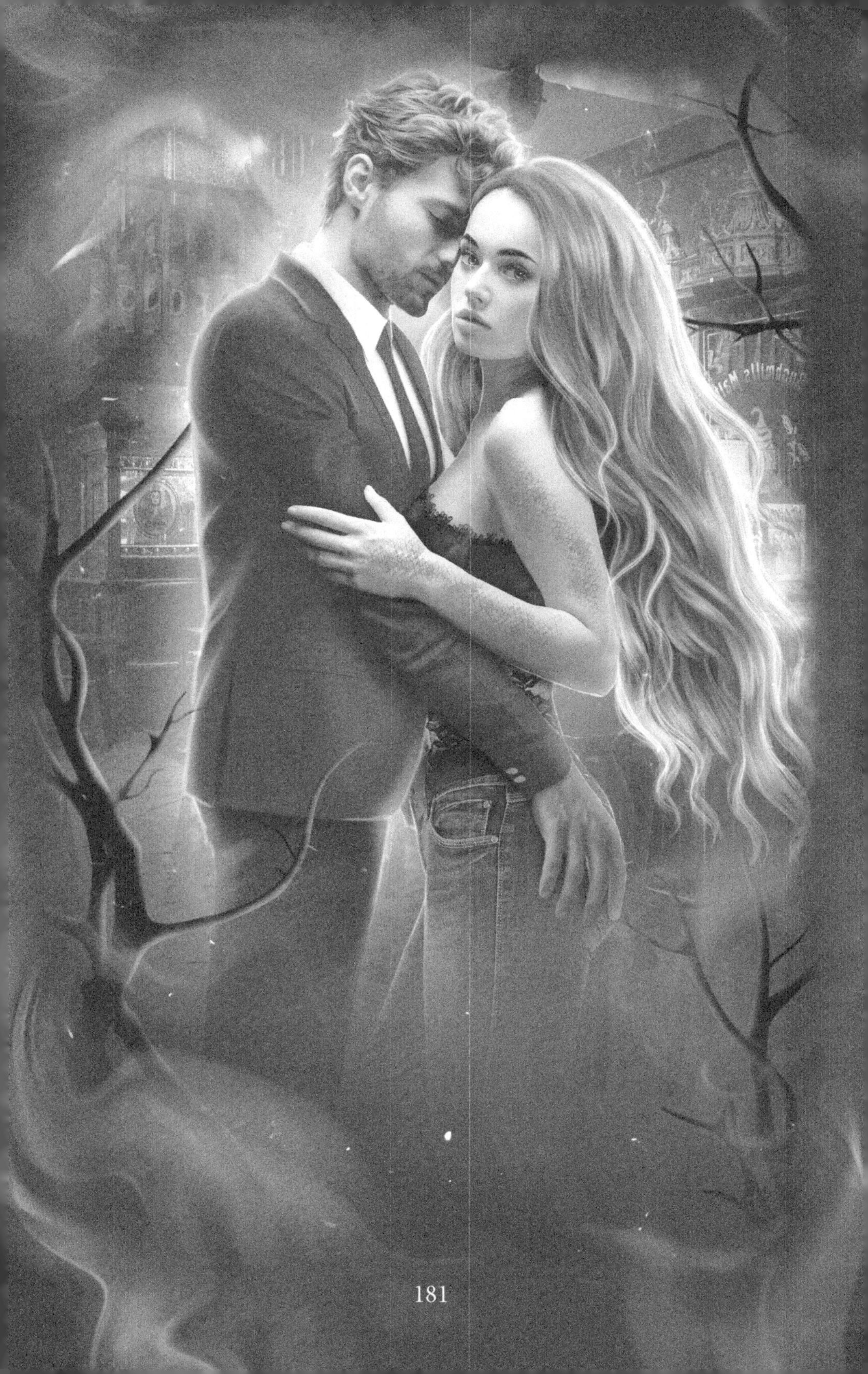

CHAPTER TWENTY

OUR VAMPIRE BARTENDER, MILENA, is waiting for us outside The Bar puffing on a cigarette when we arrive with Killian's army and Hendri in tow. I opted to catch a ride with the wolf so I wasn't tempted to shift in a car with that asshole Kavanagh and burn him until he's crunchy and crispy.

"You knew?" I ask Moe, for what seems like the hundredth time since we left Killian's. "You really knew what she'd do?" I'm beyond shocked my sister could have an inkling of what was about to transpire and just let it happen.

Moe rolls her eyes. "Don't be so indignant. You've taken lives before."

"Only to protect mine or yours, and only the damned."

She turns around in the front passenger seat of Hendri's government-issued vehicle. "This was to protect our lives. This was to defeat Natasia. The sacrifice will prevent her from grabbing power and reigning over us both. Can you imagine what life would be like under her rule as Fire Witch? None of us would escape her ire."

I know Moe is right. Deep down, I know Moe wouldn't sacrifice an innocent life unless the balance of the world didn't depend on it. "What language was she speaking?"

She frowns. "I don't see what it matters, but it was an African dialect, likely hailing from Haiti."

"I just hope you know what you're doing and what sort of magic you're messing with. You've always told me we reap what we sow, so I hope you're ready for what the Universe is going to throw our way."

Before our conversation can continue, Zarzos raps his knuckles against my window. "Lady Jayden?"

I emerge from the vehicle without any further word on the matter. "What is it, Zarzos?"

"Please allow me to check the premises with Aleki and Barzul before we enter."

"Sure," I tell the demon. "Do it to it, Z."

He bows, draws his sword like a samurai warrior, and off he goes leading the pack of demons and vampires.

"I chose well for your guard," Killian says as he saddles up beside me.

"Let's not do this."

"Macushla, when will you learn that I will not allow you to push me away?"

"I suppose I should've staked you in the kidney when I had the chance, and I might begin to feel a little better about the situation."

"Have it your way then," he says and pulls his suit jacket off. "You're not going to stop until I let you beat me to a bloody pulp." He throws his jacket to Moe, who catches it before the precious fabric can touch the ground, and then he holds his arms out wide. "Where would you like to stake me first, Macushla?"

I scoff at him. "Let me?" He smirks at me. I can't tell if he's antagonizing me or not, so I stop to consider the vampire for a moment. "What's your endgame?"

"You. Since I laid eyes on you, it's all been about you."

"Zvi," Moe pleads. "Don't do this. If his men come out, they'll jump in to save him."

"I'll order them to stand down," Killian replies.

My sister's hands go to her hips. "Until she hands you your ass." I love when she gets sassy.

Zarzos, Barzul, Aleki and the Minister's army emerge from The Bar's front door. They zip across the parking lot and form a circle around us. I smile at Killian as I rush him and tuck my upper body just in time to push my shoulder into his belly.

"Oof!" he says as he flies in the air and then lands on his back with an audible crack that can only be the sound of breaking bones. He remains on his back and looks up at me with pain in his crystal blue eyes.

A sharp pang of guilt laces its way through my chest at the visual, but for the life of me I can't understand why I care after what he did to Hannah. "After this case is over, I never want to see you again."

If I thought there was visible pain in his face before, it's nothing compared to his reaction to my words.

"Not so fast, vampire," my guard warns, and I look over just in time to see Aleki coming for me.

Killian manages to get to his feet, not quite healed from the broken vertebrae in his back, and stands between me and his right hand. "You are to protect Lady Jayden at all costs, even from me. Those are your orders, Aleki." He murmurs something else in a language far older than all the rest of us combined, and Aleki stiffens before ceasing his progress.

I'm inclined to stick my tongue out and antagonize the mountain of a man to come after me, but I really need to get inside and check on our bar. "Is it all clear?" I ask Zarzos.

He nods and leads the way to our front entrance. Inside, we find the chairs and tables overturned by someone strong enough to pick up tables and throw them across the room. Wooden bar stools are in pieces all over the place. Glass crunches under our feet, and after stepping behind the bar, I find most of our glasses are gone and likely on the floor. The jukebox is across the room and turned on its top. It looks like a tornado ripped through our place of business.

I hear Moe sniffle. "They ruined everything."

"There, there, love," Hendri wraps an arm around her to comfort her. "These things are replaceable. You aren't."

Moe and I worked hard on our establishment. We built it from scratch. Keeping a bar in business is no easy feat since they have a high failure rate. But we offer the supernatural a place to socialize and wind down after a hard week. There aren't many who could keep all of our secrets under wraps, but we manage to do that very thing. I keep it safe, and Moe makes sure the liquor and beer keep flowing. And now someone has encroached on our turf and damaged things that aren't theirs to wreck. Yes, these things are replaceable, but it'll never be the home we first built. It'll always be some second-rate version of our original idea, a tainted version of the first home we built on our own.

"We needed to renovate anyhow," Moe says as she comes to stand beside me. Her attempt at a jovial tone falls flat. She shrugs.

Zarzos slams his foot through the front glass of the jukebox and giggles. Aleki watches the demon with a strange satisfaction, almost as if he wishes he could be as wild and free as him. Killian stands at the south wall taking in the train wreck in front of him, and his army begins to pick up tables and chairs. Hendri keeps his eyes on Moe and his hand on his weapon at his side.

"Zvi?" Moe asks when I offer no reply to the room.

My hands go to my hips, my nostrils flare, and my eyes glow.

"Uh-oh," Hendri says. "I don't think that means anything good?"

"Zvi," Moe says and pulls my hand into hers, "they're only things. They can be replaced."

"But they were our things," I say, voice so low it's almost a growl. I don't have to say more for Moe to understand this isn't about materialism— it's about someone coming into our home and ruining both of our senses of safety. Considering we're both creatures that go bump in the night, the breach is that much more unsettling.

Zarzos giggles and begins bouncing up and down like a pogo stick. "Fire. Fire. The building is on fire," he sing-songs. "If you're happy and you know it, start a fire." He pauses and claps and stomps his right foot twice. "If you're happy and you know it, start a fire." Another clap and a stomp. "If you're happy and you know it, and you really wanna show it. If you're happy and you know it, start a fire."

The vampires instantly go on alert as I raise my nose to the air and smell for the scent of smoke.

Zarzos begins a variation of a dance that looks something like a rain dance, and if a demon dancing a Native dance isn't strange enough, the sprinkler system goes off as the fire alarm sounds. I have to wonder if there's more to Zarzos than meets the eye. Is he also part-shaman?

Killian is standing in front of me seconds later, looking down at me helplessly. "I have to leave the building, Macushla."

A grin overtakes my face. "Yes, or you'll be burned alive. Buh-bye now."

"You'll forgive me, Zvi." And then he's gone, and I feel like I can breathe a little easier in his absence without his intense gaze bearing down on me.

My guard heads for the staircase leading up to the second and third floors as I turn to my sister. "Go with Killian and his men. Hendri, Zarzos, Barzul, and I will check out the fire."

She nods, squeezes my hand, and then she gives Hendri a hug and a kiss on the cheek. We watch her walk to the door, and then we both dash up the stairs after Zarzos as Barzul brings up the rear. Smoke is pouring from my third-floor apartment. Great. My shit is on fire. Zarzos kicks in the door to my place and disappears inside. I duck inside the apartment behind the demon and through the thick, black clouds of smoke. I immediately go for the windows and start to break the ones that haven't been broken yet.

I don't see Barzul and Hendri again until they're lugging a fire hose inside from the hallway. God. I hope the damn thing works. It looks ancient. Moments later, water spurts from the hose and begins to beat back the fire. The entire building will go up in flames at this rate, so I venture up to the roof and call Moe.

"You're seriously calling me at a time like this?" she answers.

"Can you cloak me? I need to gather water for the fire."

"Oh," she says. "For sure. Two seconds. Let me jump inside Hendri's car for privacy."

"I'm undressing. I'll catch you on the other side," I tell her and hang up.

When the scent of Moe's magic wraps around me, I begin to shift. My claws shoot from my fingertips as my skin transforms into purple and iridescent blue scales. The concrete of the roof grows farther away as I shoot up to my full dragon height. As I reach full form, I stretch my wings and then I expand my lungs with a roar. I flap my wings in the humid October air and take flight over Atlanta.

A small lake near The Bar is the perfect location for me to quickly gather water to help extinguish the fire. I'm able to swallow a massive amount of water and breathe it much like I can fire. It will be a lot more water at once than the fire hoses can deliver. Water, fire, and smoke damage are all inevitable at this point.

I focus on the lake and dive as deeply as I can in the middle, inhaling water as I go until I can't hold any more. The water is cool and refreshing against my scales as I swim through the murkiness. When I've collected my fill, I swim to the bottom and use it as a platform to lunge from the water into the air. I accidentally knock a fisherman off his boat. After I correct his vessel, I pluck him from the water and set him to rights. He chokes and sputters, but I'm already halfway back to The Bar before he can question his invisible savior.

I'm bursting at the seams with water when I reach the roof. I land on the side and hold tightly to the ledge as I swing down and fill my entire apartment with water. I don't hang around to watch the water leak from the building. Taking flight over our city once more, I use the same route to reach the lake where I fill up again. It takes me half the time to make it back to The Bar and deliver another load to help the efforts.

Emergency vehicles and lights fill the lot and street below me, all now covered in water from my deliveries. They're all shouting and looking around for what could've possibly filled an entire apartment with water and extinguished the fire so quickly. Except Killian who is staring straight at me. If I wasn't so sure of Moe's magic, I'd think he could see me.

I turn back to the roof and shift back, dress, and carefully make my way down the scorched stairs to my apartment. I stand in the middle and have a look around at my black, smoky home. Devastation curls in my gut, but it's soon replaced with rage for Natasia and whomever else did this to us. I'll get my revenge on every last single person responsible if it's the last thing I do. There's nothing salvageable here, so I leave it behind and dart down the stairs to the bottom level.

I very carefully sneak through the back entrance to the bar kitchen and slip out undetected by authorities. I walk up the street a ways and cross before I loop back around to the massive crowd in front of The Bar. And then I locate all the key players. To my right, Aleki looks around the crowd he towers over. To my left, Killian's phone is pressed to his ear as he also searches the crowd. Sebastian moves around the perimeter of the group also seeking someone. But who?

I search for Zarzos, Barzul, Hendri, and Moe but can't locate any of them. Anxiety ripples through my chest when I look back to Killian and find myself in his worried eyes.

"Zvi!" Hendri shouts from the middle of the mass of people, his head a few inches taller than everyone else. I search through the crowd, pushing people as needed so I can reach him and Moe. I can rest easy when I know she's okay.

"Here!" I say and jump up and down with my hand in the air to show them my location. "Moe!"

The deputy wraps his hand around my arm and pulls me to him through the crowd. His green eyes are full of terror. "Where's Moe?"

A pain sears through the center of my head, temporarily blinding me. A ringing in my ears takes over. I shake my head and stick my fingers in my ears.

"Zvi? What's wrong?" Killian's voice is muffled, but I hear and smell him. I reach for him, reach for anyone to stabilize me.

"Zvi?" Hendri asks.

"Moe," I croak out as I hold my head between my hands. I fight through the pain and open my eyes, but the emergency lights create starbursts in my vision.

"Come here," Killian says, grabs my hand, pulls me to his chest. He wraps his arm around me and presses his cool lips to my forehead, and then his cheek which actually provides relief from the pain.

I'm finally able to at least squint. "Where's Moe?"

"We're looking for her," he says.

Panic shoots through me when I realize the comfort of Moe's magic is gone. "That's who you were looking for in the crowd this whole time?!"

"Macushla..." he starts, but I pull away and start my search.

"She's around here somewhere."

"Zvi, my love…" he says from behind as I pick through the crowd. I wave him off and continue looking. "Where did Hendri go?"

"Zvi, come with me."

"Where is Zarzos? Barzul?"

"They're waiting for you at the car."

"Moe!" I shout.

"Lady Jayden, please come with me."

I turn to him, already tiring of his incessant pleas. "Why? Did you find her? Do you know where she is?"

He struggles to speak, his mouth opening and closing, but no words come out. His lips thin into a sympathetic line, and then he looks all around us, a quiet reminder that we're not alone— that we're in the presence of humans. He attempts to speak once again to no avail. His angelic blue eyes close as he takes a step toward me and places his hand on my hip. "Macushla, you are bonded to her by blood."

"Yes! I am!" I say as I reach out with my senses to prove him wrong, but the magic is gone. Her warmth is gone. The bond has been broken, most likely by Natasia's magic.

Hendri emerges from the group congregating in front of The Bar. He shakes his head when he meets my gaze. "Fuck!" He marches to his car with his phone to his ear, likely to call Black Star in to assist.

"No." I say and shake my head to make sure he understands that this isn't happening.

"Lady…"

"Stop it!" I take a deep breath and look around me as onlookers start to take notice of the argument brewing between me and Killian. I'm losing it. I can't do this. I spin around looking for an escape from reality. I need to get out of here before I completely fall apart.

And then Zarzos is in front of me with the most serious expression I've ever seen him wear. "We'll find Miss Moe."

He confirms what I've feared for what seems like an eternity now. Moe is gone. The resulting pain in my body is far more than anything I've ever felt. Death has to be easier than this.

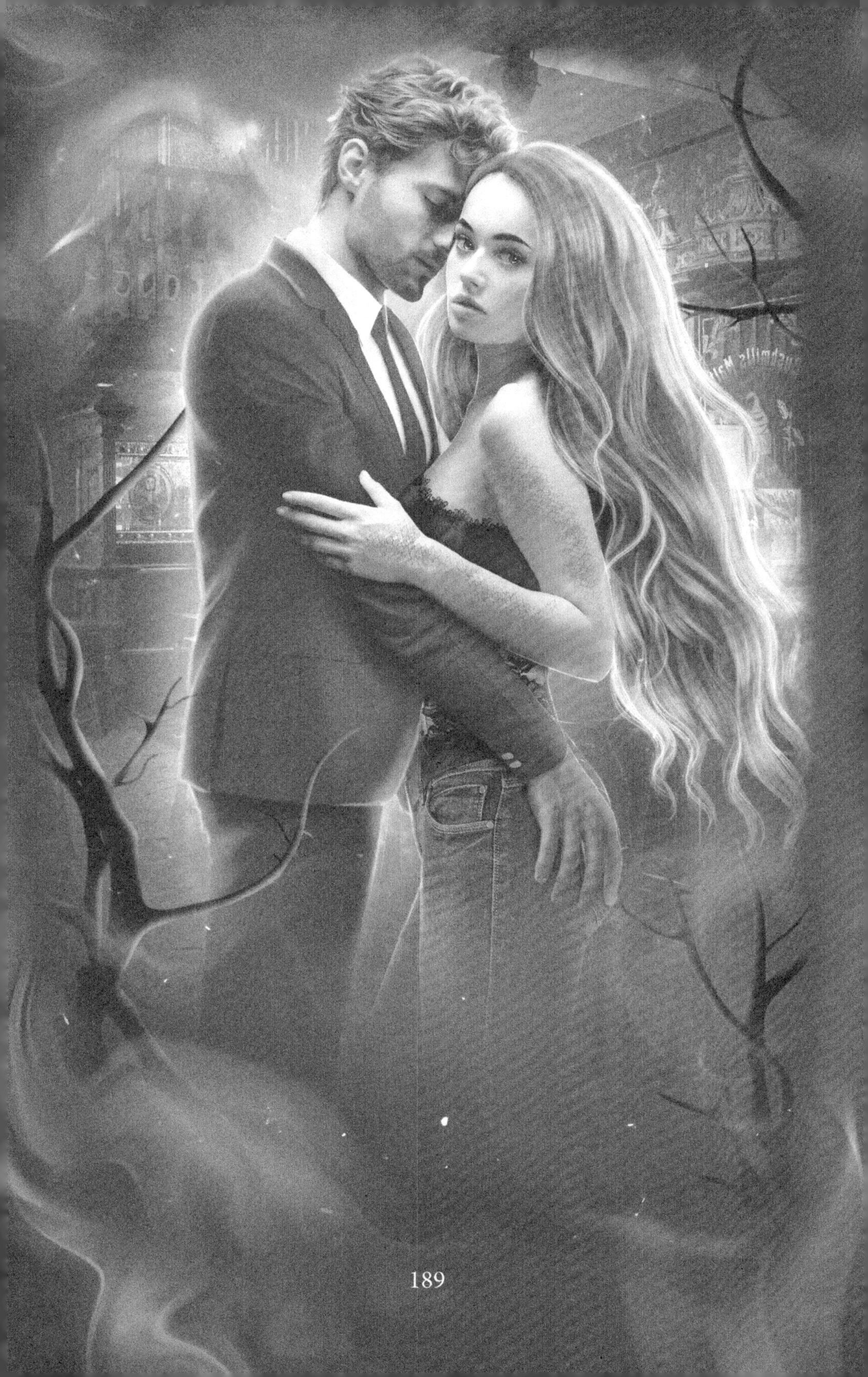

CHAPTER TWENTY-ONE

THERE ARE CERTAIN THINGS we take for granted—like the air we breathe. We won't always have the luxury of breath, but we do expect the next one to come without much thought. I've taken Moe's safety for granted for the last twenty-eight years. I've taken her being mere steps away from me each day when I wake for granted. I always assumed with my bad attitude and penchant for trouble and fighting that I would be the first to go to the other side—that she'd be the one who'd have to live without me, not the other way around. Without a connection to her through our bond, I have no way of knowing if she's still alive, but Natasia and whoever else is involved better hope like fuck she is.

I zip through the city following the deputy as he tracks a faint scent southwest of Atlanta. Killian, Zarzos, Barzul, and three dozen vampires also do what they can to spread out and cover the area around the wolf for any sign Moe has been in the area. I'm helpless on the ground, and I can't change without Moe's bond and magic. I can't risk being seen by Natasia. If I don't shift, she can't harness the power of my fire for her ritual, and without my fire, she has jack shit going for her. It's the only thing that keeps my hope alive that Moe is still breathing—the fact that Natasia needs my fire and that she knows she doesn't have a shot in hell at it if Moe is dead.

I have no idea how far we travel or how many miles we cover, but as dawn nears, the big gray wolf comes to a stop at a creek up ahead. He sits on his back legs and turns his head to look at me. "Why are you stopping?" I ask him.

A small bark escapes him, and then he nudges my hand with his nose.

"Macushla," Killian says quietly, aware that we're surrounded by his people, "the sun will rise in the next hour. We've already pushed the envelope with our distance from our daytime resting places."

"I'll keep searching," I tell him and move forward, but he hooks his hand in my elbow and pulls me to him.

His right hand slides across my lower hip and his other wraps around the back of my neck as he lays his forehead against mine. "My love, you need rest, food, and protection, now more than ever. When we find her, and we will find her, we're going to have quite the fight on our hands. I need you rested, nourished, and ready for battle. Please allow Zarzos and Sebastian to take you back to the estate while I sleep for the day."

I'm too tired to fight against his glamour wrapping around me. I'm too devastated to do much of anything but look for Moe, but my retort falls flat. "I can't stop looking."

Hendri whines and nudges my hand again as if he's disagreeing with me.

"The wolf needs food and rest as well," Killian softly reminds me, his voice bringing me comfort as he works his magic over me. "He needs you as much as you need him right now. Go to the estate together and allow my people to care for you."

Zarzos approaches. "Minister, the vampires are becoming restless."

Killian speaks without moving his blue eyes from mine. "Thank you, Zarzos. They are relieved of their search efforts until dusk tomorrow." Zarzos bows and leaves to relay the message. The Minister begins to softly sway us to a piano sonata that seems vaguely familiar.

"Where's the music coming from?" I ask as my eyes grow heavier by the second.

"It's us, my love. Listen to the beautiful music we make," he whispers against my lips. "It's just you and I now. Everyone has gone. You can close your eyes, let go, and allow me to make you feel better. And no one has to know."

I fight it with all my might—the warmth that spreads through me like lava. I want to hate the feel of his magic, magnetism, and the way he holds me like I'm precious. "Don't leave me," I beg. I don't want to be left alone feeling the way I do.

"Zvi," he says close my ear, "don't beg me, or I'll give you what you want."

I barely manage a final plea. "Please."

It's all I remember as I lose myself in a dream where my sister is alive and well behind the bar at our establishment. Killian sits at the scarred, wooden bar in front of her drinking a Midleton, and Hendri occupies the stool next to him. Zarzos sits on top of the bar gargling expensive sipping tequila like it's mouthwash.

I'm lightly jostled awake. "Where are we going?" I ask, eyes half-closed.

"It appears I can't resist you. We'll rest together, and when we rise this evening, we'll sate your appetite before we find your beloved sister." He presses his cool lips to my temple and wraps his arms around me as I drift into a sea of dreams.

*

An obnoxiously loud phone shrilly rings in my ear. God. Whose phone is that and why is it so close?

I growl in my sleep. "Knock it off."

It rings again.

I reach for my gun. "I'm gonna kill it."

Something shifts beside me, and for a half a second I question what in the hell that could be.

"Hello?" My eyes open wide at the sound of Killian's Irish lilt, but it's pitch black. I'm stuck somewhere between consciousness and a dream when he utters one word that brings it all back— the pain of the harsh reality of my sister having been kidnapped. "Natasia," he says with disgust dripping from his tongue.

The glow of his phone illuminates his face as he pulls it from his ear to look at the screen. Relief fills his blue eyes. "I've got it. If you harm one hair on her head, I'll…" Appalment flashes across his face. "She hung up on me."

He moves to his right and reaches across to click on a lamp. I soon find I'm in a king-size bed covered in black sheets. "Where are we?"

"My daytime place," he says, and fuck me, it takes everything I have in me not to look down at his naked upper body.

Why, oh, why do I want to know whether or not he's wearing underwear at a time like this? I clear my throat. "What did she say?"

"She sent proof of life."

I sit straight up in the bed and reach for his phone. A video sits inside a text message with Moe's face on it. I press play and watch her come to life. "Zvi, I'm okay," she says into the camera and then looks up and past it. "There. That's all I'm saying." The video ends with Moe crossing her arms over her chest and refusing to say more.

Tears spring to my eyes as relief courses through me. She's okay, at least for now. I still have time to find her. I play the video three more times to hear her voice and relish in the fact that she's still alive.

"Macushla," Killian says with reverence in his voice. I suck back the tears before I look at him. I don't do the best job at hiding my rare show of emotion. His kind, sympathetic eyes soften even more. "You are beautiful, my love, even when you weep."

He touches his hand to my lower back. I'm uncomfortable with his consoling me, so I scoot to the edge of the bed facing away from him. Before I can stop him, he drags me back across the bed and pulls me down to his pillow. Leaning above me, he searches my face and wipes the remnant of a tear from my left eye. "Moe is your person."

"Yes."

"She's okay."

"For now."

"I vow to return her safe and sound."

I don't have a lot of faith in the world as a whole right now, but I have at least some hope when he tells me he'll bring Moe home. Maybe it's the determination in his eyes, voice, and set of his jaw, but I believe he'll do everything in his power to bring her home safely.

"Let me be your person," he says and touches his hand to my cheek.

I don't know what possesses me to lean forward and press my lips to his, but I do. Maybe it's because I want to crawl inside him and forget how much this hurts, even if for only a little while. Perhaps it's because I've never felt so alone in the world as I do now without Moe and our bond. He can never be my person though, not really, but we can both pretend for a little while—pretend we'd work together, when in reality we both know on some level we're doomed from the start to crash and burn.

I expect him to be a perfect gentleman and stop this so I don't have to. Instead, he deepens the kiss into something I've never experienced before—a full-body astral projection where I'm standing outside my body looking at the two of us as our hands begin to move over each other's skin. His is cool underneath my touch, a welcome contrast to the higher than normal temperature of my dragon core and burning skin.

He breaks the kiss and travels down my neck, his fangs out and lightly grazing against the sensitive area. I moan at the sensation and arch my back in response, wanting, no, needing more of this feeling. I want to dive into the deep end of his pool and drown in his affection as I swim through nirvana with him. His hands meet his mouth at my chest, and then he begins to remove the olive green racerback tank over my head, his mouth landing on the newly exposed skin. He murmurs in an ancient language against the valley of my breasts. I don't have the first clue what he's saying, but they sound a lot like words of worship as he continues past my chest to my stomach.

His strong hands trace a path down my ribs as those he's holding me in place, scared I'll run, and I should. God. What am I doing?

"Macushla," he says against my lower belly, and then he snaps the button on my jeans, "if you let me have you, you'll always be mine." He slowly kisses a line across the top of my pants and cups his hand to my pussy.

"Fuck," I purr and forget that I should be running.

"Your pleasure will be mine to have and control." I want to tell him to go fuck himself. I'm not a toy for anyone to have or control, but then he interrupts my thoughts by tucking his hands in the top of my jeans and pulling them over my hips. He leans down and places a kiss on the outside of my panties. "Your panties are soaked for me." A finger slips underneath the hem. He slides it back and forth over my center, soaking the digit in me. His free hand travels to my hip and snaps the side of the garment into two pieces. He pushes the remainder to the side and buries his face between my legs. "Bend your legs, love."

I bend my legs as he settles between them and licks my pussy before parting my lips and sucking on my clit. I have no idea which sounds or words escape me, but I find myself not giving a damn either. I'm also completely okay with the fact that Killian Kavanagh is licking my hoo-hah. I might not be later on, but right now, I accept it as reality. I also accept he's quite talented at the art of oral sex. Of course, he's had two millennia to perfect it. Hell, he probably invented it considering how great he is at it.

I buck my hips and bury my hands in the hair on top of his head as I pull him closer to me. "Please," I beg.

He turns his face to my thigh and presses his lips there in a kiss. "Tsk, tsk, tsk, Love. One," he begins his explanation, "you're still overdressed. And two…" he climbs me slowly, kissing the center of my body as he goes. "… the first time I make you fall apart, I want you wrapped around me. I want to feel your heartbeat and every breath you take."

I'm so desperate for him, I bring my hips up, lock them on his sides and roll us. "You're talking too fucking much." And then I grab his very impressive cock, line him up, and begin to sink down. It's not an impossible task, but he makes it a bit tough to take control when I'm not sure we're going to physically work together in the first place. His hands rest on my hips, concern etched on his face, as he waits for my body to give way to him. He's so quiet, so patient, I begin to feel a bit self-conscious. "I can't do this."

In a flash, I'm on my back, and he's over me looking down at me like I'm made of glass. "I'll give you what you want, Macushla. I'll give you what you need."

He begins to creep down my body again, headed for the Promised Land, but I stop him. "Can we just slow down?"

His blue eyes drink me in before he closes his eyes and nods. His lips find my chest once again, but this time he fully explores my breasts with his hands and mouth. I grow more aroused by the second, but I can't seem to completely let go. Maybe it's because we've never been together before. When I purr against him out of sheer pleasure, he starts to speak to me in his ancient tongue again, a language he seems drawn to when he's turned on.

He spreads my legs wider and lines himself up as he brings his mouth to mine. "Relax, my love. Let me care for you."

I don't relax. I feel like I'm about to lose my virginity again. The first time wasn't all that great. I'm not looking for a repeat, but then I smell his chocolate scent and hear the beginning notes of our song. My heart rate slows as I relax under his spell. He massages the inside of my thighs, freeing me further from my anxiety, and then he inserts two fingers inside me. He works me over slowly, never allowing me too close to the edge of bliss before he brings me back. All the while, he tells me how beautiful I am, inside and out. Normally, I'd argue the matter, but fuck it, I'm too involved in him to care.

When he drops his glamour, he whispers against my lips, "Are you with me, Zvi?"

The fog clears from his magic. "Yeah, I'm with you."

"Be sure. I don't want you to miss a thing."

"I'm sure."

He pushes inside as gently as he can. His muscles strain and quiver as he holds himself back. "Buíochas le Dia," he growls as he slowly slides in and out, opening me wider for him. "You are the best thing I've ever felt."

I lose myself in him and the rhythm of our bodies moving together like we've been lovers our entire lives. Time lapses and the Universe freezes as we tangle in a dance as old as him. I purr as he growls, and our bodies slide against one another as our song plays somewhere on this plane with us.

My muscles begin to twitch with the anticipation of my release. My eyes close as I prepare to jump off a cliff without a chute. My core tightens. My eyes fly open when he says my name, and at that exact moment, I fall to pieces. I vaguely remember asking him for more—more of this beautiful feeling. I'm also vaguely aware of him burying his face into my shoulder and the tips of his fangs puncturing my skin as he pulses inside me.

I turn my lips to his ear, still lost in the ecstasy of the moment. "Drink." His fangs sink in deeper, stinging at first, and then the discomfort is replaced by warmth. "More," I encourage him to take more than a little nip of me.

He picks up the pace until he's fucking me at a punishing tempo. "Fuck, Zvi!" he shouts as he raises his head from my shoulder and peers down at me. "I need you again. I need to feel you again."

And as if he commanded it, I come undone again, shouting his name, begging him not to stop, and he falls apart at exactly the same time.

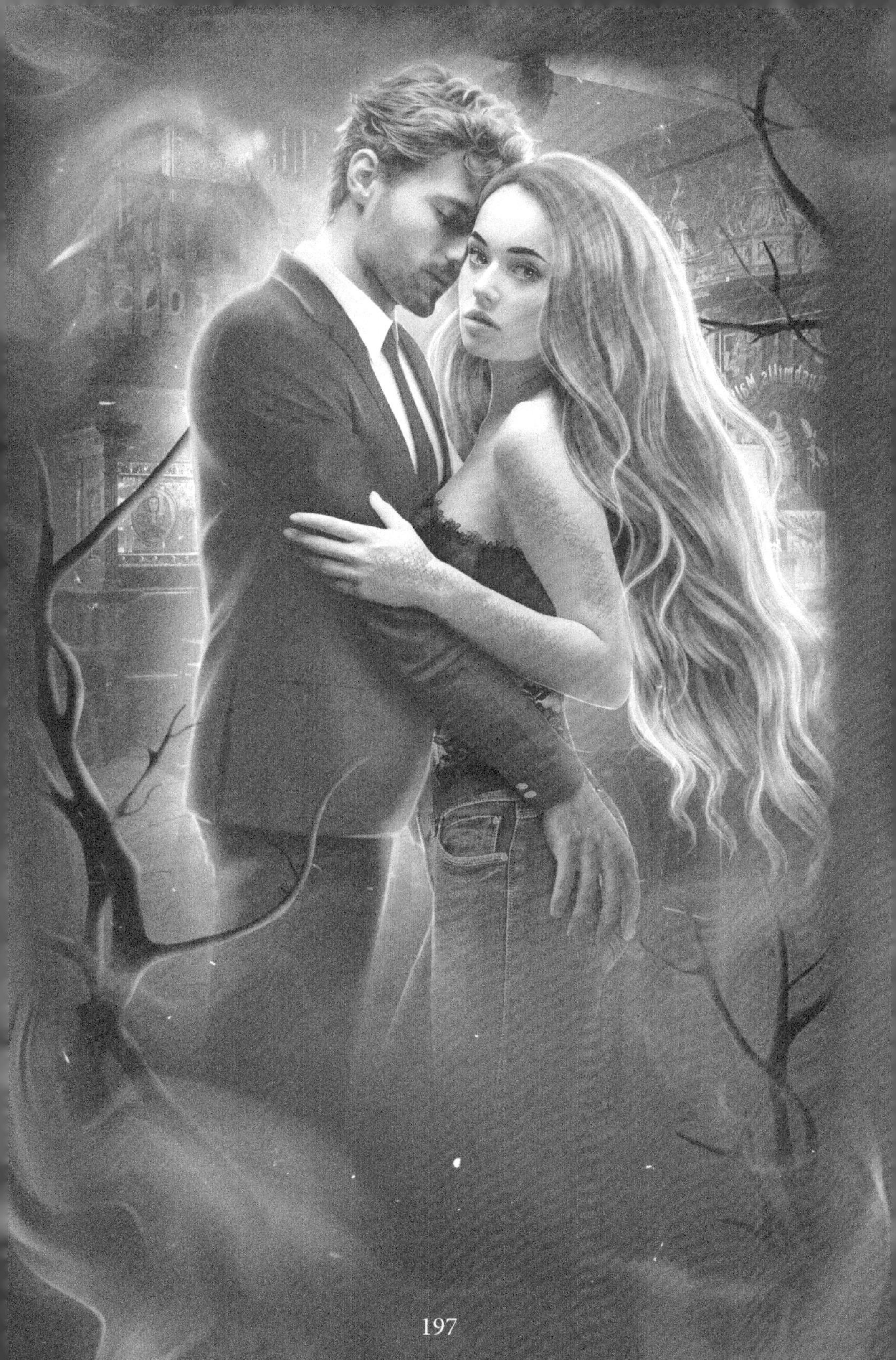

CHAPTER TWENTY-TWO

KILLIAN DRAWS LAZY CIRCLES on the small of my back as I trace a raised scar on his chest. It's a gash of an old wound, now white from time, and I imagine from changing over to vampirism.

"Did you have a choice?" I ask him.

"To become a vampire?"

I nod.

"Yes, but my master was not forthcoming about the tradeoffs of living as a vampire."

"What do you mean?"

"I didn't know anything about it, except that I would gain immortality. When you're dying, immortality can seem far more enticing than it is."

"You were dying when Gio turned you?"

"Yes, I'd been injured in battle," he says. "I was bleeding to death."

I trace over the scar again. "Here?"

His hand covers mine. "Yes, Macushla, I took a spear to the chest. Gio found me as I crawled home to my family in the late hours of the evening, hoping someone would be able to save me. Gio is quite charming to most, and he offered a dying man his last wish. Except, I didn't know I'd never see the sun again."

"You had a family?"

"I was blessed in having a rather large nuclear family. I was only a man of twenty-six when I died. It was rare for a man of my age to never have married, but I was busy protecting my clan's lands from neighbors and foreigners for many years. I was due to be wed two months after my death."

It's hard to imagine living in a time like that. It's equally difficult to imagine him with this whole other existence as a human. He was only two years younger than I am now when he was made into a vampire.

"What is it, my love? What are you thinking?" he asks.

"Did you love her?"

"The woman I was to marry?"

"Yes, her."

"I've never felt anything more than lust for a woman until I met you."

The sincerity in his voice scares me. I'm lying here open and bare for him, bleeding out emotions I've also never felt before. I'm too raw from the events of the past week and day to respond. I don't know what's real right now, or what this is I'm feeling for him. "I don't want to feel anything for you," I admit.

He kisses my forehead. "I know."

It's as if he senses the conversation is over. The intimacy, too, is over. I cut it off. It's time to shut it down. I have to get Moe back and move on with putting my life and business back together. "We should go. Hendri will want to see the video."

My clothes are scattered around the bed, and they're my excuse for pulling away. To my surprise, he allows me to go. He does lean up and press another kiss to the back of my shoulder right before I throw my tank over my head and escape the bed.

"Zvi," he calls after me.

I turn my back and finish dressing without replying.

He sighs, and then I hear him roll from the bed. I sit on the edge to put on my boots and have a look around the tiny room. There's a huge bed with a black headboard and black sheets. Matching nightstands are on either side of the bed, and there's a dresser against the south wall. Nothing adorns the four windowless walls.

"Where are we?"

"In the basement of Le Ambrogio. We're safe here."

"Where are Zarzos and Hendri?" I ask.

"Both are on their way here with my driver."

I turn and frown at him in time to see him push his arms through a white oxford shirt. The planes of his body are hard, defined, and delicious. When he died, he was in his prime.

He smirks knowingly. "Is there something I can do for you, Lady Jayden?"

I turn and try my best to ignore my growing irritation with him. "Why are we here? Is this where you sleep each day?"

"No, I don't sleep in the same place each day."

"Wise."

"Thank you."

I turn to him again and watch him work his tie into the perfect Windsor knot. His deft and capable hands remind me of the things he can do to my body. He smirks again like he knows all of my secrets, and I suppose now he does. "Why are we here?"

"I'm enlisting the help of the most ancient and powerful vampires on the continent."

"Le Ambrogio?"

"Yes, my Deputy Ministers. I wanted to catch them all at dusk, but I was too busy to meet them as they rose."

I roll my eyes. "You're never going to let this go, are you?"

He walks around the bed, stands in front of me, and offers me his hand palm out. I hesitate to take it, but I have to leave this room somehow, and it might as well be on the arm of the king fanger if I'm going to be surrounded by a bunch of the ancient critters as soon as I exit. So, I slip my hand in his and follow his guide as he gently pulls me to stand in front of him. He moves my long, purple hair to the side and leans down to kiss the spot where he bit me, and then he moves up my neck and over to my earlobe where he nibbles.

"Macushla, I know what you taste like when your pussy is wet for me. I know what you sound like when you fall apart on my cock. And I've fed from you. No, I'm not going to let it go. You are the most exquisite woman I've ever met. Why would I let you go?"

"You don't have a choice," I say, but my heart isn't in it. If I can't burn the fucker alive, I might as well get as many orgasms as I can from the situation. He'll tire of me soon enough.

There's a smile in his voice. "Come, my love. Let me be the envy of every vampire."

I'm almost a puddle as he disentangles himself from me. My spine and legs feel a lot like jelly, but I manage to pull it together and collect myself.

Killian offers me his arm on the other side of the door where we step into a concrete tunnel. "Fancy."

He doesn't offer a retort as we take a right and follow the passage to a steel door much like what you'd see in a casino, not that I have firsthand knowledge of casino safes. To the right of the door is a large digital display. Killian steps in front of it, and it first scans his eyes, then his entire hand, and finally, it takes a blood sample from a finger prick. It's the most impressive setup I've seen. I have no way of knowing how to bypass any of it, unless someone—an accomplice—was small enough to crawl between walls and chew through the wires.

"Why are you smiling like that?" Killian asks.

My brow arches. "Like what?"

"Like you're planning to take over the world."

"Where does this lead?" I ask as the door opens and exposes a small foyer with an elevator at the other end.

"It leads to Le Ambrogio headquarters."

"I got that, smart-ass."

He answers his ringing phone, and then he presses the elevator button. "We're coming up the elevator now." And then he hangs up.

While we wait for the car to arrive, he stands next to me, grazing his fingers against mine. I'd pay a lot of money to know what this fucking fanger has that gets my engine running, and I'd pay even more money to reverse it. When the car arrives, he places his hand on my lower back and guides me inside. Before the doors close, I'm spun around and backed into the corner.

He lifts my chin and brings my blues to his. He opens his mouth to say something, and then he tries again, but nothing comes out. A sea of emotions and thoughts flit across his face as he looks past my thorny front. His eyes are gentle as understanding passes through them. He whispers a simple, "Zvi". Then his eyes close slowly, and he presses his forehead to mine.

I don't hear the elevator door open nor am I aware we have an audience until I hear Zarzos giggle. Killian opens his eyes, looks into me once again, smiles, kisses me, and then he turns on his heel and escorts me out. Sebastian, Aleki, Killian's other regular henchmen, Zarzos, Barzul, and Hendri are all aptly watching us with barely suppressed grins from Le Ambrogio's expansive lobby. I'm going to have to kill them all now.

They all bow to the Minister, even Zarzos and Barzul.

"You've brought news?" Killian asks as he approaches the group.

Sebastian straightens and closes the space between. He sniffs me, smirks, and then pretends like it never happened as he pulls my hand into his. "The Fire Witch is near death."

I look to Killian. "What does this mean?"

"Her power will soon soak into the earth and is up for grabs by the first witch to complete the fire ritual."

"Moe doesn't have a shot in hell." I start to pace back and forth. "She doesn't have the blood. She has to drink the blood in order to become the Fire Witch."

"I have the goblet," Hendri advises.

"Yes, but we still need human, wolf, and witch blood."

The deputy supplies a local grocery store plastic bag with the handles tied into a knot. "Taken care of. We used Amelie-Madeline, mine, and Hannah's blood. Also, the goblet containing the blood is inside the bag."

Zarzos laughs like an excited child. "I put metal straws inside for Miss Moe, Lady Jayden."

I choke back tears at the mention of my sister and hope like hell she is able to use the demon's gesture and gift. "Considering Moe doesn't drink blood, we might also need a chaser."

The wolf pulls a flask from his back pocket. "Also taken care of." He walks it over to me and Zarzos follows like a little pup.

Zarzos laughs again when he reaches Killian and I, this time over the top and a bit maniacal as he's prone to do when he's excited. Then he starts to moonwalk as he simultaneously sings, "Bow-chica-wow-wow." When he's got it all out of his system, he moonwalks back to us and grins. "I love the smell of..." Hendri slaps a hand over Zarzos' mouth, but it's too late. We can still make out his muffled last words, because the demon doesn't let the wolf's hand deter him from speaking or spelling for that matter. "S-E-X!"

"*Oh, God*," I mutter.

"Zarzos," Killian says, smile in his voice, and then he leans forward and whispers to the demon like we aren't standing in a room full of vampires with excellent hearing, "it's impolite to talk about such matters publicly."

Confusion settles over the demon's narrow face. He turns his head to the side to look at Hendri with a question in his eyes, and then he thins his lips and looks to me with the same unspoken question in his eyes. He also leans forward, mimicking Killian and whispers in the same room of vampires. "Which matters?"

Jesus. I wave the conversation off. "It's not important. Thank you for coming. Do we have any updates or a possible location on Moe and Natasia? Do we know who the other players are yet?"

"Just Natasia. Karl is in lock-up at Black Star HQ. Everett and Greta are dead," Hendri replies.

Zarzos turns his nose to the air and sniffs. Not this again. "I smell a rat." And then he draws his sword at the same time knocking begins on the massive red double doors across the large lobby. Zarzos runs across the room and stands at attention, his sword drawn to the side, ready for battle. "Funny-smelling rat."

The knocking draws movement on the second-floor balcony which surrounds the ground floor lobby. A look up and around, and I count forty or more vampires, many of them ancient and powerful. Most of them are in suits as expensive as the Minister's. The women are also in power suits and look like they just stepped off the Congressional floor.

"What in the actual fuck?" Hendri mutters under his breath and puts his hand on his gun as he looks around to see what I see—we're really fucking outnumbered.

Zarzos' giggle is the only other sound that fills the marble room until the incessant knocking begins again.

"Is anyone going to get that?" I ask as the knocking keeps going.

"The guards are checking it out," Killian informs me.

I roll my eyes, stomp across the room, draw my gun from my side, sling the heavy door open, and stick my weapon in a man's face. "For fuck's sake, stop knocking."

He squeaks. "Lady Jayden?"

I lower my gun and find Rishi on the other side of it. "You're the wererat."

He pushes his glasses up his nose and nods. "Yes."

"Do I have to kill you today?"

His voice squeaks again. "No?"

"You're not sure?"

"I found them," he says, a smile spreading across his face. "I found your sister."

I yank him inside by the collar of his shirt, and when I do, I find about sixty more vampires surrounding the balcony above and part of the back lobby below. But eleven men stand apart from the rest. There's a dangerous air about them that not just any vampire possesses.

"Lady Jayden," Killian says and lowers his eyes as he bows to me, "the Deputy Ministers of Le Ambrogio."

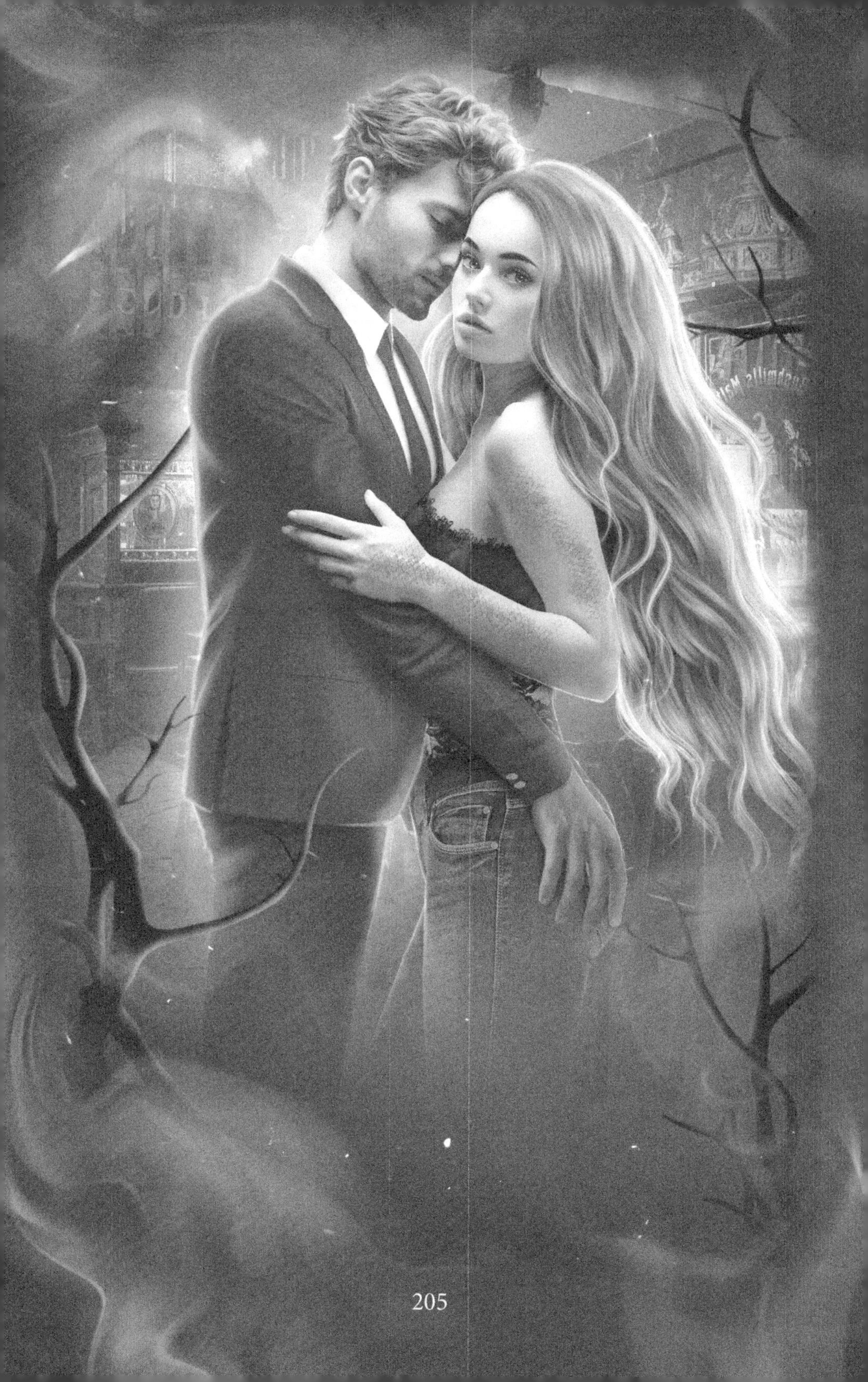

CHAPTER TWENTY-THREE

IF I WAS INTO deaders, I'd have a hard time picking my jaw off the floor. Being a member of Le Ambrogio must first require being extremely attractive.

Rishi closes the door behind us and leans over to whisper, "Your mouth is still open."

Clearing my throat, I holster my gun, close my mouth and drag Rishi across the lobby with me to where Killian and Hendri stand. Zarzos follows closely behind like I'm dragging a steak behind me.

"What is it?" I ask the demon.

He sloppily licks his lips like a drooling mastiff. "Rat."

I snap my fingers in front of his face. "Focus, grasshopper." His eyes clear of the hunger. "You cannot eat or bite Rishi."

"M'kay," Zarzos replies and hangs his head like Eeyore.

I finally release Rishi when I'm a little more sure my guard won't devour him, and then I turn to the wolf and the Minister. "He says he found Moe."

"Lady Jayden," Killian says, "I've called upon the Deputy Ministers and their employees to help bring Moe home."

My attention is called back to the fact that I'm basically at the center of 100 plus vampires' attention. I straighten my back, square my shoulders, and offer a nod to the room as my greeting.

"They'll assist with any assault efforts," he continues, "and virtually anything you want or need."

"Thank you," I say in a voice that sounds way more confident than I feel.

Killian looks up, around, and back down to the lobby as he continues a circle in the middle of the room. "Please go back to your offices and carry on with your duties while we convene with our war council."

My brows reach my forehead. "War Council?' I mutter to Hendri next to me.

He grunts. Not sure what that means.

At once, the room is filled with vampires zipping to and fro as they travel to their offices in the large six-story building, and then it's empty except for the eleven vampires behind Killian with their focus on me.

King Fanger extends his hand for me to take. "Please allow me to introduce you to the Deputy Ministers, my Love."

Normally, I'd buck at meeting the vamps. I don't want to know any more ancient, powerful vampires than I already know. It invites drama, vampire politics, and bullshit I don't want or need into my life. No, thank you. But tonight is outside of the norm, because people I would normally just as soon set on fire as knock their teeth out are willing to put their lives on the line to rescue Moe. So I graciously accept Killian's hand and allow him to lead me to the eleven gorgeous men.

The first vampire has a brilliant, white smile, and it's the first thing I notice after the long, dark lashes framing his honey brown eyes. He appears to be of African and Asian ancestry. "Tage Vang, the Deputy Minister of Louisiana," Killian says.

Tage Vang casts a brilliant smile in my direction. "Lady Jayden, the rumors of your beauty don't quite do you justice."

"Thank you," I say, genuinely endeared to him for some strange reason. Maybe it's his kind eyes. "And thank you for helping out tonight."

"Of course."

Killian moves us on to the next vampire. "Augustus Bon, DM of the Northwest."

He shakes my hand. "Please, call me August."

I don't have long to take in his inky hair, perfect five o'clock shadow, and devilish smirk before I'm ushered onto the next guy. They begin to blur after another two, but all of them are tall and handsome. There's a Scotish ginger dude, Shamus Corrigan, the DM of Michigan; Felix Valencia, DM of Mexico; Esteban Valentine, Deputy Minister of Texas; Ezra Devron, New England; Marius Jaymes, DM of the Southwest; Harlan Knight of California—tall, dark, and flirty; Adnan Mardini of Western Canada; and Bjorn Axelsson of the Midwest. It's a smorgasbord of hot men for those who prefer their lovers to be of the non-breathing type. By tomorrow I won't remember any of their names, except maybe the last one.

Killian and I come to the end of the line to a man with wavy, shoulder-length, dark hair kissed by the sun before he died his human death. His eyes are blue gray with a dark outer rim. They're as stunning as his king's. He inhales deeply, takes a step toward me, pulls my hand into his, and says, "Amadeus Fitzpatrick." And before he can finish his name, visions of him and Killian together in war and covered in dirt, invade my mind. There are other flashes of his memories that cross my brain barrier—all memories of him in battle or killing someone.

"Geez. Got it, homie. You're protective of King Fanger."

"Amadeus," Killian chastises, and the vampire releases my hand. The snaps of his past disappear with his touch.

"Forgive me, Master. I was simply trying to see if she's as formidable as they say."

I assume the master comment is for my benefit, to let me know Killian made Amadeus into not only the vampire, but the warrior I saw in his past, and therefore, a bond exists between the master and his child. It's a deep bond that can only be broken by death of the maker. Amadeus Fitzpatrick is telling me several things without saying much at all. First, he adores his master. Secondly, he's ancient as fuck, so they've been together a gazillion years. And last, he'll stop at nothing to lob my head from my body if I should ever cross Killian. I know that because he showed me him lobbing several heads off bodies without breaking a sweat.

I motion between Amadeus and myself. "Is there going to be a problem?"

His demeanor shifts. He softens a bit toward me. "He's never taken a consort." And that's all he offers in explanation of himself and his behavior—there's not a protocol in place for how to handle a consort, much less a faux-consort.

Touché.

Zarzos giggles and growls somehow at the same time sounding a lot like the Tasmanian Devil, and all of us turn to him. He's facing Rishi's side and poking him in the arm. "Rat." He giggles again, tickled to death at being in the presence of a wererat. Rishi looks like he's on the verge of a panic attack.

"Zarzos, if you eat Rishi, we'll never find Moe," I tell him.

The demon makes another giggle-growl sound and then turns on his heel like a soldier, saluting me and Killian, but he cuts his eyes at the wererat one last time.

Killian takes control of the room now containing the eleven Deputy Ministers, Killian's army, Aleki, Sebastian, Hendri, Zarzos, Barzul, and Rishi. "Rishi, can you remember exactly where they are?"

"Yes," he answers, "they have a small encampment outside the city. I wrote down the coordinates." He reaches into his back pocket, produces his wallet, and pulls a scrap piece of paper from it before handing it over to me. "It's an old empty hippie commune left over from the 1980's, north of Atlanta." He draws us a rough sketch of the property. "They were here in an abandoned red barn. Moe was tied to a vampire."

"Did you know the vampire?" Hendri asks his co-worker.

"No, I didn't, but I didn't go inside to get a closer look either. If Natasia had sensed me, I wouldn't be here."

"I'm glad you're here to tell us where to find Moe. You're going to be an excellent field agent someday," the Deputy tells him.

Rishi's eyes nearly pop from his head as his neck stiffens in terror. "Me?" he squeaks and nervously laughs. "No, I'm in IT."

The wolf reaches over and gently pats the nervous Nelly on the arm. "Talk soon."

Hendri uses a laptop to bring up the property on a satellite image, and then we plan our assault on Natasia. Rishi stands at the computer and points out key points of the property. "Vampires are located throughout the wooded part of the property that faces the highway. Demons are surrounding the barn. I was able to shift and have a peek inside."

"How's Moe?" I ask.

"She's magically bound with rope, but she was managing to sleep off and on while I was there."

I take a deep breath and try to relax a little in the knowledge that Natasia won't kill Moe until she's managed to finagle me there.

Killian's influence comes over me, calming me for once instead of riling me. I hear the song he plays for me as he whispers from across the way. "I can feel your pain, Macushla." And then a kneading sensation takes over the muscles in my shoulders. "Give us a second," he says.

I'm lost somewhere in his scent and the feel of his hands against my skin, when I realize my eyes are closed. Upon opening them, I see him staring down at me from his tall height.

"How did you do that from across the room?" I ask.

He pushes my long hair behind my ear and gently pinches the lobe. "Whisper to you?"

I try not to focus on his lips or how badly I want to kiss them. "Yes."

"Your blood is coursing through me. We're connected to each other."

"I thought a blood bond would require me to take your blood as well."

He leans down and softly kisses me. "I'm 2,000 years old and quite gifted in tracking and torturing my prey until they'd rather submit to me instead of enduring one more second of the mind fuck I put them through."

Killian Kavanagh is usually a refined vampire, and I assume he doesn't have to get his hands dirty. He has beau-coups of minions to do it for him, but the mere thought of him brutally hunting his prey turns me on. And I wish like hell it didn't.

"How are you?" he asks. "You were growing tense."

"How did you know?"

He pulls my hand to his lips and presses them to the sensitive skin. "Your blood, Macushla."

The bond is going to get old. "How long is this going to last?"

"Days."

"Fuck."

He smirks.

I frown. "We should return to the war council. I don't want to miss anything."

He pulls me flush against him, kisses the shit out of me, and releases me before he pulls me along to the lobby of Le Ambrogio.

"Ah, there you are," Amadeus greets us. "We were wondering who will lead the charge?"

"I will," Killian and I say at the same time.

Still holding my hand, he holds ours up and replies, "We will."

Hendri and Amadeus argue over the best strategy for infiltrating the demons while also avoiding bites.

"Use a sickle. It's what I do," I offer with a shrug.

"Proximity is still an issue," Amadeus says, an air of self-importance in his voice.

"Not if you're good," I reply, snark on full blast. "Scared of a little demon bite?"

"Have you ever been bitten by a demon, Lady Jayden?" Amadeus asks.

"Nope, because I'm that fucking good. Have you?"

"Yes."

I cringe. "That's tough. Well, best to avoid it a second time. You might want to stay back and let the professionals handle the demons."

The Deputy Minister's back stiffens at my insult. "I beg your pardon."

"Hey!" Hendri shouts and claps his hands together, the sound echoing through the large marble room. "You two want to have a pissing contest, do it on your own fucking time. Moe's life is in danger. We're pulling out in twenty minutes. We'll meet at the front of the property. We're Team 1. Black Star will comprise Team 2 and will come in from the creek at the back of the property."

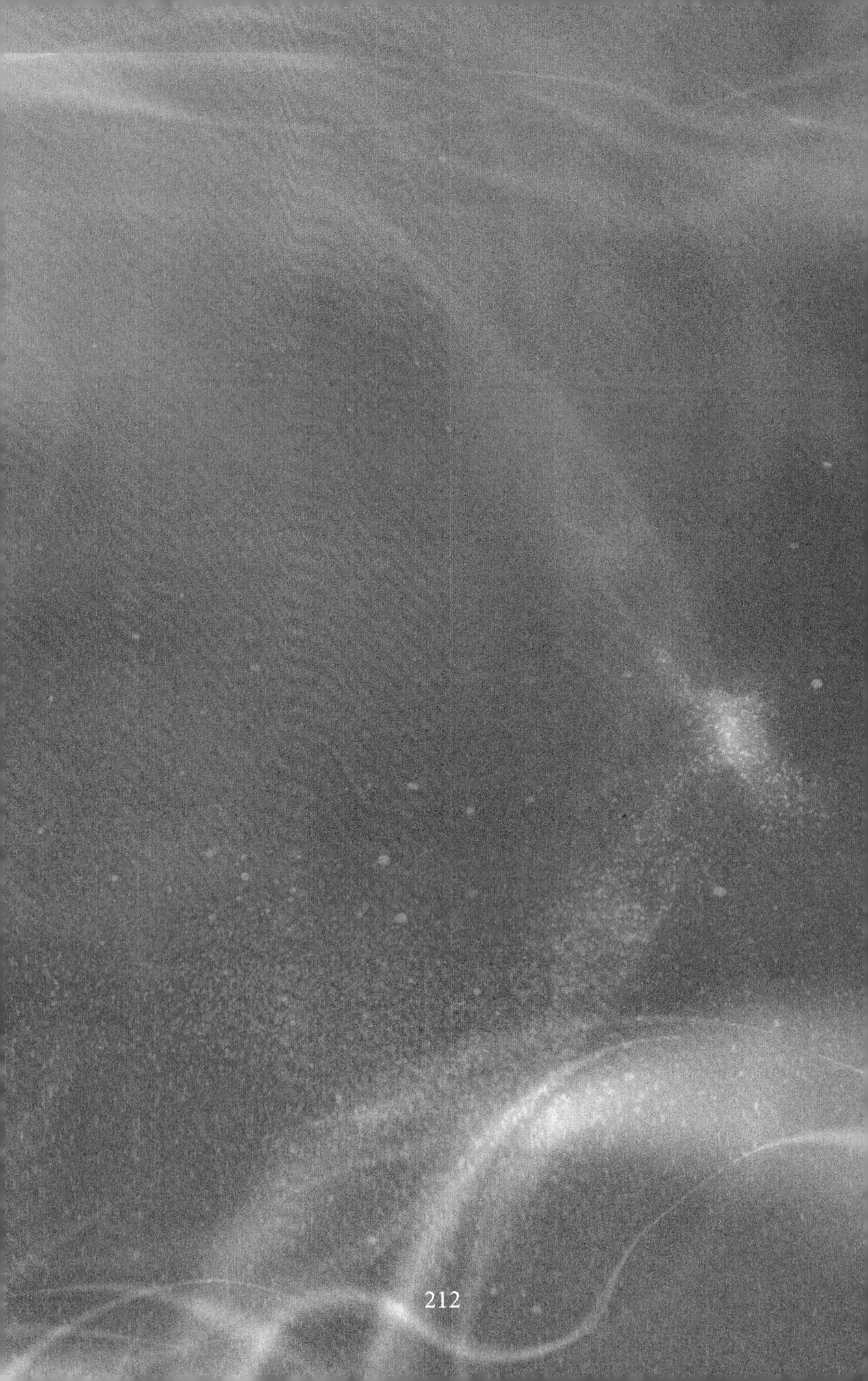

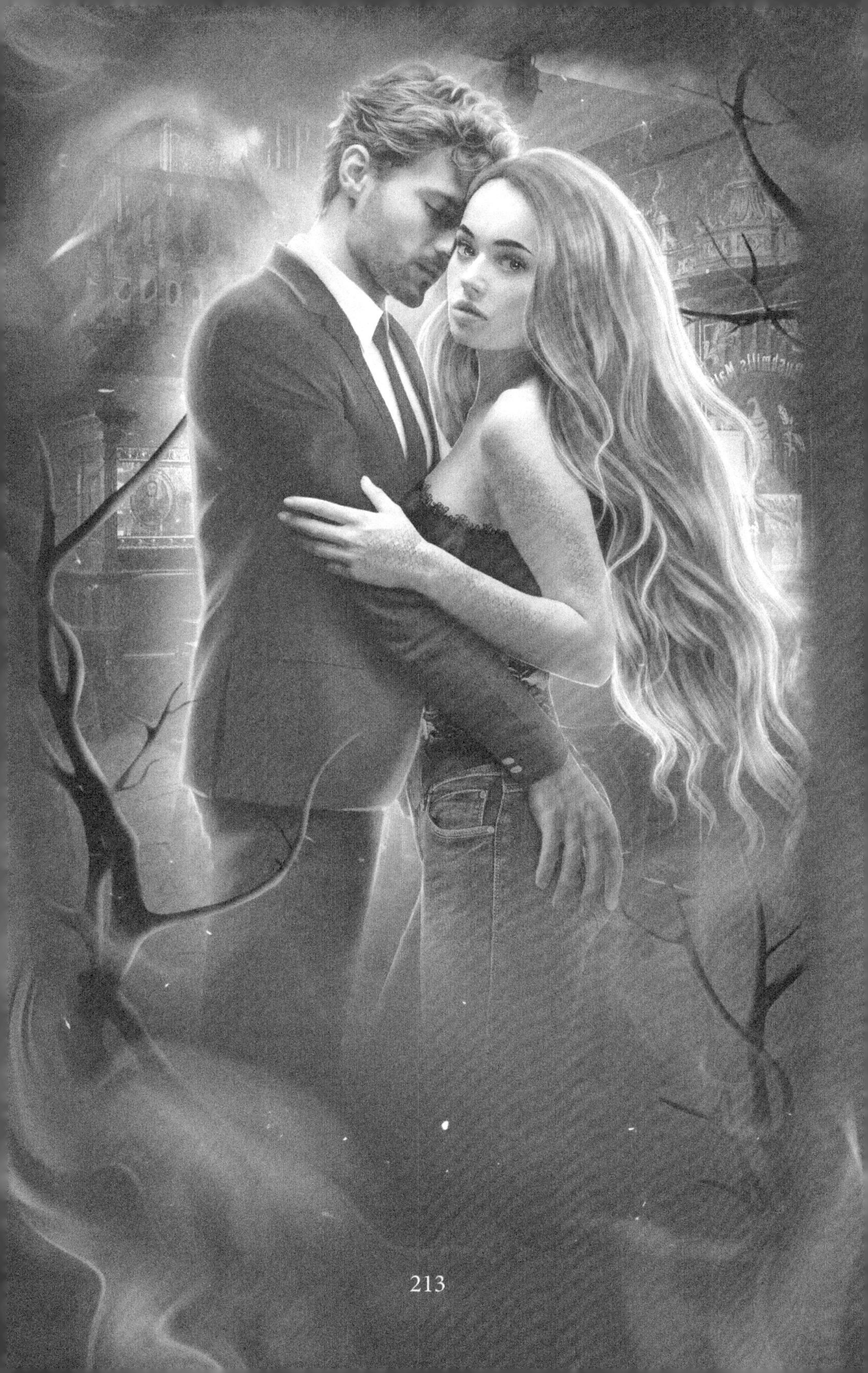

CHAPTER TWENTY-FOUR

THE WARM OCTOBER GUST sweeps across us as we step into the field just outside the big red barn Rishi described. There haven't been any vampires between here and the highway, but I can smell a lot of fangers and demons nearby. Team 1 quickly spreads wide throughout the field and rapidly descends on the structure. Killian is to my left and Zarzos to my right. Hendri's on the other side of my guard and Barzul and Killian's army bring up the rear. Behind them is an even larger army of over 100 vampires, many ancient and powerful, ready to wage war on behalf of their Minister.

Killian and I zip across the field in front of the army to check out the barn. It's dark inside and difficult to see anything through the wooden slats of the building.

"*There's no one here, Macushla,*" he says to me telepathically. "I'm never going to get used to that. Let's go back to the group."

I follow him away from the barn and back across the field to where they're spread out, standing still, not making a sound.

"Master," Killian says and breaks off to the right toward the back of the property and within the blink of an eye, he's gone.

I spin around to figure out where he got off to. "What the fuck just happened?"

"He's in trouble, Lady Jayden," Amadeus says. "Gio summoned him from nearby."

I can't say I'm surprised to hear the news. It's not like I thought Gio was a good guy, but for the life of me I can't figure out what in the hell he wants from a Fire Witch. I can however pin down Natasia's intention for Gio. "She's using his blood for the ritual."

Amadeus begins to pace. "Then the world is most certainly doomed if we don't stop her. She'll inherit any one of his abilities and all of them are dangerous for one person to have without the combination of her other inherited talents."

Hendri's hands go to his hips. "This is a clusterfuck of epic proportions. They aren't here. Kavanagh is gone, and he's likely a fucking a puppet now. I'm about to start shooting people."

Zarzos giggles and draws his sword. "Want to see if I can block the bullets with my sword?"

Hendri's face scrunches up so tight it looks like it hurts. "What?! No!" The Deputy's hands go to his face where they scrub up and down in frustration. "Jesus, Zarzos." He removes his hands and shakes them out at his side. "Okay, here's what we're gonna do…"

"And who put you in charge?" Amadeus asks with an air of superiority.

Hendri charges him. I jump in between. "Whoa there, Nelly! We're all feeling this, okay?" I look between the two men, both ready to tear the other's throat out. "Far be it for me to be the peacemaker, but we don't have a shot in hell at winning this thing if we're infighting. I need you both to get your shit together so we can rescue my sister. So, I'm the head motherfucker in charge from here on out. Either of you got a problem with that?"

Neither of them responds, and both are refusing to back down. I push at both of their chests. "Back the fuck up or you'll both have me to contend with." I put a finger in Hendri's face. "You know what you'd be up against. Don't fucking push me." I turn and stick my other finger in Amadeus' face. "You don't know, but I'll light your ass up if you don't get it together. Capeesh?"

Amadeus pulls at his jacket lapels. I don't know who fights in a freaking $2,500 suit, but there it is. Hendri huffs and walks away a few paces.

"Master," Amadeus says as he stiffens his back and looks past me into a plane I can't see.

"Not this shit again," I say and put my hands on my hips.

"Follow me, Lady Jayden," the vampire commands in a robotic voice, and then the fucker takes off toward the back of the property too. He doesn't zip away like Killian though. Amadeus walks slowly across the field, allowing us enough time to follow.

I shake my head. "Nah, I don't think I'm going to do that, homie."

"Kavanagh wouldn't lead you into a trap," the Deputy says. "Something isn't right though."

Aleki and Sebastian approach me. It takes a moment to realize they aren't themselves. "This way, Lady Jayden," they say in unison in a creepy voice.

"Uh-oh, spaghetti-O," Zarzos says and draws his sword.

"Fuckin' A," I agree.

And then the entirety of our army turns to me and says, "This way, Lady Jayden."

Zarzos' eyes grow as big as mine. "Whoa. That's creepy as fuck."

"Indeed," Hendri replies.

With dead eyes, our army turns and marches through the field and into the woods toward the back of the property. All that remains are the Dig'Dred brothers, Hendri, Rishi, and myself.

My hands go to my hips so they don't go to my hair and pull it out in frustration. "Well played, Gio, you fucking weirdo." I take a moment to gather my bearings, take a few deep breaths, and pull my big-girl panties up. I then pull my sickle from my side as I turn to the few remaining soldiers. "Let's fuck some shit up."

We take off for the back of the property, travelling through another dense piece of woodland as we go before we reach another open field. Bingo.

Gio is there to greet us. Fifty yards behind him is my sister and she's tied to Shaw Benton. Natasia is beside them, but I'm not surprised by her presence. I'm surprised by the woman standing beside Gio though.

"Helpful Helen?"

Helen laughs non-humorously. "Not quite."

"Well, are you going to put me out of my misery or are we playing that stupid game where I guess incorrectly a bunch of times before you finally tell me yourself anyway?" I ask. I have another look around but don't see Killian, Amadeus, Aleki, Sebastian, or any of the hundred or so vampires who were last seen walking this way. "Where's my posse?"

She offers me a smile—one that appears inviting and kind—but I wasn't born last night. I'm not trusting the heifer as far as I can throw her. Natasia walks over to a burning torch stuck in the ground, removes it, and throws it to the left away from everyone. A large circle ignites at once, illuminating much more of the vast field where I now see hundreds of vampires standing perfectly still, watching like vampire Stepford wives.

I keep my eye on Helen and Gio outside the circle while also keeping tabs on Natasia inside the circle with Moe and Shaw. Gio still hasn't said anything. Should I be more nervous that he's strangely quiet. "'Sup, Fucker? Cat got your tongue? You're usually so chatty, never really shutting the fuck up."

He offers a slight bow. "Lady Jayden, please meet my queen, Selene."

I recall a conversation I had with Moe a few weeks ago, which seems like an eternity ago, and after a few seconds I remember exactly where I've heard Selene's name before. "The goddess of the moon?"

Helen transforms into Selene before my eyes. She is a beautiful woman with long, perfectly curled chestnut brown hair and intense sapphire eyes like the night sky. "You've heard of me?"

"You could say that."

"So many are ignorant of their histories."

"What's going on here?" I finally ask when no one offers an explanation as to why we're all here in the first place.

"I was punished for loving Ambrogio," she says. "Cast out of Mt. Olympus and down to earth where I'm to live a human existence until I'm freed and allowed to return home." She reaches over and grabs Gio's hand, squeezes it affectionately, and smiles at him before focusing her attention back on me. "I have much work to do for us when I return."

"Can the Fire Witch send your ass back to where you came from?"

"No, but she's the only witch with enough power to give the ability to walk in the sun to a vampire."

This is news to me. "Cool story. Learn something new every day. What in the hell does that have to do with the price of nail polish in China?"

"I cannot return to my home until a vampire walks in the daylight."

I shake my head at her. "Tsk, tsk, tsk. Silly girl. I think your sentence was meant to be eternal, not become fulfilled."

Gio interrupts our powwow. "For the life of me, I cannot understand what my child sees in you."

I shrug. "I'm kind of a big deal, if I do say so myself, and while we're on the topic of you, I'd like to tell you something about you that you don't know."

I pause for dramatic flair.

"Well?" Gio asks, not appreciating my drama at all.

"You're about to have a really bad day."

Zarzos giggles to my left, Hendri begins to shift to my right, Rishi is missing in action, Barzul grunts and takes his suit jacket off in preparation for battle, and I attach my sickle to my belt. If I'm opening a can of whoop ass on the creepiest fanger of all, I'm taking his ass down with my bare fists.

Zarzos bounces up and down and makes the Tasmanian Devil sound as he prepares to do his favorite thing in the world. "Fucking shit up!" He laughs again, and then he yells, "Charge!!!"

At once, we launch ourselves across the field. Gio and I collide with one another and instantly go to the ground, roll around, and try to land punches on each other. I grunt when he lands his fist in my kidney, but I shake the pain off and land one in his throat. His hands go to his neck as he attempts to reattach his Adam's apple. I throw another punch into his nose. It spurts a crimson river down the front of him, and the stale scent of the oldest vampire's blood fills my nose.

Gio knees me in the crotch and my pelvic bone shatters into pieces. I roll off him and onto the ground while I cover my pelvis to prevent any further injury. I heal incredibly fast, but that doesn't mean I don't incur the pain of the broken bones. The healing part isn't exactly easy or painless either. He jumps to his feet after he's able to heal and staunch the bleeding. He closes the small space between us and pulls back his leg before he lets it fly at my face. I roll to the left to avoid the direct hit to the face, knowing it will clip me in the temple instead, but the blow never comes to pass.

I turn back to find Barzul holding Gio's head in his hands, ready to pull it from his shoulders.

"Barzul, no!" I scream.

Gio's eyes grow wide as he realizes he doesn't have a shot in hell if Barzul carries through.

Zarzos speaks quickly in his native tongue, and Barzul stops pulling on Gio's head like he's a Barbie Doll, but he doesn't release him.

"Release my people," I order Gio to drop his glamour and return my army to me.

Two seconds later, Killian and Aleki are by my side. Killian offers me his hand and helps me stand, although I don't manage to stand straight right off the bat. The Minister takes a few seconds to ensure I'm okay, and then he and Gio tangle up as Barzul releases him.

"Lady Jayden!" Zarzos yells. "Get Moe out of there!" he says as he points to the circle of fire.

Inside the circle, Natasia weaves her magic as she chants her incantations in Latin. One look in Moe and Shaw's direction, and I spot a large rat chewing at the magical bonds that were used to not only tie the two up, but also ensure they couldn't use any magical abilities. I fly through the wall of fire like a mad woman with a war cry on my tongue. Natasia is preoccupied with her ritual and doesn't see me in time to miss me bulldozing her at the waist.

"Oomph," she says as she flies in the air a few feet and lands flat on her back. The magic she had brewing like a cloud hanging in the air disintegrates and falls apart. When she hits the ground, she tucks and rolls away from me.

    I follow her and pull my sickle from my belt to lob her head from her body and end this once and for all, but I'm tackled to the ground from behind by a demon. As he snarls and wraps his hands around my throat, I pull my knees into my chest and bury the sole of my boot in his stomach, and then I shove him off. He flies several feet in the air before landing a few yards from me. Typically, demons are quick. They don't stay down long, but I have the advantage of surprise. Demons are always so surprised in the moments before you cut the head from the body, like they can't believe any other being bested them, and this demon is no different. His head rolls halfway across the large circle before coming to stop in front of Moe who quickly kicks the head away.

    Natasia has begun to weave her spell again, and as I'm about to charge her another time, I'm stopped by the sudden urge to shift. I look across the way to the witch and see it in her eyes—she's found a way to force me to give her my fire— and that's a very, very bad thing. Still, I do have control over which direction my fire travels, and there's no way she's getting in the direct line of it if I have anything to say about it.

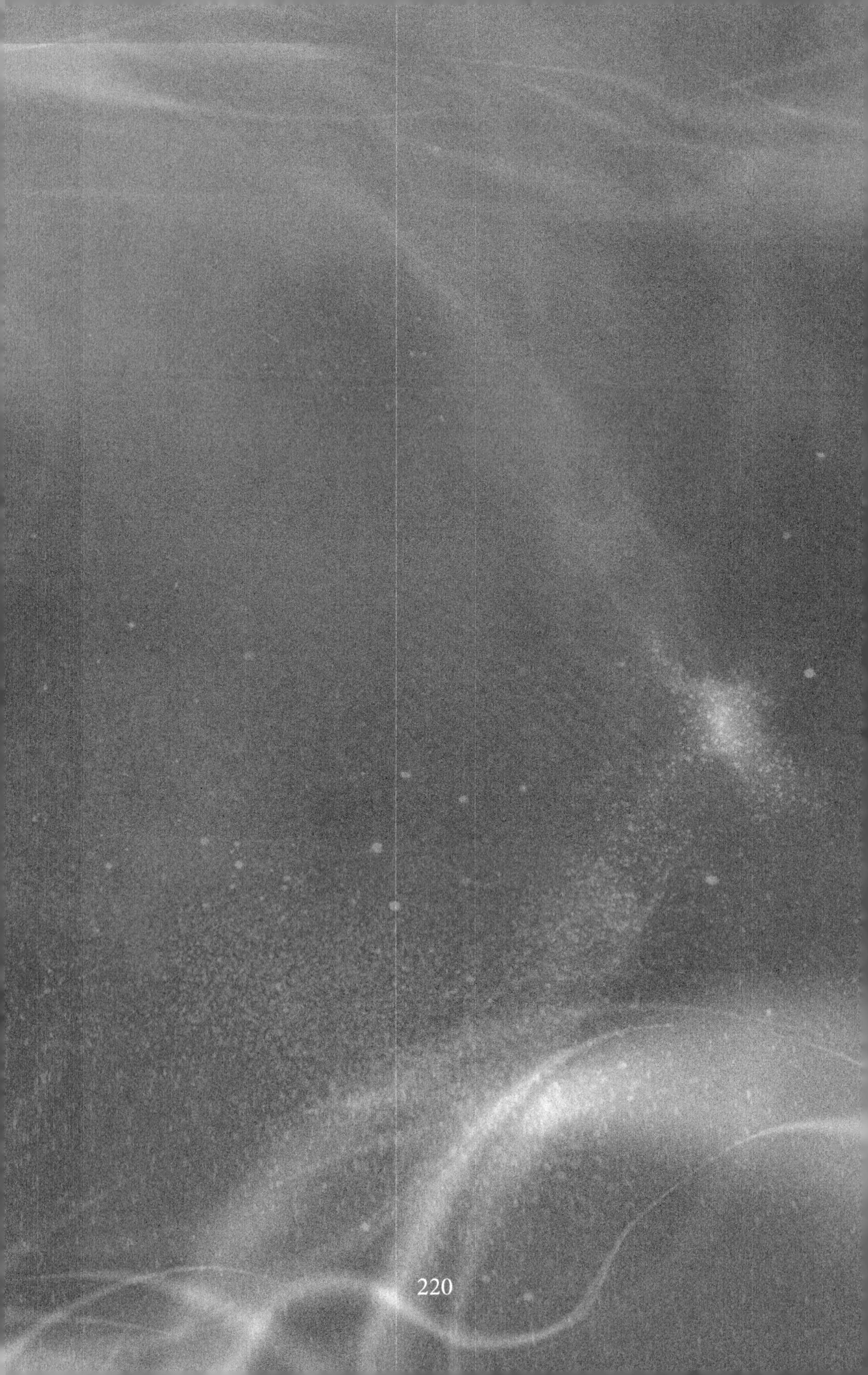

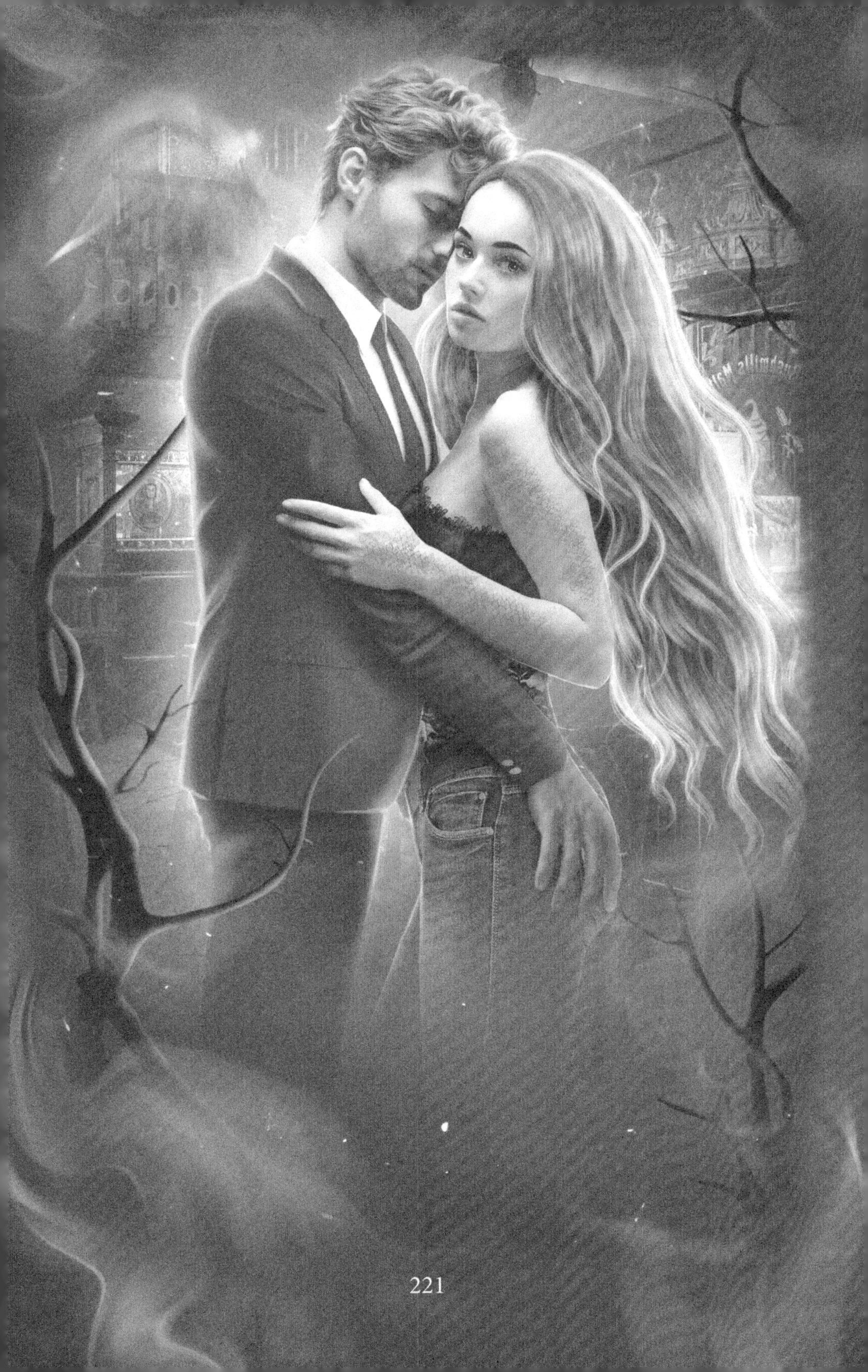

CHAPTER TWENTY-FIVE

MY CLAWS PROTRUDE FROM my nails as Natasia's magic pushes me into my other nature. My wings form on my back, and purple scales replace my human skin. I scream in pain as my bones break from being forced to shift. Natasia isn't easing me into it, letting me take my time and make it as painless as possible. I shoot into the air over everyone and flap my wings as my screams turn into roars of anger.

The entire field comes to a standstill as the fighting stops, and they all turn their heads to take in something they didn't believe existed anymore before this very moment—a dragon. And then, it's as if someone presses play. The vampires collectively panic at once, running over one another and zipping across the field to escape my path. They hide in the tree line of the forest, hoping I won't notice them. The demons on both sides cheer because they're all a bit insane when they're excited. There's still a group of vampires in the middle of the field, their backs to each other as they ready for the next onslaught of enemy combat—Aleki, Sebastian, Augustus, Tage, and Amadeus.

But Killian stands in the middle of them all, arms hanging at his side with a look of wonderment on his face. He raises his right hand to his lips, kisses his index and middle fingers, and then he lowers it to lay over his heart. "Fly away, álainn."

Fire starts to bubble in my gullet, which means I have very little time to get away before it has to come up and out. With one last look at Moe, Natasia, Hendri, and Zarzos, I turn and fly away. I have to hope and trust that Zarzos, Hendri, and Killian have my sister's safety and rightful place as the Fire Witch as their only interest and goal.

I find a large pond not far away and dive into the cool water as I push the fire from inside me. My flame is so hot, it turns a portion of it into steam. I shoot out of the water as I'm pulled back in the direction I came from. It feels like I'm being dragged by the nose. It gives me no time to gain the altitude I need to miss the tree line. I bump and practically roll across the trees, the tops of them poking and jabbing me like needles. I manage to muffle the roar of pain that leaves me, but just barely.

Shit. That hurts.

I crash land into the creek at the back of the commune property and injure my left wing on a jutting rock formation. An unintended screech of pain leaves me, but I fight like hell against it until I get to my feet and leap into the air, flapping my wings as much as I can. If I get my hands on Natasia Portnova, I'm going to break every bone in her worthless body.

I find my way back to the field, still being pulled by the witch's magic, and hover above her casting circle. I'm being forced to fly low like someone is pulling my tail to the center of the circle. My broken wing and flying this low to the ground is quickly expending my energy. I begin to tire to a point where I know if she forces me to breathe fire again, I might not be able to fight it.

Movement in the circle catches my attention as Moe and Shaw break away from each other, finally freed by Rishi, who scurries away behind Moe. Shaw's blood-curdling scream fills the night and pulls my attention back to him. There's a demon at his neck. Shit. I knock the demon away with my wing, but it's too late. A huge chunk of his neck is missing. The venom from the demon's bite will work its way through his body and cause immense pain. He'll survive it, but he'll wish he didn't.

The demon comes for me after he scrambles to his feet. I use my tail to knock him out of the casting circle. Zarzos is standing on the other side and brings his sword down on him. My guard walks through the fire and checks out the situation before walking over to Moe and Rishi. He scoops the rat up, putting him on his shoulder like a parrot, and then goes after Natasia with his new sidekick attached and likely pissing himself.

Natasia strikes Zarzos down with magic, a flash of lightning that has him retreating a few steps. Moe takes the moment and the element of surprise while Natasia is focusing on my guard to knock the dark witch's teeth out. I've never seen Moe throw a punch until she rears back and clocks Natasia right in the side of the jaw, rocking the crazy woman back a few steps.

Natasia recovers quickly and rushes my sister. She wraps her hands around Moe's throat and squeezes. I'm helpless to do anything but watch. Zarzos can't do much, but Rishi can. The wererat runs across the way to the witch and bites the bitch on the ankle. Her scream fills my ears at the same time Zarzos launches himself at her and saves Rishi from her wrath.

Hendri leaps through the fire with a bag in his mouth—the bag with the blood and the goblet. He runs it over to Moe. My sister wraps her arms around his neck as he drops the bag to the ground. Natasia runs for her and the wolf jumps in front to protect her while she digs into the contents of the bag. I flick my tail and sweep Natasia's feet from underneath her to buy Moe additional time in which to drink the blood.

Moe holds her nose and downs the concoction in one swallow. Hendri begins snarling, growling, and snipping as Natasia regains her footing and gets closer. My sister bends at the waist, and I think she's about to upchuck the blood, but she manages to keep it down.

Gross.

"Now, Lady Jayden!" Zarzos yells as he tangles with Natasia's dark cloud of magic.

It's now or never—it's time for me to do my part of the ritual. I flap my wings harder, now almost fully healed from the break, but I can't fly more than a few feet higher than I am. My flame is too wide to concentrate on just Moe, and with Hendri so close, I'd roast him, too. I roar in frustration, pissed this isn't fucking working.

The Deputy takes over, grabs the hem of Moe's shirt and drags her to the edge of the circle. I close my eyes as they run through it and hope like hell they make it to the other side in one piece.

When I open my eyes again, a swarm of robotic enemy vamps surround them. I continue to fight to fly high enough to focus my flame, but Hendri is still in my line of fire. I screech at him to leave the circle, hoping he'll understand me, but if he leaves the small open area they're encased in, the fangers will tear him limb from limb.

Killian and Tage Vang show up out of nowhere and separate Moe and Hendri. Tage pulls Hendri from the area as my muscles begin to quiver from overexertion. I flap my wings past the point of exhaustion as fire begins to bubble inside me again. Natasia breaks through the throng of vampires, chanting in Latin as Moe begins to chant in Gaelic.

"Do it, Zvi!" Killian yells at me to finish, but the fire would cover him and Natasia as well. He'd die and she could become the Fire Witch.

As the urge to release my flame grows, I crane my neck up and shoot it into the sky. The need to release begins to grow again immediately. I hold it in as Moe breaks away from Killian and runs to the other side of the throng of vampires. I aim my fire at her, but hesitate because what if this doesn't work and I kill my own sister?

"Zvi!" Moe turns and pleads.

I can't believe I'm going to do this. I take a deep breath and fill my lungs with air. In the span of half a second, before my fire can reach Moe, Natasia rushes inside the path of my flame and throws herself beside my sister. Killian is on her heels and snaps her neck as the flame engulfs all three of them.

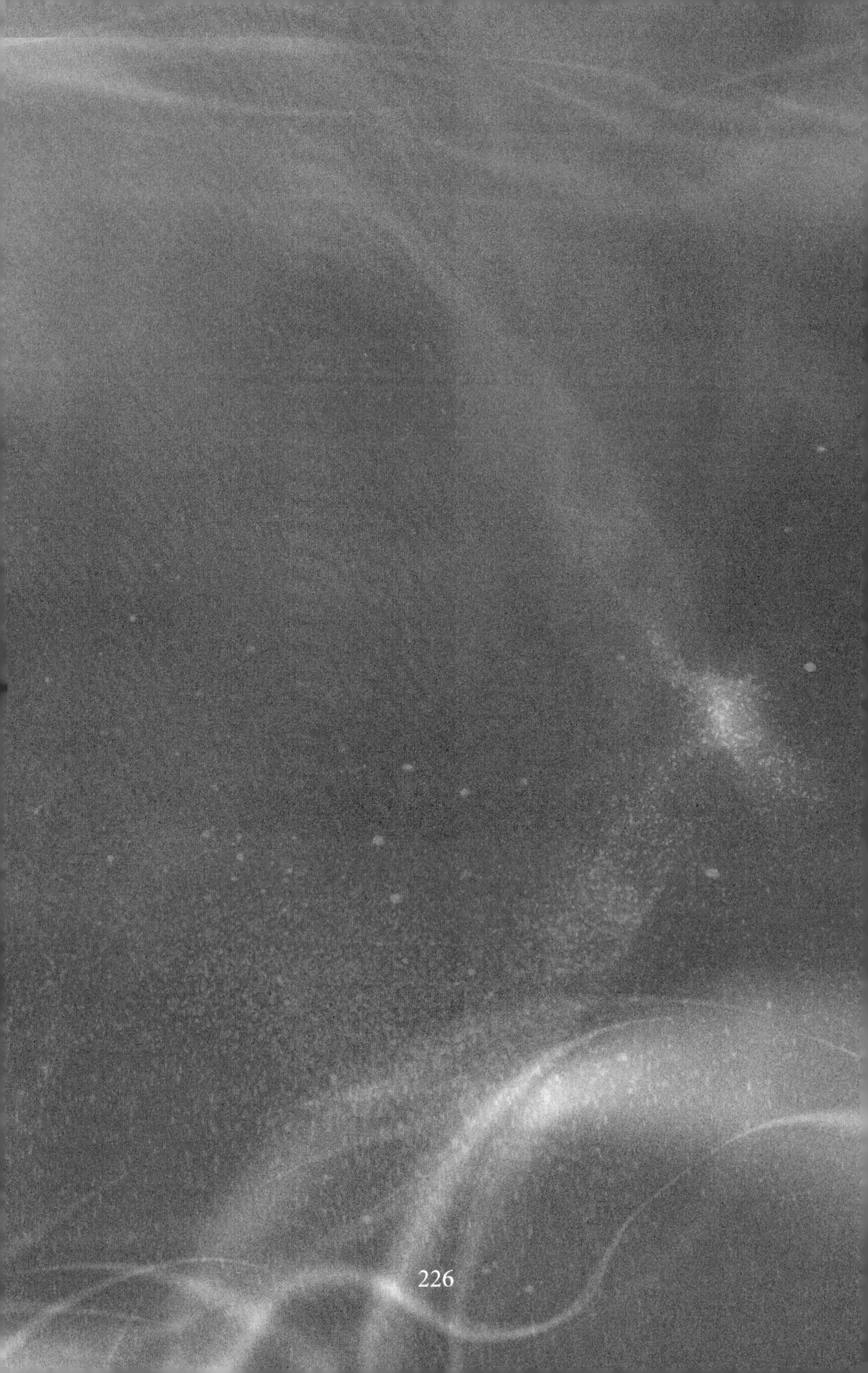

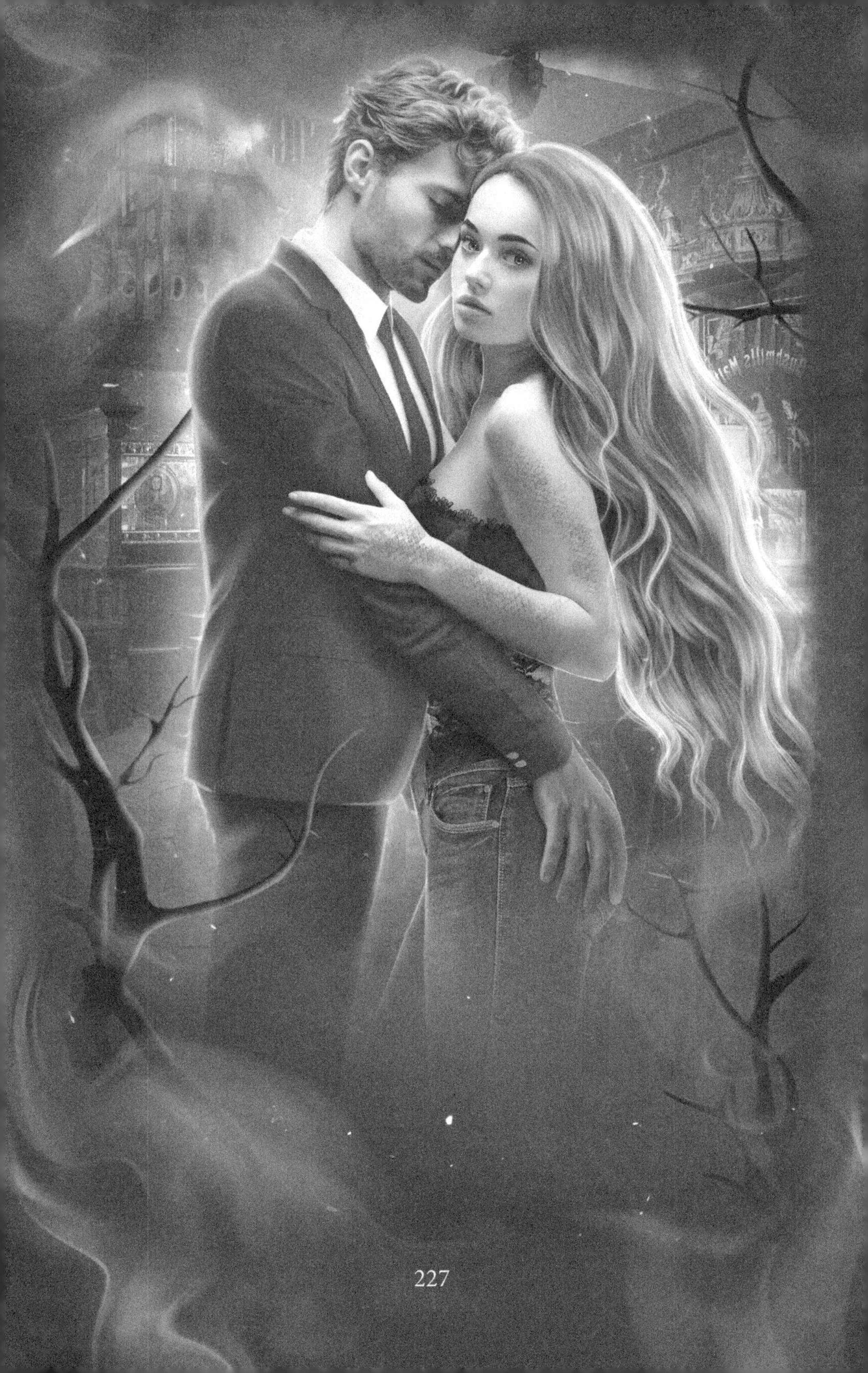

CHAPTER TWENTY-SIX

HOPE IS A FUNNY thing—it can exist, even against all odds. It doesn't mean the outcome will be what was hoped for, that a miracle will happen, but a miracle is exactly what I hope for in the small eternity it takes for the smoke to clear.

I hear Hendri's bark at the same time a helicopter flies over the field shining a light on the situation on the ground. I'm afraid to move, scared I'll crush anyone below my feet, so I remain just outside of Natasia's casting circle and several yards from the charred ground and thick smoke cloud that hangs heavy like fog. Hendri continues to bark from the general direction of the bodies, but I can't see him through the haze.

The vampires begin to emerge from the forest and creek areas on either side of the field. Slowly, they converge on us with all eyes on me. I couldn't care less that most will now know of my existence, because I won't likely be known as just a dragon. I'll be the dragon who killed her sister and Killian Kavanagh.

A bright magical light flashes in the area of the cloud and colors it blue before it vanishes. I don't know what it means. Is it what happens when the fire ritual fails? Or is it what happens when you kill an ancient vampire? I've never killed one. They're ancient for a reason—they've learned how to survive in the face of insurmountable odds.

The cloud begins to rise as I feel something climbing up my back like I'm a rock wall. I turn to find Zarzos, but the expression on his face is unreadable. I have no way of judging whether he's about to deliver two pieces of bad news or just one. My heart sinks and dread fills my stomach as it takes him forever to reach the top of my shoulder. He makes it up to it and has a seat. "I thought I'd sit with you, Lady Jayden. I'd want my best friend to sit with me while I wait, too."

A tiny little flame is the first thing I notice as the cloud rises up by my head and makes it impossible to see much more. I duck down to take in the scene below and find a naked Moe sitting on her knees with her right palm open and the tiny blue and orange flame dancing in it. The wolf kneels beside her and Barzul stands at her back protecting our new Fire Witch from anyone who would dare harm her. Killian's body lies in front of them unmoving. I don't understand. He should be ash.

Zarzos slides down my shoulder and arm, lands on the ground, draws his sword, and heads for the vampire king. "Move," he tells the vampires and demons in his path between Killian and I, "make room for Lady Jayden."

When the crowd parts for me, I get close to Killian and try to make sense of his body still being intact. I hold my breath, afraid one deep exhale from me will have his ashes scattering in the wind. Aleki, Sebastian, and each of the Le Ambrogio Deputy Ministers kneel around their king and bow their heads in respect. The scene chokes me with emotion. I killed him. I threatened to do it. I thought I meant it. I thought I meant a lot of things, but now I'm not so sure, because I'd give just about anything to look at his marbled blue eyes again and to feel all these things when I do.

My chest feels like it's being ripped apart as a stupid, gigantic tear rolls from my eye. I want to scream, to roar at the top of my lungs so the entire world also feels my pain. I can't do this. I can't look at him anymore and try to be stoic.

I slowly back away from Killian. I take in the scene below me again and when I'm sure the Dig'Dred brothers and Hendri will protect Moe, I turn and leave. I hold it in as long as I can. I make it 100 yards away before I take a running start down the field and run away from the tragedy I created behind me. My wings work up and down until I take flight and climb higher and farther away from here.

Before I can completely fly out of sight, the sobs come, and everyone below hears my devastation as my screeches and roars echo throughout the night. God. Why did that fucking fanger have to get under my skin? Why did he ever come into our bar? I was doing just fine in my quiet little life right by my lonesome. I was fine. Great. Fucking perfect.

He's such an asshole, and now the asshole is a dead fucker... again. Ugh. Who jumps in the path of a fucking flame? Who survives two millennia and just decides to end it all in a split second? Fuckity fucking fuck! If he wasn't already dead by my hand, I'd set his ancient, gorgeous ass on fire again just for being a dumb ass.

I fly out to the river and dive into the cool waters hoping it will wash it all away—erase the past two weeks and give us a different ending where my sister doesn't have to be the Fire Witch and that fucking fanger isn't dead. And it doesn't hurt so freaking much that he's gone forever.

It hurts so much that his scent is stuck in my nose and his voice in my head murmuring ancient gibberish. I turn in the river and swim against the current, push harder to tire myself out until I can go home and crash. Except, I remember I don't have a home or a bed. Everything I have is at Killian's or bought especially for me by him. His ghost is everywhere.

Macushla.

I manage to make some headway against Mother Nature. For a few minutes, I make her my bitch, but she does exactly what I need her to by exhausting my body. I hope that mental and emotional exhaustion will follow.

Macushla. I'm never getting the stupid fucking Irish accent out of my head. *Fly back to me, my Love.*

I rage inside and fly out of the water as fast as I can, the surface stinging my face and eyes as I come up. I shake the water from my body as I fly aimlessly toward the western state line. I roar as our symphony fills my ears.

Listen.

I can't help but hear it, but listen and suffer through it. My cries keep coming. This is so stupid. We slept together once, and he was an annoying, smug shit half the time. Fuck him for dying.

Zvi.

If I wasn't in my dragon form, I'd be at the hiccupping stage of crying at this point. I've never cried this hard in my life. His scent warms me from my tail to my head, stronger than it's ever been. I close my eyes and let it wash over me—his scent, his voice, our song, and the sleepy feeling I always get when I'm in his arms.

I feel the pull of my sister's magic—a familiar, comforting feeling—although it's not the bond at all. And yet, her magic has a different feel and vibe to it. I resist her pull for a few moments before I decide I need to be strong. She's just become the Fire Witch. Her life and her very existence are going to substantially change. She needs me, so I turn back for the commune.

The sky is clear this far outside the city. It's not a bad flight back as I return, and my energy and rage are dissipating as exhaustion takes over. I'll have to change back as soon as I land in the field. My stomach begins to growl from hunger, but I have no appetite for anything at all. I just want to sleep for a few weeks. It'll feel better when I wake.

I soar over the creek and then the field where the battle occurred. I dodge a few helicopters making rounds of the property. I have no idea how they're going to identify all the vampires and demons involved, but Black Star won't stop until they do.

I shift as I drop behind the empty shed at the front of the property where we first entered. I don't have a go-bag, so I peek inside the shed hoping something was left behind from its earlier use, but nothing is inside except old hay bales stacked against the far wall.

The shed door slams shut behind me. I turn on my heel.

"Macushla."

I blink in the dark shed, but I'd know that voice anywhere. I'd know his presence in a sea of beings. I close my eyes, not willing to believe it, not willing to allow myself to hope a second time.

I don't know whether to lean over and vomit from the pain or run and wrap my arms around him. I don't get to do either since the shed door opens behind him, and Black Star runs in with flashlights and guns pointed at me.

Killian, alive and well, and somehow redressed in jeans and a sweater, walks through the men with bare feet, slowly covering the ground between us. I don't let myself hope too much. He could be a ghost, because no one in Black Star seems to mind that he's walking straight for me.

When he reaches me, he removes the light-colored sweater and places it over my naked body. His hand comes to my cheek, and his forehead rests against mine. Neither of us says anything for the longest time. Either ghosts don't speak, or he doesn't know what to say any more than I do.

He sways us as our song plays softly in the background. His deep voice hums along and sends me onto another plane. The deputies and their guns disappear as he takes my hand and twirls me around until I come back to face him, his blue eyes already on me and full of things I'm not sure I'm ready for.

"Zvi," he whispers, my name thick on his tongue, and then Black Star converges on us.

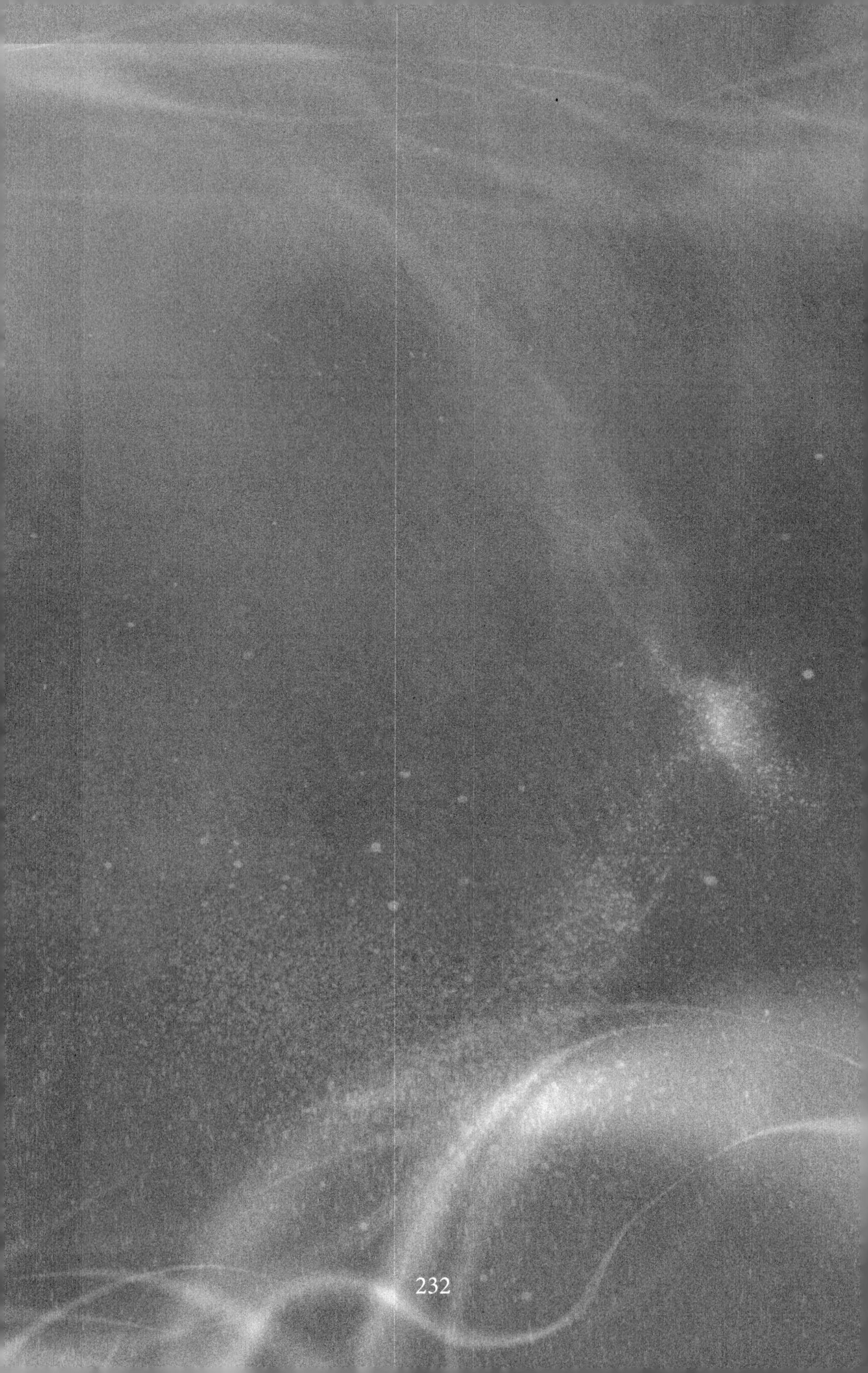

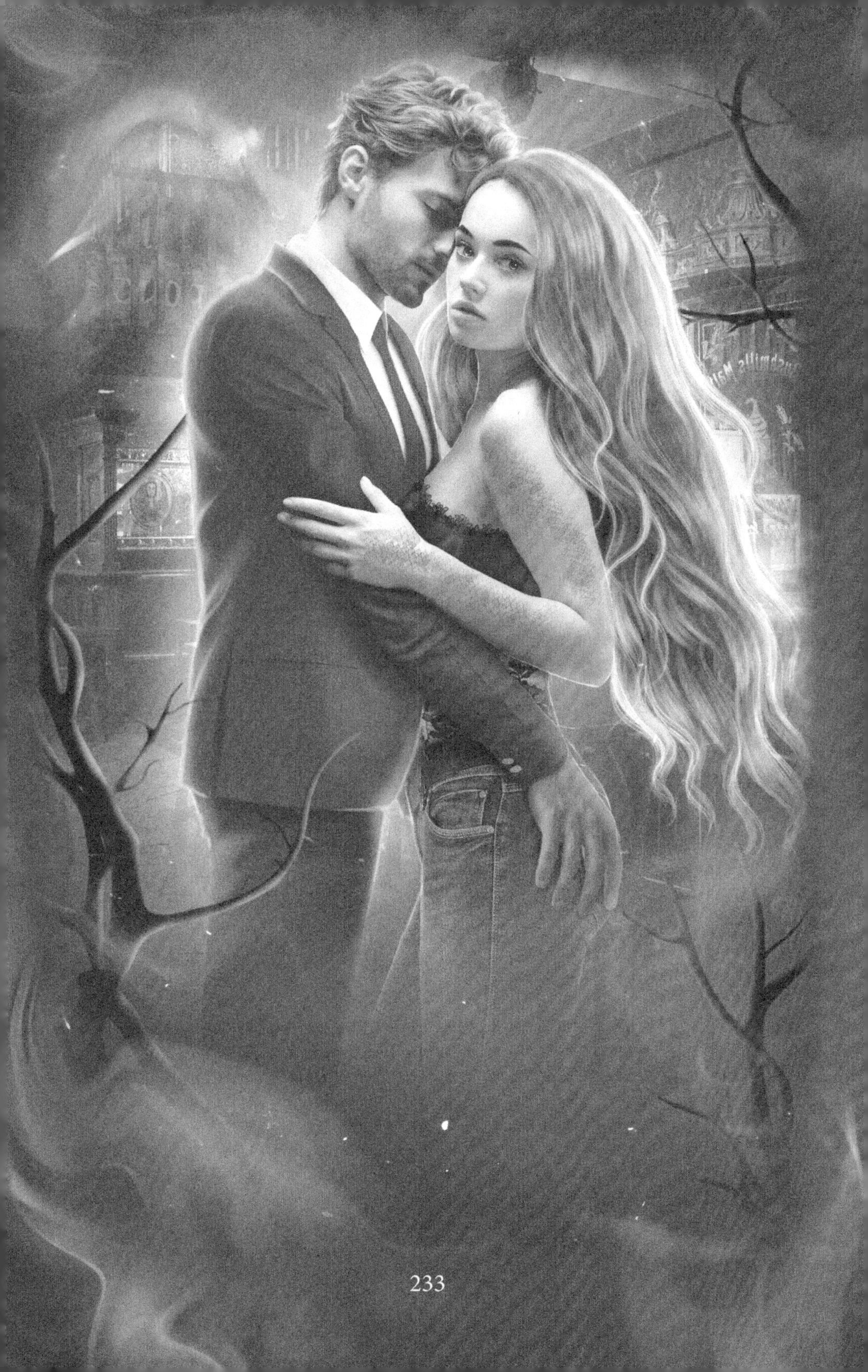

CHAPTER TWENTY-SEVEN

"HOW THE FUCK DID this happen?!!" Deputy Morris yells across the table at me.

God. I'm tired. I've never been so tired in my life. "You're going to have to be more specific."

"You're a dragon!" The dude is going to have an aneurysm.

"And you want to know how that happened?" I ask and kick my feet up on the table. I could lay my head back and sleep right here, but I'm so hungry my stomach is starting to eat itself.

"Yes!"

I stick my fingers in my ears. "Volume control is a thing. Listen, I don't know what you want me to say. I was born this way, but I'm pretty sure the stork didn't bring me to mama and papa dragon. So I guess that means mama and papa did the dirty and I was a result of their relations." I hold my hands up and smirk. "But hey, if we need to go into more detail about the birds and the bees, we can do that."

He holds a hand up to stop me. "No, thank you, smart-ass."

"Let me get this straight."

A knock comes at the interrogation room door, and Rishi sticks his head inside. When he discovers me, he smiles, and then he opens the door wide and comes in. "Been looking everywhere for you, Lady Jayden."

"Zvi. Just Zvi."

"You asked to be updated on Mr. Benton's progress?" the wererat asks.

I sit up straight. "I did."

"He's doing a little better. The wound in his neck has healed over with a few feedings, but there's nothing to be done about the venom but time. It will need to run its course."

Shaw Benton is going to be in a lot of pain for quite a while. "Thank you, Rishi. May I visit him?"

"Yes, but Zarzos is just outside and insists on escorting you down to Mr. Benton's day room in our basement."

"The vampires are staying here?" I ask.

Morris chuckles like an asshole. "Worried about your boyfriend?"

I'm not a patient person. My temper often gets the best of me, like right now. I spring from my chair, reach across the table, and pick up Morris from his chair. I drag him across the table and get in his face. "You realize I'm a fucking dragon, right? I breathe fire, have wings, and can generally fuck shit up like nobody's business."

He shakes his head, his eyes wide with fear.

"Good. I'm glad we understand each other. Now, if you'll kindly stop fucking with me, I'd really appreciate it. Toodles." I drop him on the table and leave the room to find my favorite demon waiting on me.

He bows. "Lady Jayden."

"Zvi. Just Zvi."

I've never seen Zarzos look tired, but he is today. "What time is it?"

"Almost time for the vampires to go to ground."

"I better get down to see Shaw."

Zarzos and I ride the elevator down to the basement and weave our way through a crowd of vampires waiting to be assigned a day room. There's so many of them, they'll have to share. My guard leads me to the end of a hall and knocks on the last door on the left. "Mr. Benton, I have Lady Jayden here for you."

"Come in," Shaw says from inside.

The room is small with gray walls and a bunk system attached to the wall, not that it would stop a supe from tearing it off if they feel inclined. Shaw lies on the bottom bunk, his skin a gray, sickly color, even for a vampire. An Olid healer stands, and I recognize Dr. Windsong.

"Hello," she greets, a reassuring smile on her beautiful face.

"Hello," I greet.

She and Zarzos leave without another word, and Shaw slowly speaks as soon as the door is closed behind them. "You look tired."

"You look like death."

His laugh is raspy. "I'm a vampire."

"The Olid wouldn't give you her blood?"

He shrugs his right shoulder. "You know how they are about their blood."

"What's the point in having the ability to heal people if you can't heal people? Is there anything else that would help? Anything I can get you?"

"My master's blood would help significantly, but I don't believe I'm willing to pay the high cost for it," he says.

"What will they do with Gio and Selene?"

His blue eyes, familiar to the blues I see in the mirror looking back at me, are as tired as mine, but I can also see the pain therein. "I imagine Black Star will find some place to magically tie them up for all of eternity."

"Or until a fanatic finds him and busts his ass out of jail."

"Perhaps."

Silence isn't always silent. Sometimes it's full of unspoken things—things hard to say out loud and difficult to hear. And other times silence can say a million things without saying anything at all, but this isn't one of those times.

I look down at my shoes and push the words out. "When were you going to tell me you were my father?"

"Kavanagh."

"No, I figured it out on my own. He protected your secret. Did you not want me to know?" I ask, hurt the one relative I have access to might not want me anymore now than when I was a child.

"I didn't want Gio to know. He would've used your blood to his advantage."

I frown in response. "Care to explain?"

"It's how the Minister survived. I assume he fed from you?"

I don't answer him with words. It seems like it's too intimate to share with someone else, especially the guy who helped make me.

"Did he know?" I ask. "Did he know he'd survive when he dove into my flame?"

"I doubt it, not unless he's fed on dragon blood before."

"But if you're my father, I'm only half-dragon." I have so many questions about how a vampire can father a child with a dragon, but now isn't the time for those details.

"It was enough to protect him from fire." A pregnant pause and he asks. "How did you figure it out? That I'm your father?"

"I found a picture of you and my mother in Gio's things. Your eyes—I have your eyes."

"Yes, you're the perfect mixture of Lena and I."

He begins to fade in the way vampires do when the sun is close to rising. I walk over to his bed and look down at him, his face twisted in pain, and I silently wish him well. I don't dare make a sound and disturb any peace or reprieve he might find in sleep. I quietly slip from the room and leave him to rest.

Across from Shaw's room, Zarzos holds a sleeping Killian in his arms like he would a child. "He was waiting to see you before the sun came up."

I follow Zarzos into an empty day room across the hall from Shaw's and watch as the demon gently places the King on the bottom bunk. When my guard steps into the hall, I step over to Killian and place a nearby pillow under his head, touch my hand to his handsome face as I say a silent thank you to the Universe that he drank from me. I press my lips to his forehead and leave him dead to the world.

*

The Bar has seen better days. In the daylight, the water, smoke, and fire damage look ten times worse. I stand in the middle of the bar and turn around as I take it all in.

"It can be fixed," Hendri says from the corner.

"Yeah," I agree, but I remember when we painted the walls, stained the floors, and installed the bar. Even I was excited about opening our doors. It felt great to finally have something of our own. But things are different this time around. Moe is the Fire Witch, and I'm considered a consort to a vampire king. The future is uncertain, and it's unsettling.

"How is she?" I ask of my sister, asleep on one side of a corner booth.

"Overwhelmed. Worried about you," he answers.

I make my way behind the bar and look for a salvageable bottle of anything to help me turn my brain off, but everything is broken or covered in soot.

"Liquor stores are closed at 9 a.m. I looked."

"I'll be right back," I tell him and walk outside to where I park my motorcycle. I reach inside the leather saddle bag and remove a little something I've been saving for a day much like today.

When I walk inside the bar again, I find Zarzos and Barzul at the table next to Hendri and Moe, and both Dig'Dred brothers look incredibly tired. Zarzos inclines his head in greeting, likely too exhausted to use words. Barzul grunts in my general direction. I grunt back, take a seat at the small table with the demons, and light up.

A light giggle, just a hint of the real thing, escapes my guard. "Inhale the good shit, exhale the bullshit."

"Hear, hear," I choke through the smoke and pass it to the Deputy.

He looks at me like I've lost my mind, but then he shrugs and takes my offering. "Fuck it."

Zarzos bounces on his seat twice but settles down when Hendri passes the joint in his direction. Barzul falls over asleep at the table before he can partake, and slowly, we all lay our heads down and sleep as the events of the past two weeks take their toll.

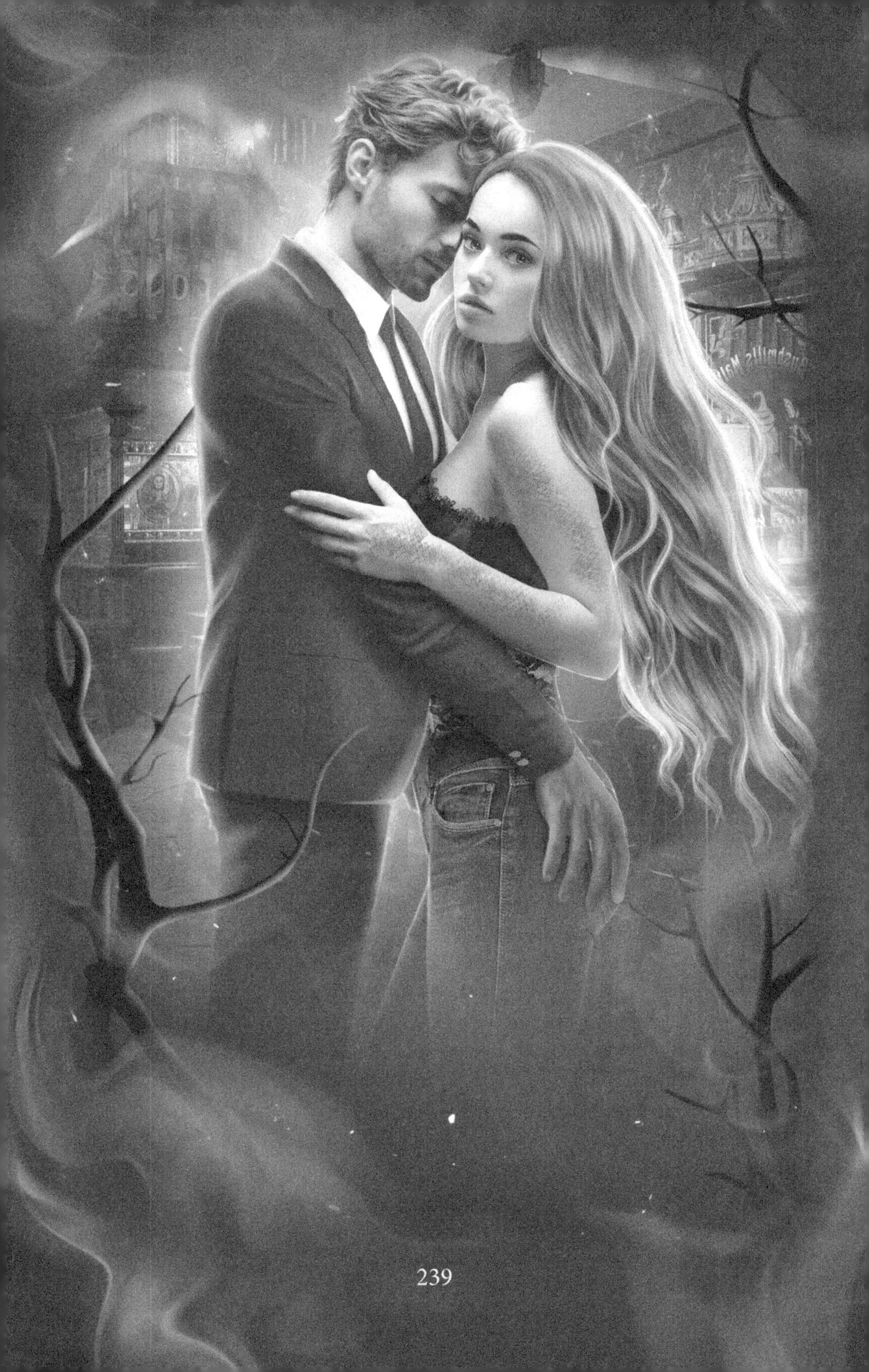

CHAPTER TWENTY-EIGHT

"WATCH THIS," MOE SAYS and blinks her eyes twice until a tiny flame appears in her hand.

We've spent the last four hours chunking debris from The Bar into the dumpster outside while Moe uses her magic to make some of the cleanup easier. Of course, her newfound power of fire might be an easier way to take care of it—just finish it off and burn it to the ground. We can build from the ground up, because throwing away my entire life is pretty fucking depressing, and we haven't even reached our apartments yet.

I look at the clock.

4:00p.m.

The vampires will be up in a few hours.

"You're sort of like a dragon now," I tell her.

She smiles at the thought. "Yeah, I guess I am."

We have a small laugh, and it feels good to have something a little lighter in my chest, if only for a moment.

"We can't sleep here," she says after a stretch of silence, but it's what she isn't saying.

"Does Hendri have a place of his own?" I ask.

"Of course."

"You should stay there."

"Zvi..."

"I can have Zarzos bring your things from Killian's."

I look at the clock again.

4:30 p.m.

"And," I continue, "we should hire the Dig'Dred brothers full-time. You're a big deal now. You'll need protection."

"You're a big deal now, too."

I shrug. "I was always a big deal."

We share another laugh and clean the liquor bottles from behind the bar.

"Where will you sleep?" she asks a while later.

I open my mouth to answer but the words don't come.

"You know you're welcome to Hendri's couch."

I don't have a home.

"It's only temporary," she assures me as though she's read my mind.

My home situation may be temporary, but everything is permanently changing. It's changing at a rapid rate. Each passing day will bring more bullshit into our lives as the witch's center shifts from New Orleans to Atlanta. The entire supernatural world will know she's the Fire Witch, and I'm the dragon that covered her in fire. There's no way life doesn't monumentally change after this.

I look at the clock again and see time has gotten away from me. 5:45 p.m.

I rap my knuckles against the wood bar twice and throw my bar towel on top. "I'm knocking off for the night."

"Don't fly too far, sister," Moe says. "I don't imagine he's going to let you go so easily."

"No," I agree, "I don't imagine so." And I don't know how I feel about it. I hug Moe tightly before I go. "Try not to burn it down for a second time."

It's already dusk when I reach my motorcycle in the lot. Karl Ekman is leaning against it. "Lady Jayden."

"Zvi. Just Zvi."

He straightens from my bike. "I've never met a dragon."

"They let you out of lock-up?"

"Apparently, I'm no longer a threat to society."

"No?"

"Natasia's dead, and the curse died with her. Gio and Selene are being shipped to the Lower Sanctum of the Abyss." He grins after he tells me.

I grin back at him, happy the guy at least is happy with the little justice he's going to get. "Doesn't seem quite like enough though, does it?"

He looks away, into the distance, and he smiles as though he's directing it at someone I can't see.

"No," he says.

I give him a moment to collect his thoughts.

"Where are you headed this evening?"

"North," I say. "I figured I'd land in North Carolina and ride the Dragon's Tail before I turn around, ride it again and head home. I might even stop in a little Alpine Village in the northern part of Georgia on my way back, take in some of the falls."

"Sounds beautiful. Mind if I tag along?"

I'm a loner by nature. Moe breaks me out of my hermit funk and gives me a person to lean on when I need it. I don't imagine Karl has anyone. There wasn't anyone who came up in his file, and since we know Helpful Helen was actually Selene and not indeed who we thought she was or Karl's girlfriend, it leaves him with no one. He was forced to murder people. His right to choose was taken away from him, and that's never okay. While I'd rather be alone with my thoughts, Karl would rather he wasn't.

"Sure. Hop on."

I swing my leg over the bike and turn the key. My Harley revs to life and fills the lot with the loud sound of my pipes. Karl follows suit as I flip on my radio and blast rock and roll from the motorcycle speakers. I find it a tad bit funny that the vampire hangs onto my shoulders in case he falls off, but I don't mention it.

For hours, Karl and I ride in companionable silence, both perfectly happy to let our hair flow in the wind down back country roads all the way to North Carolina. I stop outside of Deals' Gap and fuel up before we hit the famous bike tourist stretch of mountain road.

"How long is it?" he asks.

"The stretch is eleven miles, 318 curves."

"Wow."

"Indeed."

We shoot the breeze about nothing in particular for a few more minutes while the tank fills.

"We better hit the pavement if we're going to make it back to your place by dawn."

We ride the tail one way and then another. Karl laughs like a child as he hangs on the bike, our knees nearly touching the pavement around each curve. His laughter is infectious, so much so that I find myself laughing along with him, enjoying every single, simple moment of happiness I can milk from the experience. Maybe it's my need to have one last night as just Zvi before my life is turned upside down, but I enjoy laughing with a vampire like I haven't a care in the world. I don't think I've ever felt so carefree, however temporary it may be.

Wind therapy is what bikers call the experience—badass American horsepower between your legs, wind in your hair, and not a fuck to give. The combination somehow breeds happiness and a sense of freedom one just doesn't get from being locked in an office from nine until five.

"I've never ridden a motorcycle," Karl tells me when I stop at a late night drive-thru to grab grub. "Can I drive it?"

I chuckle. "It's not easy to drive a motorcycle. It takes practice, balance, and not tipping it over around a curve."

"How did you learn?" he asks, genuinely interested.

Sadness overtakes me at the thought of our late friend, Patrick, whom Karl killed. I figure it best not to mention it. "An old friend of mine went with me to the dealership to buy it. He drove it back to The Bar, and we practiced in the parking lot."

"I'd like to do that."

"Yeah?"

"Yes. If you don't mind?"

"Not at all." Normally, I'd tell him go fuck himself. Nobody touches my bike. Hell, the only person who has ever ridden on it is Moe. But Karl has to be the saddest vampire I've ever met. "Can I ask you a question?"

"Sure, Lady Jayden."

"Why did they choose you? Selene, Gio, and Natasha?"

"Because they thought I was weak for loving a human. They probably thought I'd follow their every command without fighting it."

"I heard you fought valiantly against her magic."

He straightens his back, the first hint of him being a little proud of himself for his efforts. "Thank you."

"We should head back to the city before the sun comes up," I remind him.

He inhales deeply. "The air is crisp up here."

There's a shift in Karl I feel immediately. "'Sup, homie?"

He won't quite meet my eyes. "Mind if we ride the Tail of the Dragon again?"

"We don't have time before you have to be underground. We can come back anytime you like though."

He still won't meet my eyes. "I miss Maribel. I've lived a long time, but I have only loved one woman, and it seems my existence means nothing without her."

"What…"

He turns to face me, finally giving me the most sincere vampire eyes I've ever seen. "My head is weary, Lady Jayden."

"There's been enough death. Let's learn how to drive a motorcycle. We can find a lot nearby, and then I can find us a cabin and lock us up tight until tonight when the sun dips again."

There's a slight shake of his head and a gentle smile. "I'll be able to see her again. Don't be sad for me. I welcome death and seeing the sun again for the first time in a very long time. And I'll welcome Maribel into my arms and gladly leave behind this existence as a creature banished to the night."

He's made up his mind, and as much as I don't condone suicide, it must be excruciating to live so long without a loved one. Also, it's not my fucking place to judge someone else's decision to end it. "So you've decided to die on the back of my motorcycle?"

He waits a minute to speak as he looks off into the distance. "I'd be honored if you'd escort me to my Maribel."

"Then you believe in an afterlife?" I ask.

"Yes, but I've been alive a very long time and experienced many cultures and religions. My afterlife is much different than anything I've been taught, but I suppose the only thing that matters to me is that she's there waiting on me. And even if it's not real, if somehow it's my consciousness living on, that it's simply her energy next to mine for all of eternity, then I'm okay with that, too."

"That's fucking beautiful, man."

I climb on the motorcycle and wait for him to follow. We ride the stretch of road two more times before the sun begins to peek over the mountain. I stop at the top of the mountain before I head home to Atlanta.

"Maribel," Karl whispers as the night sky fades into a pink hue.

"See you on the other side, homie."

And then Karl and I take his last ride. He laughs unabashedly—a belly laugh from the diaphragm, full of absolute joy. In my side mirrors, I watch him lean his head back, open his arms wide as though he's flying, and utter Maribel's name one last time. An overwhelming sadness settles over me when the back of my bike becomes lighter and I see the last of Karl's ashes scatter in the wind behind me.

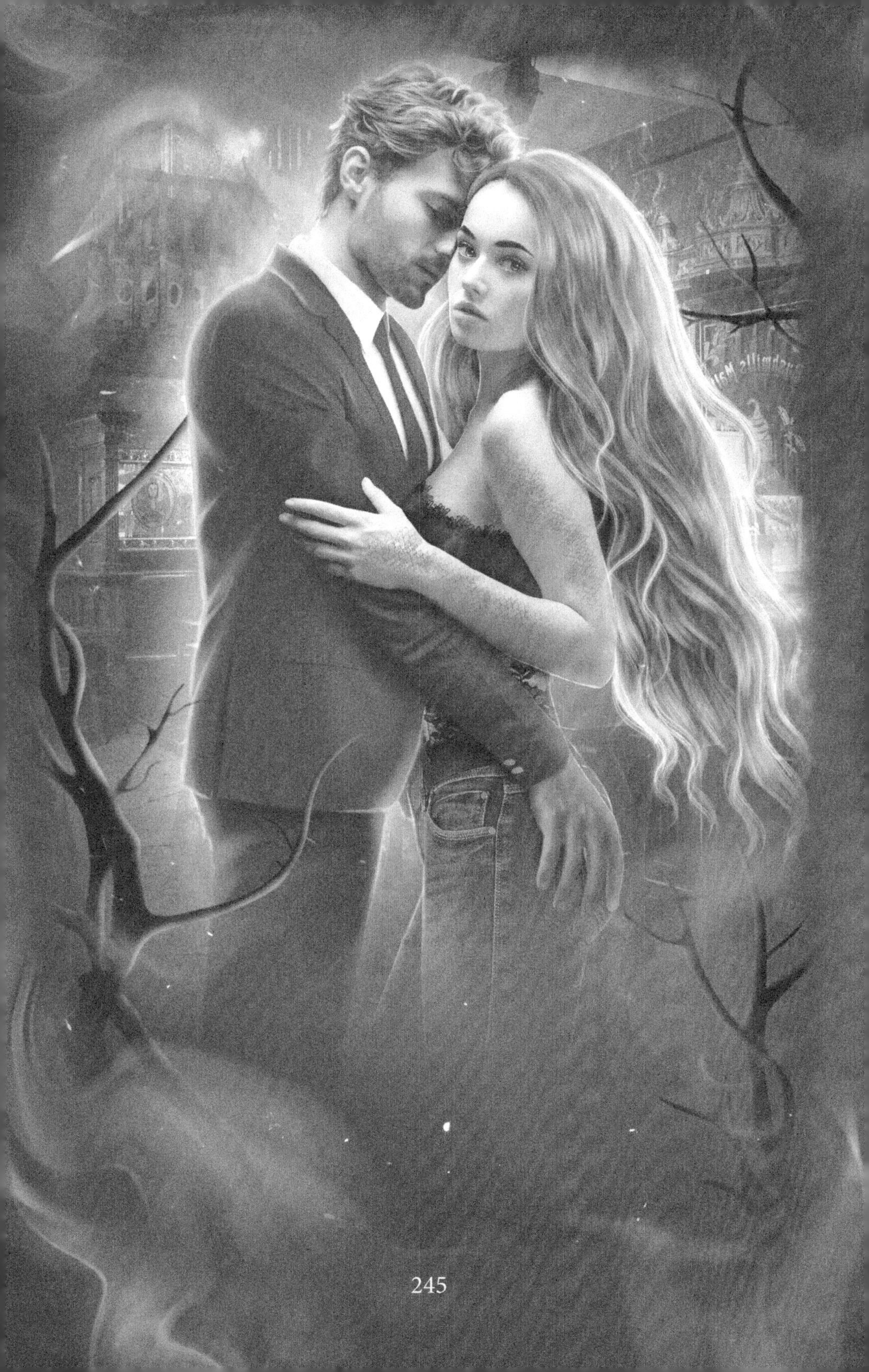

CHAPTER TWENTY-NINE

ON THE SECOND EVENING of The Bar clean-up effort, I leave before dusk to avoid a certain bloodsucker. I admit to my cowardice. But after roaming the streets on my motorcycle for most of the night, I find myself on Killian's street at two in the morning. I sit in the drive for a moment, straddling my motorcycle, taking in his mansion, and telling myself to turn around and get the hell out of here. I don't belong here, and I need to stay away from Kavanagh. Movement in an upstairs window catches my attention, but when I look up, he's gone. Still, I somehow know it was him looking down at me.

I throw my leg over my bike and trek to the door from the circular drive. Sebastian answers the door looking more pinkish in the cheeks since the last time we saw each other. "Butler, you don't look as much like a corpse as you did two days ago."

He smirks at me and stands aside to let me pass. "Lady Jayden, always a pleasure to see you. The Minister has been very worried."

"Zvi," Killian says from the top of the grand staircase. And God. I can feel his presence in the room. He zips down the steps and comes to stand beside Sebastian. "Are you well?" I try not to notice how great he looks in his fitted, white button down and gray slacks, or how the crystal blue hue of his tie matches his incredibly blue eyes. I need to ignore the expression within them.

I shrug. "All things considered."

"I'll leave you to it," Sebastian says and bows to us both before taking his exit.

We're left staring at each other not saying anything. I don't know about him, but I don't know what to say. I've never had someone invade me and my life from every direction. I've never had someone burrow underneath my skin and refuse to leave. I'm not quite sure what to do with him or how he fits into my life, but I'll never be able to forget the sacrifice he was willing to make with his own life to save Moe and ensure she became the Fire Witch. He was willing to give up immortality so that it wouldn't hurt to live without my sister. I don't remember my mother, and I grew up in foster care. I'm not accustomed to people giving a shit. I'm certainly not accustomed to someone looking past my exterior and the walls I erected long ago to protect my heart.

I could stay here all night staring at him, but the heaviness of the moment becomes too much for me. Closing my soul to him, I look away, afraid he'll see how vulnerable I am to him, but he takes three long steps to cover the space between us. His gaze bears down on me as his hand comes to my right cheek, his touch cool to my burning skin.

"Zvi, look at me, Love," he whispers.

I raise my eyes to meet his and watch him struggle to speak. With it being Killian, he could say anything. He's never held back what he's thought or how he feels. Before he can utter something that could change everything forever, I stand on my toes and kiss him. His free hand immediately comes to my left cheek and does that thing where he cradles my face like I'm precious to him. He deepens the kiss and dives inside me, parting my waters like I'm the Red Sea, commanding my soul to open to him, but I can't.

I pull away from him, remembering how much it hurt when I thought he was gone, that I'd killed him. He locks his arms around my back and keeps me from completely wrenching away.

"Let me go," I quietly demand, my voice unsteady and unsure.

"I can feel your pain, Macushla," he says against my ear. "Who hurt you, my Love?"

I push against his chest, as another memory of him lying there unmoving, burnt by my fire assaults me. He allows me to leave his arms as I yell at him, "You did!"

He immediately begins hastily reaching for me again.

"No! No." I wipe the stupid tears rolling down my face. "Stay back."

Killian stops in his tracks with his hands held up in surrender.

I suck back a sob and look away. I can't stand for him to see me this way—so open, raw, and emotional.

His voice cracks with emotion. "Zvi."

"Why did you do that? Put yourself in danger? You put yourself directly in my line of fire. You gave up, Kavanagh, and you put that on my plate."

He takes one step toward me. "I didn't give up, Macushla. I gave the world a fighting chance. I gave Moe a fighting chance."

I scoff. "Just like that?"

Another step closer. "Yes, just like that."

"Two-thousand years just down the fucking drain because… because…" I shrug my shoulders, "…because why? It felt like the day to…"

"Because!" he shouts, his lilt thick with emotion, and I swallow anything else I was going to say, the words already forgotten. I've seen him take command. I've seen him be the King, always in control and quick with a smile, but I've never witnessed him lose his composure. "Because," he repeats as he looks down at the floor between us, the first time he's been afraid to meet my gaze since we met, and then he speaks just above a whisper. "Because I've waited my entire life for you. There's nothing I wouldn't do for you, including spare your sister's life and her rightful position as the Fire Witch."

"You could've died." The mere reminder is enough to start the ridiculous waterworks up again.

He raises his eyes to me, takes a few steps to close the space between us, and then he takes my hand and places it palm down on his chest. "But I'm still here, and I'm still waiting for you. I'll wait two-thousand more years if it means I could be with you."

"Don't ever do that again."

He swallows hard and nods as he wraps his arms around me and pulls me to his chest. He presses a kiss to the top of my head. I grab a handful of his shirt and try to pull him close enough that I can crawl inside him. He sways us just like that, with me holding onto him for dear life in the middle of his mansion for anyone to see.

"Play our song," I whisper.

He hums it to me, the first indication he has musical talent, and we dance as his voice is joined by violins and cellos. One-by-one additional instruments join, adding a little something extra with each new sound, until there's a full symphony playing our song.

"Stay with me tonight," he says and moves his hands from my back to touch his hands to my face.

I lean my head back to take in his handsome face and see his intense need. I stand on my toes again and press another kiss to his lips. A few seconds later, he picks me up and carries me through the mansion, never stopping the kiss until we reach his moonlit bedroom. He places me on a dresser, giving little care or attention to the items atop it.

Killian breaks the kiss to pull my black tank over my head, and then he looks down at the exposed skin. He traces my collarbone. "So fucking beautiful." Then he places a kiss on each side along the same route his fingers took. "I could look at you all night." I begin removing his tie and unbuttoning his shirt, taking my time, kissing his lips between each button. When I push the clothing down his arms, it slides to the floor exposing the hard planes of his body. My hands wander across the skin until he shivers against my touch. "You feel like the sun."

My fingers work quickly to undo his belt and unbutton his pants before I push them to the floor and discover Killian doesn't wear underwear. I reach down and grab him as he hisses in pleasure and thrusts into my hand. His hands go to my pants and work on the belt and button, and then he removes my bra. His mouth goes to my breasts where he kisses and licks before moving on to my neck and back to my lips. And finally, he removes my panties and touches two fingers to the center of me. I nearly combust from it.

He moves us to the edge of the bed where he sits with me straddling him and my arms wrapped around his neck, kissing every inch of me he can reach. His hands travel up and down my back until he reaches my shoulders, and then he travels down to my hips. He holds onto them as he lines himself up.

"Zvi," he whispers against my lips. I open my eyes at the reverent sound of my name on his tongue. He pushes just inside, just a little taste to give me time to adjust to his length. "My entire life, Macushla."

I slide down, impatient to feel full of him, and look as deeply into him as he does into me. And then we move together, pushing and pulling, giving and taking, until we're tangled into one being incapable of being separated on this plane. Our song plays loudly in my ears, but I don't miss the sounds of pleasure he makes. I don't miss the ancient words coming from him as we ride the wave of ecstasy together, the little signs that he's as lost to this as I am— that I'm not in this alone.

"Please," I beg, ready to fall apart in his arms and find a few hours' sleep next to him. "Please."

"Not yet," he pleads back, and then he flips us over on the bed with me on my back. The change in position pushes me farther away from the precipice of bliss. "I," he begins and thrusts into me, "haven't had enough." And then he thrusts a little harder the next time, and then a little harder until his strokes are long and punishing, and I'm free-falling in his blue eyes.

Our song plays softly at first, and then it gains in volume each time he pushes inside me again until it's roaring in my ears along with his ancient curses and prayers. I climb the mountain toward the top, anticipating and needing to fall over the other side with him.

"Macushla," he cries.

I lock my legs around him as tightly as I can and flip us over to his back, and then I rock against his length. The cymbals in our personal symphony clash and clang together as we both inch toward the finish line. He bends at the waist and comes to face me, pressing his lips against mine, scraping his fangs against the bottom, and moving on to my chin. His hands push into my hair as I arch my back and moan his name. I touch my chest and grab a handful of each breast as I buck wildly, seeking a release with the king of vampires—a welcome reprieve from the events of the past few weeks.

I close my eyes as a blinding light erupts behind my lids and a lightness fills my chest and bones. "Oh, God," I say and continue moving with him as I ride out my release.

He begins to pulse inside me, whispering my name against my lips, as his eyes close and an expression of pure pleasure spreads across his beautiful face. I kiss his face, first his cheeks, then his nose, eyes, chin, and last his lips as he comes down. I purr against him when he kisses me back.

We remain that way for some time, him inside me, connected to me at the root, peppering sweet kisses all over each other's face, shoulders, and neck. When his scent wraps around me, I welcome it—the feeling of being exactly where I'm supposed to be. I close my eyes and find sleep before my head hits his shoulder.

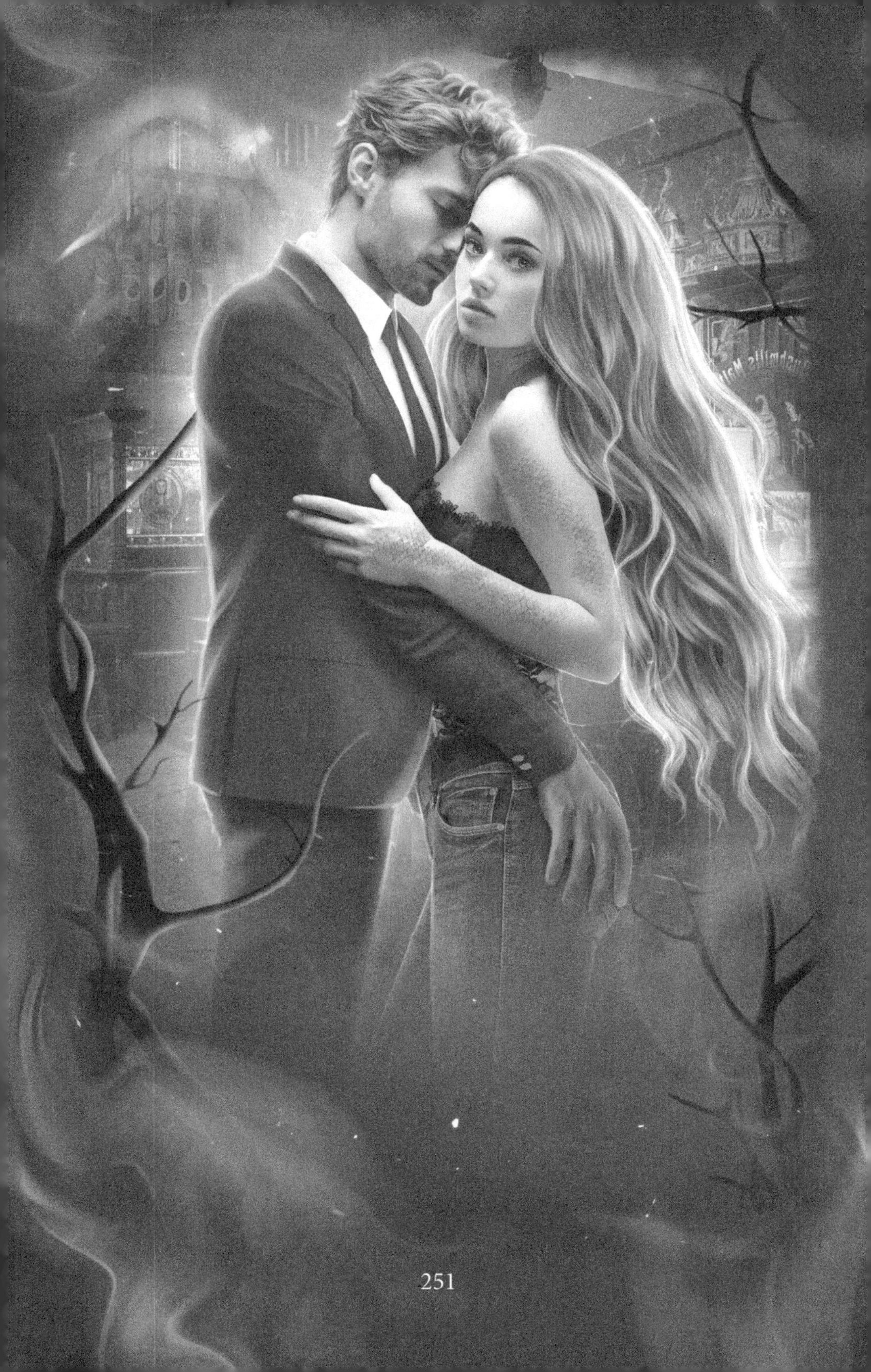

CHAPTER THIRTY

Two Months Later

ZARZOS WALKS OVER TO the new jukebox, a gift from him and Barzul, and turns on his favorite funk song. He shakes his ass across the newly stained bar floor and shows off some of his new fancy footwork. "Shake that ass, shake that ass, now."

The entire room cracks up laughing, but my guard actually has some real skill in the dance move department.

Tomorrow is our soft reopening—only friends and family—but tonight, the entire gang is here at The Bar to celebrate the installation of the jukebox. "Jukebox Party" is what Zarzos has been calling our shindig. He and Moe made paper invitations and everybody who is anybody to Zarzos received a welcome to chill at The Bar with us tonight—a much more relaxed evening than the hustle and bustle we'll endure tomorrow night when we'll be slinging food and drinks.

Killian had tonight's festivities catered for us. Sebastian volunteered to tend the bar for us—something he did for a time in New Orleans in the twenties and sorely missed. Hendri ordered Moe and I to relax while our motley crew takes care of everything.

Across the room, the king of vampires has his eye on me as he lifts a lowball glass to his lips and sips expensive whiskey. There's a smile in his eyes and a promise of things to come later in the evening. I lift my beer in the air and silently toast to those things. He lowers his glass to reveal a stupid, sexy smirk. I roll my eyes at him. He laughs, and I ignore how much I enjoy even a snippet of the sound from the other side of the bar room. Fucking fanger.

Zarzos and I pig out on meat and cheese for most of the night, and around midnight, he disappears after announcing he has a surprise for me. He's gone so long that I grow concerned that something has happened. Just about the time I stand to search for my guard, the Dig'Dred brothers walk through the front of the bar, Barzul walking backward as he helps Zarzos carry a large object. They carry it to the center of the dance floor and gently place it on the floor.

Zarzos dusts himself off, buttons his suit jacket, and waves his arms like he's Vanna White. "Tada!"

Moe and I look at each other. He's so freaking excited about his… surprise. I don't want to hurt his feelings by asking what it is.

"That's so cool, dude," I say.

Moe claps her hands. "Yeahhhh, that's awesome, Zarzos."

He bounces on his feet and nods in agreement. "Right? Can we do it tonight?"

Moe and I look at each other again. We're both at a loss for words.

Killian walks over to the surprise and eyes it closely. His hands go to his hips as he begins to shake his head. "No, Zarzos, you're not putting that on Lady Jayden." Killian turns on his heel to my favorite demon. "She's not a toy."

Zarzos mimics the Minister, hands to hips and frown on his face. "But I always wanted to ride a dragon!"

"Whoa there, Nelly! What's this about?" I ask.

Zarzos turns to me, serious as a heart attack. "I had a bridle made for you so I have something to hang onto. Genius thinking, right? Right."

I take a closer look at the surprise on the floor and see buckles and straps. "Nope."

The demon's frown deepens. "I challenge you to a duel!"

"Nuh-uh."

He huffs and stomps a foot. "I can drink you under the table."

"Maybe, but I'm not flying intoxicated. Plus, you're a demon, and therefore you have an unfair advantage."

Hendri raises his beer. "Friends don't let friends fly drunk."

"Want to spar?"

"Negative, ghost rider."

"Trivia?"

"Nah."

"Karaoke?"

I roll my eyes.

"Poker?"

I sit up a little straighter. "I'd wipe your ass in Hold 'Em."

He pulls at his tie to loosen it, walks over to my table, pulls out a chair across from me, and has a seat. "Deal the cards."

An hour later, I'm holding a Dead Man's hand—an ace of spades and an eight. There's two aces on the board, and my kicker card is decent. What's the likelihood he has the fourth ace? Not highly likely. An eight of hearts is the last card on the turn, giving me a full house. I've been getting shitty hands, so I run with it.

I push all my chips to the middle of the table. "I'm all in."

Zarzos replies to my wager by also pushing his chips in the middle of the table. "I call."

I stand from my chair and flip my cards over.

Zarzos cackles obnoxiously and stands from his chair. He dances and sings. "Shake that ass. Shake that ass. Now." Then he turns over an ace card with a ten kicker for a few seconds before turning them back over.

But something isn't quite right. "Wait a minute. There's already a ten of clubs on the board."

Zarzos grabs his ten card and shoves it in his mouth, and then he chews it up and swallows. "Nuh-uh."

I can't even be mad at the guy. He's Zarzos. "Let's go."

He jumps up and down and claps his hands together with a huge smile on his face. "Are we going to the roof?"

I nod my head toward the stairs and the entire room cheers for the demon and his efforts. Off the crowd goes to the roof, everyone crowding in the staircase to venture up to the roof. Normally, I'd change on the roof, but tonight, I'll use the parking lot of The Bar.

Killian is the only one sitting in the bar after everyone has left. "Macushla, you are fond of the demon."

"He stinks."

The vampire king laughs. "Nevertheless."

I close the space between us, but I leave enough room so he can't reach out and pull me to him as he's prone to do when we have a rare moment alone. "You should come out to the lot with me."

"What happens when I arrive?"

I pull my tank over my head. "I guess you should stop running your trap and come and see for yourself."

"You know how much I like your smart mouth."

I step out of the rest of my clothes and watch him watch me undress, his eyes straying lower and lower until he's scanned my entire body. I head for the door, pause just inside the frame, and look over my shoulder.

Other than the night I shifted under Natasia's magic, he's never seen me change. He's never seen me transform. Outside in a dark corner of the lot, I close my eyes and focus on my internal fire while he watches. Moe's magic, now stronger than ever, eases the pain of my bones breaking and morphing to accommodate my other nature.

I shoot into the air and watch as the vampire becomes the size of an ant below me. I bring my head down to him. He reaches out and touches the side of my face with his small hand. "Macushla, what a gift you have given me. Thank you."

I purr against his hand.

"Go, fly, Love. Just make sure you fly back to me."

I turn to the roof and find Zarzos precariously walking the ledge and shake my head at the demon. With a little assistance from Moe, Hendri, and Barzul, I bite down on the bridle as they strap Zarzos to me. He pulls the reins to test them out. I growl in response. I hate the stupid bridle, but I don't want to hurt his feelings.

Whatever. I look like a chump.

Once the demon is in place, I flap my wings and run the length of the building. We dive over the side and let the wind catch, and then we're flying.

"Yeehaw, motherfuckers!" Zarzos yells into the night. "It is I, the demon Zarzos Dig'Dred, and my best friend is a dragon!!!"

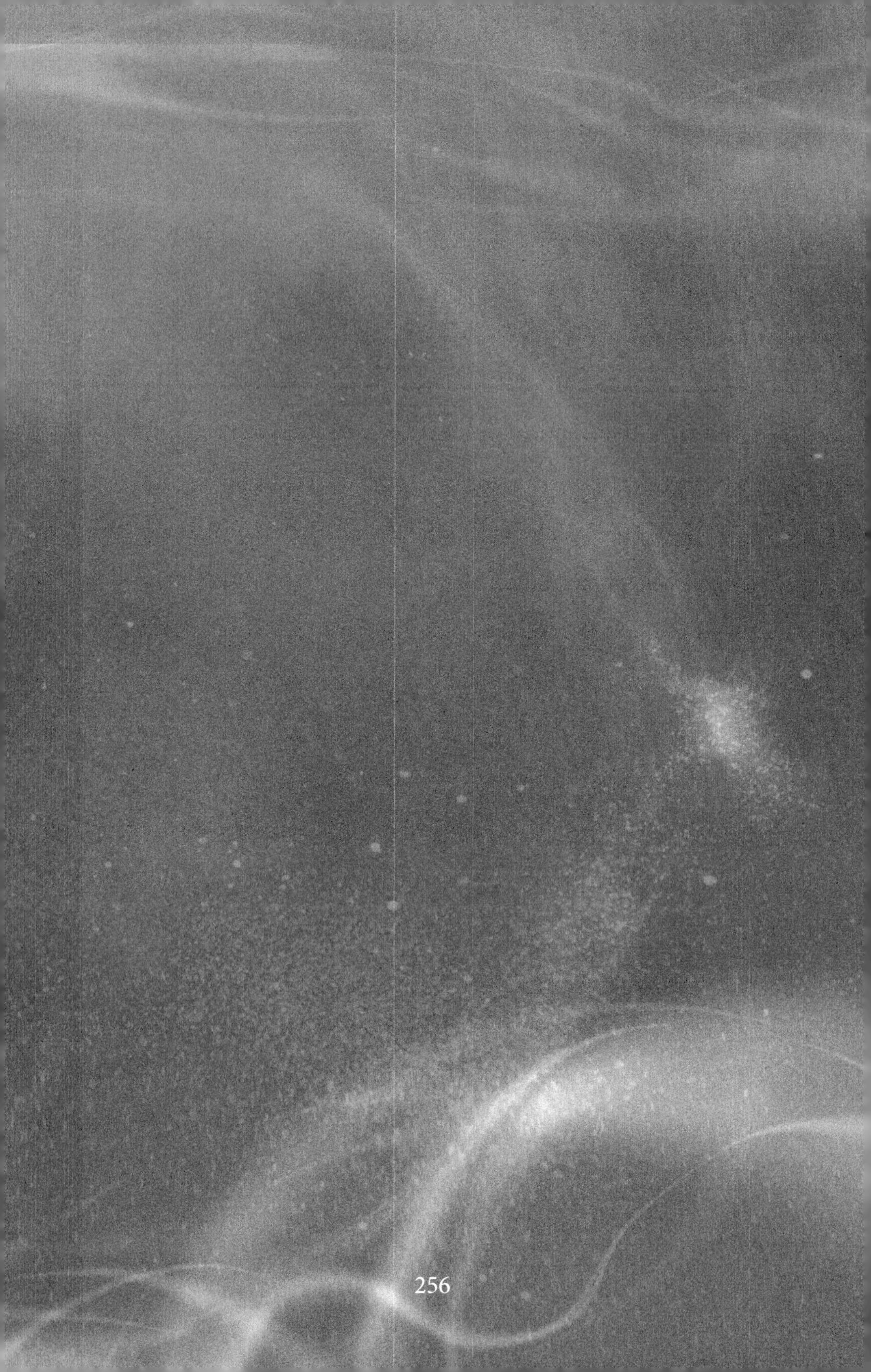

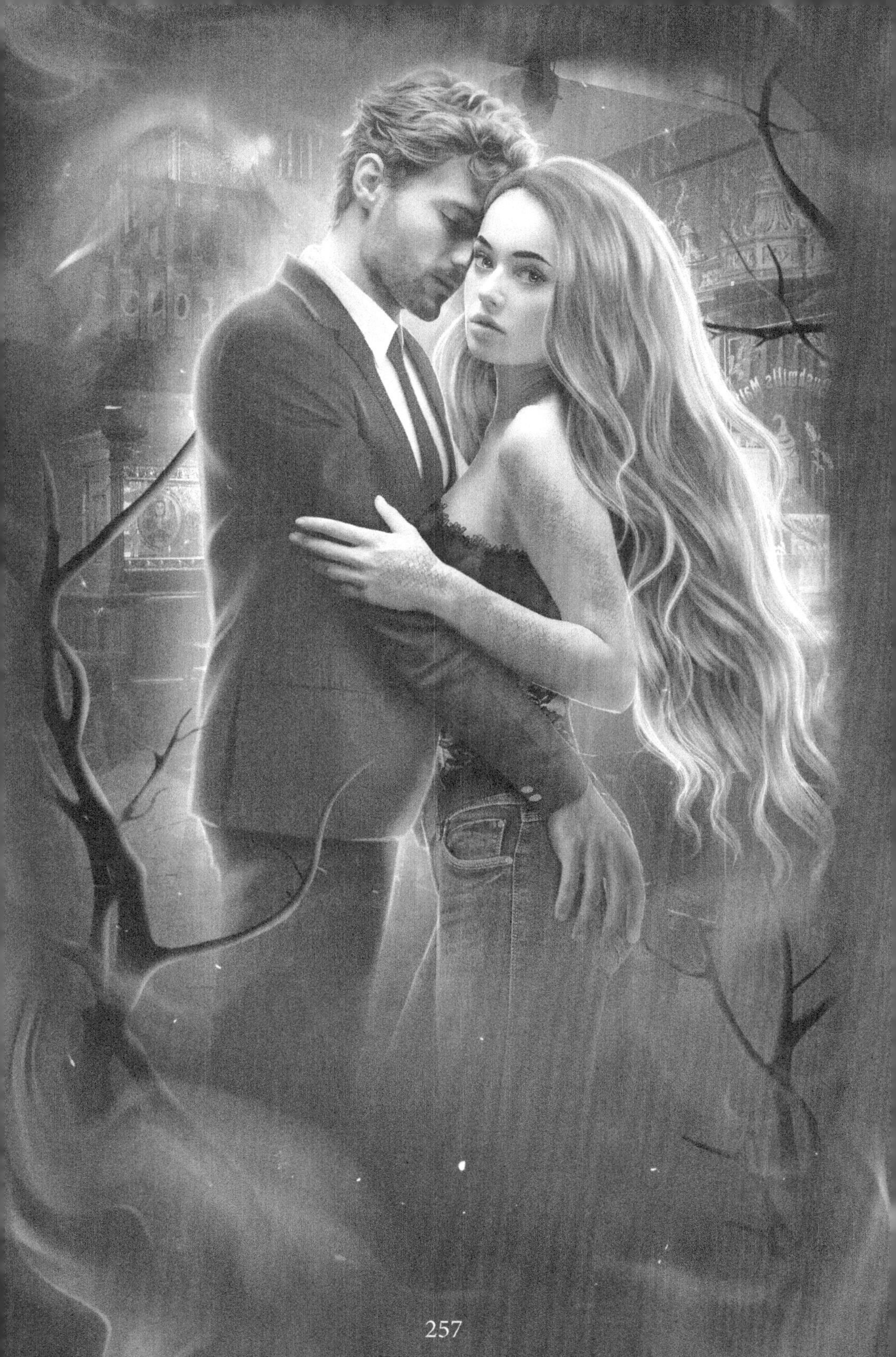

EPILOGUE

A WEEK AFTER ZARZOS and I fly over most of Georgia, because he just wanted one more turn like I'm a freaking tilt-a-whirl, Hendri walks into our bar a few hours before we open.

Moe drops a glass when she sees him. "Oh, no."

I pay closer attention to the Deputy. "Something is different and yet the same." He opens his mouth to talk, but I hold a finger up to stop him. "No, don't tell me. I'm in the mood to figure it out." He tries to speak again, but I cut him off. "Nuh-uh. I'm thinking of becoming a Black Star Deputy. I want to figure out the case for myself."

Moe snorts and lines up lemon drop shots on the bar, and then she uses the tip of her finger to set them on fire. She's been practicing controlling her fire. We're starting with baby flames. "I'm making lemon drop shots the house special." She grins.

"Gnarly," I say and refocus on the wolf.

Aleki walks in the bar, looks around until he spots me, and grimaces. He's not taking the dragon thing well. Also, we're pretty sure he now has PTSD from watching Killian roast like a pig on a spit in my fire. Of course, I think I have PTSD from it as well.

Zarzos dances through the front door with a grunting Barzul on his heels, stops beside the gigantic beast, Aleki, and bops him on the nose. Aleki reaches for his sword. Zarzos hisses at him, and then chomps his teeth as a friendly, demonic reminder that his bite can really fuck shit up.

I suppress a laugh.

Killian saunters through the door in a navy blue suit with a light blue pinstripe and a pink shirt underneath.

Hendri sighs. "I came here because…"

I shake a finger at him but don't dare take my eyes off the vampire that just walked through the door. I hate that he does it for me. There's a fuck-ton of people and supes on this planet, and I have to be attracted to the one fucker I don't want to want. I never thought I'd be a corpse humper.

"Macushla…"

I hold a finger up when bloodsucker after bloodsucker fills the room behind and around their vampire king. "You brought a lot of your homies." I blink. "Cool. I looooovvvvvvvveeeeeee surprises."

Zarzos giggles. "She totally does."

There's an apology in Killian's eyes, and I know what he's going to say before he says it. "Nope." I slice my finger across my throat. "I've already had to set your ass on fire once. I'm not doing it again. The last time you two assholes," I point a finger at the vampire king and then the Deputy, "came into our bar wearing those faces, shit hit the fan and my life was turned upside down. I knew there was something the same about you," I tell Hendri. "You're wearing that face that says, 'I've got a case'."

The wolf rolls his eyes. He knows I'm right.

"Well? Do you have a case or not?"

He opens his mouth.

"Nope! I changed my mind," I say. "We're not discussing it."

Zarzos chuckles. "She's cray."

I nod in agreement. "True story."

"Zvi," Killian tries again.

"No means no."

He zips across the room to me and looks down at me with those marbled blue eyes. "My Love, your father is missing, and we're afraid the worst has happened."

I frown at him, not quite comprehending him. "The worst?"

Killian searches my face. "Yes, Macushla. A demon broke into his home earlier in the evening and there was a struggle."

My heart sinks. Shaw is extremely unwell from the demon bite he sustained in the Battle of the Fire Witch. If he had to fight someone off, he wouldn't have been able to do it with much strength. He'd need all his strength in order to have a fighting chance against a demon.

"Zvi?" Moe calls out, concern in her voice.

"Is he dead or missing?" I ask as I stare past the crowd of people focusing on me, waiting on my reaction to the bad news.

"Without a DNA test, we can't be sure," KIllian advises.

When vampires die, they leave behind a big, inconvenient pile of ash. "Are there remains?" I ask.

The Minister's marbled blue eyes usually shine brightly enough to light up an entire room. They're slightly dulled in their brilliance tonight.

"Yes," Killian answers on a whisper.

I break eye contact, close my lids, and take a moment to breathe through the overwhelming emotions coursing through me and threatening to spill over in front of all these people. As a kid who grew up a foster child in the system, I was accustomed to not having anyone of blood relation to have my back. When I figured out Shaw was my father, I felt a little less alone. I felt like I belonged to someone, even if he's sick and unable to hold more than a twenty-minute conversation. Without knowing the true fate of my mother, I can safely assume I'm officially an orphan.

"Did anyone see it happen?" I ask.

Killian reaches out to touch the edges of my mind with his glamour. "Yes, the butler."

With both remains and a witness, the ounce of hope I still held seconds ago that my father is still alive disintegrates.

After many attempts to speak, I finally manage to find my words. "Take me to him."

THE END

ACKNOWLEDGMENTS

This book was a wild ride that lasted for three long years. So many people had a hand in the development of the story and the characters that I honestly don't know who to thank first.

I'll start with Samantha and Sandy because you both read this first and loved it before anyone else laid eyes on the manuscript. You're Zvi's biggest fans, and she's yours. I love you both so incredibly much. Thank you for the years of love and support.

Michael, you hear more about my characters than you do my "real" friends, and you endure my madness on a daily basis. Thank you for putting up with me and my insane hours and work schedule and for loving me unconditionally. Thank you for believing in me and allowing me to chase my dreams. You're the best husband a woman could ask for.

Nadine, Maria, Kella, and Mary, I couldn't have made this book what it is without your guidance and direction. Thank you for the time you spent reading and making this book the best it could be.

To my beloved Goddesses, thank you for always supporting my crazy projects and following the journeys of my characters. So many of you have been with me from the beginning, and I'm extremely grateful for each one of you. Thank you for reading.

To the readers, you are the reason I write. You are the reason I wake up and smile when I go to work each day. Thank you for reading, purchasing, supporting, and reviewing my books. you have no idea how much I appreciate each of you for your love and faith in me.

Award-winning and best-selling author Sasha Marshall is devoted to giving her readers humorous adventures with a love story sure to melt their hearts — and their minds. Her knowledge of the music industry comes from being a touring concert photographer with legendary bands such as The Allman Brother's Band and other she met along the way. A self-proclaimed free spirit, she's most often found outdoors writing a book or talking with friends. Sasha makes her home in the beautiful state of Georgia and loves to hear from her readers. Visit her website at sashamarshall.com

ALSO BY SASHA MARSHALL

Second Down Series
False Start

The Zvi Jayden Series
The Fire Witch

Guitar Face Series
Broken
There's No Crying in Rock and Roll
Walking Back to Georgia
River of Deceit
Make it Rain
There's a Woman

Holiday Novella
Mistletoe Wishes

Short Story
Wild Side